PEPI—Royal armorer to the treacherous king Hazor, this heroic Child of the Lion is called to betray his superior and perform deeds that would save the very people who may have killed his wife.

LUTI—The nineteen-year-old beauty leads a hopeless and grueling existence in the fields of Babylon . . . but when she is falsely accused of treason, she discovers her true heritage and the extraordinary powers that will forever change her destiny.

SISERA—Ruthless, bloodthirsty, this power-crazed general's foul temper and insatiable lust lead him to terrorize women and murder anyone who defies his authority . . . until his cruelty evokes the rage of a nation.

DEBORAH—A seeress who receives prophesy from the Israelite God, she sits beneath the palm trees as thousands come to hear the divine wisdom that will send mighty nations to war.

ACHILLES—The brash warrior evokes terror in the hearts of all who challenge him as he leads the ten-year battle to recapture the stunning Helen of Troy . . . but his brazen self-assurance causes him to underestimate his opponent.

HELEN OF TROY—Conqueror of hearts, this epic beauty calmly stands by as the blood of four kingdoms swirls at her feet.

Volume XIII

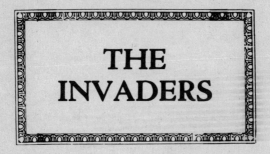

THE
INVADERS

PETER DANIELSON

 Created by the producers of
The Holts: An American Dynasty,
The First Americans, and **The White Indian.**

Book Creations Inc., Canaan, NY • Lyle Kenyon Engel, Founder

BANTAM BOOKS
NEW YORK • TORONTO • LONDON • SYDNEY • AUCKLAND

THE INVADERS

A Bantam Domain Book / published by arrangement with
Book Creations, Inc.

Bantam edition / August 1991

Produced by Book Creations, Inc.
Lyle Kenyon Engel, Founder

DOMAIN and the portrayal of a boxed "d" are trademarks
of Bantam Books, a division of Bantam Doubleday Dell
Publishing Group, Inc.

ISBN 0-553-29082-7

Published simultaneously in the United States and Canada

PRINTED IN THE UNITED STATES OF AMERICA

OPM   0 9 8 7 6 5 4 3 2 1

Author's Note

As *The Children of the Lion* Series continues into the 1990s, having begun in December 1980, I would like to acknowledge all my friends at Book Creations who have participated in its success. Some who have contributed in the past, Lyle Kenyon Engel most particularly, are no longer with us; others who have lent a hand are too numerous to mention. I must confine my thanks to those currently involved: Laurie Rosin, a gifted editor who guided the shaping of the story and the text; Betty Szeberenyi, the librarian who supplied such abundant research materials; and Judy Stockmayer and Marjie Weber, who refined and perfected the text to ensure its consistency and accuracy.

The Middle East has endured many conflicts over the millennia. It is well to remember the past, and I hope this book builds a bridge from past to present, reminding us of our heritage and the enduring thirst of man for peace.

—PETER DANIELSON

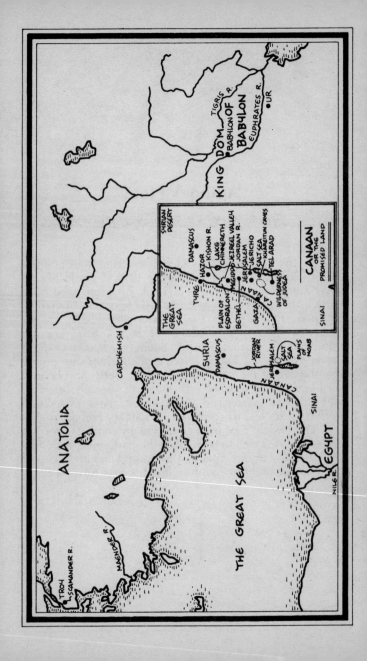

Prologue

All day long the dreaded hamseen *had blown, bringing the madness that could still be seen on many of the haggard faces around the campfire. When night fell the wind had changed direction and brought fresh air that carried the smell of the sea.*

The evening seemed softened by the sea breeze. Gulls, their huge wings spread, glided in to land on the oasis waters. Far above the western horizon sat the clouds that would bring rain. The travelers looked at them and realized the hardest part of their long journey had ended. The morrow would bring new terrain unlike the parched track they had followed through the desert wilderness.

As the lank figure of the Teller of Tales stepped out of the darkness and into the warm pool of light from the campfire, he could see the hope in their faces. He raised his long arms and bade the gathering to be silent.

"After the harsh desert, the smell of the sea," he began. "After travail, silence and rest. After sin, repentance. After bitterness, reconciliation and forgiveness. After a sundering, a healing. After the trials of life comes God's benison, although sometimes the wait seems longer than one man can bear. And the suffering seems to be more than we can endure."

He raised his voice, and his conjurer's hands wrought magic in the firelight. "So it was," he said, "for the tribes

1

of Israel in the ten years that followed the conquest of
Canaan. So it was when the children of Jacob fell away
from the Law given to them by Moses, turned their faces
from God, and felt the fire of His displeasure."

The last of the sea wind died, and the flames of the
campfire stopped dancing. "There came a time," the old
man said, "when, as man had deserted God, so God began
to desert man. The people began to forget Him and turn
toward the wretched baalim of the heathen among whom
they lived. Some even courted the favor of the evil demon
Ashtaroth. And all the strength and power that the men of
Israel had wielded suddenly left them, and they became
less than men.

"Then it was," he said in a voice that carried a hard
edge, "that the nations Joshua had conquered began to
rise from the dead, and Israel's enemies, old and new,
armed against her. In the south the warriors of Moab
swarmed across the Jordan River to enslave and oppress
Israel's southern tribes, comprised of men who had lost
the will to fight. And from the north there came a new
threat, the son of King Jabin of Hazor. As a youth he had
seen his father killed by the Israelites and his father's
army scattered. Now he wanted revenge.

"Ten years after his father's fall, the young Jabin
established a new kingdom, enslaving the men of Naphtali
and Zebulun, dishonoring their women, and oppressing
the old and the poor. Suddenly it was as if Joshua's fiery
sword had never flashed through the northern hills, had
never carved a new empire for the Israelites."

The Teller of Tales shook his bony fists. "The men of
Israel were no longer men! In their weakness they had lost
all their friends, even the Children of the Lion, who had
been their allies since the days of Abraham. They stood
naked before their enemies. Finally the cry rang out from
one end of the Promised Land to the other: 'What can we
do? Who will rise to lead us? Who will win back the power
Moses gave us?'"

The old man's hawkish eyes peered out from under
white beetling brows to scan the crowd. His thin lips
curved in a wry smile. "Well you may ask!" he said.

"*God's eyes traveled up and down the land He had given them, searching for a prophet to speak the bitter truth to His people. And among the impotent men of Israel He found no one through whom His words could rightly be spoken.*"

He paused. The crowd waited. "*So in His infinite wisdom He chose a woman to do the work the men could not do.*"

He paused again. When he spoke his voice was low and soft; a wry smile played on his thin lips; his hands wove their spell. "*Hear now,*" he said, "*of the rise of Jabin of Hazor and of his notorious general Sisera. Hear of the shame that was heaped upon Israel as the tribes fell into unholy ways.*"

"*Hear, too,*" he said, "*of the wanderings of the Children of the Lion after their exile from Israel. In Troy, Iri of Thebes's adopted son, Phorbus, carried on the struggle for Keturah's freedom . . . and in Canaan, where invaders brought war and destruction to lands that had known tranquillity, Pepi made peace with his longtime enemies. Brother fought brother, and the madness of men made a mockery of the mighty words of God!*"

"*Hear also of the woman Luti, condemned to death as a witch in the kingdom of Babylon and sent on a desperate mission to Canaan where only her magical powers can save her.*"

He paused and drank in the expectant silence as the crowd waited for the tale to begin. Then, in a strong voice full of suppressed emotion, he spoke.

PART
ONE

CHAPTER ONE

Canaan

Micah stopped the wagon and handed the reins to his friend Zuriel. "I leave you here," he said in a taut voice, then leapt lightly to the ground. "You know what to do: Deliver the tribute to the warehouses as if nothing were wrong. Remember, you know nothing, you've seen nothing, and you've heard nothing. You don't have any idea where I am or what I'm doing. Right?"

"I'll do my part," Zuriel replied quickly, but his voice betrayed his anxiety. "And I'll have our party out of the city before trouble erupts. But what about you?"

Micah did not answer, afraid for the moment to speak aloud for fear that his voice would break. The danger of his mission was becoming more real. He looked around. No longer did the city of Jericho hold any special meaning for him. Joshua, with Yahweh's help, had crushed its walls and defenses. Even after ten years of fighting with and for the Israelites, Micah felt isolated and an outsider. He cleared his throat. "Don't worry about me. Keep your mind on the assignment. I'll do what I have to do and get out. When you're away from the city, have our men blow the ram's horn throughout the hill country, then send the most reliable messengers by the fastest horses. We need to spread the news immediately that the rebellion has started."

"How will I know if you've been successful?" Zuriel asked.

Micah gave a nervous laugh. "I won't fail. I'll kill the bastard, whether I manage to get out alive or not."

"Micah, this is suicidal."

"What if it is?" He paused. He did not want to act the hero in front of Zuriel. It was the mission that mattered, not the motive. "The important thing is to stop the Moabites' main army at the Jordan. As long as we control the fords, we'll control the river. If we fail and the army crosses . . ." He shook his head sadly, then his expression became set with resolve. "I'm sure victory will be ours. And that victory is worth more than the life of one man. It really doesn't matter if I come back alive, does it?"

Zuriel could no longer suppress his admiration. "You're a true hero of Israel, Micah. And I'm proud to . . . know you."

Micah had not missed the hesitation in his friend's voice, and he knew that Zuriel had started to use the past tense as if he, Micah, were no longer among the living. Zuriel would probably be proved right before the hour passed. But what did his own life matter if they could drive the Moabite oppressors from central Canaan? What did his own life matter if by a single action he could signal the Israelite irregulars now hiding in the forests of the hill country to rise up?

Seeing the pained look in Zuriel's eyes, Micah dismissed him with a nod. "Get out of here," he ordered.

"Go with God," Zuriel said as he grasped the reins tightly.

"Which god?" Micah asked, laughing. It was an old game of theirs. It always provoked Zuriel, who was a pious and often fervent follower of Yahweh. Micah fought only for the Israelite people; their God was not his.

This time, however, Zuriel did not respond. Micah walked swiftly away from the wagon, toward the house Eglon of Moab had commandeered as his headquarters in Canaan.

He stopped after twenty steps and realized that there was no creaking of wagon wheels behind him. He turned.

The wagon had not moved. He stared at Zuriel, who sat absolutely still with the reins in his hand. Something appeared strange about his comrade. Then he saw that Zuriel, the strong soldier, was weeping.

Micah ran back and leapt up onto the wagon by vaulting off one wheel. He grasped his friend by the shoulders. "Zuriel! Do you remember the last harvest festival? When we went to the coast. Do you remember?"

Zuriel nodded, trying to stop himself from weeping.

"And do you remember that stranger we met? That grizzled old man. A sailor. Yes, he was a sailor from the north."

"The one with the scar on his face?" asked Zuriel.

"Yes, him. Do you remember what he told us about his god? About how if a soldier dies in battle for a just cause, he will live forever in a place his god has created—a place called paradise—eating lamb. And this lamb is the freshest, most succulent, and most delicately spiced meal imaginable, and paradise is never too hot or too cold, and it is crisscrossed with beautiful streams of sun-sparkled water. Do you remember?"

Zuriel nodded. His tears had stopped.

"If I do not come back, you can be sure that I am in paradise."

The two comrades embraced. Micah leapt down again. Zuriel took a deep shuddering breath, grabbed the long whip, and flicked it over the heads of the beasts. The wagon wheels began to turn. Micah stared after Zuriel until he was lost to sight; then the thought came to him: *What happens in paradise to those of us who don't like lamb?*

For more than a year Micah had delivered the Israelite tribute to their Moabite overlords. For most of that year the assassination he was about to commit was being meticulously planned and discussed and refined. As part of the strategy he had become well acquainted with the Moabite guards. They, like him, were in their twenties and shared the interests common to young men. He had spent time with them—gambling, drinking, joking. By now he knew several guards on each shift and their peculiarities: who

drank too much . . . who had a taste for the low life . . .
who was happy . . . who was disaffected.

As he approached Eglon's headquarters he spotted
Saleh, commander of the day shift, and greeted him with a
broad smile. The Moabite was a tall, rangy man, with very
long black hair and a pair of bone daggers in sheaths
around his neck. Micah knew about bone daggers; they
were deadly when thrust into human flesh but shattered
easily when deflected by bronze or iron. Saleh wore them
probably to intimidate, and they did that—they were fearsome to look at.

"Saleh," Micah said with false affability, "I didn't
expect to see you here. You haven't received your com-
mission? What went wrong? Did you bribe someone with
a black-eared goat that died before he got it home?"

"Bribe? Me?" Saleh grinned. "The gods forbid that I
should ever offend the honor of my glorious superiors by
offering any of them a bribe." He winked at Micah. "Instead call it an expression of admiration for their virtue
and their talents. Call it a love offering. In fact, old friend,
it was a fat, pregnant donkey, and it should have made a
splendid gift. But the poor, stupid beast had a breech
delivery and died. The foal was deformed and blind in one
eye. Now I'll be lucky if I'm allowed to remain with the
palace guard. The last man who fumbled one of those love
offerings is digging sewerage trenches." He shrugged philosophically. "Enough of my troubles. What brings you
here?"

"The usual," Micah answered blandly. "A love offering, as you put it, for the noble Eglon."

"If Eglon is noble, then I am the father of that deformed one-eyed foal."

Micah stepped back a bit, feigning discomfort. "Isn't
it dangerous for a captain of the guard to talk like that?"

"Only if someone hears me, my friend. And no one is
going to hear me other than you because we're short
staffed, and the nearest guardsman is fifty yards away."

Micah nodded and started toward the small stone
ramp that led to Eglon's headquarters. The walkway was
manned by one of the Moabite's personal bodyguards—a

helmeted giant, a mercenary from the Sea Peoples, grasping two short bronze-tipped thrusting spears.

"Wait, Micah!" Saleh called. "Will you be long?"

"No, not long . . ."

"Then meet me at noon."

"Where?"

"The Two Gate Tavern."

Micah realized that his deception with Saleh had gone too far. Saleh believed him to be a true friend. "I'm not interested in whores right now," he said.

"Then we can sit in the front and drink beer or wine. A tavern is a tavern. Who cares what goes on in the back?"

Micah nodded, then Saleh waved and walked off to continue his rounds. Everything was falling into place perfectly. Every step so far had gone flawlessly. A sober thought chilled him: The scheme would succeed unless Micah himself faltered. But this was not a battlefield, on which he had already been tested. Today there were no trumpets, chariots, or massed formations. This would be murder. Could he really kill an unarmed man, no matter how much he hated him? And if he succeeded, would the Israelites call upon him to murder again? Might he be called upon to kill a man he loved?

Micah stared down at his hands. His fingers were trembling. With fear or anticipation, he could not say.

CHAPTER TWO

City of Ur, Kingdom of Babylon

Luti, barefoot and dressed only in a single, coarse garment, stood shivering on the path. The sun was just beginning to rise. Shafts of sunlight were piercing the darkness around her. She listened for the familiar sound of the oxcart to take her to work but heard nothing.

It was cold, but there was no wind. As the sun rose, she could see more of the familiar surrounding landscape: the irrigation ditch, the banks of the Tigris River, and in the far distance, to the north, the towers of the great and wealthy cities. Her own city, Ur, was without the impressive buildings and the opulent gardens. It had become a stepchild, a backwater of the kingdom.

There were many reasons for Ur's fall, not least of which was the fact that the city still worshipped Astarte, the ancient goddess of love and war, rather than Marduk, the official god of Babylon since the latest tide of invaders had been driven out. Babylon was autonomous again. The kingdom had been restored, and Marduk, the storm god, was its savior. The cult of Marduk had promised the people that all the foreigners who continued to threaten the kingdom—Hittites, Assyrians, Anatolians—would be destroyed. The inhabitants of Ur, however, had refused to abandon Astarte.

Luti was nineteen years old. She had lived in the shacks of Ur for as long as she could remember, and it seemed to her that she had been waiting all her life for the oxcart to take her to the flax fields. She knew nothing about her mother or father, having been raised by an old man who refused to tell Luti how she had first come to live in his hovel. When she was twelve, he kicked her out because she had started to fight back against the beatings that he routinely administered to her. Although she knew nothing about where she had come from, she did know that she was a foreigner . . . a stranger to this land between the two great rivers.

Her hair was black, her eyes narrow, her cheekbones high, her complexion almost copper. People often asked her if she had come from the far north, where the devils lived with their shaggy ponies and their ferocious man-eating dogs. She could not answer them. Some said she was an Anatolian. Others guessed that she was a Mongol. Still others suggested that she was a Turkestani. And one even stated with authority that she had been raised in the deep forests by wild animals, which was why she had that funny birthmark on her lower back—that a bear or a lion or a tiger had used her backside as a footstool.

All Luti knew was that she could not remember living any place but Ur and that she existed without hope. There was no escape from the work and the poverty. She would never be able to save enough coins to leave. And if by some miracle she could leave, where would she go?

A strange sound suddenly filled the air. Geese! Her lovely but grim face brightened into an enormous smile. Magnificent geese were flying west in formation. She could hear them calling to each other. She could see the glimmers of their feathers, the powerful rising and falling of their wings as if they were oars in deep water. It was odd that they were not flying south toward the gulf, where the huge, rushing Tigris and Euphrates rivers emptied. Perhaps, she thought, they were winging toward the Great Sea, which she had heard about but was never able to imagine. She watched the geese until they were tiny specks in the sky. Birds had always been her secret companions. They spoke to her . . . they spread over her their mantle of beauty and

grace . . . they brought wisdom and a sense of peace into
a life of chaos and woe.

Luti was so lost in the beauty of the birds that she did
not hear the approach of the oxcart until the old wooden
wagon was almost upon her. As it slowed to a crawl, she
clambered onto it and then sat on the wooden plank next to
the old woman who called herself Asa. Luti had ridden together with Asa on this very same oxcart for as long as she
had labored in the fields. There would be no more stops. The
cart was fully loaded—four women and two young boys. It
could carry no more than six, along with the driver, who was
a eunuch employed by the Temple of Astarte in Ur.

"It will be bad today," Asa muttered as Luti squeezed
into a spot beside her. "Very bad, because I think we will
be working in the sheds."

Luti shivered. She was hopeful that the old woman was
mistaken, but she knew from bitter experience that Asa was,
in fact, rarely wrong. The old woman wore a shawl over her
head and a long, shabby dress with decorative beads, which
signified that in the distant past Asa had been a woman of
substance, a woman with a house of baked mud bricks and
a vegetable garden and perhaps some fruit trees.

It was Asa who had brought Luti to the fields, when
they had lived next to one another in small thatched huts
made of straw and mud, surrounded by hundreds of similar dwellings. It was Asa who had told Luti that there
were few work choices open to her. There was prostitu-
tion, which was dangerous and ugly. Often the girls died
young of disease or beatings. There were the northerner-
owned brick and pottery factories, which were injurious to
the lungs. And there were the fields of flax and grain
owned and administered since time immemorial by the
priests of Astarte, who paid a percentage of their profit to
the civil authority. The labor in the fields was hard, yes,
but the priests paid the workers a copper coin each week
as well as providing a midday meal.

"Did you bring a cloth?" Asa asked as the oxcart
turned onto the main road along the irrigation ditch that
led directly to the fields.

"No," Luti admitted, realizing that if Asa was right

and if they were indeed to work in the sheds adjoining the flax fields this day, then she would pay dearly for her lack of foresight.

In the sheds, the seeds of the plant were removed after the flax was crushed and pulped and before it was sent to the spinners and weavers, who would turn the flax into treasured linen. The seeds themselves were a lucrative monopoly for the priests of Astarte: The seeds were boiled to provide cooking oil; they were made into all kinds of medical poultices; and they were the basis of the many kinds of poisons for which the priests were famous—or infamous. There had even been murders in the sheds when one man had used the seeds for poison to kill another worker in a crime of passion. All one had to do to produce the deadly potion was soak the seeds in cold water for a long time and then know how to separate the acid that formed. Only cold water would do; boiling the seeds in hot water released nothing but harmless oil.

Removing the seeds was painful work. The fingers and hands of the picker became scratched and raw. If one had a cloth, Asa had instructed Luti years before, one could fold it around the fingers to prevent injury.

Luti closed her eyes and tried to get a few more minutes of blessed sleep. But Asa, angry and talkative, began to curse the driver, as if blaming him for her lot in life.

"Slow down, you cretin, or I'll make your bald head as bumpy as the road!"

He kept the cart at a steady pace.

Asa grew more furious. "You slimy toad! Which irrigation ditch spat you out?"

The eunuch looked straight ahead.

The other occupants of the cart tried to calm the old woman, but Asa would not relent. "The only thing you can do right is beat the ox, and that's only because he's your father!"

The driver did not respond at all, and his silence infuriated Asa. She rose as if to strike the eunuch from behind. The cart lurched, however, and she was thrust down so hard that the air was knocked out of her lungs and she gasped with pain. Luti, used to her friend's outbursts, put her arm around Asa while she regained her breath.

The sun was now fully up. The river was muddy and strangely calm. Asa's head lolled onto Luti's shoulder, and the old woman began to sing quietly. The others in the cart hummed along with her sad song. It was about a girl sold into slavery in some distant land and how she missed her family and friends and the fertile fields. Luti shut her eyes. The song made the pain of her loneliness acute. When the song ended, the workers rode in silence.

Suddenly, Luti heard honking sounds again. She sat up and stared skyward. The geese! They were calling to one another. Their harsh cry was strangely beautiful. They were lower now, much lower. Luti knew it was the same flock. She could tell by the leader's feathers; she could tell by the geese's formation. Why had they come back? Luti had always loved the birds flying over the flat land of Ur and had always watched them, but never had she seen a migrating flock circle back whence it came.

Then something moved in the bog by the side of the road. The movement was so sudden and swift that even the lumbering ox pulling the wagon stopped short, jolting the occupants. An archer emerged from the marshes. His bowstring was stretched taut, and the bronze tip of the nocked arrow gleamed in the sun.

Luti watched in horror as the bow sang and the arrow flew upward and impaled one of the geese. The beautiful bird fell to earth slowly, pathetically, thrashing its wings against the pain and inevitable death.

The wagon started to move again. The archer retrieved the bird and, grinning, held it up triumphantly for the occupants of the oxcart to admire.

"When was the last time you had a nice fat goose to chew on?" Asa asked bitterly.

Luti could not answer for the lump in her throat.

"Didn't you hear me, girl?"

Luti remained silent. She folded her arms and began to tremble. She knew what she had seen—an omen of disaster. The birds did not lie.

CHAPTER THREE

Canaan

"Don't you need my signature? My seal?" Nimshi asked.

Elizai the banker waved off the concern with his hand, as if it was unnecessary to deal with such matters when in the presence of such a well-connected customer. "The funds will be transferred to your account in Ashod by the first caravan heading into Philistine territory, sir. Given the numbers of bandits on the roads, you're smart not to carry gold on your person."

Nimshi's eyes quickly swept the banker's lavishly decorated room. In the old days bankers tried to hide their wealth; in the old days ostentation put clients off. "Much has changed in ten years," he remarked. "When Joshua was alive the roads were kept clear of thieves and killers. Now that Moab controls southern Canaan, one can ride for days without seeing a guard patrol. They're probably off plundering women or crops instead of keeping the peace."

The banker looked surprised. "Do you really wish the days of Joshua to return? For those of us who did not share his people's religion and customs, there was nothing but torment."

"Don't misunderstand me. I'm not entirely excusing the behavior of the Israelites then," Nimshi said. "My own family suffered at their hands. My mother and sister-by-marriage vanished during the riots in Jerusalem. I still

17

don't know if they are dead, or worse. My own younger brother joined the Israelite army, and I haven't seen or heard from him since." He paused. "My father was chief armorer to Jerusalem's military. We were well-to-do. Then we lost everything we owned in Joshua's campaign."

Elizai shook his head in sympathy, then heaved his bulk from a chair. "It was a pleasure to be of service to you, sir. It's nice to find a man who appreciates what a good banker can do in times of difficulties. Whatever one thinks of Eglon of Moab, he understands that Jericho would never have been rebuilt without loans."

Nimshi gazed at the banker and thought about the crushing taxes heaped on Israelite and Canaanite alike to repay those usurious loans. "Well, it's back to the coast for me, now that I've finished my work here. I like to be where I can smell the sea."

"I thought you lived in Ashod," the banker said.

"No, I just do business there," Nimshi replied. "I'm building a home in Ashkelon, within sight of the sea." He smiled. "Deep inside every Child of the Lion a wanderer lurks. We all have the itchy foot, whether or not we get to exercise it."

"Then you'll want to join the noon caravan for the coast. May you have a pleasant journey and return to us soon."

"I doubt that I will," Nimshi said frankly. "This trip completes the work I contracted with Eglon. Thank you for your help."

He extended his hand to the banker, whose expression had become sad with the realization that Nimshi would not be doing any more business with him in the near future. Working with any Child of the Lion was a necessary preliminary before achieving every banker's dream: to have commerce with Khalkeus of Gournia, proprietor of the family trading empire. Although the fleet had fallen on relatively hard times, there was still a great deal of money to be made from an alliance with Khalkeus.

All the Children of the Lion shared in the profits of the shipping business, the funds automatically placed in their individual accounts. Khalkeus's numerous agents in almost every seaport provided immediate access to the funds. But not all chose to enjoy the money or live in luxury on the secret island called Home. Some, in fact, had chosen quite different lives. For example, Pepi of Kerma, Nimshi's half brother, had vanished during Joshua's conquest, after his beloved wife, Tirzah, was abducted during the Jerusalem riots. Nimshi knew that Pepi had offered his services as a military armorer to the enemies of Israel. Almost everyone in the family now believed that Pepi was dead—a victim, perhaps, of the head injury he had suffered many years before.

Pepi's uncle, Iri of Thebes, had pursued a similar life-style. After learning that his wife, Keturah, was enslaved in Troy, Iri had joined the Greek forces besieging the city and worked as an armorer. Iri had attempted to gain access to Troy in order to free Keturah. He was killed in that brave but futile attempt.

Nimshi, on the other hand, had chosen—as his late father, Baufra, had—to maintain a strict neutrality in the wars of Canaan in the time-honored tradition of the armorer's creed: Make weapons for all who want them, regardless of the truth or nobility of their cause.

In fact, it had become difficult to distinguish one cause from another, right from wrong. Nimshi had not approved of the brutal recklessness with which Joshua had conquered the land a decade before. Nor had he approved of his brother Micah's decision to join Joshua's army, or his continuing enthusiasm for the Israelite cause over the years. Now that their parents were dead and Pepi was presumed so, Nimshi and Micah were their immediate family's sole survivors. Nimshi longed for his brother's company and comfort and often fantasized about pulling Micah away from the Israelites and starting a new life together. The brothers had not seen each other for ten years.

Now the Israelites, having lost their power and ascendency in the wake of the death of Joshua and Caleb, were slaves to Moab and Hazor, and Nimshi was angered by the oppressive behavior of Israel's new enemies and overlords. Nimshi did not know if this new low status would

cause Micah to cleave more closely to his adopted people
or drive him back home to Nimshi.

Gradually Micah regained control of his emotions,
going over in his mind every step of the plan. He was on a
mission of great importance . . . a mission that required
all his concentration . . . a mission that would test him to
the limit. Then he made his way to the upper floor of
Eglon's headquarters, where, he had been told, the Moabite
overlord was resting.

He found the man, huge and bloated, enjoying the
cool breezes and looking out over the long rows of newly
transplanted palms that lined the streets of the rebuilt
city.

"Ah, you finally got here," Eglon said contemptuously. "Did the transfer go smoothly? Did you short us on
the tribute?" He laughed. "No, you wouldn't do that.
You're not that stupid. Because if you did . . ." He let
the threat hang.

Micah studied the misshapen, porcine face with the
blotched skin and tiny red-rimmed eyes. He loathed the
man. But he forced calm into his voice and bowed politely. "I think your officials will find, my lord, that we
have overpaid slightly. I gave the order myself. I thought
it better than having the payment disputed. We barely
have time to harvest the crops, much less argue with your
auditors."

Eglon scowled. "You're an insolent fool, but I'll let it
go. If your accounts aren't accurate, we'll take the mistakes out on your flesh . . . slowly." He dismissed the
problem with a wave of one fat bejeweled hand. "What
else do you have for me?"

"My lord, you asked me to keep my eyes and ears
open and let you know if any of my adopted people were
plotting against you." Micah's heart was beating fast. He
felt the fear growing inside him, like a snake. His fingertips were tingling. "My lord, my throat is dry. Might I
have a drink from the wineskin I see beyond you?"

Eglon signified assent with a wave.

Micah reached for the goat's bladder, uncapped it,

and squirted the raw red wine into his throat. Then he wiped his lips and replaced the vessel. He felt with his left hand for the dagger, secure in its scabbard, concealed under his robe to the right of his navel.

Eglon was getting impatient. "Get on with it. What information do you have for me?"

"My lord, I have found evidence of a plot, but the conspirators are not Israelites. Your own guards intend to murder you."

"My guards?" Eglon was incredulous. "What are you talking about? No Moabite would ever—"

The idea of getting that close to Eglon was repugnant, but Micah had no choice. Eglon stood facing him, his huge body shapeless in its flowing garments.

"Close the doors first," Eglon commanded, his eyes glittering. "Ah, the vengeance I will visit on the conspirators . . . some bloody torture to enliven my nights!"

As Micah bolted the door with the heavy crossbar, one hand slipped down and loosened the dagger from its sheath. "Now, my lord, this must be heard by only you."

Eglon waved Micah to come closer. "Tell me everything."

"Of course, my lord, everything." Micah reached inside his garment. His fingers closed on the knife handle. He felt a sense of utter calm, as if he were walking in a familiar field. He stared at Eglon's face. At that instant nothing really mattered anymore—not the planning, not the fears, not his philosophical misgivings . . . nothing. He was going to kill this monster.

"For Yahweh and Israel," Micah grated, and his body sprang like a lethal snake uncoiling from beneath a desert rock. He brought the knife up from below with all the force he could muster.

Eglon had just enough time to blink with shock before the blade caught him in the belly and ripped upward.

Micah enjoyed watching the terror in the Moabite's eyes. Eglon's mouth fell open as the dagger, cutting through the layers of fat, found the heart.

CHAPTER FOUR

City of Ur, Kingdom of Babylon

"Didn't I tell you this would happen? Didn't I tell you we'd be in the sheds today?" Asa's voice verged on hysteria.

But Luti had grown used to Asa's odd behavior. The older woman had played an important but unpredictable role in her life. Sometimes she intimidated Luti; sometimes she consoled her. But always Asa tried to be Luti's protector, and the young woman understood this.

They started to work. The sheds were open on all sides. Two guards patrolled the perimeter of each shelter to discourage theft and to crush any disturbances among the workers. Each guard carried a lance but wore no armor. These men were veterans of far-flung expeditions, and most of them had been wounded severely. In a sense, duty in the fields was a rest cure for old soldiers. The shorter guard at Luti's shed had lost half his right ear and a part of his chin in some frontier campaign. One-Ear looked truly grotesque, and he always stared at Luti. She was used to it, but it never ceased to bother Asa.

Field laborers carried the crushed plants into the sheds in baskets and dumped them into large round basins that were scattered throughout each small shelter. Then Luti, Asa, and the others picked out the seeds and flicked them into baskets at their feet.

Seven women worked around each basin. They talked

constantly, never glancing at the basin as their hands
worked unconsciously, withdrawing the seeds by touch
alone. Their arms grew slippery from sweat and blood.

When the workers stepped back from the basins, it
served as a signal that the plants were fully separated from
the seeds and that a fresh batch of crushed, pulpy plants
needed to be provided.

At one end of each shed was a large pot mounted on a
three-legged stool. Here was the water for the workers.
Once during the day this pot was emptied of water and
filled with a milky millet stew. The grain, along with flat
cakes made from wheat not fit for the market, constituted
the workers' lunch. Although this fare was simple and
monotonous, the laborers were grateful for it, for it often
constituted their only meal of the day.

By midmorning the sun had burned off the lingering
haze, and the surrounding fields lay like enormous green
and gold blankets around the sheds. In addition to flax,
rye and barley and wheat and millet and peppers were
grown in the fields owned by the priests of the goddess
Astarte.

Asa and Luti walked out of the shed together on their
break. Asa had brought a persimmon, a special treat,
which they shared.

"Look there!" Asa pointed to an ugly brown swath of
diseased vegetation cutting through the otherwise green
adjacent field. "It widens about a foot a day. Some fields, I
heard, are even worse. What will happen if all the crops
are swallowed up by this plague?"

Luti squinted at the scar on the earth. "I heard that
one-fifth of the crops have already been lost. In the millet
fields it is very bad."

"Maybe the priests will order up another national day
of prayer," Asa said sarcastically. "Or maybe they'll hire
more astrologers."

"Where does such evil come from?" Luti asked.

But Asa, like the other Babylonians, had no answer to
the dilemma. They walked back to the shed slowly, thinking about what they had seen. The other workers and they
felt both horrified and gladdened. On the one hand, smaller

crops meant less work, and they were already pushed to the edge of their strength. Also, they could not help but feel inwardly gleeful that Astarte's hated "all-powerful" priests were being hurt in their purses. But it was a rueful, self-defeating enjoyment, and the laborers knew it; a plague threatened their very existence. They were already on the verge of starvation.

"Look at One-Ear grinning at you, Luti," Asa whispered, nudging her friend.

The poor man was obviously in love with Luti, but he never approached her—the priests forbade any fraternization between guards and workers, hopeful of preventing a conspiracy to steal produce and tools.

"If you weighed what was left of his right ear, it would be more than what was left of his brain," Asa added.

"The other one isn't too bright, either," noted Sillwa, a tall, hot-tempered woman originally from the city of Lagash on the Euphrates. "If a man wants to work for the Temple of Astarte, I think he has to pass a test proving that he is crazy or stupid." Sillwa had worked with them for only about two years. No one knew the circumstances under which she had come to Ur, but she had alluded several times to a false charge of conspiracy made against her by her husband and his family.

Luti rarely listened to Sillwa anymore; she had heard these kinds of insults for too long. They were like the refrain of a song known by heart. But this day she was paying even less attention because of the upsetting incident with the archer and the flock of geese. Luti had always listened carefully to people who knew about birds, who could tell the future by cutting a bird open, by circumscribing its wingspan on a dish of sand, or by interpreting its flight. She herself had observed birds for hours, alone in the fields before and after work. She knew that since birds inhabited the precious space between heaven and earth, they were particularly important and held within themselves a special kind of wisdom. And she knew that any expert of bird signs would say that what she had seen this very morning was an omen of evil.

"Look!" Her musings were interrupted by a whispered warning from Sillwa. Luti followed Sillwa's eyes, as did all the workers around the basin.

A short, heavyset man dressed simply but exquisitely in white linen appeared at the entrance to the shed. A heavy gold loop hung around his neck. On his right cheekbone was a small tattoo of the morning star Venus, one of the heavenly symbols of the goddess. The priests in the north had also taken to wearing such designs on their cheekbones, but theirs were of Jupiter, the planet that was Marduk's heavenly sign.

"Banniselk," Asa intoned, and there was a long, low murmur of recognition and fear among the other workers.

Banniselk was one of the high priests of the goddess Astarte. He rarely left the temple, and this was only the second time Luti had ever seen him. The first time was when she was fifteen and had attended a dance that celebrated the millet harvest. Banniselk, at that time much thinner, had blessed the crop and those who had harvested it, then had distributed hundreds of flasks of wine. Two other men now stood with the priest, talking in low tones. Luti had never seen them before.

"He struts like a peacock who has had too much to eat, doesn't he?" Asa hissed, digging furiously into the basin with her hands. "And look at his toadies, hanging on to his every word—as if a priest of Astarte has something profound to say! Well, I never heard one of them say anything worth remembering, not a blessed word."

Luti nodded out of respect for the old woman's views, although she herself was not cynical about either the goddess or her priests. She did not know if the beliefs concerning Astarte were true, but at least her ceremonies and festivals were beautiful. As a child Luti had loved to see images of the goddess—so powerful, so reassuring. She smiled, remembering her excitement when she was first taught to read the tablets and learned that each year Astarte made a dangerous trip to the underworld out of her love for humans, in order to rescue Tammuz, the god of fertility, who had been imprisoned there. If not for Astarte, Tammuz would still be chained in the netherworld. If not for the goddess's bravery and love, no flow-

ers would bloom, no beast would give birth to young, no
field would yield its crops. For those reasons, the goddess
would always be precious to Luti. As for the priests . . .
well, were they any different from the cult priests of
Marduk in the north? She doubted it.

The visitors entered the shed now, and the women
worked quietly, hopeful of overhearing what they said.
The dignitaries were joined by One-Ear, who had leaned
his lance on his foot and listened to a set of detailed
instructions.

"Perhaps they are planning to distribute extra rations?" Sillwa suggested.

"If you believe that, you're even stupider than I
thought," Asa retorted.

In response the tall woman reached down into the
basin, pulled up a clump of crushed plant, and flung it at
Asa. The older woman nimbly sidestepped the missile.
The workers tensed, breath held, waiting for the inevitable beating from a guard. But no guard approached.

The laborers waited, unmoving. But a change had
occurred: The two guards normally stationed at that shed
had been joined by four more, and Banniselk and his
sycophants had drifted back toward the perimeter, as if to
stay out of harm's way.

A second later two burly newcomers burst through
the line of guards and rushed toward a basin. The women
began to scream and scatter, but the object of their charge
was Luti. Before she could move, the two men, their linen
robes tucked up into their belts, grabbed her, flung her
down, and dragged her across the dirt floor.

It had all happened so quickly and with such ferocity
that a shocked and absolute silence prevailed, except for
Luti's cries as her head and shoulders bumped against the
ground.

Then the women screamed and threw objects at the
guards, attempting to help their friend. Luti herself recovered from the shock and screamed, "What have I done?
Why are you doing this to me?" Pain jolted through her
body, and no matter how she twisted and struggled, she
could not free herself from her tormentors' grasp.

Asa, desperate to save her companion, knocked over the water pot, picked up the three-legged stool, and hurled it toward Banniselk. The guards formed a circle to protect the priest and held their lances out threateningly.

The screaming women went on a rampage, grabbing anything they could find and throwing it, but they could not prevent the men from dragging Luti out of the shed and into an irrigation ditch by the adjoining field.

Finally, they released her. "What have I done?" Luti moaned. "Why do you hurt me?" She could see the priest of Astarte not twenty feet away, running his eyes over her. She could feel his hatred and something else . . . a sensation that made her flesh crawl.

She tried to get up, but the side of a lance smacked into her face. She could taste her own blood, and her world began to whirl and tilt. There was darkness and then light.

"Be quiet," she was told. "Stop struggling. The more you fight, the worse it will be."

She turned her head to see One-Ear. "Please," she begged him through a veil of pain, "tell me what I have done."

He did not answer.

She could hear the sounds of the women who had surged from the shed and were shouting in her defense. Her two attackers climbed out of the ditch and made for the shed area. She could hear Asa's hoarse voice: "Free her! Free her or we'll burn your sheds and flax and—"

Then Luti heard the sounds of feet running and the cries of women being beaten.

One-Ear suddenly bent close to her, his hand gently touching the side of her bloody face. "Blasphemy is the charge against you."

She did not understand what he was saying. "Please, tell me truthfully," she begged.

"Blasphemy," he repeated, his love for her obvious in his grim face as he helped her to stand. "A priest saw you bathing in the river. You have a mark on your body that—"

Luti looked up to see Asa break out of the ring of

guards and run toward One-Ear and her. A wooden plank was grasped like a weapon in her hand. Asa was coming to save her. But one of Banniselk's companions stepped calmly into her path and drove a lance through her heart. Asa dropped like a sack of grain, her eyes already wide in death, her mouth frozen.

The loudness of Luti's screams so frightened One-Ear that he jumped away. The girl collapsed without his support. The two assailants returned to the ditch and easily lifted her under the shoulders. She could see Banniselk turn on his heel and stride up the narrow path that ran perpendicular to the fields and that led to the Temple of Astarte, where all of Ur paid homage. Luti had no strength left to struggle or to comprehend. As she let herself be carried away in the procession led by the priest, the only image that came into her consciousness was the goose turning and falling and fighting against the wind currents and the barbed horror in its body, and then dropping to the earth.

CHAPTER
FIVE

Canaan

The great lump of flesh that had been the Moabite overlord named Eglon had collapsed. Micah's knife had split open Eglon's guts, and they spilled onto the floor. Micah, watching the life drain from his victim's eyes, gagged once, again, then a third time. When the wave of nausea subsided, he looked around and listened carefully: Footsteps were pounding up the stairs, then he heard urgent voices outside the bolted door.

"I heard a crash. If he fell, we better be there to pick him up."

Someone banged on the thick wooden door.

Another voice: "Why would Eglon lock the door? Who's in there with him?"

Micah felt his fear rising. He knew from the Israelites who had been rounded up to build this palace that there was a secret passage in the room. In his panic, he could not remember where it was. How to find it fast? He stared at Eglon's body and felt his gorge rise again.

The pounding and voices continued: "Something's wrong in there. You go up to the balcony and around. I'll get some help to break down this door."

Micah began his desperate search for the passage. His hands moved up and down and under the woven wall hangings as sweat poured down his face and stung his eyes. Faster and faster he worked. There had to be

something—a lever, a knob, a rope. Then his palm sank
into a recess in the wall. He groped until he found what
seemed to be a primitive handhold carved into the stone
wall beneath a woven decoration. He pulled, but nothing
happened. He pulled again, this time putting all his strength
into it. A crack, small at first, and then gradually widen-
ing, appeared in the wall. He pushed with his shoulder,
and a door swung open, revealing a very narrow staircase
leading downward into darkness. At the bottom was a
small pool of light.

Micah slid through and pulled the door shut behind
him. He tiptoed cautiously down the stairs, cursing himself for failing to retrieve his knife.

When he reached the ground floor, he found himself
in a corridor leading to a kitchen pantry. Voices came to
him from around the corner, so he quickly picked up a bag
of flour and hoisted it over one shoulder. He walked
boldly into the kitchen and through a cluster of servants.
No one gave him a glance.

He hurried along with his head down, trying to look
as if he knew where he was going. At the far end of a
kitchen storeroom was a tradesmen's entrance. If only he
could reach it!

"Micah!"

Realizing that one of the servants had recognized
him, his heart lurched.

"Where are you going?" the fellow asked as he approached. "You know you can't take that bag of flour with you."

Micah swallowed and forced his voice to sound un-
concerned. "I was looking for someone to give it to. It fell
off a cart in the street." He dumped the bag heavily on the
floor and smiled. "Take care of it for me, will you?" And
with that, he fled through the tradesmen's door.

The sunlight blinded him for a moment. He heard
screams from the roof. "Send help! Hurry! The master has
been murdered!"

Micah forced himself not to run. *Steady now,* he told
himself. *You are just taking a nice little stroll.* When he
reached a narrow alley piled high with garbage, he broke
into a trot and moved swiftly to the next cross street.

*   *   *

After taking leave of Elizai the banker, Nimshi walked through the streets of the new Jericho, an unfortified settlement that had sprung up over the gutted ruins of the old city destroyed by earthquake and Joshua's army. He saw evidence of oppression everywhere. Once-prosperous Israelite landlords now worked as common warehouse laborers or hired themselves out as beasts of burden. Their formerly bright-eyed children now begged in the streets, bellies distended with starvation. And many of their women, already reduced to selling their clothes and ornaments, now sold themselves. Each day brought newly homeless Israelites into the city, taxed off the land by the Moabites.

Joshua's long and bitter campaigns had exhausted his people. They had lost their leaders, their sense of purpose, and their religion. They became vulnerable to enemies. Nimshi could see the hopelessness in their dull eyes. Were these beggars really the same people who had swept through Canaan like a mighty wind only a decade before? Were these beaten men the same warriors who had destroyed vastly superior armies with faith in Yahweh and a battle cry on their lips?

He watched a procession of wagons filled with tribute destined for the Moabite storehouses. The Moabites extorted a large portion of the Israelites' harvests. As the wagons passed and Nimshi saw the haggard faces of the drovers, he forced himself to remember his own sufferings during Joshua's wars of conquest. He tried to harden his heart against them as his eyes followed the pitiful procession when it turned into the street of the royal warehouse and toward Eglon's headquarters.

Nimshi started on his way again, walked a few steps, then stopped abruptly. A man was walking toward him. Something about his gait and the way he held his shoulders triggered almost a numbing response in Nimshi. He found himself straining toward the man, but he was unable to move. The stranger, dressed in simple Israelite garb and peasant sandals, was eating up the distance between them quickly.

It can't be! Nimshi thought. He covered his face with his hand for a moment as if to wipe away all illusion, then he pulled the hand away quickly. *My God, it's Micah. It's Micah!*

The man was almost upon him, but he was not slowing down. His face was set. He looked straight ahead. "Micah? Micah! Stop!" Nimshi shouted. "It's me. Nimshi! Your brother! Stop!"

Micah was past him now. Nimshi reached out and grabbed his brother's shoulder, but Micah savagely beat the hand away and kept walking, without looking back, without a single change of expression that would signify recognition.

"Do you deny your own brother?" Nimshi screamed after him. "Do you love the Israelites so much that you would betray the memory of your own family? Your mother? Your father? Micah! Please stop! Talk to me!"

But Micah did not stop or turn. Nimshi felt weak. He was trembling and drenched with sweat. *What has happened to all of us?* he thought. *How could we have let this bloody and violent land destroy the love between brothers?*

Once Micah had gotten past his brother, he searched out a small hidden alcove near a building's wall to compose himself. It had taken all his strength and discipline not to respond to Nimshi's pleas, but he had had no choice. Poor Nimshi! The anguish on his face had caused a pain like a spear in Micah's heart.

Micah breathed deeply and tried to blot out the vision of his brother's expression from his consciousness. In the distance he could hear shouting. By now everyone would know that the last man to see Eglon alive was Micah the tribute bringer. He zigzagged through Jericho's alleys like a rabbit leading hunters through a boulder-covered field. At least the new Jericho had no walls to trap him; Joshua and Caleb had forbidden the construction of any new walls because Yahweh, their God, had commanded that Jericho was never to be rebuilt. The new town that had sprung up on the ruins of the old had not even borne any name for the first few years. After the Israelites had begun to embrace Canaanite ways and forget not only Yahweh's Law but Joshua's commands, the inhabitants had begun to call it by the name of the vanquished city.

Micah was trotting through a narrow alley when he spotted a cluster of city guardsmen. He slowed to a walk and then stopped, watching them carefully. A chariot drawn by a fast horse sped into view. The vehicle stopped, and the guardsmen surrounded it. Micah flattened himself against the wall. He could not hear their words, but he had no doubt as to what the men were discussing. Finally the soldiers fanned out. To his horror one soldier headed down the alley.

Micah sank back into the shadows, then did not move a muscle. The soldier did not notice his quarry until he was right on top of him. Micah leapt out of the shadows and slammed into the guardsman, driving him hard into the far wall. Both men hit the façade with a crash, but the soldier had the breath knocked out of him. Micah grabbed the soldier's dagger and pierced his heart, killing him instantly, then retrieved the weapon and hid it in his robe. Finally he dragged the body into the far shadows and covered it with garbage. As he was concealing the corpse, he found himself staring into the guardsman's glazed, staring eyes. He remembered hearing the Israelite chant: *Forgive me, I have sinned against thee.* He closed the guardsman's eyes tenderly; then, dagger in hand, he sprinted across the street and headed down another alley at a dead run. When he reached the next commercial thoroughfare he slowed to a walk and again hid his dagger in the folds of his robe.

But this time his luck failed him. He looked up and saw the sign of the Two Gate Tavern. And it was Saleh who was coming out the door. They saw each other at the same instant. It was obvious from Saleh's broad smile that he had not heard about Eglon.

"Micah!" he called happily. "Just in time to have a long drink with me."

There was no escape. A sudden horror dawned on Micah: There would be no end to the killings now. Neither friend nor foe would be exempt. His future was like a chasm of death opening before his eyes, and there was nothing he could do to change it.

He forced a smile and pulled Saleh into the alley behind the tavern. Micah could see the man's bone daggers dangling in their sheaths. "I have to tell you a secret, my friend," he said. "Come closer."

Saleh gave him a strange look but bent toward him.

Micah pulled the dagger from his robe. Just as he had done with Eglon, he brought the weapon up from below. But Saleh was wearing body armor under his uniform, and the blade struck it with a loud *clink*. Saleh staggered back, then recovered. His face was twisted with shock and confusion. "Is this a game, Micah? Are you drunk?" He stepped forward and reached out as if to keep his friend safe, to prevent Micah from hurting himself or others until he sobered up.

Micah panicked. He grasped the stolen dagger with both hands and desperately lunged, stabbing Saleh in the throat.

A fountain of bright blood gushed out, staining his robe. Now he was marked. His soul was marked as well. He watched in horror as Saleh fell to his knees, clutching his throat, desperately trying to stanch the flow. Because there was no turning back, he stabbed Saleh in the temple and felt the sharp point of the dagger break through his friend's thin skull. Saleh cried out softly, a sound Micah would hear for the rest of his life—plaintive, accusatory. Saleh shuddered once, then lay facedown, a bubbling mess in the filthy alley.

It was done. Micah shivered and cursed softly. The front of his robe was gory with blood. He tore off his clothes, leaving himself naked except for sandals and loincloth. He kicked the stolen dagger under his discarded robe and moved back out into the street. Saleh's swift and silent death had attracted no attention.

Hopeful he could pass as a body slave or, perhaps, as a day laborer, Micah discarded his leather sandals in another alley, scooped up a handful of dirt, and spread it over his torso. Feeling safer, he walked briskly down the street until a hand grabbed his arm. Micah froze with fear as strong arms hauled him through a doorway.

The door was shut behind him. The grinning face in

front of him was Nefeq's, one of his Israelite confederates inside the city. Micah exhaled and relaxed.

"God loves you, Micah!" Nefeq exclaimed, embracing him. "You did it!"

"How did you know?"

"Our man in Eglon's headquarters sent a signal—thick black smoke."

"Who is he?"

"Never mind. The less you know about him the better. Our people in the hills will have seen the signal by now. There's a unit at the river to cut off the runners sent to warn the main Moabite force. You can relax. Your part is over."

Micah held up his hand. "Not yet. I have to get out of the city."

"Not the way you look. A real body slave would be burned black by the sun. No, you'd better stay here for the night. It's a safe house. Have some food and rest. Then we'll find you some clothes, and you can be led out at dawn." Nefeq, grinning widely, embraced him again. "I can't believe you did it! You just walked into old Eglon's headquarters and killed the bastard."

The horror came back to Micah. "It was ugly. I left my knife in the pig because I couldn't bear touching him again." A paralyzing weariness spread throughout his body. "I killed a soldier, too, whom I never saw before in my life. And I killed another man . . . a man I knew, a good man. Saleh came to me as a friend . . . and he—"

Nefeq cut him short. "Was he a Moabite?"

"Yes, but—"

"The only good Moabite is a dead Moabite," Nefeq said harshly. "That's all you need to know."

The caravan wound slowly through the pass of Beth-horon above Jericho and came to rest on the tableland called the Shephelah. Nimshi fretted, impatient with the caravan's slow progress through the hills. Feelings of anxiety and dread had settled over him after that bizarre encounter with Micah. He could not relax. He could not calm his mind. What had happened to his beloved younger brother?

Finally he could sit still no longer. He separated himself from the long line of wagons and pack beasts and approached the caravan leader.

"I'm leaving the caravan," he announced. "I want to go into Ekron."

The driver shook his head. "Are you sure? The hills are full of bandits."

"I know all about the bandits," Nimshi assured him.

He urged his mount along the southward path. An hour later he turned his horse toward the dusty road to Ekron. The route led through flourishing olive groves; olive oil was one of the principal sources of Philistine wealth in the region, and every bit of spare ground was given over to the trees. As he rode, his thoughts were consumed by his encounter with Micah and his trying to comprehend the strange events. Why would Micah refuse even to recognize him?

A ram's horn sounded in the hills. A few minutes later, the hollow, atonal signal was repeated. Strange, Nimshi thought, the ram's horn was not usually blown except to proclaim a religious day or a disaster or— Suddenly it became clear to him. The Israelites were planning an operation. But what? Against whom? A revolt against Moab? Well, that was long overdue, he thought. For how much longer could the Israelites allow Moab to squeeze them dry? It dawned on him that Micah had been in Jericho on the Israelite's behalf—probably to deliver the required tribute to Eglon. But there might have been another reason for Micah to be in Jericho—a reason of such importance and danger that Micah would refuse to greet him. After all, Micah had been a soldier, not a messenger. And the Israelites had always believed that the best way to kill a snake was to cut off its head.

The implications were chilling. Had Micah been sent to assassinate the Moabite overlord? Possibilities flooded Nimshi's brain. Things were beginning to make more sense.

The Israelites had behaved so docilely when Eglon of Moab moved in and began demanding tribute. But it was not like the sons of Joshua to sit passively by forever while Moabite taxes subjected them to poverty. The worm was

turning at last, and in Nimshi's opinion, a good thing it
was. Moabite domination had been bad for business—they
refused to patrol the roads, so there had been constant
raids on caravans.

Nimshi heard the ram's horn again. That was what it
meant: revolt! And Micah was in the center of it. Nimshi
rode on, a great sadness enveloping him. He realized that
in his heart he could not care less about the Moabites, the
Israelites, the caravan raiders, the declining trade routes,
or his own business. The only thing he truly desired was
to reconstruct what was left of his family. He wanted to
live in peace, harmony, friendship, and intimacy with his
brother Micah. There had to be a way for them to reunite
and begin a new life!

The entire garrison at Jericho turned out, and runners were sent across the Jordan to summon help from the
main Moabite force stationed farther down the valley. But
the runners were ambushed by Israelite bowmen at the
ford, so no messages got through.

Next the Jericho guard appeared, and Israelite soldiers attacked them. Wave upon wave of young men,
directed by the veterans who had ridden with Joshua,
poured down from the hills. They fell upon the Moabites
with a fury, hacking and stabbing—their bloodcurdling
war cries breaking the enemy ranks. Victory belonged to
the Israelites.

In Jericho one of Eglon's aides sent up a distress
signal from the palace's roof: three puffs of smoke followed
by a pause, then three more puffs. These signals were
picked up by the Moabite army, and a unit of cavalry was
dispatched to the river. They were met by Israelite irregulars, and after a brief but bloody fight the Moabites realized they could make no headway in recapturing the ford.
So they dug in, sent runners for reinforcements, and
vowed to yield no ground.

Micah was greeted as a hero when he arrived in the
Israelite camp early the following morning. The men,
women, and children who had journeyed to the river's

edge to witness the destruction of Moabite supremacy cheered when they saw their hero. They knew that it was he who had assassinated the hated Eglon.

"Long live Micah!"

"Let Micah come forth!"

"Let Micah lead the army!"

Micah held up his hands to silence them. When they gathered around him, he said, "I'm no leader, my friends. Right here, right now, there are a hundred men better equipped than I . . . men who were born among you, of your own blood. I cannot lead. I will not lead!"

Many of the enthusiastic people would not take no for an answer, but Micah held firm. He understood that they really were not looking for a war leader. Dozens of good men had already distinguished themselves in the first hours of the revolt. What they wanted was someone who could confirm to them that this revolt was Yahweh's will. Micah could not do that. He was not an Israelite. He had been born in Jerusalem of Egyptian parents. He was not a believer.

At last the Israelites left him alone, and he crossed the Jordan to meet with the leaders of the resistance. Many of them had fought with Joshua, and some of the older men had even been with the army when it first conquered Sihon and Bashan.

Among the veterans was Shemida, Joshua's foremost adjutant. After Joshua's death, Shemida had retired, but when the ram's horn had blown, he had ignored his wife's entreaties and his lame leg and had ridden to the ford to offer his services. After all, he was only in his thirties, still a young man. He had been a special friend of the young Micah's, and now they enjoyed a happy reunion.

"We are all proud of you," he said to Micah as they embraced. "You've done a great service for our nation."

Micah shook his head sadly. He could confide in Shemida. "I didn't mind killing Eglon, but there were two others I had to kill—and one of them thought of me as a friend. He trusted me."

Shemida nodded. "Our numbers include many men who actually enjoy slashing and maiming and killing—but when it comes to a killing that has to be done right, with precision and daring and sacrifice, we reach down into the ranks and find someone who'll feel guilty about the deed. Life is filled with ironies and puzzles."

"I keep seeing Saleh's face, Shemida. He was glad to see me and was trying to help me, even as the blade struck."

Shemida looked Micah in the eyes. "Did you know, my friend, that Joshua was haunted at night by the faces of the people he'd killed? For the last months of his life he could not sleep or love his family or even think or fight properly because of the ghosts."

"I can believe it," Micah said, cringing. "When I was in the safe house in Jericho, I was afraid to close my eyes for fear I would see Saleh's face." His features twisted with misery. "Shemida, the people acted as though I was a great hero, a man to lead the Israelites into battle. I think they want me to become another Joshua."

"Be glad that you're wise enough to see that you're not. No one would ever want to be the new Joshua if they knew what the old one endured." He put a hand on Micah's shoulder. "Besides, a man doesn't choose to become a Joshua. It is God who chooses him to become one—and the price he pays is terrible." He moved away and sat down on a broad rock. "My leg doesn't let me stand for long without pain."

Micah joined his friend.

"I, like many of my comrades," Shemida went on, "keep wondering if God is going to send us another leader like Moses or Joshua, enabling us to triumph over our oppressors. But I don't think so, not now." Shemida let out a long, disgusted sigh. "Look around, my friend. Moses said that if we obeyed the Law, kept to the dietary regulations, and followed the commandments, we would prosper. But that the moment we started straying from the path, we would become weak."

"Canaanite superstitions are cropping up everywhere, aren't they?" Micah asked. "Everyone has one of those little stone *baalim* in his pocket for luck. Astrologers and diviners wander through our villages. There are even cults of Ashtaroth."

"I have an idea that what we need now, Micah, is not a great warrior to lead us in battle against the enemy. The enemy is not the Canaanites but ourselves. We have drifted away from the One God. But where are we going to find a prophet? We could create a military leader, perhaps, and he might serve us well. But only Yahweh can create a prophet. And He doesn't seem to have given us one. We'll just muddle through as best we can and remain hopeful that the tribes of Israel will find some reason to unite—for only when we become one great army can we reclaim this land as our own."

The Israelite force on the Jordan, having seen the runners go back toward Moab for reinforcements, strengthened its own ranks with every male old enough to carry a weapon. But night came with no sign of the Moabite army. It was not until dawn that the enemy troops deployed themselves opposite the Israelite force. Before the sun was high the Moabites attacked, throwing every last man into the fight.

The Israelite army wavered and then broke on the left flank. The entire line could have been thrown into chaos. Quickly the Israelite command committed its reserve force of older, more experienced fighters. They rallied the young men and closed the gap.

Great, powerful-looking Bedouins on beautifully trained Moabite stallions set upon the strengthened Israelite line, only to be cut down by Israelite infantry who had no fear of cavalry troops. They had been taught by the veterans that horses could be hamstrung or shot out from under their riders by a sharp-eyed bowman even before they reached the lines.

By day's end Moab was without a military force, and Israel had a victory. But by nightfall the civilian army that had so decisively defeated the Moabites was already fragmenting, dispersing, drifting away as the men from the various tribes headed back to their widely separated homes in the south.

Although Moab had been crushed, better than half of the Israelites in Canaan remained under the control of one enemy or another. And for these poor souls there was no army to rise against the oppressor.

Nimshi arrived in Ekron in time to visit old friends at the school for metalworkers and arrange to hire apprentices for his own forges in Ashod and Ashkelon. Unfortunately, his heart was not in his activity, and he grew very tired. Instead of continuing his schedule he went into one of the inns and, after washing up from the dusty trip, went downstairs to eat. At the bottom of the stairs the innkeeper intercepted him and pointed out a gentleman seated in the tavern who had been inquiring for him. The fellow presented a tall, commanding figure, athletic, bright-eyed, his temples flecked with gray. Nimshi thanked the innkeeper, then walked over to the table and introduced himself.

The fellow stood up and smiled. "I am Theon, your kinsman," he said. "I just missed you in Ashod. I had other business that brought me here. Imagine my surprise upon learning from an armorer friend that you were also in town."

The kinsmen clasped arms and then stepped back to study each other. "I am delighted to meet you," Nimshi said warmly. "I've heard a great deal about you and, of course, your parents."

Theon nodded. "My father was extremely fond of your mother and acted as her protector for some years."

"Of course you'll stay the night," Nimshi said. "This is a better inn than most around here, and we have a great deal of catching up to do."

"Only if you'll let me act the host," Theon said. "Don't argue. We have some business to discuss, you and I."

Business? Nimshi thought. He did not care about business now. He did not want to discuss anything but finding Micah. He wanted to sit down with his brother over some wine and talk about what they had done and what they would do in the future. He wanted to talk with Micah about God and Man and Destiny.

After Theon and Nimshi were seated, a servant brought

out platters of lamb and fresh fruits and olives and dates.
The kinsmen spoke about their families and their lives.
When the platters were cleared, the men fell silent for a
few moments. Nimshi had not voiced his concerns about
Micah.

"Now," he said at last, "tell me what brings the
illustrious adviser of noble Khalkeus of Gournia to Philistia."

"My business representative in Ashkelon is dead,"
Theon said.

"I hadn't heard, but I've been away. When did it
happen?"

"About a month ago. He was a splendid man, wise
and resourceful, with great insight into people's strengths
and weaknesses." Theon laughed kindly. "He was also one
of those rare men who could deal with liars gently . . . and
successfully."

"May his spirit find rest," Nimshi said.

Theon looked him in the eyes. "I'd like you to be his
successor."

"What? I run a forge, Theon. I'm no businessman. I
can't keep accounts. I can barely add a column of ten
figures."

"We can hire a scribe to do that for you. You have an
excellent reputation, Nimshi, and I'd like to integrate you
into our business. Everyone says that people like you,
they open up to you and feel comfortable dealing with
you. My sources tell me that you're fluent in every language of the region. I've also heard that you're a shrewd
bargainer without angering the people you're dealing with."

"But, Theon—"

"And it's about time you settled down, married, and
raised a family." Theon took a deep draught from his wine
bowl.

Nimshi realized that only a few days before he would
have leapt at this opportunity. But now all was changed.
"Let me think about it, Theon. I need some time."

Theon nodded genially, and they moved on to other
topics, enjoying each other's company. As they finished
the yogurt and fruit dessert, the tavern door flew open. A
huge man wearing a guard's uniform staggered in, obvi-

ously drunk. He waved his hands wildly and yelled his news to the entire tavern. "Eglon of Moab is dead! The Israelites slaughtered the Moabite command at Jericho! There's fighting on both sides of the Jordan."

Cheers resounded throughout the tavern, and the innkeeper offered free wine. Eglon of Moab had been universally hated.

"So it has begun," Theon remarked. "I didn't think Israel would stand for much more of this. Do you think the revolt will spread throughout Canaan?"

"Not likely," Nimshi answered. "The twelve tribes are always at odds. They won't accept any central authority, so they wind up being cut to pieces by their enemies." Nimshi thought for a minute before continuing. "And this certainly won't affect the oppression of the Israelites in the north—Jabin of Hazor hardly realizes Moab is here."

"Don't you think it will come to Jabin's attention once the Moabites are gone?"

Nimshi considered. "Yes, Jabin may very well get territorial ambitions. He knows the Israelites can't maintain a standing army. My half brother has done a good job up there. Too good," he added ruefully.

"Your half brother? Pepi? I've never met him, although my father was very fond of Pepi as a boy. Why would he arm Jabin's military when his ties to the Israelites were so strong?"

"Because Joshua's second-in-command, Caleb, put a price on Pepi's head. He moved north to Hazor to be safe from Israelite assassins. It makes me sick to think of Pepi working with Jabin and Jabin's general, Sisera, that son of a whore."

"Sisera . . . I've heard much about the man, but I've yet to hear anyone say a kind word about him."

"You won't hear one from me, either, Theon. From all accounts he's as cruel as they come."

"And Pepi's working for these people?"

"Yes. Beyond Caleb's threats, Pepi is reacting to the disappearance of his wife, Tirzah, and our mother. We've never been able to learn what happened to them, but Pepi bitterly blames the Israelites."

"This isn't good news at all," Theon said. "Maybe I can find Pepi and talk to him. But first I'm on my way to Ebla and Damascus. I'll speak to you when I get back in a month or so. Try to have a decision for me by then. By the way, how is Baufra?"

"My father died about six months ago," Nimshi replied sadly. "He, too, never recovered from my mother's disappearance."

The tavern was becoming raucous. Arguments had erupted between patrons over the relative strengths of the Israelites and Moabites. Nimshi wanted to get away from the noise, but Theon seemed unaware of the increasingly violent discourse around them. Nimshi closed his eyes and let the wine soothe him. He heard Theon talking to him again, this time about some shipping problems in the Philistine League.

He opened his eyes and nodded, pretending to listen. But a plan was forming in his head: He would find Micah and persuade him to give up his violent association with the Israelites. They would both abandon their allegiances and their possessions and go south to Gaza. In Gaza were the finest ironworkers in the world, masters of their trade. The brothers could start a new life together. They could rediscover their art and their craft. They would once again become true Children of the Lion.

Nimshi suddenly came back to reality. Theon was still talking. Should he tell Theon of his idea and decline the job offer? For a moment he was tempted. But his kinsman would not approve of the plan. Theon obviously believed that life consisted of a position of responsibility and the acquisition of wealth. As a result, Nimshi remained silent, even though Theon's considerable resources could prove helpful in locating Micah.

The din was becoming intolerable to Nimshi. He closed his eyes again. Was there any possibility his plan could be realized? Was he brave enough? Would Micah be willing to leave the Israelites? Or was the wine making him feel optimistic?

CHAPTER SIX

City of Ur, Kingdom of Babylon

Luti opened her eyes, and even that slight movement caused her pain. Her whole body ached from being dragged and beaten. She remembered immediately where she was—in the courtyard of the Temple of Astarte. The ground was covered with a fine white sand made from crushed stone. Lining the sides of the courtyard, which led to the hidden shrine of Astarte—a place only priests could enter—were large, beautifully wrought jars. Each vessel had an unusual design on it, painted in the most delicate colors, recounting symbolically some great feat of the goddess.

The courtyard was empty and quiet. Even though it was open to the outside world, the tinkling of a small bell somewhere in the distance was the only sound Luti could hear. She summoned her strength . . . to rise . . . to flee. Something pulled her down, and she fell.

Luti twisted around to stare at her leg. A stake had been driven into the ground, and a leather thong ran from the stake to her ankle. She was trapped, but if she moved slowly and carefully, she could stand.

Once she was up, she felt better. She tested the stake. It was driven very deep; she did not have the strength necessary to pull it free. Her legs and arms were caked with blood. Her eyes still smarted from the salt tears. Why had they brought her to the Temple of Astarte? Where were her friends? Where was One-Ear? Luti re-

membered what the shed guard had whispered to her:
She was a blasphemer. It was all so crazy, incomprehensi-
ble. A blasphemer? The only things she had ever blasphemed against were long hours of work and low wages
and oxcarts that never arrived on time.

A strange sound pierced the stillness of the courtyard.
Luti whirled toward it, her tethered foot straining against
the stake. A deep purple curtain that protected the secret
shrine of Astarte opened, and from behind the curtain
walked six figures. They were coming toward her!

As they approached she could see they were priests,
all wearing the high conical hats that signified that they
had access to the secret shrine.

One man held the banner with Astarte's cult symbol
on it—a magnificent black-maned lion in the midst of its
hunting leap. Its fangs were bared; all four legs stretched
out, ready to pounce on the prey; its deadly claws were
unsheathed preparatory to rending flesh. It was a symbol
that all Ur's citizens recognized. The children of Ur had
always been taught that Astarte was their mother and
father . . . that she loved them with the ferocity of a lion's
hunger . . . that if they were loyal, she would caress them
with a tender paw, but if they were betrayers, she would
scourge them with the lion's claws.

Luti sank to her knees and moaned, frightened, as
her heart beat erratically. The priests halted about ten feet
from her. Only one came closer. It was Banniselk, the
priest who had ordered her dragged from the shed. He
was carrying a staff, and he poked its point at her as if she
were a fatted animal at the market.

Then he waved his stick high, and two temple servants came running, to place bowls of watered wine and
crushed peas in front of her. Then they ran off as quickly
and silently as they had come.

Luti's thirst was enormous. She grasped the bowl of
wine and drank it in desperate gulps, spilling much of it.
As she drank, she stared at Banniselk. The priest gazed at
her calmly. There was no hint of the expression she had
seen in his eyes in the ditch outside the shed, when she

had sensed that he wanted to hurt her or ravish her, when she had believed that he was the most evil man on earth.

The other priests, Luti saw now, were old men. Gold filigree was woven into their long linen gowns. She searched their eyes for some sign as to her fate, but there was none. They observed her as if she were a strange and unfamiliar object.

Then, quickly, Banniselk touched her on the shoulder with his staff. Luti cringed. He whispered to her: "I know you. I know who you are and whence you have come. I know what you have done. You and your comrades shall pay." He dug the wood into her flesh until she cried out and fell over.

"I have done nothing! I am a simple girl who works hard in the fields. Please believe me!"

But Banniselk, ignoring her outburst, turned to the other priests. "My lords, for two years we have witnessed the progressive and unstoppable decay in our crops. The goddess withholds her divine love from us. Slowly, inexorably, our fields are losing their potency. The harvest becomes smaller and smaller. A stink in the air bodes ill fortune. My lords, we have purified ourselves and our altars. We have dedicated great storehouses of wealth to Astarte. But, alas, she has not been placated. Even the heavens conspire against us. Just ten nights ago strange, fiery objects hurtled across the path of the morning star."

Banniselk paused. The other priests murmured in agreement over his assessment of the ills that threatened the people of Ur. Banniselk circled Luti once, twice, and then positioned himself so that she was between him and the other priests.

He continued. "My lords. There was a good reason why all our prayers and sacrifices were in vain. A messenger had been sent up from the netherworld, from that land of molten death deep in the bowels of the earth. And that messenger has recruited others and poisoned the wells of our fields, minds, and hearts. The goddess will never bring us joy until we expel these demons among us."

His words prompted whispers and anguished sighs from the frightened priests. Evil was loose in the kingdom, malevolence of such force and power that it had neutralized even the priesthood.

Suddenly Banniselk sprang forward, straddling Luti with his legs. "Behold!" he screamed. He ripped the garment from her body and left her trembling and naked on the fine white sand. Then he brutally kicked her in the side so that she spun over onto her belly. "Behold!" he repeated, resting his staff on the small birthmark on her back. It was shaped like the paw of the lion.

The wide-eyed priests crowded around her, staring and pointing. Her flesh crawled when she felt their withered, clawlike fingers trace the birthmark on her skin.

Banniselk grabbed the banner the priests had carried with the cult sign of the lion. He laid the banner next to the girl. Her paw-print birthmark matched exactly the left paw of the cult's lion. It was as if someone had traced the form of the paw on the banner and then tattooed the tracing to the girl's back.

All the priests backed away, muttering, then screaming at her.

"Sorceress!"

"Demon!"

"Witch!"

Luti shrank from their screams and buried her face in her hands. She cried piteously, feeling that her heart would break.

"We will root out her accomplices in sorcery," Banniselk assured the other priests.

Luti reached back with one tentative hand to touch her birthmark. Was she going to suffer and die for something she had always considered unimportant? Nobody had ever paid attention to the stupid little mark on her body since she was six years old; one of her little friends had smeared some black mud from the Tigris onto the mark to wash it off. . . . Her one other memory pertaining to the mark was very dim: a hand tracing its outline on her back—a gentle hand. And a loving voice singing about pain and loss and the man who had given his child the mark of his passion.

CHAPTER
SEVEN

Canaan

In the morning Theon joined a caravan and traveled across the hills to Jerusalem. He spent a day in that city on business and the following morning joined another caravan, which was setting out along the road through the hill country. It would pass through Ramah and Bethel, above and west of the Jordan Valley. He had made this journey before, with his now deceased representative, to meet with the innumerable traders, merchants, artisans, and bankers who were small cogs in the family's shipping empire.

From the beginning it was obvious that something was different about this caravan. At first, the manager was reluctant to allow Theon to join, and he relented only because of the applicant's obvious affluence and imposing presence. This treatment whetted Theon's curiosity, and as the wagons slowly rolled northward toward Gibeah, he quickly befriended a hostler named Akkub and asked questions.

Akkub explained that the caravan was the property of a very rich widow from Ebla named Huldah; her husband had been a wealthy and well-known trader named Ephai. After his death Huldah had assumed management of his businesses. She had not remarried.

From time to time Theon would catch glimpses of Huldah's curtained chair, carried on the shoulders of tow-

ering Nubians who never seemed to notice the weight
they bore from dawn to dusk. The curtains were always
drawn against the harsh sun, and Akkub explained to
Theon, who was frustrated in his desire to set eyes on her,
that Huldah was protecting her very fair skin.

Just before the caravan passed Ramah, Theon saw a
long, slender, pale arm emerge from the curtains and
beckon to a man riding alongside. The rider pulled close
to the chair, listened intently, then rode back along the
column in the direction of Theon and Akkub.

Theon found himself staring at the curtains, but the
elegant hand did not reappear. He had the oddest feeling
that there had been some kind of secret signal in the
woman's gesture, meant only for him. His musings were
interrupted by the messenger, who pulled up his mount
and called: "We'll be stopping straight ahead. Put out
pickets. There are bandits in these hills."

He started to ride down the line but was stopped by
Theon's question: "Did she say why we're stopping here if
it's not safe?"

The messenger leaned over his mount's neck and
spoke softly. "There's someone she wants to see, someone
famous she's heard about."

"The Israelite seeress?" Akkub asked.

"That's the one," the messenger confirmed. "Our mistress is superstitious." He shrugged and then added, "Just
obey her. Stop when I give the signal. And make sure the
pickets go out. We're not taking any chances. The roads have
never been so safe as when the Israelites ruled the area. I
think they are going to show people that their revolt will provide safety and security as well as freedom from oppression."

After the man had ridden off, Akkub turned to Theon.
"I'll do what he says, but it's unnecessary tonight. There
aren't going to be any bandits around when the hills are
full of armed Israelites coming back from the big battle
yesterday on the Jordan."

The messenger stopped on his return to the head of
the line to speak again to Akkub. "The seeress isn't here
today. We're going to make camp tonight so our mistress
can consult her tomorrow."

Akkub cursed under his breath as the man rode away.

"This seeress must be extraordinary," Theon said to Akkub. "Or your mistress is more superstitious than you supposed."

"The seeress has a good reputation around here. She's an older woman and has already raised her children. Her husband apparently doesn't mind her making a spectacle of herself. She comes out every day, sits under a palm tree beside the road, answers people's questions, and predicts the future. She even does some healing." He paused. "They say she's got a touch of the divine about her. Not only does she dispense justice—people bring their disputes to her, and she renders judgment—but the Israelites' God is purported to speak through her occasionally."

"Through a woman?" Theon asked. "That's unusual. Thus far Yahweh has communicated only through men."

"Maybe their men aren't what they used to be, letting the Moabites and the Hazorites walk all over them. Perhaps their God has given up on the men and gone over to the woman."

When Akkub had trotted off to find a campsite, Theon reflected on his words. The God of the Israelites was speaking to a woman now! Well, wisdom often settled on odd people in surprising places. His own father, Seth, had been considered an idiot because he had not spoken until he was ten years old. Of course, he had gone on to become the brightest of all the Children of the Lion, and during one period in Seth's illustrious career the king of Babylon had given him the task of redesigning that city.

How strange and chaotic his ancestors' lives were. Yet he himself experienced none of this turmoil, having been raised in luxury and safety on the island of Home. Even when he had posed as a sea captain and trapped the famous pirate called the Minotaur, his rich and powerful family had always stood ready to protect him. Now he wondered what an unprotected life would have been like. Might colors have appeared more vivid, tastes more pungent? Victory sweeter and defeat more poignant?

An almost unbearable sadness settled over him. It was a feeling that afflicted him often lately. All his suc-

cesses, all his relationships—particularly his marriage to
Nuhara—became like ashes in his mouth. He longed for
some kind of escape. Theon closed his eyes and tried to
talk himself into feeling contented. But it was a half-
hearted effort, destined to fail.

The pickets had been set out, the campfires lighted,
the pack animals tethered. The goods had been checked
and secured. Theon sat by the fire and ate with Akkub. A
gentle breeze blew sparks up toward the clean, starry sky.
Theon nodded from time to time to show Akkub that he
was listening. But, in fact, he heard little that the hostler
was saying. His eyes were fixed on the faraway campfire
where the intriguing Huldah of Ebla sat eating alone,
attended by servants. She was so tall that except for her
fair complexion, one could have suspected that she had
Nubian blood. Her hair was gray, and her lovely face remained expressionless, giving her well-chiseled features the
curious passive quality of an Egyptian wall portrait. She
seemed withdrawn, disconnected from the world around her.

At first Theon thought this was a terrible pity; she
was extremely attractive, and any man would think her a
good catch, particularly because her beauty came accompanied by such great wealth. Then he wondered if the
coldness of her appearance might denote a coldness in her
personal relationships.

As he watched, Huldah rose and vanished with her
servants into the darkness. Theon's eyes strained after
her, but she was totally lost to sight. He felt angry and
frustrated. He had not seen enough of her. He wanted to
speculate, dream, fantasize. . . .

As the night wore on, he asked the others around the
campfire for more information about Huldah. They spoke
freely. In Ebla, they said, she was much talked about
because of her fascinating history. Only ten years before
she had been a whore in a brothel in Damascus. Later she
became the mistress of the same brothel, then its owner.
Ephai, who eventually married her, had loaned her money
when she wanted to buy more brothels. Soon they had
become partners, and from partnership had come the

marriage. She ran her own business as well as the under-side of his concerns—the taverns and brothels—while he handled the foreign ventures.

By the time Ephai died, Huldah had developed into a shrewd businesswoman. She consolidated control and learned to run the respectable half of his business as efficiently as she did her own. Since his death she had doubled the domestic enterprises, increased trade by a third, and become a power both in Damascus and in Ebla.

An admirable woman, Theon realized. But her obvious sophistication seemed at odds with her current behavior. Whatever possessed her to travel a lonely road in a backward country to seek the advice of an Israelite woman who probably had never traveled more than ten leagues from the house in which she had been born?

He could spend hours trying to find an answer, he realized, but the fire was burning low, and his companions were rolling into their blankets. Theon lay back and closed his eyes. He fell asleep quickly but not for long, waking suddenly and violently, his body drenched with sweat. Again he dropped off to sleep, only to be jolted by a nightmare. He did not remember the content of his fearful dreams, but Huldah was present in each one and had touched his body. As the night progressed and the dreams became more intrusive, he found himself repeatedly starting out toward her tent, only to stop and return. It was as if an unseen hand were pointing him in a certain direction, pushing him forward, then yanking him savagely back. Finally exhausted, he fell into a dreamless stupor, which lasted through the night.

In the early morning, flanked by friends and well-wishers from her village in the hills of Ephraim, Deborah, wife of Lappidoth, came to sit under a palm tree not a thousand paces from Huldah's caravan. Long lines of people from great distances already waited patiently for her.

It was a very diverse assembly of men, women, and children. There were Israelites from all twelve tribes. There were Canaanites and Philistines. There were Syrians from the coast and long-haired herdsmen from the

steep hill country. Many carried crippled loved ones, to
be touched by Deborah. Many brought pets who were
ill—dogs and goats and donkeys. And many barren women
were waiting, hopeful that the prophetess could make
them fertile with a prayer or a charm or a potion. Those
who had brought food ate as they waited. Some slept in
place because the line moved so slowly. Children played
along the column, laughing, running, and tossing clumps
of grass at each other.

When Deborah finished with a petitioner and the line
moved, there was a collective gasp of expectation. What
had the prophetess wrought this time? Who had been
helped? Who counseled? Was her power strong? Rumors
flew in furtive whispers.

To Huldah's great surprise, wealth and rank meant
nothing to the seeress beneath the tree. The businesswoman from Ebla was asked to stand in line like everyone
else. Since no special treatment was forthcoming, she
accepted the situation and had two of her towering servants
hold a canopy over her head to shield her from the sun.

She studied the seeress. Deborah was short and stout
and could not, even in the bloom of her vanished youth,
have been impressive or beautiful. Her face was careworn,
and wrinkles marred her brow, as if she had suffered
much privation.

Deborah was not what Huldah had expected, although
on reflection the elegant businesswoman had to admit that
someone who looked like Deborah could not afford to be a
phony. Besides, she had to be genuine, or hundreds of
people would not be waiting for hours to consult her.

As Huldah waited she recalled all the reports she had
heard about the prophetess. Most had centered around
Deborah's fierce honesty and her ability to cut through all
the deceit of human existence. Huldah had heard that
Deborah sensed the truth and love in each person and
could bring it forth with a power that she had obtained
from her God.

The line progressed slowly, and although Huldah
strained to listen, she could not overhear everything that
was being said by petitioner or seeress. Directly in front of

Huldah was a Kenite girl, perhaps in her late teens, plain
and poorly dressed and with a pitiful cast in her eye. As
the line grew shorter, the Kenite grew more distressed
and jittery, and when her turn came she almost ran away.

Finally she was persuaded to approach the prophetess. Her first words were too soft to be heard. Deborah
smiled reassuringly and said in a deep, calm voice: "There
is no rush, my dear. We have time. Yahweh made the
heaven and earth in six days, but you and I have time.
Tell me what is the matter."

The girl took a deep breath, then she blurted out a
story with alternating despair and anger. She had a friend,
she said, who lived in the Plain of Esdralon, to the north-
west of Bethel beyond Mount Tabor. And there was a
man—rich, powerful, and evil—who harassed her when
her husband was away. He made shocking, inappropriate
remarks to her and put his hands all over her body. And
there were worse violations, things so horrible one could
not even speak of them.

"I see," Deborah said calmly. "Are there any children
in your friend's household?"

"She cannot have children," the young woman replied. "At first she thought this was a curse, but now she
sees it as a blessing. This man has his way with her, and
the idea of bearing his child . . ."

"Can she confide in her husband and let him defend
her honor?" Deborah asked.

"That's the problem," the girl answered, anguished.
"The man who has been bothering her is a famous soldier.
If her husband challenges him, the soldier will kill him.
He has great power and is ruthless."

Deborah pursed her lips. "Can you tell me the name
of the soldier?"

At first the girl was too frightened to speak his name.
But the broad, encouraging face of the seeress, the kindly
eyes, the work-roughened hands folded so placidly in her
lap, gave the girl strength, and she finally blurted: "Sisera.
His name is Sisera."

For the first time Deborah's calm eyes widened, and
her expression darkened. "Your friend is not the first to

complain about Sisera. He has brought dishonor to many
women of the tribes of Zebulun and Naphtali. He is a
curse upon my people, the Kenites, and all the others who
lie under the blight of King Jabin."

The girl's voice trembled as she spoke. "I ache for my
friend, but what can she do? Her family can't move—
they're Kenite tinkers and have to live wherever their
work takes them."

Deborah was silent and closed her eyes for what
seemed a very long time. When she opened them, she
said, "Tell her to come here, to this grove, and I will tell
her what to do. God will not let her suffer much longer.
He will answer her prayers."

The girl was startled. "How did you know she was
praying to your God?"

Deborah did not answer; instead she continued with
her instructions. "Tell your friend that the Lord will eventually deliver this man into her hands. But for now she
needs strength, faith, and assurance. Only God brings
strength. Only she can provide herself with faith. But I am
here for reassurance. Tell her to come to me."

"But she can't leave. She is caught between her husband and that evil man."

"Tell her that God will whisper the answer into her
ear. What is your name, dear?"

"Basemath."

"You are a good girl, Basemath, and I will remember
you in my prayers. And your friend's name?"

"Yael. Wife of Heber the Kenite."

"Go now. Deliver my message."

Finally, it was Huldah's turn. She stood in front of
Deborah. The prophetess waited.

"I have come a long way," Huldah began.

"Many of these people have come farther," Deborah said.

Huldah bristled. "Don't compare me with those
people."

"And why not?" Deborah asked gently.

"Well, look at them! They are pathetic, standing in
line, as if you're giving out free food."

"I am giving out free food," Deborah said cryptically.

"Then maybe I'm in the wrong line. My caravan has the finest cook in Damascus, to cater solely to my whims."

"Come here, my wealthy friend!" Deborah's voice was angry. "Stand close to me. Maybe your gold will make these trees grow higher and make their fruit sweeter? Your worldly status means nothing to me! And spiritually, you are as bereft as the saddest petitioner in this line." Her tone gentled. "Now, forget the walls of gold you have built around yourself and tell me, my dear, why you have come to me."

Huldah's façade began to crumble. Her arrogance vanished. This Israelite woman was perplexing and oddly powerful. After the harsh scolding, Huldah felt an enormous compassion flowing from Deborah—compassion for her!

"I have come for your help," Huldah confessed, searching for words.

"And I am here to give you help."

"I . . . have lost something," Huldah faltered.

"And you wish me to find it for you?"

"Yes."

"What? An emerald earring? A gold necklace?" Again Deborah's voice was tinged with contempt.

It was painful for Huldah to be scorned. She reached out and grasped the seeress's hands. "No! A man. I am looking for a man I lost a long time ago."

"Is that really why you have come?"

"Yes. I loved him. But I wounded him."

"Ah. And you wish me to find him for you? To point you toward him?"

"If he is still alive."

Deborah reached out and tenderly smoothed Huldah's gray hair as she spoke gently. "I wish you to leave now. I know you have great financial and mental powers, but I cannot help you." Then the prophetess sat back and gestured to the next one in line.

Huldah was furious. "I will not leave! Why won't you help me? You have helped the others!"

"Because the others have come to me in truth. And you have not been truthful."

"I have," Huldah protested.

"No. You tell me that you are looking for a man. Perhaps you are, but that is not why you have come here. You are here because you are in despair. You want to find your lost self—a woman of grace and beauty. But you will never find that woman if you persist in making dishonesty the cornerstone of your life. Please leave. You are a fool, and you sadden me."

Huldah started to shout at the prophetess. "You can't make me leave now! You haven't done anything for me! I demand to be helped!"

Deborah dismissed her again, with a gesture.

"Please . . ." Huldah begged in a childlike voice. "Help me. Give me more time. I will pay you whatever you want. I will feed and clothe your people."

But her protests were futile. People behind her in line began to curse and mock her. Deborah's ears remained closed to her pleading. Huldah walked away, wrapped in silent rage and despair.

Theon, watching the scene, was astonished and impressed. The battle was fought by two powerful women, but Deborah's spiritual supremacy easily cut down any advantage Huldah held in the material world. He wondered how Deborah would treat him if he consulted with her. What questions would he pose? Most likely he would ask why he felt so empty at times, why the passionate love that existed at the beginning of his marriage had vanished like smoke from a fire. He would ask why he no longer felt joy at seeing the flight of a bird or the curve of a leaf or the brilliant color of a butterfly. So many questions! So much misery!

As for Huldah, his curiosity about her and his desire to know her better were intensified by this episode. What secret horrors dwelled in her heart? What were her weaknesses? What were her secrets?

Lingering to watch Deborah, Theon found he had been left behind by the caravan, which the angry Huldah had ordered to move out immediately. He had to ride at a brisk clip to catch up.

* * *

At Beth-shean, Theon requested an audience with Huldah but was refused. After that, he decided to leave the caravan, strike out on his own across the Jordan Valley, and using the ford just north of Pella, pick up the King's Highway to Damascus in the hills of Bashan. At Huldah's orders, the caravan was bypassing Bashan, but he saw no reason to do so himself. Besides, he was too old and too married to make a fool of himself over a woman.

Now he was in Hazorite territory, having left the country once administered by Moabite overlords. As he rode through the lands just south of Lake Chinnereth, he could see evidence of the heavy hand of King Jabin. Overseers and tax collectors were everywhere. Whenever he saw a prosperous-looking farm, he saw Hazorite overseers. Once he saw a young Israelite being beaten unmercifully by a Hazorite soldier. Several people were watching; no one dared do anything to stop it. Apparently General Sisera put few restraints on his military's relations with civilians.

He stopped at an inn in the town of El Hamma. Low benches lined the dark rooms, and a smell of wood shavings was in the air. Theon ordered bread and wine and relaxed. The room was empty except for a large, unkempt man three benches away, who mumbled to himself. Theon could tell by the man's large staff, leaning against the wall, that he was a sheepherder.

The herder stared at Theon as he ordered a second bowl of wine.

"Yahweh's blessing upon you, stranger," the herder said, standing unsteadily and lurching toward Theon's table.

Theon looked up. The herder's face was crisscrossed by wrinkles from exposure to the sun and wind. He wore skins fastened by leather strips, and a small dagger was strapped to his thigh.

"I am not an Israelite," Theon replied congenially, "but I will gladly accept all the blessings I can get."

The herder sank down heavily beside him. "Do you have enough coin in your pocket and love in your heart, stranger, to buy me a bowl of wine?"

Theon nodded and called for another bowl.

The herder drank it greedily and then sat back and heaved a sigh. "Many thanks. Jabin has taken my flocks, so now all I do is hate."

"Why did he take your sheep?" Theon asked.

"A whim, perhaps, or a payment of debt. Who knows? But they're gone." He stared into the bottom of the bowl. "At least my daughter is safe. I sent her away to relatives in the south. That bastard Sisera will never lay a hand on her."

Theon purchased another bowl of wine for the herder. This time he drank it slowly.

"Do you know of Sisera?" the herder asked, his voice filled with anger.

"I have heard of him. He's Jabin's general."

"Ah, you are wrong. I know soldiers; I fought with Joshua. Sisera is no soldier. He is a demon. His enemy is beauty. He exists to violate beauty, like a wolf among lambs. He lives to brutalize young women. He does to their bodies what is in his perverted mind." The herder suddenly buried his face in his hands and wept uncontrollably.

Theon reached over to console him, touching him lightly on the arm.

The herder yanked his arm away, staggered up, spat on the floor, retrieved his staff, and stumbled out the door.

Theon sat in shocked silence, unable to understand why the men of Israel put up with this insult. How could the armies of Joshua and Caleb have become so weak in less than a generation? Something had disappeared from their spirit. Would they be able to get it back? Or was it up to the women now? Would Israel have to depend on the bravery and power of women like Deborah?

But other forces were at work here, he conceded—forces he could not see, such as the ones that had led to the revolt against the Moabites in central Canaan. He would find out more about it when he finished his business in the northern cities. He would also locate Pepi and discover what had gone wrong in his heart. And he might even stop in the hill country between Ramah and Bethel again and speak to the prophetess Deborah.

*   *   *

The shadow of Mount Tabor lay on the little Kenite tent community along Wadi Kishon, below the towering Hai ruins of mighty Megiddo. The women and their small children had gathered along the stream to wash their clothes. Yael, wife of Heber the Kenite, picked up her clean laundry from the sun-warmed rocks and walked slowly homeward. Her people, the Kenites, were a desert clan from the tribes of Midian, and after Joshua's death, members of the clan lived and prospered in Judah.

As she left the stream she felt the eyes of the women following her. Their enmity for her was never spoken but always theie. They scorned her as an adulteress. They did not or could not understand the horror she faced with Sisera. It had probably never occurred to them that she was too weak to stop his violent embraces and too protective of her husband's well-being to bring her anguish to him. They were jealous of her beauty. Her lustrous black hair hung loose down her back. She wore the simple long robe of her people, fastened in the front by three shell clasps. Her beauty was delicate—soft brown eyes, slim face and body, the graceful movements of a woman who has lived close to the earth.

Heber would not be there; he was still at the Hazorite encampment at Harosheth-ha-goiim, some miles to the north, and would not be home for several days. She missed him terribly. Perhaps if God had taken pity on her and given them a child, it might have been different. A child might erase some of the loneliness. Seeing the other women's children accentuated her feelings, poignantly reminding her of her own barrenness and what a great disappointment she was to Heber. Like all men, he wanted a son to train in his trade.

She had unburdened herself to her only friend, Basemath, and the two had wept together. Basemath had promised to ask the prophetess Deborah to pray for her and to ask God to make her fertile. But in her heart Yael knew she would never have a baby of her own. All she could hope for was that some young mother would abandon her baby because the child was born deformed. Someone else's infant would give her solace even if it was crippled.

In her small tent she folded the clothing until the sound of men's voices came to her. She moved to look out the doorway. A patrol of Hazorite soldiers was riding along the streambed. Why were they there? The tax had been paid. The tents clustered along the river held nothing of value, while the city of Megiddo, rich and prosperous, was nearby, ripe for the picking.

And then she saw him. Sisera! She recognized his tall and imperious figure with the broad shoulders and arrogant stance. She did not have to see his face. It was always before her eyes: the massive head with the coarse strands of premature white in the black hair, the thick eyebrows joined across the bridge of the nose, the sardonic eyes that seemed perpetually to glitter with desire, and the thick, curly beard, which made the scowl on his face seem more animallike than human. The beard always rubbed her skin red as he forced his mouth on hers, and the last time it had left a rash that she feared Heber might notice.

Oh, God, she prayed, *please don't let him come in here. Not again. Make him change his mind and find some other pleasure.*

But even before her ears could pick up the footfalls of his horse, she knew he was going to come to her. She shuddered and for a moment considered running from him or hiding.

"I thought I saw you come in here."

She wheeled at the sound of his voice. On his face was the expression she hated. He took her elbow and shoved her ahead of him, into the center of the tent.

"Please don't. It's against my people's customs for me to be alone with you."

"Customs? They are for lesser people. Not for you and me." He closed the tent's flap, then moved toward her, his hands held out, as if he were ready to trap a stray cat. His presence filled the tent like some gigantic, snarling beast.

She backed away, pressing herself against the walls of the tent.

"Still pretending you didn't like it last time? Still pretending you love your poor stupid little husband? Don't make me laugh."

"Stay away or I'll scream," she threatened.

"Scream for whom? The other women? They're all down at the ford washing. My men are with them now, to assure us some privacy. And their husbands are all away, just as yours is."

She tried to run past him, toward the tent's opening. He caught her with one hand. Screaming was useless. Fighting would only leave bruises. And she would have to explain them to Heber when he came home. Then he would seek revenge, and the monster Sisera would kill him. There was no hope, and Yael began to cry.

He ripped the robe from her neck. The shell clasps went flying, and the act of tearing the cloth seemed to excite him. In a moment she was naked, wearing only her sandals and the necklace her husband had given her.

"Please, have mercy," she pleaded, backing away.

His hands fell like talons on her naked body. She shuddered and twisted away from him. But this inflamed him. She clamped her jaw shut and closed her eyes.

When the sun was at its zenith, Deborah, exhausted, announced that she was going to rest. The people kept their places in line and sat down to wait.

Deborah slept fitfully for a hour. She tossed and turned, and her lips moved and formed words as she slept. Her friends hovered over her and watched in concern as her eyes darted back and forth. The words she muttered made no sense. Then her eye movements became more rapid and agitated, and when she spoke, it was only a single word. She said it three times: "Barak. Barak." A pause. "Barak." And then she awoke.

When she sat up, her friends told her what she had said. She sat lost in thought. "It's a name," she finally said. "But whose? And why did God give it to me?"

CHAPTER EIGHT

City of Ur, Kingdom of Babylon

The pit was circular, ten feet deep, and five feet in diameter, with wooden planks covering the top. A guard lowered food, water, and a slop bucket by rope twice a day after removing one of the planks. Luti crouched at the bottom, huddled against the chill dampness. She had no clothing to protect her. From time to time she heard other prisoners in adjoining pits call out to one another. Who were they? Why were they there? Had they, too, been accused of blasphemy? She did not know.

Luti had lost her sense of time. She could no longer tell whether minutes or hours or days were passing. When her muscles cramped she would walk the perimeter until she grew dizzy, then try to sleep with her legs drawn up under her chin.

It was during one of these fitful naps that they came for her. The planks were pulled away, and the sudden infusion of light dazzled her eyes. A rope ladder was flung down, and voices yelled at her to climb out of the pit fast or she would be beaten. She stood, confused, still half-blinded by the light, then stumbled toward the rope ladder. Her foot slipped. Their yells became louder and more threatening. Trembling, she reached the first rung and grabbed the sides of the ladder with all her strength. She climbed rung after rung and finally reached the lip of the rim, where she was pulled out roughly by two sturdy men wearing only loin garments. Behind them she saw Banniselk.

The other prisoners called out, telling her to have courage, to be strong, as the two men dragged her to a staircase, which led up to a bright, bare room with very clean stone walls. A moment later they raised her and fastened her wrists to leather thongs on a wall. Her feet dangled six inches off the floor, so the whole weight of her body pulled on her tethered wrists, arms, and shoulders. The intense pain made her fear that her arms would be dislocated from her shoulders.

Banniselk stepped between the two muscular guards and spoke in a soft, almost kindly voice. "Now that we have discovered you, there is no point at all in resisting. You must tell me the names of your accomplices and where to find them. You must explain how you have cast this deadly spell across our land and how it can be stopped."

She rasped out her answer, gasping, as tears squeezed from between her eyelids. "I can't tell you anything. I don't know what you are talking about. I am no blasphemer. I have done nothing wrong. I work in the fields."

He laughed harshly. "Do you expect me to believe that you chose to work as a common field hand when more luxurious and less taxing occupations are open to a beautiful young woman like you? No, it is a cover for your demon ways."

"No," Luti sobbed. "I have always worked in the fields. Please believe me. I have no family—there was nowhere else for me to go, nothing else for me to do! Your goddess is my goddess. I have not conspired against Astarte." Her voice lost its strength, and her last words were barely audible.

"You are a demon in the guise of a woman," Banniselk replied, his fingers digging into the flesh of one of her arms, "and you are marked as a blasphemer by that lion's paw on your back. You mock the goddess. Misfortune walks in your footsteps. Tell me the names of your companions! Name the demons that have been released!" His face was so close to hers that she was sprayed by his spittle.

She twisted and turned in the thongs, but there was no escape. "Have mercy on me. I beg you. I am innocent."

Banniselk stepped back and nodded curtly to one of the guards, who approached Luti. He held a whip so beautiful that Luti stared at it in fascinated revulsion. She had seen whips like this before, in the market—the Bedouins made them and sold them. First, dozens of snakeskins were sewn together, then dried in the sun. Next the skins were rubbed with sheep fat and rolled and stretched to the desired length and thickness. Then they were dried again. When finished, these whips were often more than twenty feet long and had enormous striking power. They were worth a great deal of money, particularly if they were made of skins from the Syrian hills, just north of the desert. The snakes there were decorated with exquisite patterns, and their venom could paralyze a man in seconds.

At the same horrible moment that Luti realized the whip was for her, the guard flicked his thick wrist and activated a weapon of blinding speed and enormous force.

Luti screamed with pain as the whip tore a chunk of flesh from her neck.

"There is no need for this," Banniselk said, thrusting his face close again.

"I don't know anything," Luti cried.

Banniselk nodded to the guard, and the whip struck again . . . and again . . . and again. Through a haze of agony, Luti realized that the whip had finally come to rest.

"Do you want more?"

Luti realized she would have to lie to survive. She would make up any story, name any names, to stop the pain and keep herself alive, even for a little while.

"There are five of us," she whispered.

"Do you all have the mark of the lion?"

"Yes, all of us," she managed hoarsely. "We meet at midnight of each full moon at the fisherman's shack upriver . . . on the west bank near the ruins of the old temple."

Banniselk began to pace, obviously evaluating the

veracity of her confession. He stopped abruptly and swiveled toward her. "How do you perform your magic?"

"Through spells and rituals."

She waited, gasping for breath and staring at the
whip, now coiled on the floor. Would Banniselk believe
her? Did it matter anymore?

"Cut her down," Banniselk ordered.

A second later the thongs were cut, and Luti fell
heavily.

"Listen to me, witch. You will be brought to the civil
magistrate and sentenced for your crimes once we have
confirmed that what you say is true. May the goddess have
mercy on you."

They left her lying in her own blood. Her wounds
burned as if white-hot sticks were being pushed into her.
Suddenly she had a sensation that she was not alone in the
room. Her eyes darted about like a wounded animal's.
Yes, there, standing quietly in one corner, was an old
man. He was wearing neither sandals nor conical hat. His
robe was made from brown and white birds' feathers. His
beard was white, and his skin so thin and pale that blood
could be seen coursing beneath it.

He started to walk toward her.

"Please," she moaned, "I have told them what I know."

He said nothing, but when he reached her side, he
knelt slowly and with difficulty and then began to daub
her wounds with a small, saturated sponge. The pain
diminished rapidly.

"Thank you," she whispered. Up close, he looked
truly ancient, and his whole body quivered with slight
tremors. But there was strength and purpose in his hands.

"Tell me your name, child."

"Luti."

"And you have confessed to blasphemy?"

She was about to tell the old man the truth—that she
had lied to avoid more torture . . . that she had made up a
story—but she held back. He nodded, though, as if he
already understood. He finished sponging her wounds and
helped her prop herself up against the wall. From his

pocket he withdrew a small cluster of grapes, which he fed to her. Luti ate greedily.

"Thank you again," she said.

"We do not have much time, child, and you must tell me some things."

"If I can."

"Have you always had that mark on your back? Were you born with it? Or was it placed on you artificially?"

"From birth."

"And where were you born?"

"I don't know. I have lived in Ur for as long as I remember."

"Your parents?"

"Dead. I was an orphan. I was raised by strangers."

"What do you know of your father?"

"Nothing."

"Your mother?"

"Nothing."

"Do you have memories of your childhood?"

"No."

He was silent. He motioned with his hand for her to turn over. She did so, and his hand traced the contours of her birthmark.

"I am going to press my palm against your birthmark," he said. "Human hand to lion's paw. And when you feel the pressure, I want you to close your eyes and pretend that you are a child."

When she felt the pressure, she closed her eyes. Everything he said and did seemed so logical and helpful. She had the sensation that she was being gently raised and lowered, as if she were on a ship . . . and she was warm and happy, and her mother was with her. In a sky clear of clouds were flocks of birds . . . and she raised her tiny fingers to greet them. How happy she was!

Then the memory vanished. Luti opened her eyes, and for a brief moment she did not know where she was. Had her mind been playing tricks on her? She saw her own blood caked on her body and was fully back in the nightmare of reality.

"Tell me what you saw," the old man said.

She described her memory—or was it a dream?
—exactly as she had seen it in her mind.

He smiled, then asked: "Do you understand the secret world of birds?"

"Sometimes. Sometimes I feel I know their mysteries, their portents."

"Yes, it is logical. But let me explain your dream to you: You were not on a ship; you were in a cradle, strapped to the side of a horse. That is the reason for the undulating motion. You were riding on the Anatolian steppes—the plains far to the north. And your mother was leading the horse, for she was a nomad of the high plains of Anatolia. That is where you were born."

Luti was astonished. She forgot her fear. "How did my mother get to Ur? And why?"

The old man did not answer at first. He went over her wounds again with the small sponge. Finally he said, "Many unexplained mysteries surround you and your family." He climbed to his feet and shuffled away.

"Don't go, please. I don't know your name or who you are. Stay with me. I am frightened."

"I must go, child."

"What will they do to me? Will I die? I have done nothing. . . ." Her pleas trailed off in sobs.

"Take courage. All is not yet lost," he replied, and then he was gone. She remembered that as she had been dragged to the torture room, the other prisoners in the pits had said those exact words: "Take courage." But she had none left.

CHAPTER NINE

Canaan

Ten years before, Jabin's father had been killed and his palace at Hazor burned to the ground by Joshua's conquering army. When young Jabin came to power and reestablished his family's ascendancy over the north country, his first act was to order the palace rebuilt.

People of the northern tribes of Israel had been put to work on this backbreaking task. Men, women, even small children, were pressed into service, laboring long hours on short rations. Overseers, men of Sisera's army, stood nearby as the Israelites quarried and carried the limestone, forcing them to work harder and faster in the choking dust so that the rebuilding would be completed in time for the king's twenty-fifth birthday.

Jabin's armorer, Pepi, walked through the city, scowling. Everywhere he looked he saw ruthlessness and oppression, the exact factors that had caused his rift with Joshua many years before. Joshua's army had killed women and children: *"No use killing the snake if you haven't destroyed its eggs,"* was one of Joshua's favorite sayings.

Pepi had repeatedly taken him to task for massacring innocents, and that disagreement—exacerbated by Caleb's false rumors about Pepi's treasonous behavior—had forced his defection from the Israelite cause he had once served so faithfully.

But now, a decade after Joshua's death, Pepi felt no

satisfaction at seeing his erstwhile friends brought low by Jabin's rise to power. Gone, in fact, was his vindictiveness toward Israel. These people did not deserve to suffer like this.

He stopped and watched a pathetic scene: An old man was carrying large stones in the usual manner—in a back sack attached to thongs that circled his forehead. The browband had slipped, and the elderly man and the stones had fallen down together. An overseer began to beat the aged Israelite with a stick until he lost consciousness. Then another guard joined the first one, and they dragged the body off to one side as if it were a sack of refuse.

This horrid occurrence reminded Pepi of similar abuses in Kamose's Egypt, which he remembered well even though he had been only a child when Moses led the great Israelite revolt. The Habiru, as they were called then, slaves for many decades to the delta overlords, had finally won their freedom and escaped to the desert. Despite his freeman's status, Pepi had joined them. The poverty of the under-nourished Israelites and treatment they had suffered as slaves had awakened sharp feelings of resentment in him. He realized that years after their emancipation and their return to Canaan, they were in no better condition than they had been under Egypt's yoke.

He admitted this despite his position as a highly paid and supposedly loyal employee of Jabin's—arms maker to the army that had subjugated the North. But Pepi disliked the king and hated his general, Sisera, and most of the upper ranks of the court. In fact, he had no friends in Hazor except one or two of the hired help.

The stress of dealing with the king and General Sisera was detrimental to his health; one more episode of seizures from his head injury could be the end of him, and the attacks were always brought on by tension.

As he walked to the forge Pepi thought of Heber, the young Kenite who had joined his staff several days before. He had been doing odd jobs, but he showed real talent for metalworking, even though that talent was raw and untrained.

Only yesterday Pepi had pulled the Kenite out of the

ranks and put him to work on one of the smelting ovens. The fellow had caught on immediately—unlike most of the others, who had to be watched, cursed at, and even beaten for their inattention and poor products.

Today he intended to give the new worker more training, if he could. This would cause jealousy among the rest of the staff, but it was more important to find the best men to work by his side.

As Pepi approached the forge, he observed his assistants at work. The forge was being heated, the charcoal raised to white heat by foot-operated bellows, after the Egyptian fashion. The distinctive odor of the just-ignited fuel was filtering through the air—an odor that Pepi had always loved.

One of the bellows pumpers was the new man. Pepi could see he had made a stirrup for the foot pump, which had sped up the backstroke. His forge, unlike the others, was already well on the way to producing the necessary heat.

Pepi's Hazorite assistant, Melek, saw the Kenite's innovation and was bearing down on him. "What have you done to the bellows?" he demanded. "There's only one right way to do things! Stick to it!"

Young Heber's face fell. "But, sir, this seems to work better and faster."

"Don't give me any of your damned impudence," Melek warned. "Just take that thing off and do it my way—or look for work elsewhere."

"But—"

Melek cut him off in a fury and was about to strike the young man when Pepi hurried to his side and restrained him.

"What's going on here?"

"Nothing, sir," Melek replied. "This Kenite gets out of line now and then. You have to keep these idiots on their toes, or they'll ruin a week's good work."

Pepi ignored Melek and said to Heber, "Show me how the pump works with your modification."

"Yes, sir!" The Kenite, in a seated position, worked the pump with both feet. "I could do this all day with the modification, sir. If you were to use a stirrup like this, you could free half the shift for other work."

"Don't waste our time with your foolish—" Melek began. Then Pepi's hand fell on his arm, and Melek turned to him. "Please, sir, you distinctly told me—"

"I know what I said, Melek. But this young fellow has devised a better way. I want all the pumps converted immediately."

Melek grumbled under his breath, and his ears turned red.

Pepi continued, "And from now on Heber works for me, understand? Put someone else on the forge." Pepi took the Kenite by the arm and guided him away from the angry but obedient Melek. "You've had some experience at this work, am I right?"

"Not really. Mostly I've just watched. But I've repaired a lot of other people's metalwork."

"An armorer's work is primarily repair of some kind. You can learn a great deal repairing things. Among them, the importance of patience and quality."

"I haven't given up hope of learning more, sir."

Pepi stopped and looked at the young man. "You were poor when you were young, right? And had no money to buy an apprenticeship?"

Heber nodded his assent. His dark, handsome face tensed as if he were reluctant to speak to the large, imposing Child of the Lion who had befriended him.

Pepi had caught the man's hesitation. He liked young Heber. The fellow was lean and long muscled, built more like an athlete than a metalworker. Pepi, with his huge forearms and thick neck, had the more standard armorer's physique. Heber would have speed and agility, gifts desired by everyone. Quickness with one's feet meant speed with one's wrist, and that meant the ability to wield a tool of any kind, including a sword.

"What were you going to say?" Pepi asked. "You can trust me."

"Just that I couldn't afford an apprenticeship. My family hardly had enough coin to keep us all alive. We, like many other of my tribesmen, earned a little extra by passing information about the Israelites to Jabin's soldiers."

Pepi nodded nonjudgmentally. "You're still young," he noted, "and I'm going to offer you a chance to learn more and earn more. Some of the best metalworkers in my family were late starters. Seth of Thebes, for instance."

"That's a very famous name, sir, even here. Did you know him?"

"He raised me."

The Kenite's eyes were as wide as a child's. "Seth of Thebes was a great hero of mine. When I tell my wife that I've met a man who was raised by Seth and learned from him, she'll—"

"When you do," Pepi interrupted, "tell her you are going to learn metalwork from me." He laughed. "You're too old to be apprenticed; you and the little ten-year-olds wouldn't get along. No, you'll follow me around. Watch what I do. Keep your eyes and ears open. You're a bright chap. You'll pick it up quickly."

"I never dreamed of such good fortune!"

"We're past the dreaming stage. I'm going to work your fingers to the bone. We're behind schedule, although your invention will help somewhat. You don't mind hard work, do you?"

"Oh, no, sir!"

"I sense a 'but' in there somewhere. Do you have other commitments or responsibilities?"

"Well, my wife is expecting a visit from me. She lives down near Jezreel, sir. But I can send a message. She'll understand."

"I can see you love her very much. Do you have any children?"

"Not yet, sir. But it's not for lack of trying."

"When you have children, you'll be able to support them. I'm raising your salary now. Whatever it is, we'll double it."

"Thank you, sir!"

"But I expect a lot of work for that. Don't let me down. And call me Pepi." Something caught Pepi's attention, and he turned to find a court messenger standing at his elbow. He grimaced. Messengers from the king were always unwelcome. "You have business with me, Nahbi?"

"Yes, sir," Nahbi replied, bowing slightly. "The king requests your presence. Immediately, sir."

"He does, does he?" Pepi said, his eyes narrowing. "His requests are getting more peremptory with each passing day. Soon he's going to say, 'Come here, damn you,' and I'm going to run in the opposite direction. Heber, why don't you find a messenger to send your wife the news—good and bad. Tell her you won't be home for another month or so. I'm sorry, but we're going to be very busy until then." He turned and scowled at Nahbi. "Unless Jabin offends me badly enough to make me walk out, in which case we'll both be looking for work." When Heber left, Pepi's expression softened. "I'm sorry I was so abrupt, Nahbi. You're not responsible for the king's rudeness."

"That's kind of you, sir. Do I understand that you're promoting the Kenite?"

"Yes. Why? Do you know him?"

"No, but his name has come to my attention. His wife, sir . . . it appears she's having an affair with General Sisera."

Pepi's face fell. "Does Heber know? I can't believe he does."

"Apparently not, sir." Nahbi cleared his throat. "And it would appear he's the only one, poor chap. He's the laughingstock of the garrison, but no one has the guts to tell him."

"I thought Sisera never bedded the same woman twice."

"She appears to be an exception, sir. The lady must have a stomach of iron. I can't believe she actually likes him."

Pepi nodded. "So you're no friend to Sisera, either."

"He leaves a trail of brutality and terror wherever he goes. Even the old troopers are afraid of him. I have a kinsman in Damascus who has offered me work in his countinghouse. Only my wife's reluctance to leave her family has kept me here. Have you had any dealings with Sisera recently?"

"A few weeks ago."

"If you thought he was bad before, I assure you he's gotten worse. But you're safe; Jabin needs you. As for me, I stay as far out of Sisera's way as possible. But sometimes even that doesn't work."

"Well," said Pepi, "thank you for telling me about Heber. One needs to know these things."

On the way to see the king, Pepi decided that something about the Kenite's situation did not ring true. Heber was a poor man who did menial work. His wife would be an unlikely paramour for a man of lofty rank like Sisera, who could choose any woman in Jabin's kingdom.

In fact, Sisera grabbed whatever and whomever he wanted. Recently he had seduced the wife of a ranking courtier and, when challenged, had killed his lover's husband in a so-called duel. It had been no contest; the courtier was no swordsman, and Sisera had a reputation as the finest sword in Hazor. Onlookers distastefully said it was murder.

The widow, free to follow her heart's desire with Sisera, had hanged herself instead.

What was the motive for her suicide? Was it possible that she could not withstand the "ardor" of Sisera? Rumor had it that no woman chose to have him a second time. And no woman discussed his sexual peculiarities. It would be interesting, Pepi decided, to learn more about Sisera . . . if only to have another weapon against him. Sisera was a very dangerous man.

The merchant Azzur had a caravan heading into the Jezreel Valley in the morning, so Heber sought out a scribe in the marketplace and had a letter written to Yael. When the scribe read it back, it was full of flowery and ornate turns of phrase.

"That's too fancy," Heber protested. "Yael won't understand what you're saying. She'll certainly know those aren't my sentiments. Try it again in plainer words, the way I told you."

The scribe rolled his eyes and heaved a dramatic sigh. "Let's try it this way," he said, as if to a child. " 'Dear Yael: Greetings and much affection from your husband, Heber. I will be delayed a month at least. I have found employment as an armorer.' " He frowned and looked up. "Do we really want to say that? An *armorer*? That trade requires years of training."

"Well, I'll explain it to her in my next letter. She doesn't know too much about metalworking. Now just tell her I love her, and that will be it. How much do I owe you?"

The scribe named his price. His expression was lofty, even superior, while Heber counted out the coins. When the Kenite walked away, the scribe leaned over to speak with the scribe in the next stall. "The cuckold now gives himself airs." He chuckled. "Armorer indeed! Doesn't he know that the longer he stays away from that wife of his, the longer his horns will grow? Why, Sisera visits that area twice a week."

The other scribe laughed and licked his lips. "If the Kenite doesn't wake up, he's going to find a cuckoo egg in his nest."

Pepi's angry mood persisted all the way to Jabin's audience chamber. It was not soothed by his finding Sisera with Jabin. They were an odd pair—the slender, almost childlike Jabin and the fierce, large-boned, always pugnacious Sisera. Jabin, Pepi knew, prided himself on his reasonableness, on his ability to analyze and solve problems, on his compassion toward conquered peoples. But since ascending to the throne of Hazor, he had never been able to inspire the loyalty and respect he craved. Sisera, on the other hand, was violent, unpredictable, irrational, and introspective. His loyalties were fierce but precarious. His hatreds were full-blown and random. Pepi was well aware that Sisera hated him because Jabin deferred to him in certain military matters.

Now Pepi's formal bow was perfunctory. "You called

for me?" he asked, without using any of the obligatory
terms of deference.

"Sisera tells me you're falling behind in your work. If
you can't do the job on time—"

In a fury, Pepi turned on one heel and headed for the
door. "I don't need this job. I've had offers from Tyre,
Sidon, Arvad—"

"Wait!" Jabin cried out. "Let's talk this over. I didn't
mean—"

Pepi stopped at the door and turned to face him.
"The wise man means what he says and says what he
means. I haven't any time to waste on windy words."

"You see!" Sisera erupted. "The insolence one has to
put up with! You should have let me get rid of him a long
time ago."

"Get rid of him?" Jabin echoed. "I have no intention
of getting rid of the finest armorer north of the Egyptian
border. Sisera, you mistake me. And you, also, Pepi."

"Excuse me, Sire," he said while looking darkly at
Sisera. "I have to start packing."

"I meant no disrespect or offense. It's just that Sisera
was telling me that the schedule—"

"The schedule is in fine shape for an army that has no
plans for an immediate offensive. If you had been preparing to move on the Moabites, it would be another matter,
but the Israelites have driven them back across the Jordan. That puts the situation into quite another light. The
Israelites seem to have shown an initiative lacking in our
illustrious general."

"I'm sick of your damned effrontery," Sisera seethed,
his hand moving to his sword belt.

Pepi reacted with striking quickness. "Under the law
it is a criminal offense, punishable by death, to draw your
sword in the presence of the king, except in his defense.
Are you planning to claim that I threatened Jabin's life?
I'm unarmed, as you can see."

Sisera's mouth opened, but no sound came out.

Pepi continued, "Since you've reached for that sword,
you might as well try to kill me, unarmed as I am." He
kept his eyes on Sisera's sword hand; it had not moved.

"Jabin, violence offered me without provocation will have to be dealt with. I think I'll take this snake's sword away from him and ram it down his gullet. I offer my apologies for the offense against court etiquette that feeding this reptile will entail."

The men rushed together, but Jabin forced himself between them. "Stop this nonsense right now! I *order* you to end it. We'll talk things over quietly."

Slowly Sisera's hand edged away from his sword, but pure hatred burned in his eyes, and his words could not hide his suppressed rage. "Your word is my command, of course."

"If I'm no longer wanted here," Pepi said, "I have to get to the coast. The commander at Arvad offered me half again what I've been getting paid here, and since my lord the king finds that he can so easily do without my services . . ."

Jabin spoke quickly. "Sisera, leave us for a few minutes." Sisera locked eyes with Pepi. He seemed on the verge of attacking the armorer, but then he gained control of his anger, nodded, and left.

Before fifteen minutes had passed, Pepi had doubled his own salary and made room on the royal payroll for his new assistant, Heber the Kenite.

As the caravan left for the southern country, bearing Heber's letter to Yael, a man wearing the robes of the Israelite tribe of Issachar came through the Hazor city gates. His people were not under the thumb of Jabin and had fought in the uprising against the Moabite overlords at Jericho. The traveler, however, had escaped military service due to a bad knee.

As he moved through the city he tried to blend in. Occasionally he stopped to talk to other Israelites, asking the same single question again and again. No answer satisfied him until, in the early afternoon, he found a work detail from the tribe of Naphtali.

"Have you heard of a man named Barak?" he asked and braced himself for the inevitable no.

But this time one of the laborers wiped his sweaty brow and demanded, "Who wants to know?"

"I am Jerah, of the tribe of Issachar. A woman of my tribe, a prophetess named Deborah, has told me to look for a man of that name."

The worker looked suspicious. "Deborah of the Palm Trees? I've heard of her. But what could she want with such a man—*if* he could be found? These days, you understand, one cannot betray secrets, no matter how trivial they seem, to just any man, be he Israelite or not. We have been betrayed by our own before, and these are dangerous times." He jerked his head toward the towering palace of Jabin.

"I have identified myself and my purpose," Jerah said. "My life is in your hands. I don't know what more you can want of me."

"Well, if I were to lead you to someone named Barak . . ."

"Please, if you know such a man, tell me where I can find him. I have to deliver a message from Deborah. Have things come to such a pass that one child of Jacob cannot ask after another without being under suspicion?"

The local man looked at Jerah through slitted eyes. "A man wanting to find Barak should inquire along the road between Merom and Kedesh. He sells lumber to Hazor for the restoration of Jabin's palace."

The man's neighbor chimed in. "More like he acts as agent for all the men of Naphtali who sell lumber to Hazor. Ask for Barak, the son of Abinoam."

As Jerah moved off, he heard another laborer's bitter admonishment. "You fool, you told him too much."

"His mission is a righteous one," another voice said.

We shall see, Jerah thought.

In the Kenite colony, at the foot of Mount Tabor, Yael knew nothing of the good fortune that had come her husband's way. She could think of nothing but Sisera and his demands, and she was sitting alone by the river, trying to think of a way to escape. Fear and loathing of the general created a blanket of despair around her body and mind. She could not escape it.

As she sat, her eyes on the water, a familiar figure approached her.

"Basemath!" Yael cried happily. "Where have you been?"

"You won't believe the adventures I've had. I went down to visit my kin in Ephraim, and on the way back I sought out Deborah of the Palm Trees."

"A stargazer? I didn't know you believed in such things, Basemath."

"This woman is more than an astrologer. She's special. She speaks with the voice of God. My kinfolk told me about her. You should see the crowds that gather every day to consult her."

Yael nodded but remained skeptically silent.

"You're just listening out of politeness. Look at me, Yael." Basemath studied her friend's face. She saw the pallor, the trembling lips. "Sisera has been here again, hasn't he?"

Yael's eyes filled with tears.

"Yael," Basemath said, her voice urgent with concern, "you must come with me to talk to her."

Yael shook her head fiercely. "What if Heber comes home and finds me gone? How will I explain my absence?"

"I don't know, but Deborah said you'd find a way."

Yael turned on her friend in a fury. "You told her about me? How dare you!"

"She's the kind of woman you tell things to. She isn't brilliant or beautiful or rich, but she is very wise. When I told her about what is happening to you, she said: 'Tell her to come to me, right here in this little grove, and I'll tell her what to do. Make sure she knows that God will not let her go much longer without answering her prayers to Him.'"

Yael was astonished. "You told her I've been praying to Yahweh?"

"No. She already knew. She knows everything. She says that her God will deliver Sisera into your hands."

Suddenly Yael began to shiver violently.

"Yael, what is the matter? Are you ill?"

Yael shook her head and held up one hand for
Basemath to be quiet. Then the trembling ceased, and
Yael looked wide-eyed at her friend. Some color came
back into her face. "A Voice . . . it was as if a Voice spoke
in my mind with great force."

"What did It say?"

"That Heber was not coming back for some time."

"You see?" Basemath asked in awe. "The prophetess
said God would whisper into your ear."

Yael sat quietly, dangling her feet in the cool water.
"Basemath," she finally asked, "if the Voice that whispered to me told me the truth, then I am to go to see
Deborah." *This Yahweh*, she thought, *is most strange. He
is invisible and powerful, yet He speaks into the ear of a
young tinker's wife.*

"Get rid of him," Sisera snarled, "or I'll kill him. Find
another armorer."

Jabin stared with disbelief at his boyhood friend. "I'd
control my threats if I were you. Pepi supposedly bested
Caleb of Canaan, the Israelite general, more than once.
Among the Israelites Caleb was said to have been second
only to Joshua. And remember, both your father and mine
fell at the hands of Joshua."

"Lies! Caleb was a superior warrior. Pepi would have
had to kill Caleb to beat him."

"Remember, Joshua, Pepi, and Caleb were trained in
weaponry by Moses of Egypt, and Moses was trained by
Baliniri of Mari, whose weapons prowess is still a subject
for the ballad singers in the north country."

"Who cares about ballad singers? Pepi is insolent.
Why should I have to put up with his insults?"

"As a favor to me," Jabin said gently. "I need him just
now."

"There are other armorers."

"Not other Children of the Lion. Don't forget, a
member of that famous clan brings more than skill to his
employer; he strikes fear into the hearts of his enemies. As
soon as we hired him, people started to take us seriously."

Sisera gave a reluctant nod.

"Now forget about Pepi," Jabin continued. "There's another problem you and I have to discuss. Word has gotten back to me about your relations with certain women in the region."

Sisera glared at him.

"The word used, again and again, was *rape*. There were two complaints filed by women in Kedesh, and there was a woman in Beth-shemesh who committed suicide after being visited by you. She was the daughter of one of the tribal leaders, and he attributes her suicide to your abuse."

"Ridiculous."

"Then you deny these accusations, and I can trust your word that you had nothing to do with the death, the rapes, or the beatings?" Jabin had long ago accepted the fact that his general had bizarre tastes. But Sisera had to be made to understand fully that in times of political peril, certain passions had to be restrained. All he wanted to do was get this side issue out of the way, and fast, so they could devote their energy to more important matters.

Sisera's fists clenched and unclenched. "I admit I had relations with the women. But they all asked for it, virtually begged me for it. You know what I mean—the sly glance, the feigned protest and resistance, while what they want most is to be thrown on the ground and taken."

"This can cause serious ramifications. You heard what happened in Jericho—some Israelite stuck a knife in Eglon of Moab, and then a huge force of irregulars swooped down, slaughtered the city guard, and drove the stragglers all the way across the Jordan. When the Moabites finally came to their rescue, this pickup army of Israelites destroyed them. Bashan is now totally free of Moabite influence, and any Moabite found on this side of the river is put to death by stoning."

"They won't try that here," Sisera scoffed.

"Don't fool yourself. They could. So far the only thing that has prevented a serious revolt is that the Israelites don't have a leader to stop the tribes' bickering and organize them to work together."

"Nothing will ever unify that gutless, worthless rabble. In the meantime, why shouldn't I take my pleasure
where I can find it? Their women are the only interesting
aspect about the Israelites. Their men are the whipped dogs
who can't keep them satisfied. You've nothing to fear
about the Israelites living in Hazor, no matter what went
on in Jericho."

"All the same," Jabin pressed, "go easy on their women.
You can push people just so far. And these tribes think a
lot of their daughters—and their wives. Remember what I
said."

Sisera, having agreed in principle to control his passions, took his leave. *He's sold out,* he thought, filled with
disgust for Jabin. *He's backed down before Pepi.* Jabin was
too worried about what the other kings of the region—
older, secure, and more experienced—would think about
him. But why should he care about what people thought?
Anyone who made judgments based on that was unfit to
rule.

Sisera stopped in his tracks. Jabin unfit to rule? The
thought had never occurred to him before. But what need
did he have of Jabin? The king was hardly more than a
figurehead. At first his name had been useful to woo
prospective supporters who remembered Jabin's father
and who had looked back on the old days, before the
Israelites' invasion, with great nostalgia. While waving the
banner of Jabin of Hazor, it had been easy to find soldiers
and money.

The more Sisera thought about it, the more firmly he
believed that Jabin was no longer necessary to the enter-
prise. It was an exhilarating thought.

CHAPTER
TEN

City of Ur, Kingdom of Babylon

Luti had been given a simple tunic so that her naked-ness would not upset the venerable judge who presided over sentencing individuals for such serious offenses as blasphemy. It was a coarse, moth-eaten garment that had obviously been worn by other prisoners before her. It was too large and had a musty odor, and the threads along the bottom were unraveling.

She stood quietly, her wrists bound behind her back. All her wounds had been treated, and she felt little pain now, although a dull, lingering ache affected her body.

The sun was overhead and strong, blazing through the open terraced roof. She relished its warmth after her interminable hours in the penal pit. Luti understood what was about to happen to her; she was going to be con-demned to death. But because she was still in shock from the arrest, interrogation, torture, and the old man's kind-ness, the judicial proceedings seemed vague and far away.

She stood in a room in the municipal building, about half a mile from the Temple of Astarte complex, where she had been imprisoned. The same two guards who had accompanied her from the pit now stood behind her, whispering. They carried long knives thrust into belt scabbards.

One wall of the room held shelves of clay tablets, piled high, lengthwise. Two other walls were bare. From

the fourth wall hung a curtain through which officials came
and went. Just in front of the curtain was a large S-shaped
table on which several seals and stamps were arranged.
The table, made of African ebony, was very beautiful and
intricately carved.

The moment Luti saw Banniselk she averted her eyes.
She could not stand the sight of him. She had turned her
head so quickly that one of the guards lunged closer and
made certain her restraints were secure. They were, so
the guard merely cautioned her against sudden movements.

The judge entered the room and sat behind the table.
He glanced at Luti once, then ignored her. Banniselk
whispered to the judge, who appeared to listen offhand-
edly, as if he had heard it all before, a thousand times.
She had been told by one of the guards that the judge's
name was Hammur and that he was strict but fair. Hammur
was wearing a simple knee-length tunic of unbleached
linen, leather sandals, and one of the small caps often seen
in the king's court. He had very dark eyes and a square-
cut beard. Other people began to enter the large room
now. They stood or squatted along the walls.

"Bring the prisoner forward," Hammur ordered.

The two guards moved swiftly behind Luti and nudged
her toward the large table. When she was about five feet
away, he motioned to her to stop.

"Unbind her," he said.

The thongs were removed. She rubbed her wrists
briskly to get the circulation going.

Hammur spoke loudly, so everyone in the room could
hear. "Luti of Ur, you have confessed to the crime of
blasphemy against the goddess Astarte. Furthermore, you
have borne false witness to a priest of the goddess—
identifying accomplices who do not exist so as to hide
your coconspirators' true identity. Most likely, you have
done that to enable them to escape the wrath of our city
and to continue their evil works among us." He paused
and waited.

Luti did not speak. What could she tell him? That she
had been tortured? That much was obvious from her appearance. That every word in her confession was a lie?

That she had no idea what the birthmark on her back meant? That she loved the goddess and would do nothing to injure the people of Ur? No, there was nothing to say. It was too late.

At that moment terror overcame her. This judge was going to have her killed. Her whole body trembled. The birds! The flocks in the air! The beautiful, twisting, diving birds! The ripe wheat. The fishermen at dawn! All that she would never see again.

"The laws," said Hammur into the void of Luti's silence, "are clear." He stared at the spectators lining the walls. "A death sentence is required for the crime of blasphemy against a god or goddess of the realm."

There was a low, long murmur of excited assent from the onlookers. Luti cringed.

When Hammur turned to her, she felt a nearly overwhelming hatred.

"Luti of Ur, I sentence you to death. You shall be taken to the Tigris at noon tomorrow by the civil guard and be drowned there for your crimes."

The crowd in the room heard the sentence. Many voices shouted, "Honor to Astarte!"

Luti's hands were grasped harshly and the thongs wrapped around her wrists. Suddenly the room went silent, and the hands holding her relaxed. A gentle voice issued from the back of the room, riveting the attention of all present. "My lord Hammur, a mistake has been made!"

All eyes followed the old man as he shuffled slowly, painfully toward Hammur. Luti, to her astonishment and relief, recognized her ally as the elderly gentleman who had visited her after the whipping.

Hammur jumped up from his chair. "An honor!" he said fervently. "A great honor to see the esteemed Drak! Welcome to this court!"

Murmurs rippled throughout the room. The onlookers did not seem to know the newcomer.

Hammur came around the table to greet Drak. "I had heard you were ill. How glad I am that you are about again. This kingdom cannot afford the loss of one of its greatest astronomers and mathematicians."

Drak smiled. He walked to Luti and placed a comforting hand on her arm.

"Hammur," he said in his gentle voice, "this young woman is not a blasphemer. Nor is she a demon from the netherworld conspiring against the goddess or poisoning our wells. She is innocent. She is an orphan who, unknown to herself, is a member of a great and noble family."

Hammur laughed nervously. He shot a withering glance at Banniselk, who seemed equally perplexed. The crowd shifted uneasily at these startling pronouncements.

Drak continued, turning Luti and lifting her tunic as he spoke, so that all in the room could see the lion's paw birthmark.

"Long before the goddess Astarte was worshipped in this southern part of the kingdom, a family called the Children of the Lion lived and worked in Canaan—and were distinguished by this mark. While the birthmark is usually passed through the male heirs, from time to time it appears in females of the line. Another branch of the family, the Chalybians, is even more ancient, originating in the mountains far to the north—and they are great masters of the powers of the mind."

The spectators leaned forward for a better view of Luti's backside.

Drak's voice became harder, more brittle, almost accusatory. "We in the south, noble Hammur, have always been isolated. In the north, in the palaces of Babylon, the birthmark of the lion's paw is immediately recognized as belonging to a Child of the Lion. One member of that family—Seth of Thebes—was heir to the winged throne of Babylon. All of the charges against this child are rooted solely in ignorance concerning her family. I ask you now to rectify the mistake. I beg you not to send an innocent child to her death."

Hammur seemed unsure of how to reply. After a brief hesitation he said, "I have the greatest respect for you, Drak. And I assure you that I am already aware of the contributions of Seth of Thebes in rebuilding our divine city in the north. I am also familiar with the Children of the Lion and the Chalybians. Indeed, they are part of the world's great legends. But I was not aware of this family birthmark. And, even if I had been, there is absolutely no proof that the young woman is a Child of the Lion or a Chalybian. She has, from all reports, spent her whole youth working in the fields along the river. She has neither father nor mother. Surely, if she was a member of that powerful family—a large shipping and trade cartel as we all know, in addition to their numerous other virtues— they would have rescued her from such an existence. As much as I respect you, Drak, I cannot base my sentencing on anything other than facts."

"What would constitute a fact in this case, my dear Hammur?"

"Evidence that refutes the charges," the judge replied simply.

"If I proved to you that she is a Child of the Lion, that her birthmark truly identifies her as a Child of the Lion heir, would you throw out the blasphemy charge and negate her confession?"

"Of course! It would make the presence of that mark on her back merely coincidental in relation to the seal of Astarte."

Banniselk started to object, but Hammur cut him off with a sharp movement of his hand.

"Did you know of their special talents?" Drak asked.

"No, other than that they have achieved power, wealth, and sometimes notoriety in many lands."

"The art of metalworking, Hammur, is their great talent," Drak revealed. "They have a hereditary genius with metals of all kinds. It is an almost mystical ability with their hands."

"But this prisoner is a field worker!" Banniselk sputtered.

"Precisely," Drak responded calmly. "She knows nothing of metals or of tools that work metals. She knows nothing of the arts and sciences pertaining to metallurgy."

"I don't understand what you're getting at," Hammur confessed.

"If this girl could work metals without any training whatsoever, then it would obviously prove that she is a

Child of the Lion, for they are supposed to gain that genuis while still in the womb."

"A test, you mean?"

"Yes! Test her! If she can work the metal, free her. If she cannot, then she is a blasphemer. Test her!"

Hammur pondered. "A fascinating idea, Drak. Don't you agree, Banniselk?"

Are they all mad? Luti wondered. *First they condemn me to death, and now they are going to play games with me, like a fly who is tormented by a child.* She leaned over and whispered desperately in the old man's ear, "But I know nothing of metalworking. Nothing."

"We shall see," Drak said, smiling.

CHAPTER ELEVEN

Damascus

Theon had been in Damascus, the so-called Queen of Cities, for only a week, but he could not wait to get away. Far from the gorgeous center of culture it was reputed to be, it was, in fact, old, dirty, and corrupt.

The only good thing about Damascus, Theon decided, was that it was not Ebla. Ebla, a bustling, over-crowded city of a third of a million people, required a bureaucracy of fifty thousand to administer it; and these functionaries, intent on anything but service, either blocked most deals or demanded enormous bribes to facilitate them. It was very complicated doing business in Ebla.

In Damascus, however, there were no middlemen. There were only buyers and sellers . . . and in Damascus everything was bought and sold. Theon had only one more appointment left to be made in Damascus, so he sent messengers ahead and set up a meeting with Huldah, widow of Ephai.

As he wandered through the Damascus bazaars on that morning, taking careful note of what sold and what did not, his thoughts kept returning to Huldah. He had legitimate commercial reasons to meet with the woman—by helping each other, they could create a profitable relationship. But in his heart he acknowledged that there were other reasons for the visit. He wanted to speak to her face-to-face. He wanted to be physically close to her.

He stopped at a jeweler's booth, where a pair of gold anklets caught his eye. He was looking for a gift for his wife, Nuhara. The displays were being guarded by two well-armed men. He bent over to examine the anklets. "Who made these?" he inquired. "If it's who I think it is . . ."

The concessionaire grinned shrewdly. "Iri of Thebes," he boasted. "And they are from his mature period, after he left Egypt. I must say, sir, you have excellent taste. It's a pleasure to find a customer who appreciates real craftsmanship. These are one of a kind with a story behind them. Iri made them for his wife just before he lost her."

"Keturah was kidnapped by slavers," Theon said sharply. "How did her jewelry find its way to your stall?"

"Sir, I haven't any idea how, where, or why these pieces left his wife's possession. All I know is that I recognized them at once when they turned up for sale in Carchemish. I paid a hefty price at auction for them. As for Keturah, everybody knows where she is now."

"Enlighten me," Theon urged. "I like a good story." He added cynically, "And we all know that Damascus storytellers are the most imaginative in the world."

The merchant ignored the implication. "She is said to be either a slave or a freedwoman, depending on whom you happen to believe, in the royal house of Troy."

Theon nodded wearily, but his heart thudded. Over the years he had heard many rumors about Iri and Keturah, placing them somewhere in the vicinity of the Greek and Trojan conflict. But this was the first time Keturah's whereabouts had been pinpointed.

The merchant continued, "It appears Keturah was purchased as a slave some years back by Helen of Sparta, then given as a goodwill gesture to one of King Priam's daughters, a witch named Cassandra. The princess took to the girl and made her a personal servant. That much everyone agrees on. Some say Cassandra freed Keturah but that Keturah chose to remain in Troy as Cassandra's friend. Others vehemently deny that version." He stopped and peered at the anklets. "While all this speculation continues, however, what you have here, without any question whatsoever, is authentic work from the hand of the master himself. Observe the artistry . . . study the love of the material . . . enjoy how it was worked."

"And Iri?" Theon asked. "Is he still alive?"

"My sources say that Iri died years ago. My informants didn't know how it happened; he had been making arms for the Greeks. I assume his demise had to do with the war. What a waste that lunatic conflict is! And it never seems to end."

Theon believed what the jeweler had reported. He stared morosely at the gold anklets. The great metalworking tradition of the Children of the Lion would die out unless someone stepped in soon. As senior member of the clan, Theon felt responsible for helping the survivors: Pepi in Hazor, Keturah and her child in beseiged Troy, even Nimshi and Micah in Canaan. But which one first? And how? Could he enter Troy? Did he have the ability and courage and daring to act?

"I'll take the anklets," he said suddenly, dropping five gold coins on the counter.

The jeweler stepped back. "Far too much, my lord. These are fine pieces, but they are not the treasures of Babylon."

"They are treasures to me," Theon said, pushing the coins toward the merchant contemptuously, "and I am grateful for your information." He accepted the anklets and strode away. He realized, with some discomfort, that both he and the jeweler had violated the rules of the game: one paying too much and the other protesting the overpayment. It was very strange.

Huldah's town house was one of a long row along the Damascus street called Straight. When the servants ushered Theon inside, he was surprised to see the unlived-in look of an official building. Everything was too well-ordered, too clean, too empty, to be a residence.

When he was kept waiting for a long time in a small enclosed courtyard, he decided the delay was a deliberate tactic that Huldah used to demonstrate her contempt or to make him feel ill at ease so that she could strike a better

deal at his expense when the time came. At first he was
angry at the ploy, but then he realized that his motives
were far from clear with regard to this mysterious woman.

Finally Huldah appeared, tall and regal and cold.

He rose, bowed, and recited the litany of flowery
phrases that etiquette expected in Damascus. As he spoke,
Huldah stared at him with icy eyes. He watched her face,
taking careful note of the stark planes of her bone struc-
ture, her lofty and imperious air, the gray hair that her
personal servants had taken such extraordinary pains to
arrange in a perfect pattern. Every fold of her gown was
impeccably pressed, and below the hem he could see her
large but beautifully formed and meticulously pedicured
feet in sandals trimmed with gold and precious stones.

He had seen her just the once before, when he had
traveled in her caravan. Why, then, did he have the
feeling that they shared some kind of intimacy?

"I have seen you before," she said.

"I was briefly a member of your caravan in Canaan. I
was there when you visited the seeress Deborah. I left
near Lake Chinnereth."

He realized that there had been a subservience in his
voice, and it shamed him.

She looked sharply at him. "Ah, the seeress. An
interesting person. I sent a messenger to her afterward,
offering to pay her a fortune to come to Damascus. She
sent back a reply that said she was quite content to be
where she was."

"It's always interesting to find someone who can't be
bought," Theon said.

"Bought? The woman can't even be bargained with.
Plenty of people can't be bought, but they can be rented
or leased." Just then a cloud seemed to pass over her face,
as if some terrible memory had invaded her mind.

Theon remembered the gossip about her background,
how she had worked her way up from the stews of Damascus. She had been "rented" or "leased" many times.

He tried another tack. "Did you get your money's
worth from the seeress?"

"She would take no money. This, too, was interesting behavior. There seemed to be a principle involved. Men and women of principle are rare indeed, particularly among the Israelites."

Theon raised a brow. "My lady has a worse opinion of the people of Jacob than my own experience has given me. In general I have found them to be neither better nor worse than other people. Perhaps I will seek out the seeress myself, the next time I go to Canaan on business." He paused to wonder if he dared. "Perhaps I will find you there."

"Perhaps." Her voice was sharp and distant.

Theon wished he could penetrate the forbidding walls she erected around herself. Something about Huldah stirred strong feelings in him, but he did not even know who she was or whence she came. Who had she been before her days in the brothels? What had driven her to that existence?

"Let's get down to business," she said brusquely. "I tried to have you thoroughly investigated after you sought an audience with me. Do not be offended; I must be prudent. But nobody seemed to know anything about you—that, or they chose to remain silent. Yet you come to Damascus bearing letters of credit from the most prestigious bankers. A man whom no one knows—or who is so powerful that he frightens reliable informants into silence—is a man of mystery, a man about whom I must learn more before we have any dealings."

She looked at him intently, and although her eyes were still as blue as the Great Sea, a fire burned beneath the ice, touching the core of him, creating a feeling that had been forgotten since his marriage to Nuhara. He had been faithful in deed, although not always in spirit, to his wife, even though the passing years and numerous misunderstandings had sapped the ardor from their relationship. They had settled into a pattern, and he no longer ached when they were apart. She had become a vague presence, neither supportive nor annoying.

Now he was feeling passion again—passion for a woman he did not even know, a woman whose background appalled him. As she reached out and touched his hand, he felt a profound shock. Their palms met, and heat flowed out of her tall, pale, cool-looking body into his heart and loins, and he trembled uncontrollably with emotions he could not describe.

"Perhaps you would like to return later," she suggested, "and finalize our agreement." Both of them knew what she meant, and it had nothing to do with business.

He fought to remain calm. "When would you like me to come?"

"Whenever you wish," she replied, releasing his hand. "I have all the time in the world."

Theon arrived at the inn a full hour before he was supposed to meet Perida, his most trusted agent in Damascus and the man who had arranged the meeting with Huldah. Theon sat down and had two quick bowls of good Chios wine. He tried to relax, but he could not get Huldah out of his thoughts. He was obsessed with her. She had driven away other concerns and created a visceral ache that tugged powerfully at his guts.

A cold film of sweat covered his brow. His hands were shaking. The lamp across the room seemed to dance before his eyes. He blinked in a futile attempt to clear his vision. He was in the grip of something. . . . Was it an illness? he wondered, wiping his brow.

Don't! he told himself. *Forget that promise to return to her! It is a terrible idea. Don't think about her anymore.*

He gulped more wine. The dancing lamp across the room was blurred. He had always led a temperate, chaste life and was not used to drinking uncut wine.

What's the matter with me? he agonized. *Am I under a spell?* How absurd that was! He had never believed in magic, even though his father had described many strange and terrible acts that could be accomplished through the occult arts. But magic? Magic was something that fakirs played on gullible children. Then, why, all of a sudden, was every precept he lived by hanging like a millstone around his neck?

He closed his eyes and felt as though she could control his soul. He opened his eyes and tried to pick up his wine bowl, but his hand was shaking so badly he spilled it. He gripped the bowl with both hands, guided it to his mouth, and drained the contents. It was no use to fight her.

Shuddering, he stood and hailed the innkeeper. "There's a fellow who's supposed to meet me here for dinner," he said, then gave a description of Perida. "Tell him to meet me for breakfast instead." He pressed a coin into the man's hand and lurched out the door.

On the street, Theon hired a guard with a torch to find Huldah's house. Lights were burning in her upstairs windows, so he took the guard's torch, then dismissed the man and went to the door.

His knock was meant to be loud and imperious, and he was embarrassed to hear how timid it sounded. The door swung open, and Theon was surprised to see her facing him.

"I . . . I had to come," he faltered. "I don't know why."

She was wearing a wrapper over a sheer gown and was apparently getting ready for bed. But she still wore her rings and a golden choker, and her hair was exquisitely arranged, as if she were expecting him.

The light from his torch sent reflections dancing on the golden necklace, bracelets, anklets, and jeweled rings on her fingers and toes. Her hands, long fingered and beautifully kept, went to the collar of her wrapper. They undid the pin, and the cloth fell at her feet in soft folds. The torch fell from numb fingers and burned itself out on the ground. The fabric under her wrapper was so sheer he could see her full breasts, her generous hips and soft belly, and the still-golden triangle of hair.

"I willed you to return," she said, closing the door behind him. "I sent a message to you with my thoughts."

He tried to speak, but no words would come as Huldah expertly unfastened his belt and opened his garment. He stood unmoving, like a callow boy. She stepped closer, and her soft lips fell upon his.

He had never been unfaithful to Nuhara. Now he could not even remember that she existed. Huldah's soft,

fragrant-breath kiss became a hot, demanding one. Under
her manipulations his tunic fell to the marble floor. He
was naked except for his loincloth. Her insistent hands
undid that garment, and it fell to his feet. He stepped out
of his sandals, pulled her to him, and kissed her. His lips
sought her neck, her throat, her shoulders, and his hands
reached for the sheer gown that was all she wore.

"Tear it," she said in a husky voice.

He ripped it off, and she pulled him farther inside the
vestibule and to the woven rug on the floor.

They made love for six hours, longer than he thought
he could endure, but she had summoned the strength out
of him, using all the arcane arts of the courtesan. And she
had shown him ways to please a woman that did not
demand endurance. He learned that every inch of a woman's body would respond erotically if given the right stim-
ulation and that his own body was capable of sensations he
had never imagined. He had realized from the first that
Huldah was a whore; now he had learned that she had not
forgotten these skills.

How, he wondered, had he lived this long without
learning these things? He had thought he had known the
ways of women, but he had known the ways of only one of
them, and now it appeared that there was more variety to
womankind than he had imagined. But was there more to
the pleasure of the evening than her whore's skills? he
wondered. Why, for instance, did he feel no guilt about
being unfaithful to Nuhara? When he had sat in the tavern
before dinner, he had vacillated, telling himself that his
obsession with Huldah was wrong. But the moment he
had looked into her icy blue eyes, all hesitation had fallen
away, the guilt had vanished, and he had made love with
an open mind and a clear conscience.

Might she be a witch—a conjurer who could look into
his eyes and control his mind? His father had told him that
Pepi's father, Apedemek, had possessed this faculty and
had used it to seduce Neftis, who was Pepi, Nimshi, and
Micah's mother. Apedemek had used that power to cause

men to kill one another, to betray friends and country and God.

Seth had learned the knack to counteract Apedemek. If good men and bad alike could master the trick, then a woman of power like Huldah could certainly master it and use it on men. How else to explain her rapid rise from whore to madam, to courtesan, to wife and partner, to rich widow? Everyone knew the degradation endured by the unfortunate women who fell into the hands of the whore-masters of the lower ranks. They were said to be forced to entertain as many as forty men—no matter how brutal or depraved or diseased—every twenty-four hours, to suffer beatings, whippings, and every imaginable maltreatment.

The prostitutes of Damascus were said to be kept naked day and night, chained to the bed even when their meager portions of food were passed in to them. Only when one died was she unchained. The women would last two years at most before dying of suicide or disease, or going mad.

Yet this woman, if his sources were correct, had endured several years. How? Was it possible that she had learned witches' ways early on and had used them to control men's minds, to move her customers about like puppets?

Wait! he thought. *Am I sure what I thought was happening during the past six hours actually occurred? Or could she have cast a spell on me? How do I know that the experience was real and not a suggestion planted in my mind while under her influence?*

For the blink of an eye he saw Huldah as she actually was: large, very large. If a man was not in the mood, he might speak of her as being too big-boned to be beautiful. Her hands and feet were enormous. Signs of middle age were beginning to appear: wrinkles, slightly sagging breasts, rough patches of skin.

But then she caught his eye, and suddenly she became irresistibly beautiful again. All doubts were driven from his mind. Her eyes never left his as she put the tray down in the middle of the floor. Without hesitation he stretched out his hand and pulled her into his embrace.

*   *   *

When he awoke she was gone. He was lying in a
huge, comfortable bed, and someone had neatly laid out
his clothes for him. He could hear servants outside, and
when he dressed and went into the great hall, one of them
handed him a letter. There was nothing personal in the
missive; it was as if no intimacy had occurred between
them. It was a draft of a trade agreement: His ships would
make connections with Huldah's caravans at specific inter-
vals in named locations and would deliver and receive
goods. Accounts would be kept through a particular counting house, and the transfer of bills of credit or hard cash
would take place through neutral bankers.

Ordinarily, such a trade agreement would have made
Theon very happy. This was the way the family had tried
to recoup its losses in recent years—by making trade
agreements with energetic merchants and then, within the
law, taking over their businesses. But now he felt no
contentment whatsoever. Nor did he feel triumph at having successfully hidden his affiliation with Khalkeus of
Gournia from an unsuspecting trader. What he did feel
was a niggling, vague sense of danger, not to Nuhara, his
firm, or his children, the twins Gravis and Hela, safely
ensconced on the island of Home, but to himself. Why
would he be in danger?

He went out into the morning sunlight and found his
way through the streets to the inn where he was to meet
Perida. His agent was already there, a small, thin, nervous
man who kept spinning an empty bowl in his hand.

"Did it go well, sir?"

"Well enough," Theon said, showing Perida the letter.

Perida read it slowly and carefully, rubbing his chin.
He handed the letter back to Theon. "Was she suspicious?"

The question angered Theon. "Of what?" he asked
sharply.

Perida squirmed on his bench. "Well, sir, if she knew
whom you represented, she might have refused to do
business with you. After all, your family is well-known to
be a tough competitor. Please don't take this wrong, but

Khalkeus is considered a shark, and ports all around the Great Sea are littered with the remains of trading companies who were once partners with him."

Theon grinned. "Are you saying, Perida, that this agreement is merely the first step in our taking over Huldah and her wealth?"

"All I am saying, sir, is that your family is formidable."

"And so is she," Theon whispered, so quietly that Perida could not hear him.

An hour after Theon's departure, Huldah came down from her office. She called out for her maid Yabamat, who arrived at a dead run, a frightened look on her face.

"Did you give him the message?" Huldah asked.

"Yes, my lady. He took it and went away."

"Fine. Was he sad? Angry? Annoyed?"

"I couldn't read his expression, my lady. His mind seemed to be elsewhere."

"Good," Huldah said. "He was an excellent subject, which is surprising. He's very intelligent, and the smart ones usually resist having their minds directed in any way."

"Did my lady get what she wanted from him?"

"Not really. I became distracted—he was a very good lover once he relaxed. I wanted to find out more about him, and I suppose I lost the threads of my method during the passion. But it doesn't matter. I have people looking into his background."

"Oh!" the girl exclaimed. "My lady, I forgot to tell you. One of them is here now, waiting in the anteroom."

Huldah, noting how the girl avoided looking her directly in the eyes, curled her lips in a cold smile. "Send him in."

Theon peeled the fruit the innkeeper brought him for lunch, but he did not eat. A hundred conflicting thoughts were troubling him. He had the feeling that he had lost all contact with objectivity. He had kept at Huldah like a pariah dog mounting a bitch in heat. In the morning's light he felt soiled, small, and mean, as if he had fallen from a great height. Yet he knew that while one part of him was repelled by the idea of going back to her, another part thoroughly enjoyed his descent into depravity and looked forward to returning to her.

He was so lost in thought he did not even see Perida enter the tavern.

"Sir, we were able to get these back for you!" Perida said excitedly, dangling something familiar in front of his eyes.

Theon realized he was looking at the gold anklets he had purchased in the bazaar. He had forgotten all about them. "Who had them?" he asked, perplexed.

"A whore."

"I never went to a whore," Theon said.

Perida laughed. "It was I who went to the whore. We followed the standard procedure to track Huldah's people after you left. The woman sent a messenger carrying a package to a whore who used to work for her. When the whore left her house, we sneaked inside and obtained the package. Inside were the anklets you had purchased in the bazaar."

Perida waited for a response, but Theon remained silent, so the agent shrugged his shoulders, laid the items on the table, and left.

For the longest time Theon refused to pick them up. He did not even remember bringing them to Huldah's house, much less giving them to her. Now he knew she had used extraordinary powers to control his behavior. The ultimate insult was that the jewelry, which meant so much to him, obviously held no value to Huldah; otherwise she never would have given it away so easily, and to a whore. She had used the jewelry, he guessed, merely as a way to test him and her powers over him. There was no doubt in his mind that if she could cause him to relinquish Iri's artwork, and without his remembering that he had done so, she could prompt him to do anything.

Now he was frightened. What else had he done of which he had no memory?

Huldah glared at her informant. "You're certain of that?" she demanded. "You'll be very sorry if you're mistaken."

The man fidgeted in his seat. "Certain, my lady? No. But the probability is very high. It took me the entire day to gather it for you, and I accepted no information unless it was confirmed by two other sources. The man who visited you here is a high-level official in Khalkeus's shipping operation."

Huldah's large hand balled into a fist and smashed down on the table between them. "That duplicitous fool will pay for this!" she vowed in a lethal voice.

How long had he been in the tavern? Ten hours? Twenty? Theon did not know. He had drunk himself into a stupor, recovered, then became stuporous again. Now he was sipping a concoction of wine and vinegar that seemed to revive his faculties.

A thousand times during the past hours he had stood up and started out of the tavern to go to her. Each time he had turned back, ashamed of his desire for her, humiliated by his weakness. Again and again he was caught between the conflicting needs to make love to her and to be free of her.

He drained the bowl and suddenly became very still. A strange epiphany jolted him: His whole analysis of their relationship had been crude and stupid. He had been thinking in terms of seduction and power; what if it was actually love? What if it was one of those inexplicable situations in which two mature, settled people fell in love?

The tension of the past hours drained out of his body. For the first time he relaxed. There was no reason why he should not go to see a woman he loved. She would be waiting for him.

He stood, dumped a handful of coins onto the table, and lurched unsteadily out of the inn. The night was star filled, and a breeze brushed his face. She would be pleased to see him. He grinned happily.

For a moment he forgot how to find her street. He turned once, twice, and then started to walk south in a drunken, love-thick haze.

He stumbled on a loose stone, and that split second's hesitation saved his life. A fifty-pound sack of bricks dropped from the roof above and smashed into the street beside him, missing his head by inches. Trembling, he stared upward. A shadow flitted across the roof. The person who had dropped the sack was leaping from roof to roof.

Theon wanted to give chase, but his knees felt weak. At that moment he knew, with more certainty than he had ever known anything in his life, that Huldah had sent a man to kill him.

CHAPTER
TWELVE

City of Ur, Kingdom of Babylon

"Luti, are you frightened?"

Luti heard the words coming from the top of the pit, but she could see no one in the darkness. She moved to the wall of the penal hole and cowered there, terrified that it was Banniselk, come to taunt her.

The man repeated, "Luti! Are you frightened?"

No, the voice was not Banniselk's. It was friendly, compassionate. The girl moved to the center of the pit for a wider view of the circumference of the opening. She saw the silhouette of the old man they called Drak. He had moved aside a few planks covering the pit so his voice could be heard.

"Why should I be frightened?" she asked bitterly. "This test is just a game to torment me, to postpone the inevitable. I am already dead. Soon I will be drowned."

"Do you disbelieve what I said to Hammur? Do you disbelieve that you are a Child of the Lion?"

"What does it matter if I have twenty such birthmarks on my back? I can't work metal! I know nothing about metal!"

The old man did not respond. Luti could hear him shuffling slowly about the rim of the pit. She did not mean for her words to be so harsh. The old man had shown great kindness to her, but she had told the truth.

Darkness and dampness enveloped her. It was better

to be dead, she thought, than to live like this in darkness, in fear, surrounded by powerful enemies . . . except for an old man who made up outlandish stories in an attempt to save her life.

"Listen to me, child," the old man said. "Listen carefully. Tomorrow I shall be wearing a special coat made of the feathers of a nighthawk. Do you know what that is?"

"A bird. It lives in the desert. But I have never seen one."

"It is really a falcon," Drak explained, "and it hunts by night. It is very small, fast, and powerful. It hovers in the night currents and then swoops down at great speed to kill its prey. Sometimes it kills snakes, small birds, and rodents. If it is extremely hungry, it will eat the flesh of any kind of carrion."

Why was the old man telling her this now? Luti wondered. Was he losing his mind?

Drak asked urgently: "Are you listening to me?"

She folded her arms around her body and squeezed tightly to warm herself against the chill. "I am listening," she said wearily.

"The feathers of the nighthawk are beautiful. Scattered amid the dull gray hues are what seem to be sunbursts—all the colors of the rainbow shaped into spheres and circles and triangles. Sometimes, when one looks at the feathers of the nighthawk, one can see in their beauty the heavens and the planets and the shooting stars. Do you know what I am saying?"

She screamed at him. "No! I don't know what you are saying. I don't understand you at all!"

"I must go now, Luti," he said gently. And then he was gone.

She sank to her knees in the dark pit and wept bitterly.

She was brought once again to the courtroom of Hammur. The massive ebony table no longer held judicial seals. Instead a great many unfamiliar objects were arranged across its broad surface.

Her hands were untied, and she was shoved forward

by the two guards. Behind the table stood Hammur and
Banniselk, who was glaring at her. No spectators were in
the room now, and there was no sign of Drak. Odd, she
thought, because all this nonsense had been his idea. For
a moment she felt betrayed.

"Pay careful attention," Hammur said to her. He
pointed to the section of the table that contained three
necklaces, each on its own tray. "You will notice, young
woman, that each necklace is gold in color. But only one
of them is real gold. Do you understand?"

She nodded, then stared at the three objects. She had
no idea which one was the real gold necklace.

Then Hammur pointed to a large slab of slate, on
which a flame fueled by an oil wick burned in an earthen-
ware dish.

"Here is where you will do all your work," he explained. He pointed farther down the table to three small
stone hammers, each one shaped differently, but each one
set in an identical wooden handle. "These are your tools.
Only one is specifically intended for working gold."

She nodded again. Luti could identify everything that
was on the table, but what was the point of forcing her to
participate in her own death sentence? What was the
advantage in being drowned tomorrow instead of today?

"Noble Drak has not graced us with his appearance,"
noted Banniselk. "Perhaps he is ill again."

"No matter," said Hammur. "We shall follow his instructions to the letter. Are you ready to take the test,
young woman?"

Luti wanted to spit in the face of her judge, but she
grimly realized that she had to attempt the test, if only to
repay the kindness of old Drak.

Banniselk pointed a finger at her and said in an ugly
voice, "Remember, witch, you must choose the gold necklace; next you must choose the correct tool to work it; then
you must fashion it into a spear point."

Hammur turned on him angrily. "You are overstep-
ping your authority, Banniselk. The goal of the test was
not supposed to be disclosed until the moment she started."

"What does it matter? She's a witch. She'll never succeed."

The curtain rustled. The argument between the two men stopped. Drak shuffled into the room, smiling benevolently and nodding his head.

"We were worried about you, my esteemed Drak," Hammur said.

Luti noted that the old man did appear ill and was paler than usual. He did not look in her direction. He did not greet her. Instead he stood next to Banniselk behind the table.

Hammur turned to Luti and repeated the final instructions. "You must select the gold necklace. You must choose the correct tool. You must beat the gold necklace into a spear point. Do you understand?"

She shrugged. Hammur made a flourish with his hand. It was time to begin. The sudden appearance of Drak gave her a glimmer of hope . . . a possibility of success. She moved closer to the table and stared at the three necklaces. She picked up one at a time and replaced it. She glanced up at Drak, hopeful for some clue, but the old man was standing with his eyes shut. His body swayed slightly.

Luti went to the tools, picked each one up, balanced it, and then put it down. She walked to the center of the table where the flame burned and stared at it. She had no idea how to proceed. Despairing, she looked again at old Drak.

For the first time she noticed his coat of bird feathers. She remembered that he had told her about the garment made from the feathers of the nighthawk. The coat was indeed beautiful. The sunbursts of color against the gray background filled her with immense joy. She started to laugh as she drank the colors in with her eyes. A strange feeling crept over her body. She felt light and carefree, as if she held gay musical instruments—cymbals, bells, flutes, drums.

Still laughing, she turned back to the table, quickly picked up a necklace, and held it over the fire. She

grasped one of the tools and worked the softening metal
with incredible precision and speed.

Now her laugh was like a gurgling of happy sounds.
She laughed even louder, and her fingers seemed to fly as
a rustle of the bird-feather coat caught her eye. She felt
possessed of the most wonderful strength and wisdom.

She saw Drak coming around the table toward her.
The sunbursts on the coat truly were the planets moving
across the heavens.

"It's all right now, Luti. It's all over," Drak whispered to her, grasping her gently by the shoulder and
guiding her away from the table.

As the feeling of immense relief came over her, she
buried her face into his coat and began to weep powerfully, convulsively.

"Look, dear Luti. See what you have wrought," he
said.

She looked up. There, on the table, in plain view,
was a beautiful, perfectly formed golden spear point.

"You see?" Drak said to Hammur. "She has chosen
the necklace of gold; she has utilized the proper tool; she
has worked the metal professionally; and she has passed
the test. Now will you free this Child of the Lion?"

CHAPTER THIRTEEN

Canaan

Jerah, Deborah's messenger, rode into Kedesh while the sun was still high. Within minutes he had obtained a description of Barak, son of Abinoam, and was pointed toward where Barak would most likely be found, supervising the loading of logs. Jerah recognized the big, broad-shouldered Barak immediately from the descriptions he had been given.

Barak was half a head taller than anyone else working with him. He looked even younger than people had said. Nothing in his face or demeanor gave credence to what Jerah had learned from informants—that Barak had been a wild and violent youth and now was a bitter and inconfident young man.

Jerah took the luxury of studying him for a long while before approaching, noting the thick dark hair, the poorly cut and simple garments, the powerful chest and arms, the voice that was polite but tentative.

"I'm looking for Barak," Jerah said. "Barak of the tribe of Naphtali, son of Abinoam."

"I am he," Barak said. "What can I do for you?"

Jerah found himself unexpectedly tongue-tied in front of this young giant. His mission seemed ridiculous. How could he look a stranger in the eyes and tell him that God had chosen him to raise an army of ten thousand men of all the Israelites' tribes and fight a war?

"Is there anywhere that we can go to talk privately? What I have to tell you, Barak, is . . . a bit complicated."

Ten minutes later, over a plate of fruit and a couple of bowls of wine, Jerah began his story. He grew more relaxed and eloquent as the story progressed, and Barak proved to be a rapt listener. When Jerah finished, he sat back and waited for the young man's response.

It was a long time in coming, but finally Barak said, "Well, you are either insane or drunk."

Jerah laughed. "I'm neither, I assure you."

"Then give me some proof."

"There is no proof. There is only faith."

"I don't have time for faith. I push logs around all day so I might have enough to eat. Just tell me how you can be sure that I'm the man you're looking for. How can you know that Deborah really heard my name in her dream?"

Jerah took a deep breath. "I'm not sure of anything. Neither is she. But ask any priest north of Jerusalem. Ask any Israelite in Ephraim. Everyone will tell you that Deborah is a woman through whom Yahweh speaks."

"I don't listen to priests."

"Then ask the farmer in the field or the woodsman at his saw or the shepherd among his flock."

"They all know Deborah? Why have I never heard of her?"

"Because your nose is buried in your logs."

Barak stared about the tavern, confused, undecided, his powerful hands kneading one another.

Jerah pressed on. "What do you have to lose? A few days' wages? I guarantee that any conversation with Deborah is worth a whole year's wages. Perhaps you are not the man who will break Hazor's grip on our throats. But for your own sake, for the sake of your people's children growing up here with no future, you must talk to her."

Barak blew out a deep breath. "When do you want me to go?"

"Right now. I will take you to her."

Barak's face relaxed into a smile. "Do I have time to finish my wine?" he asked.

*   *   *

Sisera dismounted and strode into the tinkers' town, a grubby mix of shacks and tents clustered near the stream. When he approached Yael's tent, it was obvious that no one was at home. A neighbor woman with three children playing nearby stared at him.

"You!" the general called. "Where's the woman who lives here?"

"I don't know," she answered. "I was only asked to watch the place while she was gone."

"Did she say where she went?"

"No, sir."

"Or how long she'll be gone?"

"She told me nothing, sir. She just asked me to watch."

"Damn!" Sisera fumed. "The little bitch!"

The general turned on his heel and angrily stalked away. As he walked through the tinkers' village, Sisera realized that other women in other tents could be taken now, as he had planned to take Yael. But it was Yael he wanted. No one had ever excited him as much. Her gentleness and her delicate beauty always seemed to cry out to be crushed by his strength. When he violated her, when he caused her pain, it was as if he were shattering her soul as well as her body, and only he could heal her, if he so wished. He closed his eyes and remembered her naked, weeping. She would pay for not being in her tent when he wanted her! He ground his boot into the gravel of the stream.

Yael never quite understood why she had agreed to accompany Basemath to the hill country of Ephraim. All she knew was that since Sisera had become attracted to her, her life had been a horror. So desperate was she that she had considered ending her life. If there was even a remote chance that Deborah might help her, she was willing to try, especially since the Voice had whispered to her.

The trip was pleasant. Basemath, a nonstop talker, rattled on at such a pace that Yael had no time to think of anything bad or depressing. Basemath's good heart and eternal cheerfulness were blessings.

For the first time in her adult life, Yael was out from under the shadow of Mount Tabor, and she enjoyed the change in scenery as the road wound through the foothills. Just south of Ramah on the third day, they came to the little grove of palm trees where the prophetess held forth. Something about the atmosphere in the glen caused Basemath to fall silent. For the first time Yael found herself initiating a conversation.

"How long has she—Deborah, I mean—been coming here? Has she always held audiences like this?"

"No, not until her children were grown. She says that her first duty was to her family. Only when they could fend for themselves could she busy herself with anything else. At least that's what one of the local women told me when I was here last."

"Does she answer all questions? Settle all disputes?" Yael asked.

"I don't think so. She says that God tells her which requests and disputes are important and which are a waste of time. She can be very abrupt with those people, and they seldom bother her again."

"I hope I'm not wasting her time. I mean, who am I? I don't even share her faith. All I did was pray to Yahweh once or twice when I was desperate."

"She knew that. Don't worry; she asked for you. That makes you important." She patted Yael's hand. "See that big fellow who's talking to her now? That's unusual. Few men come here, and almost never anyone that young."

"I wonder what problem he's brought," Yael mused.

Barak's problem was Deborah herself. The woman's calmness and surety unnerved him. No matter how persistently he denied her dream, no matter how many times he claimed that he could not do her bidding, the prophetess merely smiled and affirmed her choice.

Exasperated, he spoke to her as he had never spoken to anyone else in his life: "Listen: You know nothing about me. I am violent and stupid. I know nothing of military warfare. I used to fight for bread in the bazaars because I was big and strong and had no trade. The God you speak of is a stranger. I have never been devout. I ignore the fast days. I never sacrifice. My fellow Israelites fill me with loathing. I have no friends. People ignore me or go out of their way to avoid me! How can I lead people to freedom? I cannot even take care of myself properly!" He realized he was shouting and felt ashamed.

"You demean yourself, Barak," Deborah said evenly. "I see a young man of wisdom and integrity."

"No! I am not the one you seek."

She smiled again. Her eyes swept past him, toward the gently rolling hills.

"I was stupid to come here," he said grimly.

"You could not have done otherwise. Yahweh is powerful, young man. He has given me your name. He has chosen you to stand beside Moses and Joshua and Father Abraham. Yahweh has chosen *you* to lead the children of Israel out of oppression and despair. Yahweh has chosen you to destroy Hazor."

"You frighten me, Deborah. I want to go home."

"You are home, Barak."

She had spoken with such conviction and love that he stared at her. He saw that she had extended her hand. Without thinking he grasped it and held it tightly. Her hand was small and enveloped by his own. It was the hand of a woman who had worked all her life—rough and calloused. He wanted to walk away, but he could not take his eyes from her and could not release the grip on her hand.

Something strange began to happen. . . . Everything in his vision had been blotted out by a glowing white cloud. Again he tried to release Deborah's hand, and again he found he could not. His head reeled.

Then a picture came into focus before him: A great army stood poised to strike at the head of a narrow valley. Far in the distance was the enemy force. He could hear the sound of drums, quick, insistent.

A tall, commanding man rode ahead of the army. He looked as if he had been nurtured and molded to sit on a war-horse. He had broad shoulders and massive arms, and he wore a protective leather vest. In one hand he grasped a buckler, and in the other he carried a shining, razor-sharp bronze sword. The figure was strangely familiar. . . . The man's face was his own.

"No!" he cried.

It is too late, a Voice said. *Your destiny has been chosen for you. It is clear what you must do.*

Barak could not have said whether the Voice was a man's or a woman's. It seemed to be originating inside his head. Remarkably, he remained aware that he still held Deborah's small hand.

Suddenly a surge of immense strength flowed through his hand and into his body. The power was unlike anything he had ever experienced. It was as if he had suddenly acquired the strength of a dozen soldiers. Then everything went dark.

"Deborah!" he cried, frightened. "What's happening to me? Why can't I see you?"

When Barak regained consciousness he found himself on his back on the ground. A ring of unfamiliar faces hovered over him.

"Where am I?" he asked. He sat up but was so dizzy he had to lie down again.

"Barak," Jerah said gently, "it's all right now. You fainted, but you're going to be just fine."

He remembered what had happened. "Jerah! I saw something—I felt something so powerful—"

"I know. Relax now."

"Where's Deborah?"

"She's talking to a young woman who has come a long way to see her. She'll be with you soon."

Barak struggled to rise again, but Jerah restrained him gently. "Patience. Relax if you can."

"Jerah, I've never been so frightened before."

"That's understandable. You've never been in the presence of Yahweh before." Jerah shook his head. "Neither had I. And yet I heard the Voice speaking through you."

"What will become of me? Who am I? I don't feel as if I'm the same person."

"You aren't the old Barak. All of us who saw It and heard It are changed, including Deborah and me. A terrible beauty has been born, and none of us will ever be the same again."

Deborah had taken Yael inside. "Did you see or hear anything of what was going on?" she asked the young woman, her voice shaking.

"Was the man having a fit?"

"It was something not unlike that. Please, what is your name again?"

"Yael."

"Yes, I remember now. Your friend with the cast in one eye came to see me. You are lucky to have such a good friend."

"She said you called for me."

"A very powerful man is oppressing you."

Yael nodded. "I can't tell my husband because he'd try to protect me. The man would kill him." Her voice cracked with desperation. "Poor Heber wouldn't have a chance."

Deborah wearily passed her hands over her eyes. "No man is going to kill Sisera. No man *can* kill Sisera."

"Then what is left for me? To kill myself?" Yael's whole body was trembling.

"That is not necessary," Deborah said sharply. "Sisera won't be around much longer to bother you or anyone else."

"But you said no man could kill him."

"*You* will kill him, Yael."

Yael could not believe her ears. "Are you mad? Do you know who Sisera is? Have you ever suffered from his brute power? Do you have any idea of the cruelty, the degradation, the pain?" Yael's anger rose within her. "How dare you sit so calmly, telling me to kill him? Do you have any idea what it means to be raped and beaten and forced to perform sexual perversions? How can I make you understand?" She began to weep, and the anger was sucked from her body. She stared at Deborah through her tears, like a totally dependent child stares at her mother.

Deborah moved close to the young woman, so close that their cheeks touched. "Listen to me, Yael," Deborah whispered in her ear. "Be patient. He'll come to you one day and place himself in your hands. He will be weak, and you will be strong. You will cut the tree down at the roots, I promise you."

And then the prophetess stood and walked away. Yael followed the squat woman with her eyes. Deborah had said that it would be so, but would her assurances be enough? She shuddered at what awaited her.

CHAPTER FOURTEEN

City of Ur, Kingdom of Babylon

Night had closed on the river. The large, flat-bottomed boat glided silently near the shoreline, and reeds brushed softly against the shallow hull. Four men with poles powered the vessel.

Luti lay on a woven mat, one hand dangling over the side into the water. Drak stood nearby, engrossed in the movement of the vessel through the darkness, his hands clasped behind his back.

It was difficult for the girl to believe that only a few hours before, she had been a criminal condemned to death by drowning. Now she was floating along the river, a free woman. Hammur, brusquely overruling Banniselk's strenuous objections, had released her in the custody of Drak after she had somehow transformed a gold necklace into a spear point, thereby proving that she was a Child of the Lion rather than a blasphemer against the goddess Astarte.

When she was first freed, she was ecstatic and thought of nothing but how good it was to be alive. But now, in the soft night, she began to wonder about that test. She remembered little about it—only that she laughingly performed a task of which she was not capable. Was it a miracle? Had she really absorbed the art of metalworking in her mother's womb? Did that birthmark on her back

mean that she had other powers she did not even know
about? It was all so unbelievable. What had really happened?

Drak's voice pulled Luti from her introspection.

"Look there, in the sky," he said. "The constellation
of the bull kindles itself. Did you know, child, that all
events of this world are determined by the movements of
the stars?"

"Even my torture?" Luti responded in a joshing
manner.

Drak, ignoring her remark, continued. "And the stars
are, in turn, coerced by the moon. The moon, mother of
the seasons, pays homage to the divine and immutable
sun, whose heat is the weaver of time and space. Did you
know that there is nothing on this earth—not flesh nor
soul nor spirit—that is not bound by numbers? And these
powerful numbers are revealed to us by the motion of the
stars." He raised his hands in a futile gesture. "Ah, my
dear, if only there were enough time to teach you."

Luti understood little of what Drak had said, but he
had been so passionate about sharing his subject, she felt a
new intimacy with him. It made her bold.

"I don't want to learn about the stars or my soul. I
want to know what happened to me."

"You were proven innocent," he said simply.

"No!" she cried. "Something or someone moved my
hands on the gold necklace. I did not prove my innocence.
I, Luti, vanished. Someone else took that test by directing
my mind and movements. Please, Drak, tell me what
happened."

"Some things should be left alone." He seemed very
ill at ease.

"But I want to know what preserved my life. Would
you keep that from me?"

"Very well, Luti, I shall tell you."

She waited.

Finally he spoke. "My research into your past uncov-
ered nothing about your father. Your mother, whose name
was Intup, reached Ur alone when you were still in swad-
dling clothes. I knew, of course, that your natural father
was either a Child of the Lion or, perhaps, a Chalybian,

because only those two branches of the same family carry the birthmark. I discovered in my research that you were sensitive to the mysteries of birds and their flight, so I assumed that you must be a Chalybian, for that part of the family has traditionally indulged heavily in the occult arts. In addition, you are from the north, from the steppes, from a tribe that once was under the control of the Chalybians as vassals."

He pointed to the sky as if about to show her something, but then thought better of it and returned to his story. Now he was talking very slowly, as if he wanted her to understand precisely what had happened, as if he wanted her to be excruciatingly clear about it.

"So, Luti, I wore a coat with the feathers of the nighthawk. I arranged the bursts of colors on the feathers in the configuration of your zodiacal sign, the crab. The visual clues activated the Chalybian birthright in your mind, and you were able to transcend your ignorance of metals and set into motion a remarkable series of actions that resulted in a golden spear point. That is all there is to it."

Luti was speechless for a long while, trying to absorb Drak's terse description of the event. Much of it was unfathomable to her.

"But why did you save me?" she blurted. "Why *me*?"

"Because we need each other."

"In what way?"

"You may be free for now, Luti, but Banniselk will not rest until he destroys you. The test meant nothing to him. In his eyes you are a netherworld demon poisoning the land. He will be a very powerful enemy. He will prevent you from working anywhere, including in the fields. You have no money, no land, no goods, and no family. You are alone, except for an old man who may not have long to live. But before I die, I am going to enable you to become wealthy beyond your wildest dreams, and that wealth will provide you with safety and a new life."

It all became clear: His involvement had not been altruistic at all. He had planned all this; he had saved her life, but she would be utterly dependent upon him for her survival.

"And what must I do to obtain this lifesaving wealth?" she asked bitterly.

"Help me save the kingdom of Babylon."

"Save the kingdom? I couldn't even save myself without your help!" She began to laugh, and then to weep. Again she was a victim. She started to shiver, and the old man covered her with a cloak. Suddenly, she slept. . . .

When she awoke, the boat was moored by the river's edge. Drak had not moved.

"Feeling better?" he asked.

"Much."

"Then let me tell you what my offer is, Luti. The kingdom of Babylon is in great danger from the Assyrians and others. During the next ten years we are certain to be invaded by massive forces. As things stand now, we will not survive the onslaught. If we obtain a certain weapon in the near future, however, we might survive."

"What weapon?"

"A chariot with a new type of composite iron-and-wood wheel, which enables the vehicle to move swiftly in all weather, on any terrain, increasing the speed of the conventional horse-drawn chariot by a factor of fifty."

Luti started to say something about her lack of knowledge of weapons of war, but Drak waved her to silence.

"Hear me out. If you are willing to take this assignment, you will journey across the desert to Damascus and from there, to Tyre on the coast. Then you will journey down the coast into Canaan and ultimately reach Gaza, the southernmost city of the Philistine League. It is a city very close to Egypt, both geographically and culturally. In Gaza your birthmark will enable you to find employment with armorers and locate the secret source of this weapon. Once you have obtained specific, practical information about it, you will journey back to Ur. It would be even better if you could steal a chariot and bring it to me, but that would be asking too much of you. When I have received the plans from you, I will give you one of my estates, which includes two vineyards and several orchards.

In addition, I will settle upon you an annual subsidy, paid by the state, of a thousand urns of wheat and three hundred jars of oil. Such a settlement will make you one of the richest women in the kingdom."

He moved close to Luti, and his hand caressed her head with obvious affection and care. "It will be dangerous, Luti, very dangerous—but I have confidence in you. If you succeed, you will save the people of your city and your nation from terror and rapine and slavery."

"I—I don't know what to say," Luti replied haltingly. "I want to help you after all you've done for me, but I don't think I'm capable of accomplishing what you have in mind."

"Say nothing now, child. Sleep. In the morning we'll talk more, and then you'll decide."

She stared up at this old man who had been her savior and who now wanted to send her to a foreign land to steal, to spy, to obtain a weapon of death. An image of the horrible priest Banniselk intruded into her consciousness. She shut her eyes tightly and pulled the cloak over her face. Maybe the morning would never come. Maybe she would sleep forever. But then what would become of her newfound freedom?

PART
TWO

CHAPTER FIFTEEN

Troy

I

It was the tenth year of the bloody and interminable war. Once again, as he had for nine years, the awesome Greek warrior Achilles called for games to celebrate the anniversary of the death of the Trojan hero Hector . . . and to mourn the death of his own beloved friend, Patroclus.

Hundreds of Greek ships, their dread black sails furled, were pulled up on the beach, forming a grotesque wall against the sea while protecting the huge tent city along the shore.

The games were officially opened by a speech that Achilles gave in front of his own ship. High above him were Hector's remains, nailed to the wood of the prow. But now, after ten years, no flesh remained. Hector was only a skeleton, defaced by crows and worms and discolored by the Greek soldiers who spat up at the figure.

Listless and dispirited, the Trojans watched from high atop their walled city as the torches were lighted in the Greek camp and the anniversary celebration began.

On the far side of the river, two foreign armies that had come to the aid of the defenders of the besieged city stood idle, waiting for a signal to attack the Greeks. But as the days wore on no signal came. The Nubian and Amazon armies remained in place, training, exercising, and waiting for the Greek games to conclude. Both the Nubians and the Amazons were longtime allies of the Trojans, but until now they had refused to enter the war against the Greeks. Only after they had realized that the fall of Troy would dramatically alter the balance of power and place them in great danger from the northern invaders had they marched to Troy's aid.

One morning King Priam of Troy awoke and called for his wife, Hecuba. "I've had a dream. The great god Zeus himself spoke to me, telling me to go down to the Greek ships, unarmed and alone, bearing gifts to ransom the remains of our son."

"This is insanity," Hecuba protested. "I won't let you." Tears welled in her eyes but then came a glint of resolve. "I was his mother. I bore him in my womb and suckled him and loved him more than life itself. But now it is time to think of the living. You must protect your own life."

Priam drew himself up and used the commanding voice that had recently been so conspicuous by its absence. "You have little choice in the matter but to support me in this."

Hecuba looked at him intently; at least he was close to being his old, confident self again.

"There'll be no problem," Priam continued. "Zeus told me that I would be shielded from harm. Even Achilles is not so stupid as to disobey the will of the gods. He will recognize my sincerity and grant my wish."

Hecuba remained skeptical. She longed to resist this mad notion; on the other hand, anything that returned the king's spirit was not to be dismissed, especially since the morale of Troy lay in the balance. When the king went to consult his advisers, Hecuba sought out their daughter, Cassandra, a priestess of the god Apollo.

She found the princess in her chambers, standing by her window and gazing out over the field at the inactive reinforcements. Her small, painfully thin, tense body seemed to vibrate with every movement of air.

Cassandra turned to Hecuba with surprise. "Mother! What brings you here?"

Hecuba quickly told Cassandra of Priam's vision. "I

know it seems insane for him to go into the enemy camp, but it's the only thing since your brother's death that has lifted your father out of his depression. How can I talk sense into him without driving him back into a suicidal despair? I was wondering if you might petition the gods for counsel."

Cassandra's mind raced. "I'm glad you came to me, Mother. I'll consult the gods and get back to you by nightfall. My father the king is not going to do anything today?"

"Not likely. He'll have to have his decision approved by the council. Naturally, they'll argue against it, but they, like me, would rather see him crazy than mired in despair."

"All right, Mother," Cassandra agreed. "You know his idea may be a good one. Any change in the war would be better than this deadlock. If our reinforcements get disgusted and leave, that would be a disaster." Cassandra patted her mother on the arm and guided her gently out the door. "Don't let Father change his mind, whatever you do."

But when the door was safely shut behind Hecuba, Cassandra called out not for the priests of Apollo but for her servant and friend, Keturah. The delicate, lovely blind woman hurried to Cassandra's suite.

"Did you hear that?" the princess asked. "My father wants to enter the Greeks' camp and beg Achilles for Hector's remains."

"But won't Achilles kill Priam or hold him for ransom?"

"Not if we send a herald to tell the Greeks that Zeus spoke directly to my father. The Greeks are superstitious and won't risk anything that could call down the wrath of the gods on them. My father never had a vision in his life, but the Greeks don't know that. He just had a dream, and the dream happens to provide us with an opportunity."

Keturah's face brightened and then, just as quickly, grew somber again. Cassandra realized that Keturah was thinking of being reunited with Iri's adopted son, Phorbus, who, since Iri's death, represented her only route to safety. Keturah tried to hide her desires, because she no longer trusted Cassandra completely. It had been a slow-growing disease in their mutual affection for one another. The mistrust surfaced rarely, but it was always there.

The women's relationship began to dissolve on the day that the princess had offered to adopt Keturah's son, Talus, into the royal house of Troy. Cassandra, unmarried and childless, claimed that her motives were selfless, that it was for Talus's sake; Keturah, however, had feared that the lonely princess would try to escape from Troy with Talus, leaving her maidservant behind. But Keturah could not suppress her enthusiasm now.

"Might it really be possible for us to escape from Troy?" she asked, her voice trembling with longing.

"If I can somehow manage to accompany Father when he goes down to the Greek ships, perhaps I can slip away and speak to Phorbus. I could find out if he'd be willing to fulfill his promise to Iri to protect you and Talus. If he is, Keturah, I'd go with you. Troy is doomed."

"But what would you do? How would you live?"

"That's not a problem. Apollo always finds food and shelter for his priestesses. Besides, I've taken a fancy to Phorbus. He's handsome, he's passionate, and he's strong."

Keturah was shocked. "But my lady! You are a virgin priestess of Apollo."

Cassandra made a defiant gesture. "I didn't choose to be a priestess and remain a virgin the rest of my days. Why can't I change my destiny? Why can't I have some choice in the matter? Everyone else in the world has a choice."

Seeing the pain on Keturah's face, she quickly put a consoling hand on her friend's arm. "I didn't mean that. I realize you had no choice after you were kidnapped and sold into slavery. Life doesn't reward us all equally. After all, fate made you pretty and me ugly."

"Wouldn't there be a terrible price to pay if you abandoned Apollo?" Keturah asked. "I thought that priests and priestesses who try to change destiny anger the gods."

"Don't worry about that," Cassandra said hastily. "Let's concentrate on how wonderful it will be to get out of here. Besides, I'm tired of my empty life. I want a man, a home, children. I'll risk the gods' anger for a normal life. And Phorbus had an interest in me. I saw it in his eyes."

Was this not a lie, too? Ten years before, when they had briefly met, Phorbus had been pleasant and polite; but she knew he had not looked at her the way men stared at Helen, who was ravishing, or the way men admired the still-pretty Keturah.

In her excitement, however, Cassandra was not interested in the truth. She would seize any opportunity to escape Troy and the terrible fate that awaited the captured women of the city. She was willing to do anything to escape, including lying to herself and even to Priam. She would have to fake a vision, claim to have been visited by Apollo, and told something that would further her cause.

No doubt this was dangerous. *Well*, she thought, drawing herself up. *There's no turning back now. I don't want to die. And this is the only chance I have of saving myself and Keturah and her son.*

"Wait here," she said. "I'm going to see my father."

As she opened the door she could hear Keturah's soft voice raised in concern. "My lady, please don't do anything you'll regret."

In the Greek camp Phorbus watched the games with growing alienation. He refused to celebrate the apotheosis of Patroclus, a man who had loved killing the way most men loved sex. Of course, Phorbus thought, snorting, Achilles probably would not have wanted any other kind of man for his best friend. And Phorbus certainly did not want to praise Achilles for having killed Hector, who, a decade before, was respected above all men in both warring camps, and for having nailed his remains to the ship's prow. The sight of Achilles being fawned over nauseated Phorbus.

The young armorer turned to his friend Odysseus, who had done his sporting for the day, having bested Ajax both in wrestling and, despite his age, in the footrace. Since Ajax was commonly held to be second only to Achilles in warrior skills, Odysseus had performed miraculously well.

"I can't stand any more of this," Phorbus said. "I'm going to take a walk down by the river."

Odysseus, who was in a fine mood because of his unexpected victories, said facetiously, "Don't you realize what fascinating games you'll be missing if you leave now? Why, there are three events left in which Ajax can make a fool of himself. I'm betting all my winnings that I can have him crying like a baby before the day is finished."

Phorbus laughed appreciatively. Since Iri's death, Odysseus had grown to be his closest friend. "No, the man has no dignity. Do what you must to poor Ajax, but do it without me. It's embarrassing just watching him."

Odysseus shook his head. "Suit yourself, but when Ajax starts bawling like a child and you aren't here to enjoy the spectacle, don't blame me. Damn it, man, there's more to come. Perhaps the great lord Achilles will favor us with one of his speeches."

Phorbus grimaced. Everything about Achilles repelled him. The great warrior was moody, violent, and unpredictable.

"Or one of his matchless songs," Odysseus continued. "Actually he has a voice like a madwoman, but everyone's afraid to tell him. I don't know which is worse: his voice or the racket from that wretched lyre of his. At least when his boyfriend Patroclus was alive, the lyre was tuned once in a while. Do you really want to miss Achilles singing a song in praise of the beauty of Patroclus and what his death meant to the gods?"

"You've just given me the best reason to leave now," Phorbus said, staring out at the thousands of Greek warriors who had put their weapons aside to celebrate death. It was the strangest sight he had ever seen.

II

"Finally I find an ally. You're the first person who hasn't thought I was mad." Priam smiled proudly at Cassandra.

The princess affected a pious expression. "It is Apollo himself who agrees with you, Father. He told me that he approves of your errand and that if you approach it in the right spirit, you will achieve what you want and come to no harm."

"Apollo?" Priam raised one brow. "This is the first of your revelations I can remember that was not couched in a mystical language nobody could understand."

Cassandra retorted swiftly, "I've been puzzling over the vision for hours. If I were to tell you the exact form in which it came to me, it would sound ridiculous. I've come to you now because I've finally figured out what the god was saying."

As he pondered she watched him intently, alert for signs of disbelief. In her heart—indeed, in her guts—was the sinking feeling that she had betrayed herself and committed the terrible sin of blasphemy. *Forgive me, Apollo*, she thought, *forgive me!*

But Priam had heard what he wanted to hear, so he nodded gravely. "I thank you for bringing this news to me, Daughter. It confirms that it was the true voice of Zeus speaking to me in the night, telling me that only through humiliation can I regain the body of my son." He rose from his chair. "I will leave in an hour for the Greek encampment. I've arranged for ransom gifts to be put in a cart. I will walk beside it, accompanied only by the herald Idaeus. I will take no weapons or guards."

Now! she thought. *Now is my chance! Ask him permission to go along!* But as she looked her father in the eyes, she knew that he would refuse. This was *his* pilgrimage. "Thank you for listening to me, Father."

"Any time, my dear, particularly if your prognostications are as unambiguous as this one. I will have high hopes for you, Cassandra, if your visions remain consistently intelligible. You could be of great value in running this precarious kingdom, and Troy will be eternally grateful to you."

He turned his back on her and left the room, his head held high, his confidence apparent.

Cassandra lingered, lost in thought. What could she

do? How could she get into the Greek camp? She moved
to the window and looked down into the courtyard. Servants had drawn up a cart and were piling it high with rich
gifts, which Troy's treasury could little spare, considering
the terrible toll the ten-year-old conflict had required
already. As she watched, the servants covered the cart
with a huge cloth. In Cassandra's mind an idea took form.

Phorbus could still hear the Greeks behind him, alternately cheering and jeering the contestants. He spat
derisively and walked faster, heading upstream. He wanted
to find a quiet spot, have a swim in the river, and wash
away the dust of the field. He headed for a grove of trees
near the bend of the river. It was the little copse where Iri
had died. He stopped for a moment, sending up a prayer
that his mentor and adopted father had found happiness in
the netherworld. How were Keturah and Talus faring? he
wondered, still cognizant of his responsibilities to Iri's wife
and son.

Through the trees Phorbus could see where the river
broadened and calmed and became a little pool for
swimming. He grinned and jogged toward the water, pulling off his tunic and kicking off his sandals along the way.
By the time he broke through the low bushes that surrounded the deep pond, he was naked. He leapt far out
across the water and dove in with a satisfying splash.

He came up puffing and blowing; the water flowed
ice cold down the slopes of Mount Ida. He brushed the
thick, dark hair out of his eyes and headed for the shore in
an awkward dog paddle.

Suddenly he stopped swimming as a tremor of fear
went through his body. On the far bank stood a woman
armed with a longbow. The hands that held the bow
looked strong and well formed. The arrow was nocked and
pointing at him.

He treaded water. *Now you've done it, you damn
fool*, he thought. *Now you're going to get yourself killed
for a stupid swim . . . and by a woman!*

She wore the thick quilted clothing he had seen on
the army of women that had settled before the walls of

Troy a few days before. Her hands and feet were bare, and she had taken off her helmet, so he could see her face. It was fair and lovely, though her expression was severe. Her eyes were deep blue, and her close-cropped straight hair was the color of straw.

"I come in peace," he called out. "There's no need for us to fight."

She just stood there, showing no particular inclination to shoot. Finally she let up on the bow and looked him over. "You are a pretty man," she said in a thick accent. "Come out of the water so that I can see what all of you looks like."

"Throw me my clothes," Phorbus said.

"If I throw your clothes to you, how can I get a look at you? You Greeks are odd people. Come out and stand on the bank."

Still he hesitated; she nocked the arrow again.

"Wait!" he called. "I'll do as you say!" He smiled and said lightly, in spite of his thudding heart, "Can I have a look at you?"

She dropped the bow to her side. "Stand on the bank, and I will do as you ask. It is a hot day, and the water looks refreshing."

Any one of the local Trojan girls from the nearby villages would have been annoyingly coy and awkward in the situation. This woman, however, said everything so matter-of-factly. She was not flirting.

"I'm coming out," he announced. He paddled to the bank opposite her and stood up, very conscious of his nakedness. He fought the impulse to cover his genitals with his hands. "Now you know," he said, feeling stupid. "I have the usual number of hands and legs and everything else."

She shrugged. "You are a very pretty man. This is the right word, *pretty* . . . no? You wait." She put her bow and arrow on the ground and stripped very efficiently. Then she stood looking at him, her hands on her slim hips.

He gawked at the amazing sight: She had only one breast. Where the other breast should have been was a long-healed scar, whitish on the skin. But the rest of her body was the most beautiful he had ever seen. She was smoothly muscled. Her thighs were long, a runner's, perfectly formed. The one remaining breast was small but rounded.

As he watched, she began to caress herself slowly, sensually but totally unself-consciously. His own body responded instantly, and he covered himself.

She smiled, knowing she had accomplished the intended effect, and dived into the pond. At first Phorbus looked around for his tunic, then decided against covering himself and dived in beside her. Kicking and paddling underwater, he swam beneath her and emerged on the other side.

Laughing, she turned over to float on her back. Without hesitation she spread her legs and opened herself to him. Treading water, he reached up and laid his hand on the patch of soft hair between her legs.

"Yes," she encouraged. "Good. Good."

What had begun in the water ended on dry land. Phorbus, who had made love to many young women, found in this unexpected liaison an erotic passion that he never knew existed. It was as if she had ushered him into a different kind of world where every touch and taste brought forth a new intensity and beauty and joy.

For a long time afterward they sat in the grass in silence, naked, opposite one another.

"I have never met a woman like you, Myrrha," Phorbus finally said.

"How do you mean?" she asked. "Women are women."

"Many women don't take their pleasure as easily and naturally as you do."

"I do not understand." She rolled over on her belly and stared at him, perplexed.

He gazed down her body, at the long legs and the smooth buttocks. "Most women I've known made me pursue them. When we made love, they acted as if they were doing me a favor."

"They do not like to lie with a man?"

"Yes, of course they do. But they pretend that they

don't. They act as if sex was something strange. Well, maybe not strange, exactly . . . I'm really not making myself very clear, I'm afraid."

"I do not understand. What I want, I go and get."

"So do I. That's the way it is with men here."

"And with women in Scythia," she said. "I think I would not like being a woman here or where you come from."

"Scythia," he repeated. "What do people call themselves there? I mean I've never heard of you."

"We are called the Sauromatae. Where I live, women ride and use the bow and the javelin." She smiled. "We are not allowed to lose our virginity until we have killed three of our enemies."

Phorbus sat up suddenly. It shocked him that this lovely young woman had already murdered three men.

She saw his reaction and laughed. "I have killed many. I am a warrior. It is what I do."

"And that wound on your chest?"

"Wound?" she asked. "No, Phorbus, this was done on purpose. Our mothers perform this ritual on us when we are young. The right breast would get in the way of the bowstring." She reached out one strong, beautiful hand and grasped his arm. "You have an arm of oak. Are you a fighter, too? Will I have to kill you when my queen orders us into battle against you?"

"No, look at my hands and guess what I do for a living. Look at my palms and the forearms."

"You make metal," she said.

"Yes, and it would be a waste of a man with my skills to make him fight. If I were to get killed, who would repair swords and make new ones?"

She smiled. "But you know how to fight?"

"Yes. I was trained by the same man who taught me to make arms."

To his surprise, she got up and pulled him to his feet. "Come. Let us fight."

"Fight? No!"

"No, I mean play. We use sticks. Show me how you can fight."

She broke boughs off two trees and handed one to
him. They started to fence, and he thought: *Look at me,
stark naked and fencing like a child! We are both crazy!*

But it was not crazy. It was fun. She was his match,
so neither could land a blow. They fought until they were
tired, and then they dived into the water to wash off the
sweat and begin their love games again.

Finally, in the late afternoon, they had to return to
their respective camps. They dressed, and Phorbus moved
off slowly, reluctantly, then turned and called her back.
"Will I see you again?"

She laughed. "Perhaps. If the war does not begin
again too quickly. Send a message by one of the people
from the village. Ask for Myrrha, captain of the Second
Troop."

"Captain?" he asked, incredulous. Just as he was about
to question her further, she turned and walked away with
a brisk military stride. He watched her go, his body tingling. "What an astonishing woman," he whispered to
himself.

III

The games had stopped at the end of the day, and
now in the Greek encampment, cooking fires were blazing
brightly. Everyone was sitting around bragging, complaining, or reminiscing. Phorbus looked around but could not
find Odysseus. He had little desire for the company of any
of the other men. Since an armorer could associate with
whomever he chose, Phorbus sought out the dinner fire of
some common soldiers. But he kept to himself. He ate his
meal silently, thinking, remembering.

Soon the men around him were talking about the
women's army and making obscene jokes or speculating
what would really happen when they met the Sauromatae
in combat.

"They won't last five minutes!"

"What a stupid idea, sending women against us!"

"Now the Nubians—they're another matter. They'll put up a real battle."

Everyone contributed his thoughts. Phorbus began to pay attention.

"I'd rather fight the women," another Greek slurred. "At least when you've whipped them, there'll be another kind of sport. When you've beaten a Nubian, what is there to do? He fights naked. There isn't even any armor to steal off his body."

"Maybe the women are ugly up close. Who knows what they look like under those padded outfits? For all we know, they could be men. They sure don't act like women."

"Tell you what," someone suggested from beyond the firelight. "Why don't some of us go there tonight, grab one or two Sauromatae, bring them back here, and find out for ourselves? The worst that could happen would be we'd all get the clap."

"I don't know," someone else said. "They could be as ugly as pigs. And then what would we do with them?"

Phorbus had heard enough. He got up. "Back where I come from," he said angrily, "we waited until we caught a pig before we ate him."

A burly soldier bristled. "What's that supposed to mean?" he demanded.

Another man grabbed the soldier's arm. "Leave the armorer alone. You don't want any trouble with him."

The burly fellow shook him off. "You heard what I said, tinker." His voice was slurred with drink. "What do you know about those sluts in the Trojan camp?"

Phorbus shot him a look of contempt. "They're as tough as wolves, and any of them would eat someone like you for breakfast, if she had a mind to.

"If you came up against one of them in battle, she'd have you disarmed and gutted before you could finish your first feint and lunge. And as for bedding them, the Sauromatae mate when and whom they please. If they don't want you, you won't get any. If they do want you, you won't have any choice in the matter. They'll throw you, mount you, and give you the damnedest ride you've ever had." Phorbus smirked. "You may even be able to get it up for a change."

"Watch your mouth, tinker."

"As for what they look like, they make the most beautiful girl in your village look like a brood sow."

The drunken soldier came at Phorbus furiously, but Phorbus sent him spinning with one hard shove to the chest.

"Somebody put this little buttercup to bed," he said, "before he mouths off to the wrong person and gets his throat slit."

Idaeus the herald arrived at the Greek camp well after dark. One of the pickets intercepted him and brought him to the main campfire, where the brothers Agamemnon and Menelaus, heads of the Greek expedition, were holding court. Idaeus recited King Priam's message while Agamemnon poked his dagger into the burning embers and slowly rotated it. Finally he spoke to his brother.

"What do you think? Will Achilles agree to give up his treasured war trophy?"

"I don't know," Menelaus said. He turned to Idaeus. "Go to the log fire, and someone will give you food. We'll have an answer for you soon." Then he turned back to Agamemnon. "Achilles has been in a very strange mood lately. I don't know if this is a good time to talk to him."

Agamemnon pondered. "He might be in a good frame of mind today; he and Odysseus won nearly every competition. But *you'd* better talk to him about Priam's offer. Achilles and I are never on good terms. I don't want him taking something I said the wrong way and throwing one of his temper tantrums."

Menelaus took a long drink from his wine bowl. "I'd talk to him if I were sober. It takes all my wits to steer clear of every subject he takes exception to. We need someone who's sensitive but not afraid to speak up . . . and someone who's been avoiding the grape tonight."

"Odysseus?"

"The very man."

*   *   *

After the altercation with the drunken soldier, Phorbus went to find Odysseus. The captain from Ithaca was sitting on the deck of his own beached flagship, looking out to sea.

"May I come up?" Phorbus called.

"Of course. But don't bring anyone with you. I can take your company but no one else's."

Phorbus climbed up and sat down beside Odysseus on the dry deck. "Your face points toward Ithaca," he remarked.

"At this time of night my thoughts are always on Penelope. How I miss her! I miss her passion and her tenderness. What an ass I was to leave home for this foolish war. I even long for her hot temper."

"I used to think I liked passive, controllable women," Phorbus said.

Odysseus turned to him. "And something has changed your mind?" When Phorbus didn't answer, he continued, "You've met a woman! One who spoke her mind. Am I right?"

Phorbus nodded.

"Tell me about her. I need a good story to distract me. You can even lie a little."

"I couldn't think up a lie that would come up to the truth," Phorbus said.

"I'm listening."

After Phorbus told the story simply, without coloring the details, he stopped for a moment, then continued, his voice filled with awe. "Who would have imagined anything like that? Fighting with sticks, naked? And I swear to you, Odysseus, she was good. May the gods help any man who goes up against the Sauromatae. And Myrrha claims she isn't even the best fighter in camp. Or the prettiest. That her queen Penthesilea takes the palm on every count."

"Modest, too," Odysseus noted.

"I thought I liked my women soft and yielding. This one is as hard as I am. Even her breast had muscles."

"I've heard tales about the Sauromatae," Odysseus said, "but I always thought someone was stretching the truth. On the mainland they are called Amazons, and the word is that they are indeed fierce fighters." He chuckled. "The rumor was that they did something else fiercely, too."

"I'm squeezed dry."

Odysseus clapped him on the back and laughed. "You think you're a dead man, and you can't come back alive. Believe me: Tomorrow you'll find you're a stallion once more, ready to work twice as hard to please her."

"I hope so," Phorbus said. "I want to see her again, tomorrow if I can."

"The games have another day or two yet to run. There'll be no fighting until they're over. Something may happen to prolong the truce further."

"Wait," Phorbus whispered urgently. He cocked his head and listened. "Who goes there?" he demanded.

"Agamemnon. Is Odysseus with you?"

Odysseus cursed under his breath, then said, "I'm here. What's the matter?"

"Priam sent a message. He wants to come into camp tomorrow under a flag of truce and beg Achilles to give him what's left of Hector."

"How does this concern me?"

Agamemnon sounded annoyed. "There's no use letting Priam come if we don't clear it with Achilles first. And you know how proud he is about having killed Hector and disgraced his corpse. I'd like you to . . ."

Odysseus looked at Phorbus and said softly, "I may be able to get you more time to play with your Sauromatae warrior, my friend." He called down to Agamemnon. "All right, I'll talk to the bastard and shame him into it. I'll make him think he's a fine, magnanimous fellow to do old Priam a favor."

"I knew I could count on you!"

"And I'd better find him now, before he's too drunk to listen." As Agamemnon vanished from sight, Odysseus gave Phorbus a conspiratorial grin. "If Achilles lets Priam have his son, he also has to give the king time to bury the remains—nine or ten days for a prince."

"Odysseus," Phorbus enthused, "you have made me a very happy man."

In the camp of the Sauromatae, Myrrha's unusually pensive behavior drew attention. Queen Penthesilea and the warrior woman Clonia watched her across the fire's dancing flames.

"I understand that some of our girls have been making friends with the Nubians," Penthesilea remarked.

Clonia barked a laugh. " 'Making friends'? Is that what you call it? My lady, have you seen the physique of those fellows? I don't blame anyone for satisfying her curiosity."

When Myrrha did not respond, Bremusa, another warrior, pressed on: "I was down in the ranks before sundown. You could tell just by looking at the women which ones had 'satisfied their curiosity.' Their eyes were glassy." She waited a beat, then added loudly, "Another way to tell was that they were as quiet as mice." She paused. "Myrrha! Aren't you speaking to us tonight?"

For the first time Myrrha looked at them. "If you have to know, I met a Greek today. I fenced with him."

" 'Fenced'? That's a new name for it!" Clonia squealed.

"We did *that*, too. But you should know that this one wasn't a soldier, and yet he was the equal with a sword of any woman in our camp. When it comes to fighting these Greeks, we're going to have our hands full."

Myrrha's comments stilled the banter around the fire. Her companions had never heard the captain voice pessimism. Or was it fear? Or was it love?

IV

"Give him back his son?" Achilles asked in a sour, alcoholic voice. "Why would I do that? Priam's an old fool. I've got half a mind to hitch up the horses and drag the skeleton around the gates of Troy, as I did just after I killed Hector, so that my chariot wheels can serenade the dead and the living."

Patiently Odysseus let Achilles rave while Phorbus stood quietly by the tent wall. Achilles lounged on a divan made of the shields of his Trojan victims and overlaid with a magnificent woven tapestry. Even when under the spell of too much wine, the exalted warrior exuded the physical strength and quickness that made him so feared. He was the ultimate fighting machine: beautiful and lean, with alert eyes that scanned the horizon for potential danger.

When Achilles finally ran out of breath, Odysseus spoke. "You should give Priam back his son to display your magnanimity."

Achilles stared at him in surprise. "Speak."

As Odysseus turned, Phorbus could see his face clearly in the firelight; he winked solemnly at Phorbus. "You are aware, my lord," he said to Achilles, using formal address despite their equal rank, "that the great deeds performed at Troy will be praised in song for many generations after our bones have been laid to rest. Bards will sing of us long after the walls of Troy are rubble and grass grows through the broken bricks."

Achilles was impatient. "Get to the meat of it."

"Very well," Odysseus said. "We will be remembered not only for whom we killed in combat but by how we behaved off the battlefield. And imagine, my lord, how people will react when the storytellers, centuries from now, describe how Prince Achilles, despite his undeniable right to dishonor the body of the fallen Hector, decided instead to show mercy to a broken old man. You will be honored as a mighty warrior and a man of limitless compassion whose heart was touched with a divine nature."

Achilles leapt off the divan with the grace and speed of a panther. His eyes were bright. "Yes! You are right, Odysseus!" He whirled in the air, then landed heavily on the divan. "I'll do it! Let the world know that I am greater than the Trojans in compassion as well as strength."

"I'll tell the herald to return with Priam in the morning," Odysseus said. "We'll make a great occasion of it."

But Achilles, consumed by visions of future homage, was no longer listening.

"Come along," Odysseus said to Phorbus. When they were out of earshot Odysseus stopped. "Well, you'll have some time with your girlfriend. Make the best of it, because when the funeral rites for Hector are over, she will be our enemy to the death."

Phorbus's face twisted with misery. "Maybe I can convince her to leave the army."

"Don't count on that," Odysseus said. "I know the Sauromatae by reputation. Fighting comes above all else to them because it is a mystical compact with the gods. The warriors display indisputable loyalty to their queen." Odysseus put a consoling hand on Phorbus's shoulder. "Enjoy your good fortune while you may, my friend. Nothing lasts in this world, particularly in Troy."

In the morning, the herald Idaeus returned with King Priam, who wore the coarse clothing of a peasant and walked humbly beside a cart piled high with riches and covered with a cloth. As the cart wound its way through the long, orderly rows of the Greek tent city, a slim hand reached out from under the cloth. A dark head, close-cropped like a boy's, poked out.

Seeing that no one was looking, Cassandra scrambled out from under the cover and looked around. She wore the short tunic of a boy, and with her narrow hips and flat bosom, she looked like one. Making a swift decision, the princess of Troy turned to jog toward the fields where the games were held.

At the edge of the encampment, she hailed a passing soldier. "Here, friend," she said in her best Greek accent. "Where might I find the forge of Phorbus the armorer?"

The soldier glared down at her. "Everybody knows how to find Phorbus. Who are you that you don't know?"

Cassandra improvised quickly. "I bring him a message from a young woman."

The soldier grinned knowingly. "The man killer, eh? I'm sure you'll be welcomed. His forge is just down the road beyond the big olive tree. But I'm not sure you'll find him. He may have gone to meet her already."

Cassandra was puzzled. *Man killer? Meet her already?* What was the soldier talking about?

Phorbus was sitting in the little grove by the river when Myrrha arrived. She was dressed in a simple tunic but wore her battle sword.

"I was afraid you would not come," he said, jumping up as soon as he saw her.

"I nearly didn't." She showed no inclination to embrace him. "Queen Penthesilea and the other captains went to the palace to reassure the Trojan women, who are afraid they will be raped by the conquering Greeks."

"And you believe otherwise?" Phorbus asked.

She shrugged. "Why should the Trojan women feel so certain that the Greeks will win? Are the Greeks so fierce? Must everyone feel afraid of Achilles? Just because he killed Hector doesn't mean he'll do as well against the Nubians and Sauromatae."

To his surprise, as she spoke of fighting, she moved closer, and her hand reached down to fondle him. It had an immediate effect.

"You are not like the men I have known," she breathed. "I would not have come back for another. I have come back for you."

Her other hand went to her shoulder and unfastened her tunic. It fell around her feet. Her eyes were on his, grave, solemn, unblinking. "Please," she said. "Make love to me now, Phorbus."

Although Achilles fully intended to grant Priam's request, he pretended to have difficulty making up his mind. Thus the old man was forced to humble himself and beg Achilles to accept the rich bribes. Everything Priam said prompted Achilles to deliver an arrogant speech. Finally, as sundown neared, the bargain was made.

Achilles ordered Hector's skeleton to be taken down, washed, clothed, and anointed with oils. It was put on the wagon under a cloth that hid it from the king's eyes. Then

Achilles made another speech, this one filled with compassion for the old king, his deceased son, and all soldiers on both sides of the war. He called for a sheep to be slaughtered and a feast to be prepared for Priam.

Odysseus had watched the whole thing, alternately sighing and snorting. When he had had enough he got up and barely missed colliding with a boy.

"Sorry," Odysseus said, "I didn't see—" As he took hold of the boy's arm to steady himself, Odysseus peered into the young face. "Why, you're no boy!"

"Please," Cassandra begged in a low voice. "Don't tell."

He led her away toward the beach and his own flagship. "Princess Cassandra!" Odysseus said. "I recognized you from seeing you atop Troy's wall. Phorbus pointed you out to me."

"And I know who you are. Iri spoke to his wife about you. He said you were an honorable man."

"What are you doing here? Don't you realize what danger you are in?"

"I came to see Phorbus," she said.

"Why?"

She frowned. "It seemed so sensible back in Troy, but now . . ." She took a deep breath. "Phorbus swore to help Keturah and her son escape. I know Troy is doomed. I . . . have my own way of knowing."

Odysseus understood immediately. "That's good news for me; I want to go home to my wife. But it's disastrous for you."

"I don't want to die. Iri said if he died, it would be up to Phorbus to help Keturah and Talus escape."

Odysseus nodded. "Because Iri adopted Phorbus, it's a blood obligation. Besides, Phorbus would keep the promise. He's a trustworthy man."

Cassandra gave a nervous smile. "If Keturah and Talus escape, I want to go with them. I don't want to die. You know what will happen to the women of Troy."

"You wanted to ask Phorbus to rescue the three of you?"

"Yes. I think Phorbus likes me. I could tell it in his eyes. I'd make a good wife for him, really."

Poor fool, he thought, *poor, foolish dreamer.* When he spoke his voice had a sad, gentle tone. "He's not in camp now and will be gone for the rest of the day."

"That's all right. My father will stay the night."

"Where will you sleep? I gather Priam doesn't know you're here. He'd hardly approve of your disguise."

"Well, I was hoping that when Phorbus came back . . ."

Odysseus quickly turned his head away from her and said: "I'll fix a bed for you aboard my ship. You'll be safe there until morning."

V

Queen Penthesilea and her Sauromatae women met Priam's nephew who was the commander of the Nubian forces, before the gates of Troy to plan their strategy. "We must put on a show of fighting strength to impress the court," the Nubian said. "The Trojan nobles have lost heart, and we must convince them that with our help they can win."

He was so well-spoken, he rose in Penthesilea's opinion. She had mistakenly believed that his relationship to Priam was the basis for his position of command. But his Greek was even better than her own, and the light of keen intelligence shone in his dark eyes. She nodded her agreement.

"You and I will fight with sword and buckler," she suggested, "and we must take care not to inflict any wounds that might interfere with our ability to fight the Greeks. Agreed?" She put out her white hand, and it was engulfed by his huge, meaty one. The look she gave him was appreciative and flattering.

Odysseus was still awake, lying on his bedroll and gazing into the last glowing embers of the fire, when Phorbus returned to camp from his rendezvous.

"You've put in a long day," Odysseus remarked. "You ought to sleep like the dead tonight."

Phorbus shook his head and sat down cross-legged, facing the fire. "I won't sleep a wink." His face was dark and perplexed.

Odysseus sat up. "Need to talk?"

Phorbus began several sentences before he finally found the words. "I've never met anyone like Myrrha in my life. I'm dazzled. And I have every reason to think that she feels as strongly about me."

"Ah, I know the feeling. It was the same for me with Penelope."

"She's a soldier, a captain, and that means she could share my life. We could travel together, hire out together. I'd make the arms, and she'd use them."

Odysseus chuckled. "So you're making plans already. Have you talked them over with her?"

"That's the trouble," Phorbus confessed. "I don't know how to bring it up. Some things we can talk about easily, but . . . well . . . personal things . . ."

"If she leaves the Sauromatae, which is probably the only women's army left in the whole world, where would she fit in?"

Obviously that had not occurred to Phorbus. "Usually commanders don't care who an armorer is as long as he makes good swords. I assumed an officer would feel the same about his soldiers."

"And if someone did hire her and would let you stay, do you think the two of you could be happy?"

Phorbus's face clouded over. "I could be. But I'm not sure about Myrrha."

"Why not?"

"She knows only the society that raised her. She has been taught to feel contempt for anyone else's way of life."

"The differences between you loom larger the more you consider them." Odysseus's tone was gentle.

"But, Odysseus! This is something I want! I love her very much."

"What about Keturah and her son? How will they fit into this fantasy of yours?"

"Fantasy? Is it no more than that?"

"It will be until you talk it over with the girl."

"Odysseus, stop trying to discourage me."

"If I don't remind you of your promise to Iri, your conscience will. And your conscience won't be so kind to you. It will gnaw away at your guts night and day and never give you a moment's rest."

"I know, damn it! My life is not my own, with the blood oath to Iri hanging over my head."

"Let me tell you what happened today. Princess Cassandra showed up here."

"Why would she do a stupid thing like that?"

"To see you. She wants to be included when you rescue Keturah. She also thinks she'd make a good wife for you."

"Wife?" Phorbus erupted. "You have to be joking!"

"No more than she is, my young friend. She has her own fantasy. Of course, in the bottom of her heart she knows it's hopeless. But she wants so much to believe."

"Whatever can have given her an idea like—?"

"You seem to have been kind to her, Phorbus. You probably treated her not like a skinny, unmarried woman with a body like a boy's—who in ten years will have a body like an old man's—but like a fellow human being."

Phorbus dragged a hand across his forehead and groaned. "How do I break the news to her?"

"What news? That you have no interest in being her consort? Or that you won't take her along when the time comes? She seems to think you already agreed to the latter."

"I may have. We were under great pressure then. Iri and I went inside Troy. Guards could have discovered us and had our heads at any moment. Besides, Keturah owed Cassandra a lot, and Iri was very grateful to her. If the princess wanted to escape death, I'm sure it sounded like a reasonable request at the time."

"You see? It is a complicated affair. You'd better start thinking how to extricate yourself. She's sleeping on board my boat." He let the words sink in. "In the morning she has to be given some answers that will not offend her, that

will keep her as your ally . . . because when you take
Keturah and Talus, you'll need Cassandra's help."

The Trojan nobles and their families had gathered in
the great hall of Priam's palace to watch the mock combat
of the two mercenary generals. The opponents made a
splendid sight under the torches that lit the huge room
almost to the brightness of day. Penthesilea was all woman,
slim and supple in light armor that gleamed like the sun,
all speed and balance, dancing like a maenad and laughing
merrily. The Nubian commander was tall and powerful,
startlingly naked and armed only with a long buckler made
from the spotted skin of an exotic animal and bearing a
sword twice the length of Penthesilea's. His motions were
slow but forceful. The mock contest between them was
magnificent and dazzling in the sheer beauty of their
leaping bodies and in the incredible skill of their swordsmanship. Neither general landed a single blow.

When the performance was over, they bowed to enthusiastic applause. As the clapping abated, Penthesilea
held up her hand and spoke.

"My lords and ladies, I, Penthesilea of the Sauromatae,
bring to Troy an army of women that has never lost a
battle. My colleague from Nubia, Priam's nephew, is the
greatest warrior south of Thebes and a man famous all
along the Nile for his military prowess. He brings to Troy
an army before which even the great king of Egypt has
given way.

"Troy has suffered terrible losses, which have sapped
the spirit of your warriors and brought sorrow and suffering into every home. You fear that the Greeks will soon
breach the walls of your city."

A low murmur of assent filled the hall.

"Although the Sauromatae and Nubians have nearly
doubled the size of your standing army, you continue to
fret and worry." She raised her voice, and its power
reached to every corner of the great room. "You fear
Achilles!"

The murmur became a low, agitated rumble, which
threatened to escalate to a roar.

"Achilles! The bane of our existence," a voice called.

"Achilles the Unkillable!" another nobleman cried out. "The man who killed Hector, the greatest warrior Troy has produced! What can you do to rid us of this terror?"

"Hear me!" Penthesilea demanded. "Priam will bring back Hector's remains, and ten days of mourning will pass before the king's son can be buried. After that the war will begin again. And when it does, I, Penthesilea, queen of the Sauromatae, will kill Achilles."

For a moment the stunned gathering was silent; then the Trojans began to cheer. The rafters rang with shouts of praise.

But when the cheering died and the crowd dispersed, the Nubian commander turned to Penthesilea. "I am not familiar with your customs, but among my people, boasts come back to haunt the person who makes them."

She arrogantly returned the giant's stare. "I know my strengths. I know what I can do."

"Yes," he said, gazing down at her from his enormous height. "And I know mine. But does either of us know Achilles's?"

VI

Odysseus shook Cassandra awake just as dawn was peeking over Mount Ida. "Princess, get up. You have to leave now."

She sat up, rubbing her eyes. "But I haven't spoken to Phorbus yet."

"He got in very late, and before he went to sleep a messenger from Agamemnon sent him away to buy ore. I didn't get an opportunity to talk with him before he left."

"Oh, Odysseus! And I came all this way and took so many risks! And for nothing? It's not fair."

He steeled himself. "I'm sure Phorbus would have liked to have seen you, but these things don't always work out. Come now. I have to smuggle you out of here and back inside the gates of Troy before someone notices you're gone."

"You're going to take me yourself?" she asked, astonished. "That's very kind of you."

You don't know how kind, he thought. "Come, Princess. The longer we wait, the more dangerous it will be."

Priam was preparing to leave the Greek camp, and Achilles could not resist putting salt on an open wound.

"Priam," he said, using the familiar form of address to the old, heartsick king, "tell me how many days you'll need to bury Hector. I'll restrain my men for a reasonable period, of course, but I can't hold them back forever."

Priam's face was ashen. "Allow me eleven days. Wood must be fetched from beyond Mount Ida for his pyre. On the tenth day we will bury him and hold the funeral feast. On the eleventh we will heap the burial mound high. On the twelfth we will be ready to fight again."

"So be it," Achilles agreed.

With no guard of honor, no drums or trumpets, and no accompanying priests, what was left of Hector was carried across the field of battle and home to Troy. Priam walked beside the wagon, while Idaeus led the horses.

The king had taken one sorrowing look under the coverlet at the skeletal remains of his son. He had been washed and anointed. Somehow the bones had resisted decay, and Hector, as far as Priam was concerned, was still the prince of Troy. He was at peace.

Atop the walls of Troy, the guards and watchmen noted that the burden in the cart had changed. The transfer had been made. The city gates were opened, and an honor guard galloped out to escort the king and his terrible burden home.

Priam refused to ride, though the guards brought the king's horse. Since he insisted upon walking beside the cart, the honor guard dismounted and walked behind him. The drums beat, the horns blew, and on the high walls of the great city the women wailed as the king brought his son home.

The procession grew as the Trojans joined the line of royal mourners following the cart.

Odysseus, standing in a copse by the riverbank, gently pushed Cassandra out toward the procession. "Go! Here's your chance!"

She obeyed, but first she looked back. "Thank you, Odysseus. And give my love to Phorbus. Tell him I'll be waiting for him."

His heart sank with pity. He turned abruptly to go back to his ship.

On the way he ran into Phorbus, who was hurrying to meet Myrrha by the river. "I did it," Odysseus said sourly, "but don't you ever ask me to do anything like that again."

Phorbus was shamefaced. "I should have told her myself but—"

Odysseus cut him off brutally. "I felt like a swine. Do your own dirty work from now on. Take responsibility for your own actions. You've taken the coward's way out, Phorbus. You've betrayed Iri and Cassandra, but most of all you've betrayed yourself."

The news about the temporary truce spread quickly on both sides. A holiday atmosphere prevailed in the Greek camp. Phorbus was not the only man to venture among the Sauromatae. Little by little the two armies began to test each other's prowess in a very different manner from the way they would on the battlefield.

The Greek soldiers who preferred the love of men made forays into the camp of the Nubians to find like-minded lovers. And the Greeks and Nubians who preferred women partners went to the Sauromatae camp for satisfaction.

As the armies fraternized, gossip spread. Despite the oath of secrecy that Penthesilea had demanded, one of her women told of the vow made to the court of Troy—that the queen would kill Achilles.

By late afternoon of that day, the story had found its way back to the peerless Greek warrior. He listened in astonishment as one of Agamemnon's men passed along a slightly embroidered version.

"Are you sure?" he demanded, incredulous. "How could anyone—and a woman, in particular—make such a foolish and rash boast?"

"The person I heard it from," the man replied, "claimed to have heard it with her own ears."

"And the Nubian commander?" Achilles asked. "Did he do any such bragging?"

"He seems to have kept his mouth shut."

Achilles's disbelief turned to rage. "Imagine some bitch queen who has fought only barbarians somewhere on the edge of the Scythian wilderness boasting that she can fight me! Does she not know who I am? Does she underestimate the power of a Greek warrior? I promise you this: She will drown in her own blood and spittle!"

"I'm sure you're right, my lord," the informer said.

Achilles ignored him. His voice grew very low—a sign that he was on the verge of murderous violence. "There'll be no more of this fraternization. No more trips to the women's camp. And no more visiting the Nubians, either. The next soldier who becomes the catamite of one of those bastards will spend the rest of his life as a eunuch. We have only ten days before the war recommences, and we're going to use them well. Every dawn we'll turn out for drill. We'll run until we drop. We'll hone our fighting skills and our formations. There will be no sexual interludes of any kind. We are going to have roasted bitch on a stick."

His words sent the whole camp into a flurry of activity. Then Achilles isolated himself in his tent, wrapped his cloak around his head, and lost himself in dreams of battle.

Keturah waited anxiously as Cassandra told her tale. "I didn't get to talk to him," the princess explained, "but his friend Odysseus assured me that one of these days Phorbus is coming up here to rescue us, and he's going to take all three of us away from Troy. Think of it, Keturah! You'll be able to go to that wonderful island Iri told you

about. Your son will be able to get the best education as
an arms maker."

"Yes, it will be wonderful," Keturah replied. But her
voice sounded tentative. Having been disappointed once,
she shied away from getting her hopes up again. "I'm
really looking forward to it, my lady."

"You'll have your own home, Keturah. You'll be rich.
Richer than you ever had hope of being. Just think of it!
And I'll have Phorbus."

Keturah listened and took note. Something was wrong
with the story. She just did not believe that Cassandra had
made her dangerous journey into the Greek camp and had
not spoken with Phorbus, if even for only a minute. She
realized that while she did love and honor her friend and
mistress, she did not trust Cassandra at all. In fact, she no
longer trusted the rich and the powerful; she did not trust
a virgin in love, as Cassandra was.

What had really happened? Had Cassandra told
Phorbus of her plan to adopt Talus? To steal Keturah's
own beloved son? Had she plotted with Phorbus to take
the boy and abandon the blind woman because she would
be too great a hindrance during the escape? Could Phorbus
be trusted? Did he still honor Iri's memory, or could his
loyalty be bought?

Keturah folded her arms across her chest and began
to sway. Her doubts tormented her. What was the truth?

VII

Achilles's order against fraternization with the enemy
during the truce had an immediate and devastating effect
on the Greek army's morale. Those who had been taking
trips across the Scamander River to meet with their new
paramours now found themselves with nothing to do but
cause trouble. Fights erupted throughout the camp as
petty arguments exploded into fisticuffs or stabbings.

Defying the rule, Phorbus sneaked to the river every
day to see Myrrha. His infatuation with the enigmatic

woman grew into love. For a while the sheer animal gratification of their physical union was enough to keep his mind contented while they were together. But at night, when he lay sleepless, staring at the stars, there was time to worry.

If only he had talked to Cassandra instead of asking Odysseus to do it! If only he could have a private conversation with Keturah! She would understand his need to live his own life! She would absolve him of the oath and fend for herself.

By the end of the first week of the truce, the burden lay heavily upon him, even when he was with his beloved.

Myrrha rolled out from under him with a snarl. "What is the matter with you? Is there another woman? You have other women back at camp?" She sat up and her eyes bored into him like spear shafts. "No? Then tell me what."

"I'm sorry," he said haltingly. "This hasn't happened to me before."

"No other woman? A boy maybe?" Her powerful hands gripped his biceps and shook him. "You like boys?"

"No. I've got a lot of important things on my mind."

"Liar!" She got up and brushed herself off. Her body caught the dappled light through the trees above, so her naked skin was the color of a fawn's coat. "I go back to camp and find a Nubian. Or maybe I will lie with a woman."

"Myrrha!" He jumped up and spoke to her back as she bent over, grabbing for her discarded clothing. "You and I have to talk. I'm serious. It's important."

She turned and faced him with blazing blue eyes. "Important, you say? Important?" She stood with her fists on her hips, feet splayed, glaring at him.

He felt miserable. "In a few days we'll have to fight each other."

"You say you don't fight, Phorbus. You say you make arms." The angrier she grew, the broader her accent became.

"You know what I mean. Your people will fight my

people. I don't want to see some Greek stabbing away at you."

"I take care of myself," she said. "How does this concern you?"

"Curse it! I don't want you getting yourself killed. You don't know how strong Achilles and his men are. You're a good fighter, I know that. But Achilles . . ."

Her expression softened.

"I'm worried about you," he said. "I have dreams about going out in the field and finding your body."

"You worry about me?"

"Yes. I realize that you've never known any life except among the Sauromatae. But there are many other ways to live."

"There's no problem. You come over to our side. Then we not be enemies."

"I couldn't do that—not and keep my honor. But if you—"

"Ah!" she said. "Now I see. You want me to leave my sisters. You want me to leave the army of Penthesilea."

"Yes! Then we can go away together." Now was the time to tell her about his responsibility to Keturah. But he did not. He was too nervous about his tenuous position with Myrrha.

She looked at him, incredulous. "You want me to go away now? Not to finish the war?"

He nodded.

"You think your honor is important—but mine is not?"

"That's not what I mean. Myrrha, I want to be with you, don't you understand? I don't want it to end."

"Phorbus," she said, taking his hand and holding it to her cheek, "man and woman meet and come together. When war comes, they are parted. Nothing lasts. You know this. Let's enjoy what we have. Forget tomorrow." Her other hand touched him intimately, and he responded. "That is better. Now you come to me." Her naked breast brushed his chest as she pulled him to her. Her lips were hot and demanding.

*   *   *

In the Greek camp, the preparations for war escalated. Discipline was tightened and morale restored. A new spirit infused the invaders. The officers roamed the camp, their eyes sharp and tempers honed, on the lookout for the least sign of softness or slackness. Any infraction of the rules was punishable by whippings.

Every man in the camp counted the days and grew more impatient as the moment of the renewed attack on the Trojans approached.

Things were different in the defenders' camp. The Nubians and the Sauromatae were ordered to protect the city against a possible sneak attack; some Trojans believed that the capricious Achilles might suddenly change his mind regarding his pledge of peace during the funeral rites.

A great lassitude, a spirit of inevitable defeat hung over Troy. Queen Penthesilea's exhibition and her brave boast had been for the benefit of the civilians. The Trojan army knew better. They knew that the end was near.

Keturah's timid desire for a confrontation with Cassandra was growing. She had to know the truth. Finally, one day as she sat sewing on the princess's old clothing that was to be donated to the widows of the fallen, she forced herself to speak of what was in her heart.

"My lady," she said, trying to keep her voice as matter-of-fact as possible, "would it be possible for me to ask a question, please?"

"Question?" Cassandra said. Her mind was elsewhere. She alternated, these days, between fanciful daydreams of a life outside Troy—a life with Phorbus—and her terrible knowledge that Troy was doomed. "Go ahead," she said absently.

Keturah caught the tone of her mistress's voice. "My lady," she quavered, "when you were in the Greek camp, did you perhaps meet with Phorbus for only a minute, the meeting so brief that you forgot to mention it?"

There was no answer.

She swallowed hard and tried again, raising her voice

a little. "My lady, I was asking about Phorbus. I thought
maybe . . . you were so tired . . . I thought perhaps you
had actually talked to him and just forgot to tell me.
Perhaps because you didn't want to raise my hopes of
escape?"

"Can't it wait, dear? I'm trying to think."

Keturah's face closed up like a night-blooming flower.
"Yes, my lady," she said. "I won't bother you again."

Dutifully she went back to her work. Realizing she
would get no answers from Cassandra, she grew more
frightened and confused. Another fearful thought assailed
her: Perhaps Cassandra had told Phorbus she was dead.

She admonished herself; she was starting to think in a
crazy fashion. She had to get control. But it would also be
wise, she decided, to show herself on the walls so that
Phorbus could see her.

PART
THREE

CHAPTER SIXTEEN

Canaan

The two brothers were a day's journey south of Mount Carmel, at the place called Emeq Hafer. To the west, as far as their eyes could see, was the Great Sea—rolling swells that reached the shore in a slow rhythm. To the east were gentle hills, covered with rocks and sparse vegetation. A few stunted wild fruit trees formed grotesque shapes near the water.

It was late morning. A cool breeze blew in from the water. Both brothers were wearing the long garment of the herdsman, with the hood thrown back. They carried one bedroll each, in which were wrapped all their possessions. Nimshi had no weapon. Micah had a long knife concealed inside his garment.

Nimshi had never felt so good in his life. After Theon had made the generous job offer, Nimshi had realized that nothing was more important than finding his younger brother. He had found Micah in an Israelite camp and described his plan: They would give up all their current alliances and travel together to Gaza, where they would start a new life.

To Nimshi's astonishment, Micah had jumped at the chance. What he had expected to be a very difficult problem, persuading his brother to leave the Israelites, had turned out to be no problem at all. Now they were on the road. Now they were a family again, reunited and traveling south to the city where metalworking was an art form.

161

But things were not as they had been. The once easy and loving relationship they had enjoyed as children and adolescents was gone. Having been apart and living in vastly different cultures for more than ten years had changed them both. A core of danger burned in Micah's eyes. Nimshi was crestfallen to realize that he felt afraid of his younger brother. He did not ask about Micah's role in the rebellion against Eglon of Moab, and Micah never offered to explain. They were, Nimshi finally admitted to himself, essentially strangers who had to become reacquainted. Their relationship had to be rebuilt, if possible.

"Nimshi! Look!"

Nimshi followed the line of Micah's pointing finger. Two fishermen were hauling in a net at the water's edge, and the skiff they were using for a pulley had capsized in the surf.

"Let's help them," Nimshi said, and the brothers ran down the slope and plunged into the water.

Quickly they righted the craft, then held it steady so the fishermen could bring in the net. As they stood there, stabilizing the sleek wooden craft and staring at the catch of fish jumping and bubbling in the net, Nimshi found his eyes welling with tears.

"Are you hurt? Why are you crying?" Micah asked, concerned.

"It is nothing," Nimshi responded, wiping his tears away with the sleeve of his robe. "I was just thinking how wonderful it would have been if our mother and father were still alive and could see us now, working together as friends, helping fellow human beings in need. Do you realize, Micah, how this sight would have made them glad?"

"They're dead, Nimshi. Stop your foolish illusions."

"I know they are dead. I was just wondering what they would feel if they were still alive."

The fishermen thanked them, and one handed Nimshi a large fish just removed from the net. The two brothers moved away from the beach and laid the fish on a grassy slope.

"What do we do with it?" Micah asked, touching it with his toe.

Nimshi laughed. "We eat it." He had forgotten that the Israelites rarely ate fish. "Give me your knife, Micah."

Using the long, sharp knife, Nimshi slit the fish and carefully removed the spinal bone and guts. Then he dug a narrow but deep hole and kindled a fire at the bottom. When the fire was intense, he gathered several large stones and dropped them into the hole. When the stones were heated, he pulled grass, placed the fish on a mat of the grass, and set it on the stones.

"This," he told Micah, "is the way the Sea Peoples cook their catch. It is simple and quick, and it makes the fish delicious, particularly if you have a little olive oil and salt."

"We have neither," Micah reminded him dubiously.

Minutes later, the brothers, squatting over the hole, lifted flesh from the fish and consumed it until only the charred tail lay on the stones.

"Was it good?"

"Very good, Nimshi. I had forgotten that you are a man of the world, a man who travels."

"We make a good team."

Micah scowled at Nimshi's words. He pulled the knife away from his brother, cleaned it carefully in the grass, and then thrust it into his robe again.

"Micah, why are you angry? What did I say wrong?"

But Micah folded his robe about him and would not respond. Again Nimshi was forced to realize that the future would not be idyllic. It was increasingly obvious that Micah had been emotionally scarred during his service with the Israelites. He, Nimshi, knew nothing about how his brother thought, what he liked, what he aspired to, how he wished to live, and what visions he held in his heart.

Yes, Nimshi realized helplessly, *I must think before I speak. May the gods give me strength!*

II

"I feel like a fool," Barak complained. "How can I go through with this? Everyone will see through me."

Jerah did not answer for a moment. Instead he assessed the crowd that he had assembled in Rehob. "It's a chance we have to take, isn't it? Unless you mean to break your promise to Deborah."

Barak frowned. "You know exactly where to strike my vulnerable parts. Of course I can't go back on my word to Deborah. My promise to her is a promise to God. Do you think I can deny the vision I had?"

"No," Jerah answered, "I don't suppose you can. That's all the more reason to clench your teeth and go out there."

"But I've never spoken in front of a crowd—not like this one, anyway. I have harangued a dozen growers, but only because they were mad at me for making concessions when I negotiated with Jabin's buyers. That was different; I knew exactly what I was doing. All I had to do was explain why I had done it, and the growers saw the logic."

"Indeed?" Jerah asked dryly. He glanced at the crowd and then looked at Barak. "And why do you suppose you were able to convince the growers?"

"Because under the circumstances what I had done was the only thing I could do."

Jerah let Barak's words settle. "Do I really have to explain further, or have you already figured it out for yourself?"

"What?"

"Isn't it a similar situation? Is there anything else the Israelites can do but rid themselves of their oppressors? Anything other than what Deborah has suggested? Anything other than what your vision has dictated?"

Barak looked at him, a blank expression on his young face.

"Go out there and speak to them," Jerah urged. "They've come some distance, at some expense and inconvenience, and they're at risk just gathering here. They deserve the best you can give them. Remember, no one rounded them up and forced them to come. No priests or tribal leaders sent them. They represent no one but themselves. They need strong words to bring them together. They want affirmation of their courage so they might break the yoke that is strangling them and crushing their families."

"But I have no skill with words!"

"All the better. Look them in the eyes and tell them

the truth. They don't need pretty speeches. They need honesty."

Finally Jerah almost had to push Barak out from behind the trees.

He blinked at the crowd and tried to estimate their number. Several hundred, he guessed. Swallowing hard, clenching his powerful fists, he began. "My countrymen and friends—"

"Louder!" someone called from halfway back in the crowd.

Barak nodded, cleared his throat, and tried again. "Friends! I am Barak, son of Abinoam of the tribe of Naphtali. Some of you know me; some do not. I am not a soldier, an orator, or a great man to whom everyone listens—"

Another voice shouted, "Forget what you aren't. Tell us what you are and why we have done the right thing by coming to hear you."

"Yes!" another man cried. "Get to the point."

Barak took a deep, shuddering breath as he realized he was losing them. His heart was pounding. "You want to know who I am and why I'm here? I'm a man who thinks Yahweh spoke to him."

A few scattered catcalls and laughs rang out.

He raised his voice above them. "But I am also a man who knows—*knows!*—that Deborah of the Palm Trees has spoken to him." His words were strong from his growing anger. "Does anyone here know that name?"

From the murmurs amid the crowd, Barak sensed a slight shift of the tide in his favor. He continued, "Deborah is the prophetess of Yahweh. Everyone in the central tribal territories knows her reputation, and I can see that a few of you are familiar with it. Deborah summoned me to meet with her."

The murmurs he heard now, he fancied, were interested, the faces before him appeared receptive.

"Deborah told me that Yahweh hears our cries of pain and sees our wrongs and oppressions. He knows that we labor under the yoke of Hazor, that we groan under the lash of Sisera, that we are debased by the cruel hand of Jabin."

A low groan of assent rolled through the assemblage.

"Our sins have been great. We have fallen away from the Law of Moses. We have toyed with false gods and lain with women of other faiths. The covenant of Sinai is now alien to us. We do not know who we are." For the first time he felt that he had them. "Yet God is merciful, for we are His chosen people. He sees our sufferings and takes pity on us. And where He has once punished us for our sins, now He holds the hope that He may reward us for our return to the faith."

He scanned the faces before him. They *were* interested. "And what reward will Yahweh give us?" he asked. "Will He make us rich, famous, or powerful? Will every man be a king? Will everything we touch turn to gold?" He shook his head. "No, my friends. Because we do not need these things. We do not need to be given what our own industry and brains can provide. What we need is for the obstacles in our path to be removed."

They knew exactly of whom he spoke, and he was pleased that he had gotten his point across so well. "I know our numbers are few up here in the northern tribes, and we are widely scattered. But if we pull together, we would be more than enough to take control of our future. In fact, there would be more than one Israelite man for every Hazorite soldier our enemy can send against us."

From out of the crowd came an objection. "But we have no trained fighters! We have no arms!"

Barak was quick to agree. "Yes, and when our fathers were in Egypt, they had no leader—and God sent them one. When Joshua led our people they had no siege equipment to breach the walls of Jericho—and God knocked them down Himself."

A new sound came up from the crowd; it was one of hope.

"It is true!" someone shouted. "When we walked in the path of righteousness, when we followed the Law, God took care of us."

"He gave us what we needed when we needed it," another voice called.

"I will tell you what Deborah told me," Barak continued, heartened. " 'When the time comes to move, you will know. God will put a sword in your hand, and you will know how to use it.' I told her that this would take a miracle. And she said, 'Then He will give you one. But it will not look like a miracle. It will look like a reward for your hard work and good faith!' "

This inspired cheers from the audience. "Tell us what you want of us! Tell us, Barak!" they shouted.

He held up both hands until they were silent. "There are among us men of experience who fought with Joshua to conquer Canaan. Will they step forward?"

A dozen men, a few of them gray haired, walked to the front.

Barak said to them, "Will you train us, my friends? Will you show us how to fight?"

"We will!" one veteran cried. "But get us weapons!"

"I will. Begin by teaching our young men the drill with wooden sticks, and when you have them fighting skillfully with weapons of wood, I will find them weapons of metal."

Some of the veterans looked skeptical, but they all nodded.

"Send out the call," Barak exhorted, "to all the young men of Zebulun, of Naphtali, and of the other northern tribes. I'll recruit more from Ephraim and Benjamin, where the men already know the ways of war because they drove Moab out of Jericho."

They barely heard his last words as the cheers rang forth.

In the crowd was a man who, although he was not even of Israelite blood, listened carefully to Barak's speech and pondered it with great concentration as he walked away.

Heber the Kenite had been sent to the area to buy charcoal for Pepi's forges, and he had merely followed the crowd to the clearing for curiosity's sake.

Now he wondered what to do about what he had heard. Under the laws of Jabin of Hazor, this was treason, punishable by death. In the past, the Kenites in Heber's village had been informants against the Israelites. Yet he found himself absolutely unwilling to turn them in. He had been profoundly moved by Barak's sincere though unpolished speech. Jabin and his men did rule with a too-heavy hand. Heber had witnessed cruelty and harshness with his own eyes. He thought about Sisera and the way he treated all the conquered peoples, particularly their women. It was wicked.

No, he would not turn these people in to the authorities. Instead, he wished them good luck. As a matter of fact, if there was any way he could throw help their way without getting himself in trouble with the officials of Hazor or with his master, Pepi, he would do so. And perhaps even Pepi would relent in his long-standing hatred of Israel and see the justice of their cause.

After the speech, Barak was mobbed by well-wishers. When he finally extricated himself, he was exhausted and wanted desperately to be alone. Jerah understood and led the young man to a small grove, then left him to recover.

Barak knelt. He needed to pray, but he really did not know to whom. To Yahweh? Deborah? He fully understood that he had unleashed forces that would lead to the death and mutilation of men, women, and children. The responsibility weighed heavy on him. He wished that Deborah could have been there to hear and advise him.

As he knelt, for the first time he began to perceive a sense of his own power. If he could address hundreds of people he did not know and sway them to his beliefs, what else could he do? He even began to believe that if Yahweh did place a sword in his hand, he would know how to use it: He would grasp it as if it were an old friend. He was becoming a leader of men, not unlike Moses. His legs began to tremble at his own arrogance . . . comparing himself with Moses. He called out to Jerah, who came quickly in the manner of a slave and handed him a piece of fruit to slake his parched mouth.

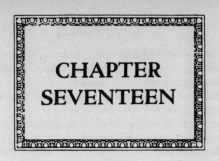

CHAPTER SEVENTEEN

City of Ur, Kingdom of Babylon

"You will leave tomorrow for Damascus, Luti, and then travel on to Gaza. It is five hundred miles from Ur to Damascus across a very forbidding desert—beastly hot during the day and freezing at night. I have reserved a place for you on a caravan that is transporting dried fruit."

Drak and Luti strolled through the formal gardens that ringed the northern approach to Ur. While these gardens did not have the reputation of the famous hanging gardens in the north, they did contain some of the most beautiful and breathtakingly exotic plants in the world, brought to the city at great expense.

Luti moderated her pace to keep up with the slowness of Drak; the old man led her from plot to plot and from trellis to trellis, commenting on all the species, explaining how they had been obtained. It was a warm day, and she frequently dipped her hand into one of the pools and brought forth some water, which she spread across Drak's neck, hands, and wrists. She had never felt so kindly toward him.

"Tell me about your decision, Luti," he requested after they had stopped to sit on a bench in a grove of flowering bushes. "I really did not believe in my heart that you would accept my offer."

She laughed. "Why not? I need to be safe. You spoke wisdom to me. You said that only the very rich are protected from the likes of Banniselk, and you offered me riches and protection. All I have to do to earn them is travel thousands of miles, stealing, robbing, and blaspheming."

"Shame on you for making fun of an old man, Luti. Tell me the truth."

"The truth is simply this: I accepted your offer because it seemed to mean very much to you. You want to obtain this weapon so Ur and the other cities of the kingdom will survive. I will honor your desire because you saved my life. You gave me faith again and showed me that I am capable of astonishing feats. I owe you much more than a chariot with iron-and-wood wheels."

"Thank you. Stay here, child. I must take care of some business. I will return shortly, and we can talk more about your adventure." The old man's watery eyes literally twinkled. He rose and shuffled away.

When Drak was out of sight, Luti walked deeper into the water gardens. She loved to watch the water plants as they clung precariously to the weeds. She enjoyed gazing at the brilliant floating flowers. And for a while she relished the opportunity to take childlike delight in the gardens—sitting carefree in the sun and dangling her toes in the pools. It was odd, she thought, that there were no other visitors to the gardens. She stood and wandered aimlessly, thinking of her upcoming journey. It was so incredible, she realized; she was no longer a field-worker with no future. Now she was embarking on a mission that would determine the very future of the kingdom of Babylon. And if she was successful, she would acquire enormous wealth.

Suddenly, a shadow crossed her eyes, frightening her. She turned, but no one was there. Had it been a bird? Had a twig been swept up in the light breeze?

She walked on. Again the shadow crossed her, this time on her body so that she could see a shape against her white tunic and on the brilliantly painted alabaster whiteness of the gardens. Fear paralyzed her. She was alone. She wondered if Banniselk was stalking her—or, if not he, some assassin who could fulfill Banniselk's pact of spite and hatred. He would never let her live in peace in Ur!

She thought of screaming, but who would hear? Where was the assassin? How would he kill her? Slowly, warily, she edged toward one of the porticos, which was overgrown with vines. There might be safety there until Drak came back. No one of Banniselk's followers would attempt violence against her while Drak was present.

Her every limb was trembling, and she could barely walk. Her clothes were drenched with sweat. She had suffered so much and survived! *Please, Astarte, hear my plea! Help me!*

Only ten more feet, and she was safe. Only ten more feet, and she could hide behind the wooden beams and scan the entire garden in safety until Drak returned.

Something touched her on the back. She whirled so swiftly that she fell down, and before she could make another move two powerful hands had jerked her into a standing position. She was staring into the most horrible visage she had ever encountered. The man's skin was burned black. Silver ornaments, attached to the skin with naked pins, dangled from one side of his face. He was wearing long, sweeping, dark-colored robes, and a sword in its scabbard lay across his back, jutting up from behind his neck. His hair was long and disheveled, and it smelled of some kind of oil or butter. His eyes were bloodshot, and there were scars on the lids.

She started to scream. One of the beast's hands went to her mouth and almost choked the breath out of her. The beast's other hand seemed to caress her neck. Banniselk had indeed summoned an assassin from the netherworld. It was no use struggling. The man was too powerful. She relaxed in his grip, resolved to die with courage and in silence.

"What's going on here?" She heard Drak's voice and, astonished, opened her eyes.

"Oh," said Drak, matter-of-factly, "I see you've met. Luti, this is Occa, a Bedouin. He will accompany you through the desert. He is deaf and dumb, but believe me, he makes up for those deficiencies in loyalty, bravery, and sheer intelligence."

Luti laughed and cried simultaneously.

CHAPTER EIGHTEEN

Canaan

I

Pepi had left his horses with hostlers at the city gates and walked through the streets of Megiddo. As he passed along the crowded, winding streets of the ancient city, he saw evidence everywhere of the heavy hand of Jabin. Even though he had won concessions from the king in his last audience, Pepi was feeling guilty about continuing his association with Jabin.

He looked around: The Israelites were at the absolute bottom of the social pyramid, and Pepi watched a work detail slog its way past him. These men were being used as beasts of burden, staggering under loads that bent the smallest and weakest of them almost double. On their legs were shackles, and when their labor in the city was done, he knew they would be chained together and taken to a labor camp.

His curiosity aroused, he caught up with an underofficer who was supervising the detail. "Officer, how did these men come to be prisoners?"

"What business is that of yours?" the soldier snarled. "Move along."

Pepi began to identify himself; then it occurred to him that a stranger might learn more than an official in Jabin's government. "I beg your pardon, but as a free citizen I have the right to ask a question."

172

The officer broke stride to face him. "I told you to move along. I'll give you one last chance, and then I'll turn you over to the guards. Do you want to be on a work detail like this one?"

Pepi remained calm. "Is this the way an underofficer talks to a citizen of means in Megiddo? Is this what justice in Megiddo has come to under the reign of Jabin of Hazor?"

The guardsman looked Pepi up and down and noted his expensive clothes. "I'll let you go this time, but the next time I hear questions out of you, you'll regret it." He gave Pepi a hard look and stalked away.

I ought to do this more often, Pepi thought. *I should find out what is really happening.* He continued down the street on the heels of the dreary parade of prisoners until a man hailed him from the open half-door of a shop.

Pepi stopped. "Yes?"

"You asked what those men's offenses were, sir?" the merchant inquired.

"Why, yes, and I certainly didn't expect that kind of rudeness from a mere underofficer of the guard."

The shopkeeper shook his head. "It's that way most of the time now. The soldiers are obeying Jabin's orders—or at least Sisera says they are. A man from this street was hauled away by guards the other day for complaining when one of Sisera's drunken soldiers kicked over his stand in the marketplace. And he hasn't come back yet."

Pepi frowned. "You keep up with what goes on around here?"

"Yes, sir. And I can tell you that those prisoners—the ones you asked about, the Israelites—their offense was in owning land."

"When did owning land become an offense?"

"When your land stands in the way of a military encampment Sisera wants to build in the Jezreel Valley. If he doesn't want to pay you for it, sir—"

"And all those people were—"

"He arrested whole families. That's why some of them are too old to be bearing burdens and others are too young. And the lot of the men is an easy one compared to that of the women."

Pepi feigned shock, keeping in character as an innocent citizen, although anything Sisera or Jabin did would not surprise him.

"First they're given to Sisera. He breaks them in. Then they're given to the common soldiers. Sisera doesn't want his men coming into the cities and lying with whores and contracting diseases. He stocks the army brothels with the wives of poor wretches like those you saw."

"That's an outrage! Look, my friend, I'm here on business, and I'm not without influence—even though that boorish fool didn't realize it. If you and any of your friends need help—"

"Thank you, sir. Why don't you join my friends and me at the Golden Lion tonight? But I'll need your assurance that no harm will come to the people who express their opinions honestly."

Pepi nodded. "I promise to honor their confidence. I want to learn more. I'll be there."

"Then I'll arrange for delivery. Would a month be soon enough, Pepi?" the tin dealer asked.

"Yes. I'll expect delivery this time next month."

"If not earlier. And, Pepi, I thought you would want to know: I would not give credit to Jabin of Hazor if your own good reputation did not back it."

"Jabin has not been paying his debts recently?"

"Well, no, he hasn't—or at any rate his representatives haven't. Sisera has been running up bills in the city and refusing to pay them. And there's no recourse. More than one merchant who pressed him for payment wound up wearing a leg chain."

Pepi pondered for a moment. "Would you be talking about Israelite merchants in particular?"

"Why, yes. Mind you, I'm not of their number and have no reason to favor them, but the problems of the Israelites may become my own problems one of these days. Business is business, and justice is justice, and when a man dishonors one account, he may well decide to dishonor another."

"I understand. I'll have a talk with Jabin."

"Anything you could do would be appreciated, sir. And if you have the time, there is a meeting you might find interesting this evening at the Golden Lion. A group of merchants and concerned citizens are getting together to discuss such issues."

"I'll be there," Pepi said. "Good day."

"A good day to you, sir."

Once back out on the street, Pepi was struck by the coincidence of being invited twice in one day to the same meeting. He realized that he had no intention of discussing the tin dealer's problems with Jabin or of attending any meeting. As he strolled, he allowed himself a rare moment of introspection. He had chosen to give his loyalty to a king who did not deserve it, while severing his ties with the Israelites, who had been so good to him and his mother long ago. He winced, coming to terms with the fact that the last ten years of his life had been wasted. They had brought him nothing, and he had given nothing to the people around him.

He had become a walking corpse, and he knew just when he had died: on the day when he had ridden back from Ashod to Jerusalem expecting to find his wife, Tirzah, and his mother, Neftis, safe because Joshua had spared the city. But when Pepi had returned, he found the Jerusalem army destroyed in a battle north of the city. The citizens, now without protection, had panicked. The panic had become a riot, and in the chaos many people had disappeared. Among them were Neftis and Tirzah.

Despite his grief and anger, Pepi had forced himself to overcome his terrible temper and his tendency to give rein to his feelings. Emotion brought on the splitting, blinding headaches. Only rigid control kept him from suffering blackouts. He refused to permit himself an attack of temper. Even his sparring matches with Sisera were cold and passionless. Pepi also had chosen to remain celibate. Not only did he still love Tirzah, he had also learned that the moment of sexual climax brought almost unendurable pain and near blackouts.

So for ten years Pepi had avoided pleasure and pain and close human contacts. For ten years he had worked for the worst kind of swine, men for whom he felt nothing but contempt, simply because their agendas had included the subjugation and humiliation of the Israelites, his childhood friends and his recent enemies—and for whom he now felt only sympathy.

He stopped walking as an idea came to him: Was it time, perhaps, for a change of alliance? Was it time to visit the Golden Lion?

II

In the Valley of Jezreel, Sisera surveyed the land he had stolen from the Israelites, then turned to his able lieutenant, Telem, and said, "This site couldn't be better. It has its own water, it commands the heights, and it stands in the middle of every route from Beth-shean and the Jordan, all the way down this corridor to the sea. I could put a toll on the road and have no trouble accumulating a treasury that could finance all future military campaigns."

Telem smiled. "This site would also make for a good city," he said. "There's enough room to build a defensive wall right along here. And you could run the main axes of the city down the middle, both ways, and start laying it out from those points. And in the meantime the army would be right here."

"Wonderful idea! A city! With my name on it! It would command the whole valley. After all, this is the most reliable route for large caravans, and the road goes to Damascus and Ebla. In the middle it passes through the Jordan Valley and links up with the great road that runs south through Jericho before cutting westward to Jerusalem and the cities of the Philistine League. And it connects with the Moabite and Edomite tracks on the far side of the river, and *they* go all the way to Ezion-geber."

"And thence across the Red Sea, sir, to Egypt."

"Yes, yes. Imagine every caravan on that whole route having to pass through! But I'll have to build another fortress or two in the Jordan Valley itself, to control that north-south traffic, won't I?"

"That's all controlled by the Israelites now, sir, since they beat the Moabites."

"Temporary," Sisera noted. "As soon as the work is begun on our fortress here—and I intend to press a lot more of those Israelite swine into service to build this place—I'm going to lead an expedition down into central Canaan and whip those bastards into shape. Moab was lax and let itself be surprised by some ragtag irregulars. Now the Israelites think they're safe just because they managed to assassinate Eglon and ambush the Moabites at the fords of the river. Well, they've never been up against well-trained regulars."

"Besides," Telem pointed out, "the irregulars that fought the Moabites have been dispersed. The gallant war heroes are back in their fields, pushing a plow and looking at the rear end of a donkey."

"All the better. We'll hit the Israelite farms one at a time. We won't allow them the chance to unite and make a stand."

Telem cleared his throat. "There is one problem I thought I ought to bring up."

"What is it?"

"Well, sir, there have been rumors about an influential Israelite woman who is talking treason."

Sisera threw back his head and laughed. "What sort of treason can a woman talk? Who would listen to her?"

Telem proceeded cautiously. "Apparently quite a few listen to her, sir. They think she's a prophetess."

"That's nonsense."

"She has a sizable following," Telem said doggedly. "And apparently she's been saying scandalous things about King Jabin and the rein of Hazor over her people."

"*Her* people?" Sisera stared at him in surprise. "I've never heard of an Israelite woman leader."

"I admit it's unusual, sir, but as you and I know, their men don't amount to much."

"You can say that again! Sometimes I wish there was a bit of the old blood in them, just to give us a decent challenge. I wonder why they degenerated so fast. My suspicion is that while the army was away, some sleazy little Canaanite dog of a philanderer was sneaking into their settlements and impregnating the women." He chuckled. "Their women love it. They won't admit it, but they do."

This was not a subject Telem enjoyed talking about. The other officers would kid him unmercifully about serving under the worst molester in the North and call him a pimp, a panderer, and worse. "Yes, sir. But as I was saying, this Deborah woman—"

"Ah! What does she look like? If she's pretty, I should have someone bring her to me."

"I heard the scout's report, sir. She's short and fat."

"Forget it, then."

"Do I understand that you'd prefer I left the woman alone, sir?"

"Not at all. Keep an eye on her. Send a spy down there to snoop around, learn what she's up to."

"Yes, sir. I'll get right on it, sir. I think we have located an Israelite who can be bought cheaply."

Sisera stretched. "This talk of women has me in the mood for love. I was thinking of seeing that little Kenite woman. She was gone the last time I was in the area, but maybe she's back."

"Sorry, sir, but you had planned to inspect the troops in an hour."

"Damn! Then I'll go see the Kenite in the morning."

Telem controlled his shudder and saluted.

That evening Pepi found a large crowd in the street, blocking access to the Golden Lion. "What are you all doing here?" he asked, trying to open the door.

"It's all right, sir," a familiar voice called. The speaker

stepped into the light, and Pepi recognized the shop-keeper whom he had spoken to earlier. "We're here to discuss the, uh, subject you and I talked about this morning. We're about to go to a warehouse by the eastern wall of the city. The walls are thick. We post guards at the doors so we can speak safely. You're welcome to join us."

"Lead the way," Pepi said. "I'm your man."

A man confronted Pepi immediately. "Sir, why do you wish to help us? Why should we trust you?"

Other men agreed, questioning Pepi's motives and sincerity. He was not offended.

"As a boy," he said, "I came all the way from Egypt with your people, sharing your sorrows and triumphs, your dangers and worries. It seems so long ago. And although your leaders and I fell out, I still remember my friends and find myself in sympathy with your plight. The question now is, how can we change things? Jabin hates your people as much as Sisera does. I promise you, my affiliations have been confused of late, but my heart tells me that I'm back where I belong."

Satisfied, they led Pepi to the warehouse. To Pepi's surprise, more than half the men in the room—all were Israelites, judging from the cut of their clothing—stripped to their loincloths.

When the men turned, Pepi understood: Across their bared backs were the marks of the lash—not one or two stripes, but in some cases dozens of disfiguring lesions. One man's back was crisscrossed in many directions, from many separate beatings.

"What brought all this on?" Pepi demanded. "Have you people been found guilty of sedition?"

"Not yet," a spokesman replied. "Although ample reason for sedition—even rebellion!—exists, as you can see with your own eyes. These men were whipped for objecting to Sisera's conduct . . . for protesting when he stole our land and livestock, our homes, our possessions . . . for speaking out when he made whores of our wives and daughters . . . for standing up for ourselves when he desecrated our altars and mocked our faith."

"Enough!" Pepi said, holding up his hands. "I know

Sisera. I know him well enough to despise him. And yes, I know of some of the offenses you complain about. The wife of a good worker of mine was raped by Sisera. I suspect she's kept it secret from her husband out of shame. At first I believed Sisera's claim that the woman had come willingly to his bed. Now I know better." He looked around at the somber faces. "What can we do about this? If Sisera were to be killed, he'd be replaced by another man who could be even worse. Until Jabin himself falls . . ."

Pepi spent the night tossing and turning and staring at the ceiling. Once the heretical notion had wormed its way into his mind, it could not be dislodged or ignored. It overrode every other thought that entered his brain.

Jabin was the key. If the king had not provided good bloodlines and the memory of his father's reign to attract the rich landowners of the North to his cause, Sisera could never have attained power. He would have remained a competent but essentially second-rate mercenary, blocked from advancement by the mental instability that manifested itself in savagery.

And who was Jabin? A man hardly better than Sisera. Ultimately the responsibility for everything that happened in the kingdom, no matter who the perpetrator was, lay with the king. Everything was done with his authority and in his name.

Jabin was not ignorant of Sisera's atrocious excesses. Every week, at his public divan, new complaints were made and tablets filed, but nothing had been done about the matter—unless one of Sisera's flunkies decided to take reprisals against the complainers.

Jabin, of course, wanted life to continue unchanged. He had gotten what he wanted by the restoration of his father's line to the throne of Hazor and the subjugation of the hated Israelites who, in Joshua's day, had killed his father and Sisera's and conquered the northland. Left to his own devices, he probably would not seek further aggrandizement. Sisera, however, with the streak of peasant shrewdness he had inherited from his father, realized that an idle army is a decaying army. The only solution was an army kept in top form with further conquests, a relentless gobbling up of land and the destruction of lives.

Now, as Pepi sat up in the pink light of dawn and rubbed his burning eyes, he realized that this was the real reason for the construction of the new camp in the Jezreel Valley. The settlement would command the route from the Jordan to the sea and provide rich sources of revenue to pay for Sisera's next move—and that would obviously be against the hill country, which the Israelites called the land of Ephraim and Benjamin.

Pepi cursed himself for not having suspected Sisera's scheme before. Now that the Moabites were out of the region, Sisera wanted it. And with a huge encampment in the valley beside the Kishon River, he could build and train a striking force. With one major campaign he could take all the cities as far south as Jerusalem without encountering any organized resistance as long as he stayed away from the lands controlled by the Philistine League. If Sisera were clever—and if no new opposition arose—the lands of Hazor could be doubled within a year.

As Pepi dressed and looked out his window at the rising sun, he made a commitment: It was time for him to lay aside the bitterness and resentment he had harbored against the Israelites. All the people who had wronged him were now dead: Caleb, Joshua, their subordinates. . . .

No, that was not quite true. Shemida, Joshua's quietly efficient executive officer, was still alive. But some said that Shemida's conscience had been troubled, also, in those terrible days when Joshua was putting the cities of Canaan to the sword, along with all their men, women, and children.

Perhaps it was time to pay Shemida a call. But how? No one would help him to find Shemida. Perhaps the crowd he had met with the night before would send a letter of endorsement along with him. No, he was still in Jabin's employ, and the men from the meeting would wait for him to prove himself before giving him any endorsements.

Then how to find Shemida? An idea came to him. He knew many shopkeepers in Succoth, near the mines. He had stayed on good terms with everyone in the region. If anyone would know where Shemida was, they would. Shemida was a folk hero.

And while going to Succoth, he would ride down the Jezreel Valley and look over Sisera's budding camp. Perhaps he could even look in on Heber's wife. If he found Sisera with the woman, he would step in and make sure Sisera left her alone.

Lieutenant Telem looked past the guard and through the open doorway of his tent to where the would-be informant was waiting. "What do you think?" he asked the guard in a quiet voice that did not carry. "Do you think the Israelite is all right?"

The guard was a grizzled veteran with a scarred face. He had lost one eye in a fight, but it was obvious that the remaining one did not miss much. He snorted. "None of the bastards are all right. Could you say that a man who would sell out his own people can be all right?"

"But can we rely on him?"

"Only if we watch him closely. He needs money; he's stuck on some slut in Megiddo. I know who she is, and I wouldn't touch her with an army pike. She's already taken him for everything he has, and some things he doesn't have, if you get my meaning. Now he has to replace the money he stole from his boss before anyone notices that it's gone." He snorted again. "He's a fool."

"Pay off the debt. Make sure the money goes back to whomever he stole it from and that nobody gets caught. You think the woman will keep him desperate for money?"

"The slut will drain him dry."

"Good. I want him hungry enough to stab his own father in the back."

The guard nodded. "Where are you going to send him?"

"The hill country," Telem explained. "I want him to ask questions about Deborah. And if there's anything seditious going on, I want to know about it."

"Right, sir. I've heard the rumors. Something's happening that we need to know about. The young Israelite men disappear for a night, and they aren't going to prayer services. So far we haven't been able to track them."

"We'll put this fellow on it. He's a disgusting-looking specimen, isn't he? No wonder he's desperate enough to let a whore milk him that way. He has the face of a diseased rat. What's his name?"

"Ishbak, sir."

"Bring him in."

The man would not look Telem directly in the eyes. *This is a bad sign,* the lieutenant thought. If it meant that he could not look his kinsmen and countrymen in the eyes, either, who could trust him with information?

"I understand you want to make some money," Telem began.

"Yes, sir," the man replied, sending his weasel's face into twitches. "I need money bad, sir. I have debts that have to be repaid. If they aren't paid within three days—"

"Listen: If you're willing to go all the way with me, I'll see that your debts are repaid tomorrow!"

Ishbak's eyes bulged. "Tomorrow, sir?"

"You heard me. And after that you'll be making good money. But in return, you have to be my man and nobody else's. That requires a solemn bond. My work is serious and important. If I found out that you let me down, that you withheld information or warned the people I've asked you to watch for me—"

"Oh, no, sir! Never!"

"—you'd be a dead man before dawn."

"Never, sir!"

"If you provide us with good information on a steady basis, we'll be good to you. You'll be richer than you ever dreamed." Telem knew that what he was saying was absurd. The blood money this poor fool would be getting would not last a day in his hands. Every last bit would go to the slut; he would be left with nothing except the knowledge that he had sold out his people.

"Now," Telem continued, "here's what I want you to do."

III

"I can't get over how much better you look, Yael,"
Basemath remarked. "You're blooming. When Heber comes
home, he's going to fall in love with you all over again."

Yael blushed. The two women stood in the chill water
of the Kishon, washing their clothing. Yael carefully laid
her wet garments in a pile on a flat rock and rolled them
up to carry to the bank. "I feel as if I can face life again.
And I owe it all to you."

"Oh, no, really—"

"Yes, I do!" she said emphatically. "How fortunate I
am to have a good friend like you. The other women won't
even look at me when I pass."

"Self-righteous old fools," Basemath muttered, gathering her own clothing. "So help me, some people . . ."

"They say I've whored," Yael quavered. "They say
I've given myself willingly to that horrible man."

"Don't worry about them. Remember, your life has
changed. Deborah said so. And she told you not to worry
anymore."

"I have to keep trying to remember that. Otherwise I
don't know how I'd go on. Whenever I think about—"

"Don't, Yael. If you start—" Basemath stopped dead.
"Yael. There's a horseman coming." Her hand went over
her mouth in horror. "You don't suppose—"

Yael craned her neck and squinted through the dappled shade of the overhanging trees. "Please, God, don't
let it be—" Then her face relaxed. "No, it's not anyone I
know. And he's in civilian clothing."

The well-dressed traveler came closer. His horse moved
slowly, surefootedly. Fifty paces away, the man dismounted
and let his horse drink from the stream before looking
toward the women.

"Yael," Basemath whispered, "we're here all by ourselves, and suddenly this stranger . . ."

"He doesn't look dangerous," Yael told her.

The fellow began to walk slowly in their direction.
"Excuse me," he said politely. "Would either of you be

able to tell me where I might find the wife of Heber the Kenite?"

Basemath shot Yael a suspicious glance. "Don't speak to him," she warned in a low voice.

But Yael held up her hand. She smiled and raised her voice. "Pardon my caution, sir, but could you explain why you want to find her?"

"Certainly." The man bowed. "I have a message from her husband. My name is Pepi of Kerma, and I'm Heber's employer. I happened to be nearby arranging for a metals shipment, and—"

Yael looked down in embarrassment at her coarse clothing and bare feet. "Oh! I had no idea! This is such a surprise! If I had known you were coming . . . This is such an honor!"

"The honor is mine," he said, bowing formally as if she were royalty. "Your husband is a fine man, and I'm delighted to have him working for me. He's going to be a master of his craft and a credit to his profession someday. He's training as an armorer, and already he shows enormous promise."

"An armorer? Oh, Basemath! Did you hear that?" Yael squealed. "I received a message from him, saying he couldn't come home as soon as he had hoped. . . ." She looked wistful.

Pepi smiled. "I can see I've got to give him a week off soon. He can tell you all about it himself. Heber speaks highly of you, but now I see that he was being modest. Your husband is now on the royal payroll, and I'm adding a bonus of my own. By the end of the year, you'll be able to buy some land."

Yael looked at Basemath. Her mouth hung open, and her eyes were wide. "Am I dreaming? Or is it all coming true already?"

"Is . . . is there anything I can do for you while I'm here?" Pepi asked. "Any problems you need help with?"

"N-no," Yael replied. "Thank you. Just tell my husband that I'm fine."

*   *   *

"I told you it'll be taken care of," Ishbak said nervously to his employer. "Tomorrow. You don't have to worry. I'm good for the money."

"I need it for the tax payment in two days, or I'm dead! Do you know what happens in Megiddo when you don't make the tax payment on time?"

"Please!" Ishbak pleaded. "You'll have the money. I assure you."

"How could you have taken money that doesn't belong to you? I've been good to you, Ishbak. You can't say I haven't treated you kindly. I took you in when no one else would hire you, and yet you do something like this to me. How could you—"

"The payment is guaranteed by a very high government official whose name I'm not at liberty to divulge. If you were to hear who it was, you'd understand why I'm so confident."

"Confident? You don't look confident. You look shifty eyed. How do I know you won't just skip town with this supposed payment and leave me hanging?"

"You have my word."

"Your word? Ha! How valuable do you think that is?" His employer looked him in the eyes, and Ishbak looked away. "What did you do with the money you stole from me? Did you gamble it away? Did you give it to that whore?"

"She's not a whore!"

"Oh, no," the merchant drawled sarcastically. "She's a sweet young flower who just accidentally shows her body to men in a tavern every night! A flower who'll go home with any man who has a piece of silver in his pocket!"

"You don't know anything of the kind," Ishbak said, his voice quavering. "I told you you'll have the money tomorrow, before sundown. I promise you." He inched backward out the door.

"Before sundown? I thought you said before noon."

"It's a promise. Before sundown."

Ishbak fled. When he finally arrived at Samal's house, he was out of breath and leaned against the wall until he stopped gasping.

The street was quiet. It was midmorning, after the first deliveries had already been made, and there were no merchants moving around. He could hear singing from the roof. Samal could not carry a tune, but somehow that made her even more endearing to him.

He felt his heart; the pounding had stopped. He cleared his throat. "Samal," he said, to see how it sounded. "Samal, it's me, Ishbak." His voice was nasal and reedy; he could not do anything about it, and he hated the fact. Why did one man get a handsome face and a rich, deep voice, while he got neither? It was not fair. He squared his narrow shoulders and stuck out his thin chest. Then, throwing caution to the wind, he marched up the stairs to Samal's rooms.

The door was open, and he stuck his head inside. A semitransparent curtain had been hung up, and through it he could glimpse the outline of her body, naked and brown. She was bathing! His heart began to beat fast again. He could see the round globes of her breasts. Her hands caressed them. As she turned, in the center of her body he could see a hot patch of black.

"Chemosh, is that you?" her voice called out, throaty, urgent. "I thought you had gone already. Come here and scrub my back, darling."

Ishbak swallowed hard. "It's me," he answered in a harsh croak. "Ishbak."

"Oh." Her voice was flat, devoid of emotion. "Ishbak. Could you come back later? This afternoon, perhaps?"

He gazed at her body with longing. "You'll be gone this afternoon," Ishbak whined. "You always are. Who's Chemosh?"

"A friend of mine," she replied. "You don't know him. Why did you come today, Ishbak? You never come until the end of the week."

"That's what I wanted to talk to you about," he said. He cleared his throat, trying to sound authoritative. "I've been blessed with a change of fortune."

"How nice, Ishbak."

He balled his fists. She had not heard a word. "I'm

going to be making a great deal more money. I just accepted a job that—"

"More money?" she asked. "Did you bring me a present, Ishbak? You never come without bringing me a present."

"Not today," he said, feeling a fool. Why did he not enjoy a sense of triumph? Why did he always appear to be a bumbling, overeager idiot? "In a few days things will be very different." He grew bold. "Would you like me to wash your back?"

"My back? Oh, I suppose so. Come stand over here."

He hated it when she was coy. He knew that this damned Chemosh fellow, whoever he was, would not have to bring her presents every visit. He wondered what Chemosh looked like. Probably handsome with strong arms and a black beard. And a deep voice. Probably a filthy, uncircumcised pig of a foreigner.

He went around the curtain, took the sponge, and slid it down her back. Meanwhile his free hand crept around her waist.

Samal slapped his hand away. "Ishbak! Stop it!"

He withdrew his hand and stood quivering with rage and humiliation. Was this his only reward for betrayal?

Yael was singing happily when she came home, her arms full of the dry clothes. Pepi had seemed so nice! How fortunate that Heber had found a man who would help him up the ladder. Their fortunes *had* changed for the better. And all thanks to Basemath, who had insisted she see—

As she stepped inside the tent a hard hand fell on her arm and held her in a grip of iron.

"Sisera!" she cried out.

"Glad to see me?"

She tried desperately to break loose, but he held her with one hand as if she were a toy. His other hand then ripped the robe off her body, and she stood there naked, trembling. He eased her against the wall of the tent, his hands now on her breasts, his fingers digging savagely into her nipples. She started to scream, but his mouth covered hers, choking her.

When she bit the tongue that was thrust between her lips, he pulled back and slapped her hard across the face, sending her hurtling across the tent and onto the floor. Her mouth was dripping blood, and she could hardly breathe from the fear and the pain.

Grinning, he dropped his sword to the ground and then his clothes. The sight of his nakedness made her cringe. How was it possible that even for a moment she had believed the prophetess? She could not protect herself from this beast, much less kill him. She could do nothing.

"I know you were waiting for me," he said, leering, moving toward her. "I know that when you think of me you pant like a bitch in heat. I'm going to make love to you as if we're dogs. That's what you've always wanted, isn't it—that I take you on all fours."

Gathering all her strength, she scuttled toward the door. She never made it. The weight of his flesh crushed her once again to the floor. The salt from her tears mingled with the blood from her mouth.

IV

Runners spread the news from one end of the Hazorite domain to the other, and when Jerah and Barak arrived in En-harod, the awaiting locals spirited them away to a prearranged meeting place in the hills.

Now, as Barak looked out over the sea of faces, he realized this was an even bigger turnout than the one the day before. Among the Israelites gathered on the hillside, waiting to hear him speak, he could see men whose distinctive dress identified them as being from the tribes of Issachar and Ephraim. That meant that the rebellion had spread to the southern tribes, as he had hoped it would. If an army capable of tackling Sisera's legions was formed, the participation of the southern tribes would be imperative.

For the hundredth time since Deborah had sent him out, Barak thought that his people might succeed in this fantastic quest. He was well aware that all the odds were against it: Hazor had the manpower, the weapons, and the training; but the Israelites had the inestimable will and the help of Yahweh.

Unfortunately, all the tribes' secret organizational work and military training had to be done under the watchful eyes of Sisera's soldiers. Soon they would realize that something was amiss, that the young Israelite men were disappearing at odd times. Or a spy might worm his way into the camp and report back to Jabin and Sisera. Then there would be real problems. The rebels had no weapons other than the farm implements they carried to their meetings. If Sisera's soldiers were to stage a raid before the Israelites procured weapons and learned how to use them, the uprising would be quashed before it had begun, and the casualties would be terrible.

He turned to Jerah. "I wonder if our security precautions are sufficient."

Jerah understood and frowned. "I assume that the people at these gatherings know each other. But I don't see anyone on the lookout for strangers—do you?"

"No, and we're taking a chance every time. It's too late to do anything today, but mention our concern to the organizers from now on."

The young man mounted the hastily constructed little platform and held up his hands for silence. "My friends," he called out, "we've all experienced the brutal hand of Hazor. We know who the enemy is, but we haven't known what to do about him. Until I was called to the Palm Trees by Deborah, I hadn't any idea, either. But now my own audiences have begun to teach me." He studied their faces. "Are there among you any soldiers from Joshua's campaigns?"

About thirty men stepped out of the crowd of hundreds and stood before him. One of them spoke in a surprisingly powerful voice. "We are all the veterans who could assemble on short notice. The next time our numbers will be greater."

Barak smiled and gestured toward the thirty men. "These are the leaders who will teach us how to fight. Let me be brutally honest: I cannot teach you how to use weapons. Until now my battles have been eye-gouging, hair-pulling, leg-twisting brawls in the marketplace."

The assemblage laughed appreciatively.

"I'm standing here before you because Deborah has told me that Yahweh will assemble an army around me. But who am I to be so honored? I am nobody. That, my friends, is why you can trust me—because I am nobody, because Yahweh has confirmed that I am the fool who will lead you, and because Yahweh has ordained that the veterans will get us ready for the most important fight of our lives."

A commotion in the rear of the crowd interrupted his words. He craned his neck to see. Men were shouting angrily. "What's going on back there?" he yelled.

The organizers surged toward the fracas, and Barak could see that a tall man was being surrounded.

"Traitor!"

"We've found a spy here! A spy from Hazor!"

"Bring him here!" Jerah demanded. "Let's have a look at him."

Several men hauled the interloper, struggling, to the front. As they passed, Barak could see several men lunge out from the sidelines to strike the prisoner.

"Don't hurt him," Barak called out. "Maybe we can learn something from him."

The captive was dragged up onto the platform. He was tall, middle-aged, athletically built, well dressed. He had the broad shoulders and big arms of a laborer.

"I recognize him!" a veteran shouted. "He used to live among us, but now he's an official at Jabin's court!"

Barak stood facing the man. "Who are you?" he demanded.

The captive, fully as tall as the Israelite, looked at Barak, then defiantly surveyed the crowd. "I am Pepi of Kerma. I am chief armorer to Jabin of Hazor and to the army of Sisera."

From the crowd came angry shouts and gestures, and

for a moment it seemed as though people were going to pull Pepi down into the crowd and beat him to death.

"Are your people going to kill me? Or would you like to hear me out first?"

Barak raised his hand to calm the crowd. He replied softly to Pepi. "It depends. Do you have anything to say in your defense? We find you here in our midst, a man who broke with Joshua in the days of our fathers and left the camp of Israel to live with the enemy."

"I had no choice," Pepi explained. "I was driven out. Caleb poisoned Joshua's mind against me with lies."

"Don't listen to him!" another veteran cried out. "Give him to us, Barak!"

But Barak waved away the soldier's demand. His eyes were locked on Pepi's. "It wasn't any lie of Caleb's that kept you working for Jabin of Hazor for ten years, though, was it?"

"No," Pepi admitted. "I was bitter. I blamed your people for the fall of Jerusalem and the disappearance of my wife and mother. Now I've been repulsed by the outrages of Jabin and Sisera. And I've taken another look at your people—people I grew up with but who turned on me. I finally decided that whatever injustices you'd committed, you'd paid for them a long time ago. As for Jabin and Sisera—who could feel sympathy for their cause? They haven't any purpose except that of accumulating power, which they abuse. I've been listening to your people's grievances. I attended a meeting of rebels last night in Megiddo."

"And what did you think of what they had to say?"

"Don't listen to the bastard!" someone cried.

Barak again signaled for quiet. "My friends, I have already heard a report of this meeting. The men who met Pepi of Kerma trusted him."

"Then you know," Pepi said, "what they told me and how I responded. I thought the Israelites' oppression would ease if Sisera were assassinated. But now I realize it isn't Sisera. Jabin must be gotten rid of."

Barak nodded. "My friends, did you hear that? That's

sedition! That's treason! If this man were an enemy, would he speak so in front of witnesses?"

Ishbak was in the crowd, listening halfheartedly and still stinging from Samal's rebuke. He suddenly perked up and shouldered his way forward until he was close to the platform. This meeting Pepi and Barak were talking about was juicy information; it would make his superiors happy. This was the kind of tip Lieutenant Telem and General Sisera were paying for. It showed evidence of a widespread conspiracy, which went right to the heart of the kingdom.

Even better was Pepi's involvement. Everyone knew about the tension between Jabin's armorer and the general. There would probably be a bonus in it for him when Sisera heard that news.

When Barak's recruiting speech was over and the crowd had drifted away, the young leader and Jerah took Pepi to the home of a fellow conspirator, a man of the tribe of Issachar.

"Now," Barak said as they sat down to bowls of watered wine, "how can we work together?"

Pepi thought for a moment. "Why is it that you don't have weapons, whereas the people who defeated the Moabites were armed?"

"They took weapons from the Moabites," Jerah explained, "and they also captured the Moabite armory in Jericho."

"Are there enough weapons for your army?" Pepi asked.

Barak frowned. "Not by half. You know the size of Sisera's army—you armed it yourself."

"Right. And unless luck is on your side, you're going to need many more men than Sisera has. You've got the older fellows training the young recruits?"

"Yes. The veterans have come forward gladly."

"Good. Now what do *you* know of soldiering?"

"Nothing," Barak confessed.

"But if you are going to lead this army. . ." Pepi

seemed disgusted. "You can't be serious about this. How can you lead the army when you have no experience with arms or strategy?"

"I couldn't believe it, either. I thought I was on a crazy chase. But Deborah is certain that I am the one. And when I was with her, I had this vision."

Pepi's look softened. "Tell me about it."

Barak quickly explained, then said, "Afterward, well, the vision was so powerful, I knew in my heart that . . . It is very hard to describe what happened. My mission was given to me by Deborah, but it was confirmed by the Voice of Yahweh."

Pepi nodded and appeared more accepting of Barak's leadership. "I believe you. You described it exactly the way Moses spoke of his first vision of Yahweh."

"Moses!" Jerah exclaimed. "You knew Moses?"

"He was like a grandfather to me. That settles it! Accept your mission gladly, Barak. It is your destiny, as sure as leading us all out of Egypt was Moses's." He pounded the table between them and stood up. "Come. I'll give you your first lesson in swordsmanship."

"I thought you were an armorer, not a soldier," Barak protested.

"Come on, get up," Pepi urged. "The way of the sword is best taught man to man, master to pupil. Moses learned from Baliniri; I learned from Moses; you learn from me. In two steps your technique comes from one of history's greatest soldiers. That's an impeccable lineage, my friend. When will you ever get such an opportunity again?"

Barak looked at Jerah as he got up. "How can I resist?" he asked, grinning.

"You can't," Jerah replied seriously. "Deborah said you'd be ready when the time came. And Deborah, it appears, is never wrong."

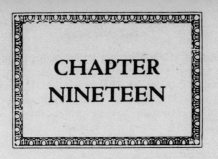

CHAPTER NINETEEN

Damascus

Heresh came out to greet his guest. "Theon!" he said with a big smile. "Welcome back to Damascus! I am delighted to see you. How was your trip across the desert from Babylon?"

"It was splendid," Theon said, laughing, as Heresh's assistant bowed and backed out the door, leaving the two businessmen alone. "I was followed everywhere by spies. Apparently I was considered a dangerous threat to the state, even though Babylon's official attitude toward me couldn't have been more correct and polite."

The banker clapped his hands, and a servant entered, carrying a tray with cups and a jar of fine Chios wine. "How has the house of Khalkeus come to represent danger to the court of Babylon?" Heresh asked.

"It wasn't my connection with Khalkeus that unnerved them," Theon replied. "You may have heard that my father, Seth, was unofficially king of Babylon after the death of his father-in-law, who had declared him heir. Father's reign lasted an hour at most, until the Hittites conquered the city and Father had to escape. But he *was* king, and since I'm his son, alive and well—"

Heresh guffawed. "They saw you as a pretender to the throne?"

Theon nodded as he took a drink of the wine. "Despite my unsolicited protests. There's a native-born king now. I suppose his bloodlines are good enough, but he's a

nervous sort and couldn't get it out of his head that some
of his enemies were going to talk me into fronting a
revolutionary movement." He paused and shook his head.
"Babylon is a political mess. The various religious cults are
at each other's throats, and several factions—both inside
the kingdom and out—are in foment."

"But all in all, it's not that bad an idea, Theon, being
a king," Heresh teased.

"You must be joking," Theon replied. "Who in his
right mind would want that job when he could have mine?
I can roam the world as I please, stop as long as I like
wherever I wish, and whenever I stop I'm always among
good friends like you. What king can do that? He's surrounded by guards, courtiers, and advisers who tell him
what to do and have only their own interests at heart.
When I tire of travel, I can go home to a kingdom on an
island, a place more lavish than anything Babylon can
provide, and there I can enjoy the company of my wife
and children without any responsibilities."

"It does sound ideal. But what did you think of
Babylon?"

"It's lovely, of course. To my surprise, the king had
found some of my father's old designs and had had a few of
them built. The so-called Seth buildings became very popular,
and now there's a whole school of Seth architecture there."

Heresh raised his cup high. "To Seth! May his shadow
lie over Babylon forever."

"Now," Theon said, putting his cup down and lowering his voice, "how is our little plan progressing?"

"Very well, I'd say," the banker replied quietly.

Theon composed his face. He had to suppress his
excitement whenever he spoke about Huldah. She had
been on his mind constantly during the trip to Babylon.
He knew why she had tried to murder him in that dark
alley. Granted, he had not told her that he represented
the commercial empire of Khalkeus, so when she learned
his identity, she most likely believed that he had insinu-
ated himself into her bed only to obtain a trading contract
and planned next to destroy her piecemeal as a competitor.

But there was much more to it than that: There was

the spell she had cast over him and the many bizarre
things he had done under her influence. Above all, there
was his erotic obsession with her that he could not shake.
Her face and body, her sophistication, her liberating sexual practices still held him in sway, no matter how hard he
fought to regain equilibrium.

"For the first time," the banker said, "the woman has
begun to run into difficulties. Because of your influence,
her loan requests are being refused. The only ones she can
get are at usurious rates. Her credit, for reasons she
cannot understand, is suddenly shaky."

Theon was at once pleased with Heresh's progress
and heartsick for Huldah's sake. "Good. How has she
reacted?"

"She's had to sell off some properties—and at prices
by no means advantageous to her—to cover payments on
called loans. Foreign markets are unexpectedly closed to
her. Her representatives are considered pariahs in cities
where they had been respected and honored. She's lost a
number of important trade accounts."

Theon appreciated the irony: Huldah had tried to
murder him because she was afraid just such a situation
would develop when she joined Khalkeus as a trading
partner. But because of Theon's infatuation, it would not
have worked out that way; he would have extended his
protection to her. Now, however, the die was cast. Because of her orders to have him killed, she was sunk into
the very chaos she thought she was smart enough to avoid.

"If we're finished discussing Huldah," Heresh said,
"there's someone I want you to meet. He has news of your
kin."

Theon nodded assent, and Heresh clapped his hands
again. The servant, ever vigilant, materialized at his elbow. Heresh whispered something in the fellow's ear, and
the servant scurried off. "Anyhow," the banker continued,
"she is stuck with three boatloads of goods that she could
sell at a profit only in Greek waters—and the Greeks
won't do business with her because of your instructions."

"If Huldah is as sharp as I think she is, she'll find a
way of disguising her own shipments."

"Yes," Heresh agreed, "but it'll take time. She's got enormous capital tied up in those shipments, and until they actually move, she can't get any money." His smile took a slightly malicious turn: a banker's smile, half-lamb, half-jackal. "The moment she sought loans to carry her through, I had the rates raised all over Damascus. The interest she's paying now is so high, she'll have to drive extraordinary bargains wherever she sells the cargo, or she'll wind up with substantial losses."

"Splendid," Theon approved. "You have the killer instinct. I think I'll put you in charge of Damascus."

"Sir, I'm honored! But where is this supposed to end? Are we supposed to drive the woman out of business or only to her knees?"

"I won't know until I've talked to her," Theon replied.

"Is it wise to meet with her personally? I remember your telling me about her powers."

"I don't have to worry about that now. I looked up some former associates of my father's in Babylon. They gave me advice about handling a woman of her talents."

"But isn't it dangerous?"

"Perhaps," Theon allowed. "My remedy may not be as powerful as I think. But the only way I can test it out is face-to-face."

Heresh looked concerned. "Sir, when do you intend to do this?"

"Soon. Very soon."

"Then allow me to make certain that you're surrounded by some of our best men, just in case."

The servant reappeared and bowed low. "The trader Ner of Carchemish, as you requested."

Theon and Heresh rose to greet the man, who was dressed in the distinctive garb of a seafarer.

"I am honored," Ner said.

"Theon, of the house of Khalkeus," Heresh said, introducing them. "Son of Seth of Thebes."

"Indeed an honor!" Ner said fervently. "Heresh, I am trebly in your debt. Who on all the Great Sea does not know these illustrious names? Sirs: What can a poor man like me do for you?"

"Be seated for one thing," Theon invited. "Heresh tells me you found news of my kin."

"Yes. Iri of Thebes went to Troy with the Greek expedition."

"I'd heard that. The family trade with Troy was broken off some years ago when Priam couldn't guarantee shipments would reach him without being captured by the besiegers. So my kinsman was one of the men menacing our own ships? There's an irony for you, Heresh!"

Ner looked ill at ease. "It appears, sir, that Iri was killed by a poisoned arrow."

"I have heard that he died, also, from a jeweler carrying Iri's wares. But the man didn't tell me who killed him or how." He pondered for a moment. "I didn't know the Trojans used poison arrows."

"Only one of them does, sir. Prince Paris."

Theon looked down into his wine cup and shook his head sadly. "I'm grateful for another confirmation of Iri's death. I really couldn't act on rumors, and I feel a responsibility to see that all family members are safe. I have probably been too protective of my own well-being. Otherwise, I would have gone to Troy, after Iri and Keturah."

"Sir," Ner said, "there's more. His wife, sir? The blind woman? And his son. Iri did find them."

Theon sat up, and his expression brightened. "They were reunited?"

"In a way, sir. His wife and boy were inside Troy. Iri stole into the palace and saw Keturah briefly before he was murdered."

"Keturah and the child are still inside Troy?"

"Yes, but the war's about over. The Trojans can't last another six months."

Theon looked at Heresh. "Keturah's the widow of one of our own, and the boy is a Child of the Lion. The family must take care of them. I have to get them to safety before the Greeks' final offensive."

"You can't go alone!" Heresh looked shocked.

"Of course not, man. I'll take a detachment of our men along." He turned back to Ner. "Is there anything else you want to tell me?"

"Apparently you have a new relative, sir. Iri adopted his assistant, a young man named Phorbus. Phorbus has sworn to get Iri's wife and child out of the city."

"Then there isn't much time. If Phorbus succeeds before I get there, I'll miss them, and the search will begin anew. An adopted son, eh? I don't recall there having been another adopted Child of the Lion. Well, I suppose blood isn't everything. If Iri thought Phorbus good enough to bring into the family, that's enough of a recommendation for me."

"I'll inquire when another caravan is leaving for the coast," Heresh offered.

"Let's finish this business with Huldah immediately," Theon ordered.

"What do you mean?" Huldah asked Yasarum the banker. "That loan isn't due yet."

"Madam, I assure you that it is," Yasarum replied coolly. "It is most unfortunate."

"But I counted on you to make the transfer of funds two weeks ago. If that had been done—"

"There were no funds to transfer, madam."

"What do you mean? I have enough money on deposit to buy a hundred houses."

"You did, madam, but your failed speculations in the grain market—"

"There was more than enough to cover those."

"—and the collapse of the cartel in which you invested, the one that was going to corner the market in precious metals—"

"Collapse? When did it collapse?"

"Yesterday, madam."

"Why wasn't I informed? How could you have let this—"

"No banker has control over that sort of thing, madam. The market is precarious at best. Your investments are always at risk. Certainly you know that."

"I'm the most conservative investor in the city. How could so many of my enterprises have failed in so short a time?"

"I'm sure I don't know, madam. The market is notoriously unstable just now."

"Why? Nothing has happened to bring about this—" Her face went blank. Then the light of understanding slowly dawned in her eyes. "Something's wrong here. It's all too convenient. Unless something drastic happens quickly, I'm ruined. Have your other investors suffered losses of comparable magnitude recently, Yasarum?"

The banker drew himself up haughtily. "Madam, I cannot divulge—"

"You know what I'm talking about! I'm not asking for specifics about any individual. I want patterns. Are there any patterns in this? Or am I being singled out?"

"Well, madam, I'm afraid it does seem as if Fortune has picked you out for disfavor during this particular time."

Her eyes blazed. "This isn't coincidental. I smell a rat somewhere."

"Madam, I can't imagine—"

Huldah realized that she could no longer play cat and mouse with this fool. She had to have accurate information immediately. She straightened, standing as tall and as relaxed as she could. She spoke one word to herself, a very ancient word, and repeated it silently. A force began to move up her spine. She felt it slithering like a snake along her vertebrae, ever upward, bringing her enormous power. Ordinarily she considered it unnecessary—even dangerous—to wield this kind of force on members of the business community. But she had no alternative.

"Tell me," she demanded, her eyes boring into his, "what connection, if any, does this firm have with the house of Khalkeus of Gournia?"

The banker blinked. His face went white. The blood and the will seemed to have been sucked out of his body. He answered her questions as if he were a naughty child.

When she had milked the banker dry of information, she knew who had planned her downfall and why. It was, in retrospect, not unexpected—but the suddenness and the deviousness shocked her.

Before she left she implanted instructions in Yasarum's mind to cover her losses by juggling accounts. This would enable her to transfer her stolen funds to another bank—one of the few in Damascus that was not controlled wholly or in part by the Children of the Lion.

She went immediately to see Kabiata of Haran, another banker. After a furious argument followed by another session of mind control, Huldah had repaired her situation to the point at which her affairs could limp along without coming to a crisis. But she was forced to dispose quickly of valuable properties at below market price to meet her current obligations. It was a crushing defeat. She had obviously underestimated the power of Theon's family.

Theon was evidently seeking revenge for the murder attempt on him. No doubt he believed her wrath stemmed from his affiliation with Khalkeus of Gournia. No, she decided, Theon would never be able to understand her all-consuming hatred of the Children of the Lion. But her enmity had nothing to do with business. Commerce meant nothing to her when compared with the crimes of which Theon's clan was guilty! For it was only the Children of the Lion—powerful, wealthy, influential—who could have rescued her from her horrible fate and her years in the brothels. Yet it was that family, which so prided itself on taking care of its own, that had absolutely abandoned her after the fall of Jerusalem. And for that, she could never, would never, forgive!

By midafternoon she was home again, poring over her accounts, cursing at her scribes, sending runners throughout the city with reassuring messages to her associates.

She explained her strategy to Bunukian, her chief scribe. "As of tomorrow we'll do no more business with Kabiata's bank or Yasarum's. I expect problems with the magistrates. Fortunately I've enough money left on deposit in the neutral banks to cover the necessary bribes."

"To which banks are you having the funds transferred?" the scribe asked.

"To the bank of Heresh, I thought."

"My lady, of all the bankers in the city, Heresh is closest to Khalkeus! It's my understanding that Heresh is very much in the confidence of Theon, Khalkeus's right-hand man in the region."

The mention of Theon's name drew a look of angry hatred. "Oh, is he?" she asked. "How very convenient."

"Why, yes, my lady. As a matter of fact, Theon and Heresh were seen together today in Damascus."

Huldah's smile was icy and lethal. "This is interesting. Where might Theon be staying while he's in town?"

"I think he could be reached through Heresh. Would you like me to summon him?"

"No, Bunukian. I may pay him a visit myself tonight."

"You must certainly mean tomorrow. It would be highly irregular—"

"Tonight it is. Yabamat!" She clapped her hands for her maid, who scurried in. "Summon the litter bearers, and then come back and dress me. I'm going out."

On the way home from a dinner party celebrating Heresh's appointment as the firm's representative, Theon thought about the situation in Troy. It seemed inevitable that he make a hurried journey to rescue Iri's wife and child. Perhaps on the way to the sea he could stop by Hazor and visit Pepi, who probably needed all the help he could get.

Approaching Heresh's house they could see litter bearers standing in front. The servants and chair obviously belonged to a guest of some standing.

As they neared the door, Theon called out to one of his own servants, "Find out whose men those are."

But his question was answered almost before the words were out of his mouth. The litter's curtain parted, and a familiar, tall, and haughty figure stood silhouetted against the chair. Theon could not see her face, but he could feel her eyes burning into him. His whole body trembled violently. As he fought to control himself, his nails dug into his palms. He wanted to punch her. He wanted to kiss her. He wanted to drive a dagger into her eye. He wanted to bury his lips between her snow white breasts. Finally he was under control, but the cost was blood dripping down his palms.

"Huldah!" he said, keeping his voice even and polite. "What a pleasant surprise. May I present Heresh the banker, who—"

"I know who he is," she snapped, her voice dripping acid. "Congratulations to both of you. You've had a devastating effect on my finances."

"I certainly hope so," said Theon with exaggerated politeness. "Heresh, my friend, would it be too much of an imposition if the lady and I were to withdraw? Some private conversation is in order."

"Certainly," Heresh said. He gestured, and a servant stepped forward. "Take my guests to the large sitting room, please."

Alone, they faced each other. There was an excitement in the air, a potential for violence, for trickery, even for love.

"You! You and your cursed family!" Huldah said bitterly. "They are a blight on the earth."

"Was that why you tried to have me murdered? Not because I lied to you but because I am a member of the family? Tell me, Huldah, do you have a grudge against us? How have the Children of the Lion offended you?"

She laughed harshly. "First you try to ruin me, and then you wonder what you've done wrong. I suppose it's too much to expect you'd make good the losses you inflicted on me."

"How could I do that? Besides, you've already stolen most of it back. You're a remarkable businesswoman. At least two local banks will soon be found insolvent, and if I'm any judge of your methods, it'll be a long time before any suspicion will fall on you. And then you'll worm out of that and charm a judge or two. Just be careful you don't use your little tricks on someone who's a member of the Order of Chalybians."

"Order of Chalybians? What's that?" she demanded.

"Oh, come now. You know all about them, don't you? The moment your little spell really started to work, I knew there was only one possible way you could have acquired the ability. It was from your husband, Ephai, wasn't it? I asked around in Babylon. They said a man named Ephai was apprenticed to one of the wandering Chalybian masters thirty years ago, although he did not advance far before his master died. So he learned none of the moral precepts of the order—or, for that matter, none of the advanced occult practices. Then, like a fool, he taught the tricks to you."

"Go on," she urged. "This is hugely entertaining."

"At first I guessed that you'd learned the method earlier, perhaps from one of the men who frequented your brothels. I thought you might have used it on Ephai himself, to get him to marry you."

Her eyes blazed. "Ephai loved me! We were equal partners almost from the first. It didn't take any Chalybian magic to win him over."

"I'm sure it didn't," Theon said. "I myself was taken with you even before you started using it on me. You were the first woman who ever tempted me to cheat on my wife."

Her lips curled in a contemptuous sneer. "You can't expect me to believe that."

"And since now is the time for truth, you never really had me totally under your spell."

"You fool, you did just as I wanted you to."

"Try me now, Huldah. Try to control me. I took a few lessons from the masters of Babylon because I knew I would see you again. Come, Huldah," he said, walking slowly toward her. "Use your eyes on me again. Try to make me your slave."

She shrank back for a moment, but then pulled herself together and gathered strength. She stood tall and looked him in the eyes.

Theon tensed, then took a deep breath and relaxed as he had been instructed to do in Babylon; Huldah's power could be deflected merely by his relaxing and blinking his eyes—tiny, constant blinks.

"Theon, son of Seth," she intoned, "your strength is mine. I have taken it all away. Your hands are weak." Her voice was soothing and seductive, measured and calm. "Now hold up your hand for me." She locked her fingers with his, palm to palm. "Squeeze as hard as you can. You will find that your power is gone, that your hand is as weak as a child's."

He squeezed but without strength.

"You see?" she said, triumphant. "You are under my control. I am your master."

Then the pressure from his hand suddenly increased as their eyes remained locked.

"Ow! You're hurting me!" she cried, twisting away.

He grinned and let go, but his eyes did not leave hers. "Huldah," he said quietly, "take the brooches from your hair. Let it fall as it does when you prepare for bed."

She found herself obeying him, unable to do otherwise. "Plait it, the way the women do it in your home country."

When she came to, she was sitting on a bench at one end of the big room, facing a bronze mirror.

"Look," he said. "See who you have become."

She looked in the mirror. The woman before her seemed twenty years younger, with braids hanging down on either side of her face, the way they had when she was a girl, far away across the Great Sea, in a land much colder, more mountainous than this. She burst into tears and covered her face with her hands like the child she still was, inside the protective shell she had built up.

"Look at me, Theon," she said, sobbing. "I am no longer Huldah. You have stripped her away from me, and I thank you for that. Once again I am Tirzah, abandoned wife of your kinsman Pepi."

Theon's eyes widened in astonishment. "I knew I could destroy Huldah, but I had no idea who would appear."

She looked up at him with eyes that brimmed with tears. "I didn't want anyone to know. Ever!"

Theon sat down beside her and took her hands. His voice was congested with wonder and dismay. "Oh, gods, are you really Tirzah? Pepi's wife?"

She heaved a shuddering sigh. "I thought I could start a new life and forget the old. Pepi didn't look for me. He didn't come to save me. None of you did, with all your self-congratulatory claims of close kinship. I had to extricate myself. I had to save my own life."

Theon embraced her. He rubbed her back and spoke in a low and soothing voice, as the masters in Babylon had instructed him. "Tell me everything, darling. I want to know."

She took a deep breath and rested her cheek on his shoulder. "When the kidnappers took Neftis and me from Jerusalem, they beat us and tied us up and threw us in the back of a wagon. I never had any idea where we were. We traveled by day. At night they would take us out and have their pleasure on us. When the masters were through, they gave us to the servants and the slaves. Neftis couldn't stand it. She had already gone mad when Pepi, Nimshi, and Micah had left. She killed herself, but I wanted to live, if only to get revenge."

"And did you take your revenge?"

"No. I never found the kidnappers. When I got rich I put men on their trail, but by then the trail was cold."

He stroked her tense neck. "Go on."

"The bastards sold me to a brothel in Damascus. I lived for three years chained naked to a bed and forced to service any and all comers in any fashion they chose. I had no idea men's minds moved in such dark corners. But all the time I kept telling myself, 'Pepi will find me. Pepi will rescue me.' He never came. And I learned to cater to every ugly craving men are capable of."

She sat back, and as Theon watched, her expression kept changing: One moment she was an avenging demon; the next she was a child whose innocence had been cruelly sullied.

"The other women weakened and died—some by their own hand, some beaten to death, some horribly diseased—but I grew hard and strong. I don't know how I was spared from disease. Luck, I suppose. My mistress finally let me off the chain. At first it was only so I might cater to the most exotic tastes, then it was to run the brothel for her. As she prospered, she gave me more authority. When she died I learned that she had deeded the place to me.

"That's when I went to Ephai. He loaned me money to buy new places, where the whores were treated well and kept clean. Eventually we became partners. Finally I ran all his affairs in Damascus; then we branched out to Ebla. But it wasn't until he died that I really began to prosper. Then I could run the entire business in my own way."

"And that's when you and I locked horns."

"Yes. Once I learned that you were the commercial representative of the Children of the Lion, I wanted to kill you. Duplicity alone would not have caused me to act in such a manner. But it was *your* family, Pepi's family, who had abandoned me." Her voice filled with sarcasm and hurt. "The great and powerful family called the Children of the Lion could make kingdoms fall and trading empires quake—but they couldn't find one poor woman."

He stroked her cheek. "Now that you know who we are, darling, what would you have me do?"

She could not answer. She just sighed and closed her eyes. "I am worthless," she said sadly. "When I was kidnapped it was not even worth my husband's effort to find me and save me. I am Tirzah no more. Tirzah is dead. I never think of her." She began to cry from deep in her soul. "Why did you make me think of her again? I was happy leaving her dead, dead and forgotten, just like Pepi."

"My dear," he said gently, pulling her back into his arms. "Pepi is alive."

Her eyes snapped open, and her body stiffened.

"He did look for you," Theon continued. "But he kept suffering from blackouts, so he paid men to search. They looked for years but could find no trace of you. You must understand: You yourself hired men to find the slavers who abducted you, and they failed."

She was silent, but her face reflected anger, rage, and resentment.

"He's spent the last ten years working for men he despises," Theon said, "believing in nothing, trying to forget. He has nothing to do with the family. He has no friends, no woman, nothing. Huldah . . . Tirzah, if he could see you again—"

"No!" she said, drawing away from him. Her eyes shone with fear. "He must never learn what happened to me! Never!"

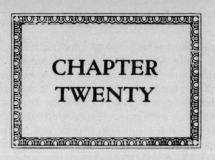

CHAPTER TWENTY

Canaan

"Are you ill, Micah?"

"No. Why do you ask?"

Nimshi poked at the fire with his stick. The brothers were southeast of Ashkelon and would reach their destination in one day's travel. They had decided to take a short detour, however, and visit the market town of Beror Hayli in the morning. Once they bedded down for the night, Nimshi began to worry about his brother, who had been increasingly silent and moody.

"I'm concerned because you are so quiet."

"I have always been quiet, Nimshi," Micah said. "Perhaps when you dreamed up this plan for us, you created in your mind an idealized version of me. Then, when I accepted your offer and we began the journey, you found that the real Micah did not measure up to your version. And you became very uncomfortable."

Nimshi realized there was wisdom in what Micah was saying, and he felt foolish. "Are you sorry that you have come with me?"

"No, Nimshi. Not at all."

"Sometimes I get the feeling that you resent your decision, that I cajoled you into doing something that you really didn't want to do."

"Nonsense. I was a hired killer for the Israelites. You

were a merchant who lived to turn a profit. Both of our lives were futile. We had to make a change."

Nimshi pushed sand over the fire so that it was extinguished. Then he lay back and stared at the night sky.

"I think we will buy some fruit in a marketplace rather than eat what we've been pulling off trees." He expected some response from Micah, but there was none. "Do you remember the fruit salad with poppy seeds that Mother used to make?" Nimshi waited, but then he heard soft rhythmic breathing. Micah had fallen asleep.

When they entered Beror Hayli the market stalls were just being set up. It was a small town, one of the dozens licensed by the Philistine League for commerce in fruits, vegetables, oil, lumber, fabrics, livestock, and pottery.

They strolled around, buying small red onions, figs, and large whitish grapes. When the sun was overhead they lunched in a large black tent, drinking rich goat's milk and eating cheese and raisins.

As they were leaving the town after lunch to continue their trek to Gaza, Micah stopped abruptly in front of a stall handling pottery. He admired the beautifully formed and painted objects.

"Have you never seen Philistine pottery before?" Nimshi asked.

"No, never," Micah replied, awed.

"Look at the figures," Nimshi suggested, picking up a simple wine bowl and holding it up above Micah's eyes so that the sunlight brought the decoration into sharp focus.

"I have never seen the human figure painted in such a manner," Micah whispered, and he stared with reverence at the thin, perfectly painted red bodies on the black surfaces. "Look! That one is flinging a spear."

"The Greeks call it a javelin, Micah."

"Is this pottery Greek?"

"It is Philistine," Nimshi explained, "and their culture is Greek. But no one really knows where they came from other than that they arrived from the north by sea."

"I have never seen such colors or forms among the

Israelites' pottery. Yahweh does not like images." Micah took the wine bowl in his own hands and turned it around.

"Watch it!" a very angry voice boomed out from behind them. "You can't just pick up what you want and spin it around your head! This merchandise is breakable."

The vendor was a short, powerfully built man who wore a leather apron. He snatched the wine bowl out of Micah's hands and pushed him aside.

Micah exploded into a cold, swift, murderous fury. He drew his knife with one hand and caught the vendor around the neck with the other hand, then flung the man to the ground. The bowl fell and shattered.

"Micah, don't!" Nimshi cried out in horror as Micah pressed his knife into the trembling vendor's neck.

Nimshi rushed to his brother's side and clutched his knife arm while begging his brother to relax.

But Micah's arm remained poised, powerful, murderous. The point had already pierced the vendor's throat, and a thin stream of blood trickled into the dirt. Finally, after Nimshi expended all his strength, the knife point was lowered, the hand around the neck loosened, and the panting, whimpering vendor staggered away.

Nimshi sat hard on the ground, trying to stop shaking.

"Sorry," Micah said to him, and then calmly and carefully cleaned the knife blade before replacing the weapon inside his robe.

For the first time since he had been reunited with his brother, Nimshi had witnessed the eruption of explosive, irrational hatred and attack. For the first time, Nimshi could believe that Micah was Eglon's murderer. For the first time, Nimshi realized that his brother was still a killer.

Who is this madman? he wondered. *What have I gotten myself into?*

For the first time, Nimshi feared for his own life.

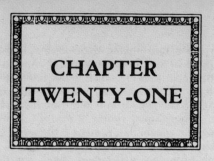

CHAPTER TWENTY-ONE

Syrian Desert

Luti had to cut the sandals from her feet at the close of her first day in the desert. The hard, flat ground was studded with tiny stones that became wedged between the soles of her feet and the sandal, quickly bringing blood, which hardened on the leather.

When she had finished the operation, she wrapped wet rags around her bruised and raw feet and watched as the men and donkeys settled down for the night around the cooking fires.

Occa, the deaf-mute Bedouin, squatted nearby. He had built a small fire, over which he was roasting a chunk of meat. He grinned fiercely at her.

Luti did not know whether Drak had sent him along to protect her or to spy on her. One thing was certain: Occa never let her out of his sight. While he could not speak or hear, his eyesight and other sensitivities were acute; the slightest movement, a minor shift of the wind currents, and his chin would come up and his eyes would dart around.

Luti realized that no one on the caravan had spoken to her. It was, she thought, because people were afraid of Occa. His appearance was very bizarre and threatening, and the sword that lay across his back was enormous.

An hour after sunset, the night became cold. Wind gusted across the camp, picking up the tiny stones from the desert floor and flinging them against beast and man. Luti wrapped herself in a blanket and chewed sadly on a piece of the meat that Occa had given her. She wondered what kind of meat it was and where he had obtained it. Soon the camp was very quiet, and the drovers had banked the fires.

There was a movement in the darkness. Occa leapt to his feet, but it was only a drover carrying a bowl filled with an evil-smelling substance. He was a burly young man with long hair and a silver bracelet on one wrist. His long whip was hung around his neck for quick retrieval. He stopped several paces from Luti.

"Your feet look very bad," he said kindly, "so I brought you something for them. This lunatic Bedouin won't help you; they spend their lives barefoot." He placed the bowl on the ground beside her. "When you get up in the morning, smear some of this on the bottoms of your feet and rub the rest all over your sandals. You'll blister for a day or two, but you won't bleed. And then it'll be all right."

She thanked him. Then she asked: "Why is everyone afraid of my companion?"

He laughed as if she were joking. "This desert is littered with the bodies of drovers, and the raiders are always Bedouins. Not your man's tribe, perhaps, but related ones. When a drover sees a Bedouin, he naturally keeps away." The drover started to leave, then turned back and said, "Of course, if we all reach Damascus alive, we'll love him." He laughed again and vanished into the darkness.

The drover had been right. After the third day her feet were fine, and Luti settled into the tedium of the desert march. The days were hot and slow; the nights were cold and fast. She fell asleep immediately from exhaustion and awoke at first light when Occa touched her shoulder.

Sometimes she was allowed the luxury of riding on a donkey, and while the change was enjoyable, the beast's motion made her ill, and she could not remain on its back for too long. For some reason Occa preferred that she walk, and when she climbed off a donkey's back, he would whirl and wield his sword. She had not the slightest idea what his dance meant.

On the seventh day of the journey they came upon four corpses just off the trail—a man, a woman, and two young children. The family had probably entered the desert ill prepared and had died of thirst. Although they could not have been dead for more than a day or two, most of the flesh had already been eaten from their bones. Vultures, crows, and ravens circled overhead or strutted territorially near the remains. In the distance, the sleek low bodies of golden jackals could be seen.

Something mysterious surrounded the tragedy, and the drovers studied the remains and whispered among themselves. Why had the family not taken enough water? Where were their pack animals?

The drovers covered the bodies with empty fruit sacks, and the caravan began to move again.

Luti, however, could not make herself leave. Something about the family made her stay. She felt unable to abandon the poor group, as if they needed her. Occa squatted nearby, rocking on his heels and staring at the bodies.

The vultures returned, gliding downward on the desert air, their wings outstretched. Then they abruptly flew off as if a predator were in their midst. The sound of their desperate flapping filled the thin desert air.

Luti stared around, looking for whatever had frightened them, but she saw nothing. Then, staring into the sky, her eyes shielded by her hands to cut the glare, she noticed four dark specks approaching. Within moments, the specks became identifiable as ravens, which settled down, one on each body. They were magnificent birds, large and black with yellow-ringed eyes and massive, bluish claws.

Luti waited for them to rip through the sackcloth and consume what was left of the corpses. Surprisingly, however, they made no move to scavenge. Instead, the ravens stared intently at her. Unnerved, she waved her arms and yelled at them to fly away. Still they stared. Feeling very uncomfortable, she picked up some small stones and flung them at the ravens. Still they sat calmly on the bodies and stared at Luti. Frightened now, she fled from the macabre scene and rejoined the caravan. Occa was at her heels.

During the day she could not stop thinking about the ravens and corpses. When night fell she wrapped herself against the cold and slept. She woke suddenly near midnight. The camp was absolutely still, and Occa was fast asleep, so Luti had no clue as to what had interrupted her rest.

She sat up and gazed at the night sky, splendid in its mantle of stars. For the first time, the significance of the ravens dawned on her with stark clarity. She shivered because the ravens were warning her of something terrible: The birds had not eaten of those corpses because there would be many other corpses soon—the caravan was about to be attacked.

She screamed and ran through the camp, warning her traveling companions. She woke them and kicked them until they heard what she had to say. The drovers laughed at her and told her she was a crazy woman, made hysterical by the macabre sight of the day before. When she refused to quiet down, they angrily threw things at her.

Finally, realizing it was futile to warn these people, she gathered her few belongings and left the camp, followed by a confused Occa.

An hour before dawn, her prediction came true. Bedouins on swift horses swept down on the caravan from the northern steppes. They slaughtered everyone in minutes, murdering the drovers with a single swipe of their sharp swords.

Luti and Occa watched it all from a safe distance. The raiders stripped the travelers' bodies of all clothing, jewels, and weapons, gathered the bags of fruit and other produce, murdered the donkeys, and left as quickly as they had come.

When the slaughter was over and the Bedouins gone, Luti, in a state of shock, could not move. She watched as

Occa returned to the caravan and searched for water. When it was obvious the raiders had taken it all, he drained the blood from the donkey corpses into the empty waterskins. Then he held them up triumphantly for her to see. It dawned on her, in her confusion and distress, that he still intended to get her to Damascus on schedule.

PART
FOUR

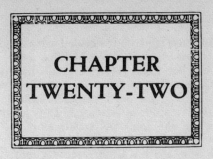

CHAPTER TWENTY-TWO

Troy

I

Hector's remains were honored in the manner befitting Trojan royalty. The day the truce was to end dawned bright. In the encampment of the Sauromatae, Myrrha rose and stood naked in the chill morning air. All around her the other women warriors were stirring. It was a mark of the new self-discipline that prevailed in the camp of the Sauromatae that all of them arose from single beds. The sharp smell of smoke was in the air.

"Whose turn is it to wake the queen?" Myrrha asked. "Yours, darling," the warrior Clonia replied, a sympathetic smile on her pert face. "I woke her yesterday."

Bremusa sat up, the coverlet falling off her hard-muscled body. "Go naked," she suggested. "Give her a passionate kiss to awaken her. Then we can all enjoy another hour's sleep, waiting for the two of you to have a morning tussle."

Myrrha frowned and reached for her tunic. "I'll forget I heard that. Besides, you're the one who likes to couple with your own kind . . . when you can find someone desperate enough."

"Why, you—" Bremusa made motions of preparing to fight.

Myrrha watched calmly. "Come on, if you're going to do anything but bluster. I haven't had my morning exercise yet."

But Bremusa apparently decided against fighting. She sat where she was and glared at Myrrha.

Wearing her tunic, Myrrha strode barefoot up the slope to Queen Penthesilea's quarters. Her wide-paced gait was that of a seasoned soldier accustomed to long marches—her relaxed, well-balanced body leaning slightly forward, while she remained totally alert to everything going on around her.

When she arrived at the queen's tent, she found Penthesilea already up and dressed in the quilted undergarments worn to pad armor.

"Ah, my lady, you're awake," Myrrha said, turning to go.

The queen caught her arm. "Last night I had a dream, an excellent omen. Today is going to be a great day in the field, a day of victory and thanksgiving. We'll all be heroes."

"My lady," Myrrha said tentatively, "is a dream enough?"

"This one was," Penthesilea replied confidently. "My father, Ares, appeared to me and said to go to war with a light heart and to fight my way to Achilles as quickly as possible, killing all who stand in my way."

"My lady," Myrrha said, "I've been speaking with someone who knows Achilles. He believes we can match the ordinary Greek soldier, but he warns us to stay away from Achilles. The man can't be killed."

Penthesilea tossed her head. "I don't believe it. Everyone is vulnerable. He's never run up against his equal before, that's all. And he's been fighting people who are their own worst enemies. Hector didn't face an indestructible monster; he came up against a man he feared. Just as you cannot make love with someone you fear, so you cannot effectively do battle with someone who frightens you."

"My lady," Myrrha said as diplomatically as possible, "the outcome of the encounter proved that Hector had every reason to fear Achilles. He—"

"No, Myrrha!" the queen interrupted. "I believe my dream, and I'm not afraid. The voice of Ares was strong and persuasive. Why should I fear Achilles or any man?

And if I don't fear him, how can he defeat me? Today, when we go after the Greeks, I will seek out Achilles and kill him. Then the war will be over."

"That might well be, my queen," Myrrha said, trying to remain deferential.

Penthesilea clapped her on the shoulder. "I'm the one who leads a charmed life today. And Achilles had better watch out."

In the Greek camp Ajax and Achilles had been drinking far into the night, toasting the combat readiness of their legions. After Achilles, Ajax, a giant of a man, was the most feared warrior in the Greek camp. Beyond his military skills, Ajax was also sociable, poetic, and given to long philosophical discussions, which only Achilles could tolerate. When the wake-up order came, neither man could get up.

Achilles snarled at the young soldier whom Agamemnon had sent to rouse him. "Get out of here before I remove your ears and make you eat them."

"But, sir," the soldier bravely said, "I have specific orders from King Agamemnon to get all the commanders up."

Achilles rose on one elbow and gave the young fellow a hate-filled glare from painfully bloodshot eyes. "If you are not out of my sight by the time I count to three, I will add your nose to the menu." To emphasize his words, he slid his sword halfway out of its jeweled scabbard.

The recruit beat a hasty retreat, only to earn a second cursing out from Menelaus and Agamemnon when he reported back to them.

When Menelaus had vented his anger, he turned scowling to his brother. "Forget those drunken louts. We'll beat the Trojans today, with or without Achilles and Ajax. We'll hit them until they crumble."

"But without Achilles . . ." Agamemnon moaned.

"I said forget him! Even if he is too hung over to fight, we have plenty of men in sharp form, and they'll make up for his absence."

"But—"

"Forget him!"

*   *   *

The news found its way to Odysseus's tents beside
the black ships. "I tell you, Phorbus," he grumbled, "I've
had enough of tiptoeing around Achilles and his moods."

Phorbus said nothing. He was sitting on a piece of
driftwood and staring morosely into the tiny fire he had
built.

"What's the matter with you?" Odysseus demanded.
"This is going to be a big day—well, for everybody but
Ajax and Achilles."

"I had an awful dream last night," Phorbus confided.
"I dreamed that I had to fight Myrrha and . . . I killed her."

Odysseus studied the young man's woeful expression.
"So you finally understand that she isn't going to quit her
army and run away with you; that she considers her own
honor as important to her as yours is to you; that you can't
snap your fingers and have her come running."

"Don't tease me. I'm not in the mood for humor."

"I know you're not. I'm not trying to be funny. This is
the reality of your situation."

Phorbus turned a miserable-looking face toward his
friend. "Don't you think I know it? I was awake most of
the night agonizing over my situation, and when I finally
dozed off, I had that cursed dream."

Odysseus picked up a stick and stirred the sluggish
fire that had been kindled at dawn to stave off the damp
and cold of a morning by the sea. "One of the most
unpleasant steps to wisdom is recognizing when there's
nothing to be done about certain situations. You just have
to accept them."

"But—"

"Listen to me: Myrrha's a warrior. She neither knows
nor wants any other life. Accept it! As for your fling with
her, consider it a present from the gods because they felt
kindly toward you at that moment. Now she has to get
back to her job." He stabbed a finger at Phorbus to
punctuate his words. "As you do to yours. You told me
that Menelaus has some weapons for you to repair, and he
wants a new sword."

"He doesn't need a new weapon. Let him steal one from some Trojan he's killed. Of course that will require Menelaus to get off his lazy behind and do some fighting for a change."

Odysseus nodded. "The rich and powerful pick the fights, while everybody else takes the risks, does the killing, and in the end gets next to nothing." He snorted. "Just watch: Menelaus will come out of this richer. He'll have Helen—yes, he'll take her back and gladly—and Sparta will get its treasure returned. Then Menelaus will gain the choicest bits from the treasure of Troy, too. He'll live happily to a great old age, while the rest of us die broke and miserable, nursing the wounds we received in this godforsaken war."

"What can we do about it?"

Odysseus's eyes glowed with a secret. "The answer rests with a man called Epeius in the village. He was a master builder."

"What are you going to have him build?"

"I'll tell you soon. First I have to find some lumber for him."

"Does this mean you're going to back out of the day's fighting?" Phorbus asked. "Agamemnon will be furious."

"He doesn't need me. He's fighting women today—and I don't want to be the one who kills your girlfriend."

"May I come with you?"

"No, stay here," Odysseus said. "You have those repairs to do. And if something happens to your girl, you'll want to be nearby."

He threw a cape over his shoulders and strode away without looking back.

II

Priam, still mourning his beloved son Hector, had not intended to watch the Trojans return to the field; but Cassandra was insistent that he do so.

"There's no use moping about here, Father. Come up

to the top of the wall. Your soldiers and the reinforcements will expect to see you there."

"I've no heart for it. I had a terrible dream, an evil
omen."

"You're the one who calls other people superstitious
fools for believing their dreams!"

"I know," Priam admitted, "but this one was so vivid.
I must have fallen asleep while I was praying to Father
Zeus. I asked him to give strength to the arm of the queen
of the Sauromatae and let her rout the Greeks."

"A worthy prayer, Father. One that Zeus is sure to
listen to."

"So I thought, also," Priam said. "But then, in my
dream, I heard an eagle scream. When I looked up I saw
the great bird whipping past me. It was as close to me as
you are right now, Daughter. In his talons he was carrying
a mangled dove. Oh, Cassandra, I just know—"

"Nonsense," the princess scoffed. "I know the ways of
portents and omens. It was just a dream, nothing more.
Come, get dressed. You owe it to your subjects."

The old man nodded sadly. "There's only one argument that can reach me anymore, and that concerns my
duty." He sighed. "Call my manservant. I'll dress and be
on the wall in a few minutes."

"Don't let me down," she said. "I'm counting on you.
We all are."

As Cassandra went down the hall past her own rooms
to the staircase that led to the top of the city wall, her
footsteps alerted Keturah. The blind woman poked her
head out into the corridor and asked: "Princess, are you
going to watch the fighting?"

"Yes, the king will join me there."

"My lady, would you be so kind as to take me with
you?"

Cassandra scowled. She had not intended to spend
the morning describing the battle. She thought for a moment, sighed, and gave in. "I didn't offer to do so because
I thought you would find it disturbing." She saw a strange
expression of hope and wariness on Keturah's face.

"I am hopeful that Phorbus might catch sight of me,

my lady. Perhaps if he saw me, it would remind him of his promise to Iri to rescue Talus and me."

She doesn't trust me as a go-between with Phorbus, Cassandra thought. It was sad, very sad.

The Greeks turned out at only three-quarters strength because they were fighting women and did not take the task seriously. As the ranks of the Sauromatae came into sight and faced them across the field, the Greek soldiers gestured obscenely, with much crotch grabbing, whistles, and catcalls.

Then Queen Penthesilea appeared, riding a magnificent horse. The sight of her with the morning sun gleaming on her shining helmet gave the Trojans and her own troops heart.

"Soldiers of Troy and of the Sauromatae!" she cried. "Are you ready?"

The answer was a confident roar from male and female throats. It was echoed by the women and children gathered on the wall, and Priam waved his blessing.

"On to victory!" she cried in a voice that carried across the field.

Urging her horse onward, she cut the air with her gleaming sword. Behind her the Trojan force marched forward.

As Keturah clung to her arm, Cassandra watched Priam with concern. He seemed depressed, resigned.

Cassandra, however, was excited. "Queen Penthesilea's magnificent, Keturah! She rode right through the Greek line, swinging her sword and leaving numerous bodies in her wake. Then she dismounted and killed three Greeks very easily. Now she's fighting—who's the man, Father? Molion? Yes, it is he. Hector once told me that Molion is a mighty man with a sword. But Penthesilea is his equal! She's got a wrist of iron!"

Cassandra sneaked another look at her father. In Priam's eyes was a new alertness. She hurried on, as much for his benefit as for Keturah's. "She's beating down his guard!

She's stabbed him in the shoulder! Now she's cutting his throat! She's finishing him off!"

As Molion fell, a cheer rose from the wall. At last there was something to celebrate! As the Sauromatae queen, hardly pausing to catch her breath, fought like a demon against another Greek warrior, the excitement grew. Soon everyone on the wall was cheering, including Priam himself.

The Greeks could not believe what was happening. The Trojans, meanwhile, given heart by the women's valor, were fighting as they had not since Hector's death.

A Greek commander named Meges bellowed to a countryman, "What has come over these Trojans? I thought the bastards were beaten when Hector was killed."

Through clenched teeth his comrade replied, "It's the same thing that made them brave before: Achilles isn't here. The 'great' man is sleeping off a great drunk."

Suddenly Meges found himself facing three Trojans, and he had to give ground as he looked for a weak point in the line. His countryman, meanwhile, faced two women warriors. They were slim and delicately built, but their sword arms were extraordinarily skilled. He barely turned aside one of their deadly thrusts and parried another before taking a wound in the throat.

Penthesilea had killed fourteen men and wounded many more. The blood lust was upon her. With Clonia on one flank and Myrrha on the other, she engaged one Greek warrior after another. Suddenly on her left she saw Menippus, one of the biggest and strongest Greeks, advancing on Clonia. Clonia was a full head shorter than the hulking Menippus.

"Watch out!" Penthesilea cried out to her comrade. The queen tried to come to Clonia's aid, but three blocky Greeks materialized in front of her, blocking her advance.

Out of the corner of her eye she could see Clonia parrying the gigantic Menippus's every thrust and laughing merrily at his relative slowness and clumsiness.

The queen chuckled appreciatively and went back to her own fight, confident that Clonia could take care of herself. In a moment Penthesilea spotted a hole in her left-hand opponent's guard. Instantly she feinted high and lunged low, catching the man in the guts. He gasped and fell, stumbling backward. When he hit the ground he was dead, and his magnificent bronze war helmet with the horsehair plume rolled loose on the hard ground. The queen lifted it on the tip of her sword and held it high contemptuously for all to see. Then she flung it far and fought on.

As the wives of the Trojan warriors watched the Sauromatae outfighting their men, new feelings stirred in their hearts. At first they spoke in quiet voices so the princess Cassandra could not hear them:

"Isn't Penthesilea magnificent? She's better than any of the men on the field!"

"And yet she's just a mercenary," another marveled. "She's not fighting for her home or her family."

"Doesn't she shame us, the women of Troy, as thoroughly as she shames our husbands?" asked a third.

"What do you mean?" one of the other wives demanded.

"We ought to be down there fighting beside her!" a young wife said. "All of us have at least one kinsman or loved one to avenge. And if our men are defeated, what awaits us but rape and slavery? Shouldn't we be down there with sword and buckler, fighting for our homes and children, too?"

"But where should we get weapons? How could we—"

The answer was buried in the din that arose, as the women turned to one another and enthusiastically echoed the cry to battle.

Finally a rasping voice cut through the chaos. It was Theano's, a white-haired woman who was the eldest of the gathered wives. "And which of you 'warriors' plans to take on Achilles?" Her withering, cutting contempt elicited only silence. "I know. You think Penthesilea will take care of Achilles the Unkillable. So, then, who among you will challenge Agamemnon?"

There was silence still.

"And mighty Ajax, whose strength is almost equal to Achilles's own?"

No one volunteered.

"And which of you will match swords with wily Odysseus?" Theano snorted. "You, with no training in the swords? With puny muscles fit for the spindle and the sewing needle, not for the bearing of heavy swords? Your arms grow weary holding a child at your breast, yet you plan to wield a massive battle-ax? Ha! There's hardly a one of you other than Princess Cassandra who even knows how to sit a horse, much less wield a spear."

"But the women down there—" someone protested.

"Those women know how to fight! Penthesilea and her army have done nothing for years but fight. They're as out of place in the nursery as you would be on the field of war. But they're not threatening to cook dinner or nurse a child; so, unlike you, they won't make fools of themselves." She paused.

No one disputed her words.

Then she continued, pointing a bony finger at the women. "I'm ashamed of all of you, sounding as if you didn't have a lick of sense! Leave war to our men! They're still unconquered! Things have not come to such a pass that they need help from the likes of us."

III

Myrrha scanned the ranks of the Greeks surrounding her. She feared that Phorbus might suddenly loom before her. What would she do if that happened? Would she kill him? She honestly did not know. In sight of the queen and the others, she could not spare him or refuse to fight. And Phorbus, in front of his comrades, could not turn his back on her.

She looked right and left but could see no sign of him. She pressed forward to stand beside Penthesilea and engaged the soldier threatening the queen's left flank. Myrrha felt confident and strong. As long as Phorbus did not appear on the field, new strength seemed to flow into her arms and legs with every new opponent she confronted.

"Die, Greek, die!" she sang out in a strong, clear voice. She lunged, and her blade caught her adversary in the soft place beneath the rib cage and sank to the hilt.

Beyond Penthesilea, Clonia and the huge Greek Menippus had fought to a standstill. Now, however, Menippus seemed to gather new power, and he counterattacked, driving the small woman back. She retreated but remained alert for an opportunity. When he lunged at her and missed, she found her chance at last. His sword held high, he had left an opening between his arm and body armor. Quickly she parried his thrust and followed through with a strong thrust of her own. Her sword slipped between the first two ribs and caught him in the lung. Menippus fell heavily, the blood bubbling out of his mouth. Clonia pulled her blade free and hacked at his exposed neck, burying the point in his throat.

From nearby, Podarces saw his friend Menippus fall. He loosed a mighty roar of rage. With a single wild swing he nearly decapitated one woman in front of him, and his backswing disarmed another woman he had been fighting. As the woman scrambled in the dirt for her fallen sword, Podarces charged through the crowd toward Clonia.

Myrrha watched all this and wanted to help Clonia, but she herself was suddenly in trouble. A new Greek warrior had engaged her, and his hands were lightning quick and his wrists strong. She suspected that he had been instructed by the same person who had trained Phorbus. She could get no advantage on him, and he drove her back and back.

She unexpectedly heard Penthesilea's voice: "Let me take him!"

The queen appeared, her eyes gleaming through the holes of her helmet. She pressed the attack, forcing the Greek to defend himself.

Myrrha stood openmouthed, watching the queen's offensive. Penthesilea seemed possessed, and for an instant Myrrha believed the dream the queen of the

Sauromatae had told her about. It was as if Ares himself animated her arm.

Beyond Penthesilea, however, Clonia was in trouble. Mighty Podarces was beating down her guard, forcing her on the defensive, and driving her back up a slope. His rage and anguish at Menippus's death fueled his strength. The path behind Clonia was strewn with bodies, and she was in great danger of tripping over them.

"Clonia, be careful behind you!" Myrrha shouted.

Distracted, Clonia took her eyes off Podarces for a moment. It was all the time the big man needed to lunge and bury his sword in her.

She screamed and fell. Myrrha pressed forward, fighting past one Greek after another, but it was too late. Even Penthesilea, stepping in and slashing at Podarces, could not reach Clonia in time. The last blow was a smashing one to her temple, which broke the woman's skull and killed her instantly.

"Damn you all!" Myrrha screamed at the Greeks. "Damn all you bastards!"

Taking her place beside her queen, she fought more ferociously than ever before.

The death of Clonia gave new heart to the Greeks. Until now they almost believed that the women warriors led charmed lives. Or had their misplaced gallantry simply made them reluctant to fight and kill women?

Now, with the first Sauromatae dead, the spell was broken. The men began to fight in earnest. One Greek warrior, nicked by a woman's sword stroke, let out a howl and then killed his opponent with a single fierce stab through the eye slits in her helmet. She died the moment the sword penetrated the core of her brain.

Bremusa had the misfortune to take on a Greek commander named Idomeneus. She was no match for him at all, and his strong wrist plucked the sword from her hand and tossed it high in the air. She blinked and took a thrust in the throat.

The women Euandra and Thermodoa died, then Derimachia and Alcibea at the same instant, with a single swing of a Greek blade. The tide seemed to have turned. The women's army was being chopped to bits by the furious Greeks. Penthesilea fought on undaunted, with Myrrha at her side. By the end of the day the queen had killed forty-eight men and wounded more than she could count.

When at last the armies withdrew from the field for the night, the queen was a hero, cheered by the citizens of Troy. Even Priam joined in the rejoicing and called for a feast in her honor.

Despite the accolades heaped on her, Penthesilea was saddened. Looking around, seeing the holes in her ranks, she knew that her own triumph had been achieved at the expense of more than half her army. Twelve of her most trusted lieutenants and captains were dead. Of the inner circle of leaders, only Myrrha was alive and unharmed. Thus, instead of retiring to bathe and change for the celebratory dinner, she mounted the walls and called out to the Greeks as they straggled home, carrying the bodies of their dead.

"There you go, skulking home like the jackals you are! Today you have paid for the grief you brought to Priam! Tomorrow you will pay for the lives of my women who fell today! I challenge you to bring me your best. Bring me the wily Odysseus! Bring me the mighty Ajax. And above all bring me the coward Achilles, who stayed away today because he dared not measure his strength and will against mine!"

Her words carried. The Greeks heard, as did the Trojans. Both armies were amazed by the queen's audacity. Penthesilea had challenged the will of the gods.

Cassandra and Keturah were among the last to come down from the city wall. Only one other Trojan noble, with a pensive look on his face, remained there, studying the emptying battlefield.

The princess strode to his side and viewed him with revulsion. "Well, Paris, I hope you're proud of yourself! While you, alone of the Trojan men, hid up here shooting arrows from cover like a coward, your place was taken by women! Women who fought like the man you're not!"

He showed no sign of having taken offense at the contempt in Cassandra's voice. He stood and slowly stretched. "You're not only a scolding fishwife, Cassandra, you're also a fool. The Greeks cut the Sauromatae to pieces. By day's end, Sister, the women's army could hardly even be said to exist."

"You demean your betters, women braver than you."

He shrugged and picked up his bow. "Penthesilea had her moment," he allowed, "and I don't begrudge her this night of glory. But the day of reckoning will come sooner than she thinks."

"What do you mean?" Cassandra demanded. "She was magnificent! Are you suggesting it was all a fluke?"

Paris made a wry face. "You heard her challenge. Can't you imagine what's going to happen when Achilles hears about it?"

"Curse Achilles!"

"I entirely agree. I don't like the man, either. That's why, one of these days, when all the bragging and blustering is finished and Penthesilea is dead and buried, *I'm* going to kill him."

"You? Don't make me laugh!"

"Of all the people in Troy, Sister, I'm the one most likely to kill him. I don't make myself vulnerable to his terrible wrath by issuing stupid challenges."

His words infuriated Cassandra. She shook her fist and glared at him. "You *don't* fight him. That's how you remain invulnerable. You just stand here and shoot your arrows."

"Exactly, Sister."

"Don't call me sister, you . . . peasant bastard!"

"My bloodlines are as good as yours. And you know I'm right: The man who kills Achilles will be the man who refuses to fight *his* fight but chooses his own ground and makes his own rules."

"Rules that have nothing to do with honor!"

"I spit on honor. It is imperative that we kill Achilles and break the back of the Greek assault."

"And how are you planning to manage that?"

He smiled. "Wait and see."

Phorbus had lost sight of Myrrha and was worried
about her. He had seen her comrades fall, so now he
accompanied the litter bearers into the field. A light evening mist had arisen, covering the area. Every rise looked
like an island in the midst of a ghostly sea. He went from
one bloody corpse to the next. Whenever he saw one of
the fallen women, his heart stopped as he bent over and
raised the visor of the helmet. Then, each time, he breathed
a sigh of relief when the face was a stranger's.

Suddenly a woman warrior appeared before him. She
was covered with dust and the blood of the men she had
killed. Her helmet was off, but she grasped a sword. As he
approached, he could see that her face was wet with tears.

"Myrrha!" he cried, running forward, his arms outstretched. "Thanks to all the gods! I had feared you were—"

"Stand back or I'll kill you!"

"You can't mean that. I came searching for you, praying
that you'd lived through the day."

"Stay away," she warned with a menacing wave of
her sword. "Go, or I will kill you. You are my enemy
now."

He stood rooted to the ground, staring at her in
horror.

She waved one hand at the bodies surrounding her.
Tears streamed down her filthy face, leaving tracks. "My
friends. My sisters. All dead. Greeks killed them! Greeks
like you!"

"But I didn't fight. I was back at the camp."

"Then you are coward, worse than the killers who did
this."

Her shoulders were bowed with hatred and grief as
she stalked off into the mist and vanished from his view.
Phorbus felt as if some demon had drained all the strength
and hope from his body.

IV

Within an hour of the battle's end, Achilles heard three different accounts of Penthesilea's challenge, each more heavily embroidered than the last.

"Let the ugly bitch rave on like a harpy whose time of the month has come," he said. "Tomorrow will be time enough for her comeuppance. I don't intend to waste my breath on her or to think about her until I've had a good night's sleep. Then we'll see about those insults and threats."

His manservant placed a bowl of grapes by Achilles's elbow, but the bowl was sent flying a second later by a powerful kick. The headache that had accompanied his hangover was gone, but his stomach was still queasy, and he was in a foul mood.

"Is there anything else I can bring you, my lord?" the servant asked, staring nervously at the overturned bowl.

"Shine my greaves," Achilles said, flinging the heavy leg armor at the man with such force that it knocked him over. "I want," Achilles shouted at him, "the bitch to be able to see her own face in the armor before she dies."

In the camp of the Amazons, Penthesilea and Myrrha, her new second-in-command, surveyed their losses. The army had been cut in half and could no longer support the entire left flank of the attack.

"What shall we do?" Myrrha asked, looking at bodies laid out around the fires. "The Trojans want to integrate us into their force."

"Over my dead body," Penthesilea said, her eyes flashing. "I'll never allow it. There has to be another solution."

"But what?"

"I don't know." Suddenly she smiled. "Yes, I do. Summon the Nubian commander to me."

Odysseus returned to camp, cursing. He limped past half a dozen ranking princelings without acknowledging their existence. He snarled at a group of exhausted sol-

diers who crossed his path. He cursed a camp follower
who was doing laundry.

Finding Phorbus in a glum mood did not help
Odysseus's disposition. "What are you moping for?" he
asked.

"Myrrha blames me for the whole thing."

"For what? Did Achilles kill her mistress?"

"No, no. Penthesilea was magnificent, and our illustrious Achilles never left his tent. But our army finally cut
her unit to shreds. And the Nubians never even joined the
fray. Myrrha's the only Sauromatae officer who survived."

"Someday you'll realize how lucky you are. Who wants
a woman with a body as hard as a man's? Women are
supposed to be soft and yielding."

"Don't make sport of me."

"I'm not. I'm just telling you to give thanks to the
gods. Ow! I twisted my ankle coming home in the dark.
I'm not going to be fit to fight for days."

"How did your business go? What about the master
builder you were going to see?"

"I think he more or less understands what I want.
Didn't Iri teach you a bit about boatbuilding?"

"Theon was the boatbuilder in the family, but Iri did
teach me a few things about construction. Why? Is this
fellow building you a boat?"

Odysseus chuckled. "He's building me a way to get
home, all right. But it's no boat."

And that was all he would say about his plan.

In the morning, when the Trojan forces deployed, the
left flank consisted of an odd mixture of the survivors of
the women's troops, in their armor, and the Nubians,
towering and naked.

Word had come through Penthesilea's spies that Achilles had heard and accepted her challenge.

She called Myrrha to her side. "I know you are looking forward to your first command, but indulge me, my
sister, and stay by my side while I fight the great Greek
warrior—even if it means carrying my spears."

Myrrha did not let her disappointment show. She had

hoped to distinguish herself today as a commander of troops, and now her mistress was asking her to act as a body servant. "As you wish, my queen."

Odysseus's ankle had not improved during the night, so he had not suited up for battle. Phorbus and he stood on a hillock overlooking the Scamander River, watching the two sides prepare for war.

"I can't see enough from here," Odysseus complained. "You've got two good legs. Climb that tree, will you, to get a better view?"

Phorbus climbed quickly up the tree and settled himself on a large limb, his legs dangling.

"I can see Myrrha," he called down. "That's strange. . . . She's not commanding a troop. She seems to be joining the queen."

"Too bad," Odysseus remarked. "The closer she is to Penthesilea when she meets Achilles, the smaller her chance of surviving the day."

"Then you don't think Penthesilea . . ."

"Anything can happen, my friend. She might win. And the sun can suddenly start moving backward. And the birds can start flying upside down. And you can get a job designing swords for the king of Egypt."

"Odysseus!"

"Just don't get your hopes up, Phorbus."

Then the drums began to beat, and the armies marched forward.

Achilles and Ajax had divided the enemy line before them so that now Ajax faced the main Trojan force, while Achilles stood opposite the combined Sauromatae and Nubian forces. As the armies came toward each other, Achilles raced ahead, outdistancing his troops and reaching the Nubian lines before any of his men could catch up with him.

Letting out a powerful battle cry, he engaged two huge Nubians simultaneously, and with his first sword stroke showed both foreigners how he had earned his reputation. The two Nubians were a full head taller than he, and their reach far exceeded his. Yet he parried one man's spear thrust with his shield and slipped under the other man's guard to plant his spear in the Nubian's stomach for the first kill of the day.

The other Nubian pressed the attack, clutching his massive sword with both hands and flailing at the Greek. Achilles nimbly avoided each stroke. When the Nubian stopped for a moment to gather his strength, Achilles flicked up the visor of his helmet. All could see his face; all could see his strange smile. Was it sheer happiness at being in combat? Or was it the madness of blood lust? Standing there, he was mocking the Nubian, waiting for him to recover. The Nubian lunged again with an infuriated roar, but Achilles sidestepped and swung his sword low and fast. The Nubian fell writhing to the ground, his left foot almost severed from the ankle.

The proud Greek preened himself as he stared at the fallen Nubian. Tall and powerful, his muscles straining against the skin, his limbs perfectly formed and beautiful, Achilles indeed seemed sent by the gods to bring death and destruction to his hapless foes.

He was about to move forward and kill the wounded Nubian when he heard a piercing war cry. He looked up to see a slim warrior in gleaming armor hurl a spear at him. Instinctively he raised his shield, and the spear glanced off it. He knew immediately who his opponent was. Although the queen's face was hidden by her helmet, his men had given him vivid descriptions of Penthesilea's armor.

As he watched, a woman at her side handed her another spear; Penthesilea took aim and launched it at him. This time it fell short.

Achilles studied her for a moment as if he were evaluating a horse. Then he guffawed. "Woman! How did you summon the courage to fight me? I am the greatest of all the Greek warriors! Even the mighty Hector trembled and fell before me! Have the gods stolen your reason?"

In answer she reached for yet another throwing spear.

Without another word he hurled a lance at her. He

had never aimed straighter nor cast with more power. The
object became a blur to the human eye.

The lance smashed into Penthesilea with a sickening
thud, splintering bone and sinew and flesh as it entered
above her missing breast. It had sliced through her body
armor as if it were leather, not bronze.

The spear dropped from her hand. Her eyes glazed
over. Yet she refused to fall. She stood wavering, impaled,
glaring at him, trying desperately to find the strength to
draw her battle-ax and continue the fight.

But like a lion who falls on a wounded gazelle, Achilles ran and leapt on her, screaming his shattering war cry.
He snatched up one of the queen's own spears and ran her
through.

Myrrha looked on with horror, unable to believe her
eyes. No man could have such strength. At last her soldier's reflexes took over. Grasping a spear, she ran toward
Achilles and flung the weapon from a distance of merely
five feet.

He deflected it easily with his shield. She stared
uncomprehendingly at the now useless spear on the ground,
then she looked up at him. His face was a mask of bore-
dom and contempt. He came toward her, his sword held
out in front of him, the bright, deadly point circling slowly
as it homed in on her throat.

"No!" Phorbus screamed. His whole body was
trembling. The sweat on his palms made it hard for him to
remain steady on the tree limb.

"Come down, lad," Odysseus called up gently. "There's
nothing you can do. It's over now. It's all over."

Achilles stepped over the fallen Myrrha as if she were
a sack of grain. He walked to the motionless body of
Penthesilea and spat on her chest. "Where are your boasts
now, you bitch? I should take your pretty armor and leave
you to stink and rot and draw the dogs and crows!"

As Greek soldiers created a protective ring around
him, Achilles bent to pull off Penthesilea's helmet. When
he did, her hair spilled forth, and for the first time he saw

the face of the woman he had killed. He blanched. His
eyes opened wide, and he let out a startled gasp.

"She's beautiful," he said in a trembling whisper. "As
beautiful as a goddess."

Her hair was the color of honey. It lay softly against
the sides of her face. The pain and shock had left her eyes,
but still open, they seemed to be staring at some distant
point . . . to be watching something beautiful, something
calming. Her exquisite skin, now pale, was without blemish.

Achilles knelt, driving the point of his sword deep
into the ground beside him. Then he wept.

V

As the leaderless women's army fell back in disarray,
the Greek units poured into the gap. Achilles, however,
still surrounded by his bodyguard, remained kneeling in
front of the woman he had slain, tears streaming down his
face, hypnotized by her beauty and daring. He cursed
himself for having killed her instead of taking her to bed.

Whereas the Sauromatae had failed, the Nubians
wrought havoc among the Greeks, hacking away with their
primitive but surprisingly effective weapons. Greek after
Greek fell under the flashing sword of the Nubian commander, whose skill was more than equal to any challenge.

As the Nubian giant advanced through the gap his
men had cut in the Greek line, he came upon the detachment from Pylos, where old King Nestor—whose friends
had unsuccessfully urged him not to take the field—stood,
flanked by two of his comrades in arms. The old man
gaped, thunderstruck at the prowess of the huge Nubian
commander, and missed the opportunity to escape.

The Nubian, as Priam's nephew, was quick to recognize Nestor because of the distinctive armor worn by all
the chieftains and kings among the Greeks. The Nubian
bared his teeth in a savage grin.

The sight of a ferocious warrior would have caused
many a younger man to turn and run; but old Nestor was

ready to die if the gods willed it. He stood his ground,
even when the Nubian, loosing a savage cry, killed first
one, then the other, of his bodyguards.

The old man knew that death was near, but he smiled
and assumed a fighting stance, shield forward, spear at the
ready, and his skinny, arthritic legs · bent in a fighting
crouch. "Here I am!" he cried.

The foreign commander looked down at Nestor—tiny,
aged, and feeble looking—and marveled that the old man
opposed him. He spoke in a deep voice: "Nestor, I can't
fight you. You're older than my father. Fall back. Don't
make me kill you."

"You have killed my son," Nestor said calmly. "I will
sell my life dearly." He looked around him. "Unless there
is a hero on our side willing to take my place."

As the battle raged around him, Achilles remained
kneeling over the dead woman, marveling at her beauty,
at the calm and peace of her lifeless face. His reverie was
disrupted by Thersites, the ugliest man in the Greek
army, who came lumbering past. A string of insults issued
from his misshapen mouth.

"Look at Achilles! The great hero! Ha! Mourning after
a dead whore, one who made sport of him before a thousand people! But now that he's killed her, he weeps and
pretends he'd rather have bedded her!"

His words roused Achilles from Penthesilea's side.
That this hunchback, with his twisted nose, pockmarked
face, and perverted mind, should speak thusly was intolerable. He jumped up, sprang forward, and struck at Thersites
with his bare fist.

Thersites half turned in an attempt to dodge the
blow, but his movement only made the punch more deadly;
it fell on his temple and crushed his skull. The hunchback
tottered for a moment and then collapsed.

A Greek soldier knelt over him. "He's dead, sir," the
young man said in amazement. "You've killed him with a
single blow, bare-handed."

"So perish all who would speak ill of Penthesilea,"
Achilles vowed. Then he grabbed two spears from a trooper

in his bodyguard and trotted off to where old King Nestor faced the Nubian giant.

The deaths of Penthesilea and Myrrha threw Cassandra into dark despair. Glumly she watched the Nubian giant and Achilles circling each other and feinting, both unwilling to make the first move and expose himself. Nestor, having been replaced by Achilles, tottered off to safety.

"It's all over," Cassandra moaned. "Penthesilea was our last hope, Keturah."

The blind woman stood by miserably, not knowing how to console her friend. "I'm sure our army will rally, my lady," she said lamely. "They haven't let us down so far."

Cassandra looked around and saw Paris standing, as usual, at the parapet, an arrow nocked but his bow unbent. "How dare you hide up here when even women are willing to die for Troy!" she shrieked at him. "How a coward like you can show his face is beyond my comprehension!"

Paris smiled. "Let anyone get within range of my bow, and you'll see who's the coward and who's the hero." He did not take his eyes off the battlefield below. "If only the Nubian would fall back to the city walls and let me get a good shot in . . ."

Cassandra sighed so deeply, it sounded like a sob.

"My lady," Keturah said, "the prince might be right. If someone were to kill Achilles, perhaps the Greeks would go away at last. Iri always used to tell me—"

Enraged, Cassandra turned on her. "Damn your Iri! He's dead! We need a live hero! Not a dead fool!"

Then she wished with all her heart she could call back her words—anything to take the stricken look off her friend's face.

The battle between Achilles and the Nubian commander pitted two men of unbelievable strength and dexterity. Each warrior quickly inflicted a superficial wound on the other, but then the confrontation became stalemated. Time after time they rushed together, only to wind

up spear to sword, unable to drive the other back. Finally
Achilles used his sword, but the stroke missed his adversary's head by a mere hand span. The Nubian giant's spear
glanced off Achilles's armor and fell to the ground.

Then came a lull in the larger battle, and the two
sides, exhausted, withdrew to watch their champions battle each other.

Now both were armed with swords, oversized and of
great weight. Blades clashed, sparks flew . . . and yet no
new blood was spilled. The sinews of the two warriors
stood out in their muscular flesh, like ropes that had been
twisted to the breaking point.

With startling suddenness, the end came. Priam's
nephew attempted a maneuver that had worked for him
many times before—feinting high only to lunge low. But
he had never faced an adversary with the blinding speed
and faultless instincts of Achilles. The Greek leapt lightly
and jumped over the stroke. The moment he landed, he
whirled and threw his weight behind the sword that he
plunged into the Nubian's stomach.

The foreign giant staggered backward, pulling the
sword from Achilles's hand. He stood swaying for a long
moment, but he was a dead man, and both of them knew
it. He tried to speak and could not. He pitched forward
and landed at Achilles's feet.

The Greek stared down at him for a long time, kicking him contemptuously once in a while. He circled the
body, once, twice, then *three* times, and then suddenly
loosed a ferocious cry of triumph, which seemed to bounce
against the heavens. He wheeled toward the watching
enemy and addressed them:

"Trojans, you sent your best warriors against me, and
I have killed them all. You sent me Hector, and I slew
him. You have enlisted the aid of two heroes from distant
lands, and they, too, have died. I have killed them both in
one day!"

He yanked the bloody sword from the Nubian's body
and waved it high.

"Hear me, Trojans!" he cried, marching toward the
walls. "It doesn't matter to me whether you open the

gates or I have to tear them off their hinges. Before we're all a week older, I'll be inside Troy."

He looked up and saw the defenders' stricken faces. Their fear filled his heart with vengeful joy. He walked along the perimeter of the wall, shouting curses and insults at the citizens above him.

"Cowards! Weaklings! Has it come to this? Must Trojans hire foreigners to fight for them? Foreigners—and women." He laughed raucously. "Women? Weak creatures who should have stayed in the nursery!"

From atop the wall a bowstring sang. Achilles staggered and looked down in disbelief. A Trojan arrow protruded from his heel.

He looked up to the walls. Prince Paris saluted him with elaborate formality. The smile on Paris's handsome face was as cold as the winter snows.

VI

With a snarl of rage Achilles reached down and yanked the arrow from his foot. He straightened and, staring up at Paris, broke the bolt in two, then tossed the pieces away.

"The bee stings the lion," Achilles roared, "and then flies away." He raised his bloody sword in defiance. "Yet the lion remains a lion, and the bee remains a bee."

Paris smiled a little too sweetly, which enraged Achilles all the more. He turned away from the city walls to face the Trojan and Nubian soldiers still in the field. "Enough of buzzing vermin! Send me *men* to fight! Surely Troy still has some men brave enough to rise to a challenge!"

From the Trojan ranks stepped one man. "I am Orythaon," he said boldly "friend of Hector's."

After a moment of pained shock on hearing Cassandra's words, Keturah felt her way along the wall to the stairs. Cassandra walked beside her. "Keturah! Please, darling! I didn't mean to speak to you that way! Forgive me! I'd do anything in the world to keep from hurting you."

Keturah felt her way down the hall. She refused to face Cassandra or speak to her.

Watching the expression of grief and suppressed rage on Keturah's face, Cassandra realized that she had alienated the only friend she had ever had and might never be forgiven. The loss seemed too much to bear.

"Please, Keturah," she sobbed, pulling at her friend's robe until the cloth ripped. The sight of the torn cloth caught at her heart. She felt worthless and brutal. Keturah owned almost nothing in the world. To ruin one of her last few possessions was the act, Cassandra realized with horror, of a selfish, hateful bitch.

She caught at Keturah's arm. The blind woman dutifully stopped but refused to turn. "Keturah! I'm sorry. I'll give you a new robe. I'll give you anything you want. Only please don't hate me. If you hate me, I'll die. You're the only person in the world I love! Can't you forgive me? I never meant to do you any harm. I never meant to insult Iri. Please!"

Keturah's sightless eyes stared straight ahead. She had retreated into some safe place where no one could hurt her again. "May I go now, my lady?" she asked in a toneless voice. "May I return to my room?"

Phorbus was still perched in the tree. From this vantage point he watched as Achilles, having killed Hector's friend Orythaon with a sweeping stroke that pierced the Trojan's temple, hacked his way through the next rank of defenders.

"Odysseus!" Phorbus called. "Achilles doesn't seem to be hurt. Now he's killed Hipponous. It's true: Achilles is invulnerable!"

Odysseus expelled a disgusted sigh. "He'll be dead within a moment or two. They can start making his coffin. He's already a corpse. Don't you remember what happened to Iri? Paris poisons all his arrows. You've seen that damned cowardly peacock shooting from atop the city wall, not risking his own neck." He spat on the ground. "Trust Achilles and his accursed pride to do something stupid, like wandering within the range of Paris's bow."

"But—"

"Watch him, Phorbus. He's probably slowing already. The coldness will creep into his limbs, starting with his feet, then working slowly up his legs. In a minute or two he'll have trouble walking."

"Look!" Phorbus exclaimed. "He's stopped. His legs are wobbling!"

Odysseus spat again. "Just as I predicted. Now I've got to go out and fight, in spite of my limp. And all for the sake of a stupid son of a bitch who won't stay out of range of—"

"Go out there? Why?"

"Don't be an ass, Phorbus. The Trojans will try to grab Achilles's body so they can do the same barbarous things to him that he did to Hector. They'll want to drag him behind a horse, then nail his corpse to a wall. They're committed to trying, and no matter what we think of the whole ridiculous mess, we're honor bound to try to stop them. Grab your sword and come on."

"You want *me* to save his body? Not on your life! He killed Myrrha!"

"It's the proper thing. Come on. Don't let it bother you—any of it. Maybe I'll tell you the secret I've been keeping. It won't cure your pain, but you may draw some half-baked comfort from it nevertheless."

Paris watched Achilles die, but the Trojan prince felt surprisingly devoid of triumph. Nor did he feel any relief that the Trojans who had blamed him for starting the war would now thank him for helping to end it. Paris knew in his heart that his abduction of Helen from Sparta was only an excuse for the invasion; the Greeks had always wanted to have Troy. It was a rich city that controlled a vital trade route.

At first, Paris watched almost emotionlessly as the poisoned arrow did its work. The deadly potion was acting as it always had, so Achilles was dying by inches. The whiplike arms were losing their resiliency; the farseeing eyes were blurring; the powerful legs, which had made Achilles the fleetest of all men, were trembling.

When Achilles finally collapsed to the ground and the crested bronze helmet rolled crazily off and bounced along the field, Paris experienced a strange sadness. It was as if he were watching the death of all men. It was as if he had played a part in murdering the qualities that both Greeks and Trojans revered: beauty, grace, speed, loyalty, and courage. He turned quickly away, confused.

The mighty Ajax was the first to reach the body of Achilles in the shadow of the walls, and he had to hack his way through half a dozen Trojans to get there. In a rage fueled by grief, he picked up a fist-sized rock and hurled it with deadly accuracy at Paris.

The Trojan prince was looking the other way when the rock struck him, crushing his helmet and knocking it from his head. When he fell out of sight behind the wall, Ajax laughed derisively and swung his sword wildly.

By this time Odysseus had limped to Ajax's side and taken up his position in the defensive circle around Achilles's body. As there seemed to be no need for him, Phorbus wandered around the field, looking for his beloved Myrrha. A bare fifty yards from the circle lay the Sauromatae warrior.

Myrrha! Her helmet had fallen off—or perhaps some Greek had taken it—and her lovely face was perfect in death. To his eyes it looked as if she had just drifted off to sleep, and it was all he could do not to bend over her slim body and awaken her with a kiss.

Myrrha! For the first time in Phorbus's life, he wanted to die—anything to join her!

"Myrrha! Come back!" he whispered.

But her brave spirit had departed, and part of him was gone with her, just as a piece of his soul had disappeared when Iri had been killed. He was not a whole man anymore. What would be left of him, he wondered, by the time he was Odysseus's age? Would he be a burned-out hulk with no feelings?

He was still standing over his lover's body when Odysseus, who had been replaced in the circle by younger, fitter men, limped his way over, a sour scowl on his grizzled face.

"Come on, friend," he said in as gentle a tone as he could muster. "Leave her to her own people. They'll want to honor her according to their own customs. She'd want it that way." Odysseus, seeing her perfect face, allowed himself a moment of weary wisdom. "There indeed was a waste. But she lived by war. You couldn't have pried her away from it, no matter how hard you tried."

Phorbus tried to speak, but his voice failed. He cleared his constricted throat loudly and wiped his eyes.

"Phorbus," Odysseus said quietly, "forgive me for doubting your feelings for her. In a few hours, you and your woman experienced a greater, truer, more profound love than do some couples who stay together for many years."

"Don't apologize, my friend," Phorbus said brokenly. "You are right. It is all a waste—so sad, so stupid."

Odysseus gripped his friend's arm. "Now you've seen what war brings—nothing but loss. Are you fed up with it? Ready for an end to it?"

Phorbus looked at him with eyes full of shock and hurt. Then he nodded.

"Then come along with me," Odysseus urged. "I'll tell you what I'm going to do to end the war."

"I don't understand," Phorbus said. "I thought that Achilles's death would have ended the war."

"No, my friend. Nothing will release us but total victory, and that requires getting inside Troy."

"What are you up to?" Phorbus asked, confused.

"Come down to the village, and I'll show you. If this doesn't work, nothing will."

PART
FIVE

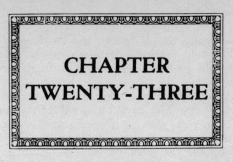

CHAPTER TWENTY-THREE

Damascus

The sound of wagon wheels jolted Luti from a deep sleep. She sat up and looked around. The first rays of light were filtering through the open-air hostel where she and Occa had spent the night. But the Bedouin was gone. She called his name, but there was no response.

She was about to call his name again, when she sheepishly remembered that he could not hear or speak.

Around her, the city of Damascus was awakening to another day. Food vendors had already begun their strange piercing yells in languages she could not understand. Luti had never been in a place where so many different languages were spoken. It was bewildering.

She was hungry and wanted to wash, but she could not do anything until Occa came back. Why had he vanished? She grew furious, but then her anger cooled with the realization that if it was not for the strange Bedouin, she never would have survived the desert trek. He had watched over her and made certain she had food and drink.

As the morning progressed, the sounds of the city became more intense. This was nothing like Ur; Damascus was bedlam, and she was glad that they would be leaving for the coast when Occa got back. She wanted to be near water.

Occa suddenly appeared in front of her, frightening

her, once again, by his bizarre and threatening appearance. She could never become used to the silver ornaments that dangled from one side of his face. They always made her cringe.

He was clearly excited and motioned persistently for her to follow him. She started to say that they must leave for the coast now, but she realized again the futility of trying to explain anything to a deaf man.

Frustrated, she gathered her belongings and reluctantly followed him. They walked through a marketplace, then through some residential areas, and finally emerged in a very old section of the city. Ramshackle huts and stables had been thrown up. She could hear the sounds of blacksmiths' hammers and could smell the dung of pack animals.

Occa led her to a low stable, which was gloomy and damp. After holding up his hand to signal that she should wait outside, he vanished, then reappeared leading the two most beautiful horses she had ever laid eyes on. One was dappled, the other pure white. They were long limbed and slender, and their necks arched with power.

Luti was bewildered. Why was he showing her these horses? She tried to indicate that she did not understand. In reply, his face broke into an enormous smile and he signaled to her until she understood that they now owned these horses.

"Beautiful, aren't they?" asked a deep, mellifluous voice from the shadows.

Luti swiveled and stared at the speaker, who walked leisurely to the horses and patted them gently on the flanks.

"There's been some mistake," Luti said to the horse dealer.

"Well, your friend did get a very good deal," the fellow acknowledged.

"But he wasn't supposed to buy horses," she explained, desperate.

What kind of lunatic had Drak stuck her with? Luti wondered. If Drak had wanted them to buy horses in

Damascus, he would have told her. And where had the Bedouin gotten the money for these magnificent animals?

She snatched the horses' reins from Occa and handed them to the dealer. "Please give his money back. He cannot hear or speak, and he cannot know what he was doing."

The horse dealer's eyes opened wide with fear. Luti turned in reaction to see that her Bedouin protector had drawn the long, curved sword from the scabbard on his back and was pointing it threateningly at both of them.

"Talk to him!" the horse dealer pleaded with Luti. "Tell him to put it away. Keep the horses!"

"He doesn't hear anything you say," she reminded.

"Well, do something, woman!"

Luti slowly raised her hands, tentatively smiled at Occa, then dropped the reins to show him that they would keep the horses.

Occa stepped toward them, the sword point moving slowly back and forth. Never had he looked so ferocious. His eyes gleamed against his blackened face; his silver ornaments jangled against his cheek. Then, just as suddenly as he had drawn his weapon, he lowered it and began to draw on the damp ground outside the stable.

"It's a map," the horse dealer said.

"Of what?" Luti asked.

"I can't make it out yet. Are you traveling to a specific destination?"

"Yes," Luti replied. "We are going to the coast and then south to Gaza. . . ."

Finished, Occa stepped back and grinned proudly. He pointed his blade at the horses and then back to the map he had etched in the ground.

In general Luti understood what he was trying to convey: The horses were needed for their journey. She moved closer to the map and stared down at it. She had no idea what it signified. She turned to the horse dealer and asked for help.

He knelt and studied it. "Well," he said, "he is going to Gaza, but he's taking a different route. He's moving down the east bank of the Jordan to the Sea of Salt, around the southern tip of the Sea of Salt, into the Wilderness of Judea, and then west to Gaza. It is a much more difficult journey than the coastal route, but it may get you to your destination more quickly."

Luti stared up at Occa, who did not return her gaze. She saw him now in a new light. She had thought that Drak had sent him along merely as a bodyguard, but now it appeared he had been given his own set of instructions by the elderly mathematician. Perhaps, she thought, Drak had given her instructions to take the coastal journey to Gaza only as a deception . . . that he had commanded Occa to change the course of the journey because their mission was so dangerous, it was necessary to throw people off the track.

Then another thought came to her, making her feel sick with dread. What if Drak had enemies who would stop at nothing to obtain one of the secret chariots? And what if Occa was *their* man? She felt the muzzle of one of the horses burrowing into her shoulder. She turned and scratched the horse's neck and stared into its doleful eyes. At least the horse was not frightened!

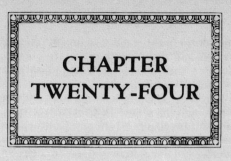

CHAPTER TWENTY-FOUR

Canaan

"Someone has been asking about you," Kish warned quietly.

Pepi did not reply. He picked up the wooden bowl and drank some of the milk. It was sour. He slid it across the inn table toward Kish. It was not that Pepi did not trust Kish; he trusted all conspirators who were recommended by Barak in the plot against Jabin. It was just that this particular fellow made him nervous. He was so obviously a hunted man, his shoulders thrust out, eyes squinting, hand always near the dagger. Kish was a frightened patriot, and they were the most dangerous kind.

"He said," Kish continued, "that he is of your family."

"Did he give a name?" Pepi asked.

"Theon. He also said that he wouldn't be in the valley for long . . . that he is leaving soon for the Great Sea."

"Theon? I've never met him."

Kish's eyes darted around the inn. "Let's get on with our business."

Pepi suppressed his curiosity concerning Theon's unexpected visit; there were much more urgent matters at hand. "Tell me, Kish, have you seen—or heard anything of—Shemida, Joshua's old assistant?"

Kish's brows furrowed. "Shemida? Why, yes. He was involved with the revolt against the Moabites."

"Then please get a message to him for me: Tell him to go see Deborah the prophetess, up near—"

"I know where to find Deborah," Kish retorted angrily, as if Pepi had insulted him.

"Listen, Kish. You seem not to trust me completely. We can't get anything done when there's no trust. Believe me, I'm in the revolt up to my neck. Sure, I have been avoiding the Israelites for a long time. But if Jabin can be brought down, I'm going to be the man to help and by any means necessary."

"Forgive me," Kish said quickly. "I have been too suspicious. Living a fugitive's existence, continually being hunted by the Hazorite guards, makes me very wary. Sometimes I find myself not trusting even Barak. Anyway, tell me: How large an army do you think it would take to defeat Sisera's units?"

"Deborah says ten thousand troops—if we can count on the participation of those who defeated the Moabites."

"Ah, Ehud, Zuriel, and that lot."

"Yes. They've got the captured Moabite weapons, but supposedly not enough to arm us all. That's why I need to find Shemida. He can coordinate the effort. And while he's recruiting the various tribe members, I can make a deal for arms."

A voice from behind them suddenly spoke up. "Arms? Did I heard my kinsman ask about arms?"

Pepi wheeled around. "Theon?"

"Yes! You must be Pepi!"

The two kinsmen embraced and then clapped each other on the back happily.

"I've been looking for you," Theon said. "I heard about your arrival from the caravan brokers. I'd been wanting to see how you're doing. I'm sorry it's taken me such a long time to meet you, Pepi."

"Much too long," Pepi agreed. "But the fault is half mine. Boats travel in two directions, you know."

"Did I hear you mention arms dealing?" Theon asked. "I never pass up an opportunity to talk business."

"You heard right. Here, sit down with us."

Pepi made room on the bench and introduced Theon

to Kish, who squirmed nervously, unsure about trusting the newcomer.

"Since when does Jabin need arms?" Theon asked.

"They're not for Jabin," Pepi replied.

Theon appeared startled for a moment, and then he smiled. "Well, Pepi, it appears you've had a change of heart."

"Do you have access to any arms now, Theon?"

"Of course. The family warehouses in Damascus are packed with arms orders that can't be delivered because of the Trojan war. We lost a couple of shipments to raids near Troy. So now we tell our clients in that area to prepay and provide security for our ships. A few contracts have been canceled for that reason, which will act to your benefit."

Pepi felt a growing excitement at the news. If an arms cache of great size could be obtained quickly and at a good price, the Israelite cause would take a giant step forward.

"How soon can you deliver it?" Pepi asked.

"A few days, a week at the most. All I have to do is give orders that it be loaded and shipped."

"I'll take the entire cache," Pepi said.

Kish scowled. "Without first asking the price?"

"My family wouldn't cheat me. So what better way could I spend my money than on mending my relationship with the Israelites? Besides, I'm a rich man, perhaps without much longer to live. The physicians in Hazor have told me a dozen times that I wouldn't last six months."

"So you're willing to put up the whole price for enough arms to outfit an army of at least five thousand men?" Kish asked.

"He can afford it," Theon assured Kish. Then he turned to Pepi. "During the past ten years the family has distributed your share of the profits to an account in Home. But"—he glanced at Kish for a moment—"you're sure you want to commit your resources to something like this?"

"To freedom?" Pepi asked. "To reconciliation? Yes!"

Theon pursed his lips. "Well . . . I think we can make a deal."

"Then here's my hand."

"Wait. Don't you want to hear the price?"

"How much do I owe you?"

Theon smiled. "A plate of good Jezreel olives, flatbread, a bowl of wine, and an order of figs."

"What nonsense are you talking? I asked for the price."

"You just heard it, Pepi."

"But—"

"The family has a profound attachment to freedom and reconciliation, also. We've been linked to the Israelites for generations. Consider it our family's donation to the cause."

"I can't believe it! Thank you, Theon!"

"Don't mention it. Now, how about that food? I haven't eaten in hours, and I've a long trip in front of me."

After Pepi and Kish had left, Theon sat for a long time in silence. He wondered what Pepi would have said if he knew Tirzah was alive. What would Pepi have done if he knew that Theon had slept with her, had loved her, however briefly, with a passion that certainly equaled Pepi's own from so many years before? Oddly enough, Theon did not feel as if he had betrayed Pepi but that he had become a brother to him.

Theon smiled. The camaraderie he felt had inspired him to pay for the Israelites' weapons himself; Pepi did not know it, but the family business had been affected by the long war in Troy. But it was important that Pepi be reintegrated emotionally into the family, and Theon was hopeful that his act of generosity would foster the relationship.

He was glad to have found Pepi, even though the armorer looked like death itself. Pepi would not live much longer—that much was clear—so Theon was doubly glad that his kinsman had come full circle and returned to his first real loyalty, the Israelites.

It was interesting, Theon thought, how so many generations of the family had been enmeshed with the Israelites. He had heard that Pepi's half brother Micah had vanished from the Israelite camp after performing many feats of valor for them against Moab. And Theon had also learned

that Nimshi had left town. Were the brothers together? he
wondered. He hoped so; nothing was as important as
family affection and loyalty.

Theon passed his hand over his face as if he had felt a
sudden pain. Why had he promised Huldah not to tell
Pepi that she was still alive? Why had he felt more loyal to
her than to Pepi, who was family? At every moment
during their conversation he had wanted to blurt out his
startling information. How Pepi would have rejoiced! But
he had said nothing.

Theon poked at the olives in the bowl but did not eat.
Had Huldah's marriage to Ephai nullified her marriage to
Pepi? A great sadness came over him. He knew he was
trying to soothe his conscience and pretend that Pepi had
no claim to the woman now. But his conscience was not
going to be calmed easily. After everything that had happened he realized that he desired Pepi's wife.

But now a fast galley was waiting for him at Acco, to
take him to Troy. He needed to rescue Iri's offspring and
wife, and now was the time to do it. His relationship with
Huldah would have to wait.

CHAPTER
TWENTY-FIVE

Gaza

Micah pointed. "Look there!"

Nimshi stared at the two massive black tents that had been thrown up between low whitewashed houses. The morning sun was blazingly hot, and the two brothers were dazed by the brilliance of the light and colors. Everything in Gaza seemed to be violent. And yet, at the same time, there were pockets of gentleness: rows of fruit trees, flocks of strange-looking sheep bleating in the streets, a profusion of purple and white flowers in a small roof garden.

Gaza was the wealthiest city in the Philistine League, which was why Nimshi had chosen it as the place to start their new life together. In addition to the tariffs exacted from the land traders, dozens of ships were anchored in the shallow marshy harbor, loading and unloading fabric, foodstuffs, and weapons. All these vessels paid loading and docking fees. In the city squares crouched the drovers who controlled the caravans that constantly entered or left the city on their way north to Canaan and Syria or east to the desert kingdoms or south into Egypt.

The brothers strolled through a neighborhood that seemed populated by Egyptians. Nimshi listened intently to conversations around him. As a child he had heard his mother speak Coptic, the Egyptian tongue, and now he was able to pick out a few words that he understood. Micah, however, remembered nothing of Coptic.

"Now that we're here," Micah said, "what shall we do?"

"Let's rest awhile and then look for forges. We don't have many coins left. We need work."

Micah laughed. He showed his brother the straps of one of his sandals: They were worn through completely and flapped like a dog's ear.

The brothers spread their blanket rolls in the city square. Micah dozed in the sun, but Nimshi just rested in the city square and enjoyed an enormous sense of accomplishment, even though his clothes were tattered and his money almost gone. They had reached their destination!

From time to time he nervously studied Micah's face. His brother's moods frightened him. What horrors had Micah suffered during his years with the army? Nimshi was afraid to ask.

Micah suddenly awoke and sat up. "Watch out!" he whispered urgently.

Two Philistine soldiers on patrol had turned into the square. They were dressed in the Greek manner—very short tunics with high sandals. Their leather helmets were reinforced with a bronze rim. Short, broad swords were sheathed at their sides, and one of them carried a throwing spear.

Micah tensed, and his eyes became slits. His right hand went inside the folds of his robe to grasp his long knife.

Sweat poured down Nimshi's face. "Micah! What are you doing? Calm down!"

Because his words did not seem to register, he jammed his elbow hard into Micah's side. Micah grunted, then relaxed.

The two Philistines slowed and looked at the brothers. Nimshi smiled congenially and nodded in greeting. The soldiers stopped and stared at Micah. The guard with the spear pulled the weapon from his shoulder and pushed the point against Micah's shredded sandal, then he and his companion laughed derisively.

Nimshi closed his eyes and prayed that Micah would do nothing rash. When the soldiers walked on, he was

thankful and found himself trembling. If Micah had suffered another irrational outburst and attacked them—and
there had been absolutely no provocation for doing that—
the brothers would have ended up in a swamp with cut
throats.

"Close call," Micah breathed.

"It wasn't a close call. You just think it was one. This
is Gaza, an open city. Strangers and travelers are welcomed, and we had committed no crime. Why do you
keep acting as if someone is after us? Micah, listen to me!
We are freemen looking for work. Can you understand
that? Now relax! Keep your knife in your robe!"

Late that afternoon, following a sighting of a bluish
curl of smoke that signaled charcoal and ore being burned,
Nimshi and Micah entered a small section of the city
where iron forges were set up. Only two of the forges
were being worked; the others had been shut down and
banked for the day.

Nimshi walked to the larger forge, which was supervised by a barrel-chested man wearing a white cloth over
his head. On the ground beside the forge were enormous
iron objects.

"What are those?" Micah asked, marveling at the
objects' thickness and size. "I've never seen anything like
them."

Nimshi glanced at them. "They're the undercarriage
of siege catapults and are used to launch large stones and
Greek fire into fortifications. They're even used on ships
now."

"Right you are!" the voice of the supervisor cut in.
"We're making seventy-six of them on contract for the
Egyptians."

He walked over to the two brothers and studied them
frankly. "My name is Arum. What do you vagabonds
want?"

"A job," Nimshi answered quickly.

Arum found this very funny. He yelled out to his
forge workers, "These two bums want to work. Should we
give them a job?" He did not wait for an answer. He

turned to the brothers. "We need all the help we can get, but you two look too puny to lug these iron beasts to the storage shed and then load them on wagons going south."

"We're not looking for donkey work," said Micah.

"Then what are you looking for?"

"Ironwork apprenticeships. We know a little, but we're willing to learn more. We're nephews of Iri of Thebes. Perhaps you've heard of—"

"Children of the Lion?" Arum asked, astonished. Then he laughed. "If you two are the nephews of Iri of Thebes, then I'm the sister of Ramses the Second. The next thing you'll tell me is that you have a lion-paw birthmark on your back! If you want to work at my forge, I'll decide the kind of work you'll do. Otherwise, get out of here. Children of the Lion? Gods! Why do I always get saddled with lunatics?" He grumbled and stomped off.

"Well," said Nimshi, grinning, "it's a start."

"Let's do it," Micah agreed.

The two brothers walked slowly toward the forge to begin their donkey work.

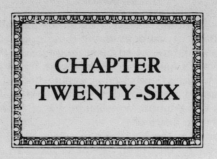

CHAPTER TWENTY-SIX

Canaan

I

Jerah had been traveling tirelessly in the hills populated by the tribes of Ephraim and Benjamin. He made numerous speeches, met with tribal leaders, and asked for the Israelites' aid in ridding their people of the cruel yoke of Hazor's domination.

In the Benjamite foothills Jerah met with Shemida, former aide to the legendary commander Joshua. Shemida, aware of Jerah's mission to recruit his participation and pick his brain, had brought along Ehud and other leaders of the successful uprising against the Moabites.

Shemida heard Jerah out and then asked questions. "What I don't understand," he began, "is how you expect to fight a war without weapons."

"We've been promised arms," Jerah answered.

"By whom?" Ehud wanted to know. "We captured weapons from the Moabites, but if Yahweh specified through Deborah that an army of ten thousand men is needed, we can arm fewer than half that number."

"Which tribes are with you so far?" Shemida asked.

Jerah hesitated. "We have men of Issachar, Naphtali, and Zebulun, and even some men of Ephraim have joined us. The chiefs of Gilead have turned us down, and Dan and Asher as well."

Shemida shook his head knowingly: "We had problems with those tribes refusing to help out during my war, too," he recalled. "What of Reuben?"

"Another problem," Jerah admitted. "They want to sit and argue and think it over. By the time they make up their minds, we'll be fighting Jabin's grandchildren."

Shemida looked at Ehud and the others. "I don't think there's any doubt as to what we have to do. We'll join you."

"Wonderful! When can you—"

"These arms you've been promised—"

"Believe it or not, the chief armorer of Jabin himself has secretly come over to our side. He is in Succoth right now, bargaining for arms."

Ehud's jaw dropped. "Pepi? Pepi of Kerma?"

"Yes," Jerah confirmed. "He's attended several meetings with our people, and now he's willing to undermine Jabin. We knew he and Sisera hated each other."

Shemida thought for a long while. "I'm not quite sure what to think of Pepi's supposed defection. After ten years of bitterness and working for our worst enemy, what would induce him to change sides? He always blamed us for the loss of his wife and his mother. And his hatred of Joshua's ways and Caleb was always intense."

Jerah shrugged. "He appears sincere. And he's changed. Mellowed. He's lost that edge of cynicism."

Shemida fell silent again, awkwardly shifting his bad leg. "To be sure, he had a good reason for feeling bitter toward us. Joshua was much misled by Caleb, who was jealous of Pepi and took every opportunity to discredit him. He convinced Joshua that Pepi had sold us out."

"Were the stories untrue?" Ehud asked Shemida.

"I can't say for a certainty. I do know that when Caleb reported that Pepi was living in the home of the magistrate of Jericho, supposedly selling our secrets, he was actually under medical care. He suffered from falling fits."

"Are you sure?" Ehud asked, skeptical. "Because my father said—"

Shemida sighed. "I knew your father well. He was a valiant fighter, but even his best friend wouldn't have called him the most intelligent man in the army. He was always coming around with some ridiculous exaggeration or distortion of the truth."

Ehud bristled for a moment. Then his anger subsided. "I suppose you're right."

"Although I can't prove it," Shemida continued, "I think Pepi was unjustly maligned. If he's finally forgiving us and coming to our side, we should rejoice; it's a forgiveness we may not entirely deserve. But what do you need me for? I can't fight."

Jerah's heart leapt. "Accompany me to Bethel. Come talk with Deborah and obey her the way I do."

After her midday rest Deborah returned to her favorite place beneath the palm trees and looked out at the never-ending queue. She recognized a familiar face in the line.

"Is that Barak?" she called out, astonished.

Her assistant craned her neck to see. "I think so. Shall I get him?"

"No, let him wait his turn, like everyone else. I can't make any exceptions. I was just surprised to see him. He has his mission."

"Let me bring him to you. The others will understand. Surely he has important business—"

"All these people are here on business that's important to them. They are here to speak with Yahweh through me and to receive His blessings and forgiveness. God has not revealed to me that He has any hierarchy in these matters. Let Barak wait."

At the encampment in Jezreel, Lieutenant Telem reported to General Sisera. "I have evidence that the Israelites are plotting a rebellion."

Sisera laughed. "Rebellion? Nonsense."

"Sir, it's true. My spy, Ishbak, has infiltrated their gatherings. The Israelites are meeting every evening to practice the use of arms."

"What arms? How can they learn to use something they haven't got? Really, this is the most stupid—"

"Sir!" Telem had learned to be persistent in dealing

with the restless and inattentive Sisera, who heard what he wanted to hear and ignored the rest. "If you'd just listen . . ."

"Oh, all right," Sisera said, but he gave little sign of paying attention. Instead he paced, trying to balance a rock on his custom-made dagger with the silver-inlaid handle, too full of nervous energy to concentrate.

"Well, sir, my spy has attended several rallies in which new fighters were recruited, and he's even sat in on one training session conducted by veterans from Joshua's army—the army, sir, that conquered Canaan and killed your father and the king's."

"Those buzzards have come out of retirement?"

"The spy also reports that the revolutionary cabal includes someone from the inner circle of the government of Hazor. A traitor, sir, is selling us out."

"A traitor?" Sisera stopped pacing. "Who?"

"My spy says he's inquiring discreetly as to the traitor's identity, but my guess is that he already knows and is trying to extort more money from me."

"Get me two guard units! We'll swoop down on these seditious bastards and kill every last—"

"If you please, sir, wouldn't it be better to wait and get a list of these meetings so we can raid all of them at the same time? We'll spread the net wide enough so we get the traitor, also."

"Good idea," Sisera approved. "Tell your spy to redouble his efforts. Promise him a rich reward. I want the whole cabal in my hand by week's end."

The second installment of Ishbak's pay went the same way as the first: He was out of debt now, but after the debts and his rent had been paid, there was little left for the only thing that was important to him: the dancer Samal.

Once again he mounted the stairs to the woman's apartment, and after checking the heft of his now-depleted purse, he took a deep breath and knocked on the door.

A familiar voice rang out. "Chemosh, darling, could you see who that is? I don't have anything on."

Her words aroused Ishbak's lust and quashed it at the same time. Who was this cursed Chemosh? The door opened, revealing a large, hairy man in a hastily donned loincloth.

"It's you," he snarled. "Samal! The little rat's here!"

"Ask him if he's got any money, darling." Then she decided to ask herself. "Ishbak, dear," she called, "did you bring any money? The landlord's been asking—"

Ishbak tried to stuff his purse back into his garment, but the big man saw it, grabbed it, and tested its weight in his palm. "It ought to be enough. If not, maybe the landlord will accept partial payment on account."

"Look here!" Ishbak protested in the squeaky voice he hated so much. "You can't just—"

Samal suddenly appeared in the doorway, wearing a robe so thin he could see through it. He could see her pink nipples and fought to keep his eyes from straying lower.

"Ishbak! How good to see you, dear. You came in the nick of time. I'm having the most dreadful trouble with the landlord. He's threatening to evict me. You wouldn't want that to happen, would you, dear? To your own little Samal?"

"No, but—"

"Then you surely won't begrudge me the money. I'll give it to Chemosh for safekeeping. And you can visit me . . . tomorrow. No, the day after. No, not then, either—I have to have my hair done that day. The end of the week. Yes, do come at the end of the week. But, darling Ishbak, let's not have another situation like the last time. It's unkind to get a lady aroused and not be able to satisfy her. Isn't that right, Chemosh?"

"Samal!" Ishbak cried out in a strangled voice. "Don't talk about things like that in front of—"

"Please, dear, go away now. I've got to get ready for my job. Will you be there tonight, Ishbak? I'll dance just for you."

Then she slammed the door in his face, leaving him alone with his shame and rage.

II

"But I don't understand," Deborah told Barak. "Jerah said that Pepi of Kerma has been training you while the old soldiers from Joshua's day have been instructing the young men, and you're all coming along splendidly. Why would you want to be replaced as leader of the revolt?"

Barak fidgeted. "I am not capable of leading the rebellion. I am too unsure of myself. You need a more experienced man, someone wise, whom all will listen to gladly. Forgive me, Deborah, but I cannot lead young men to their death."

He looked at her imploringly. His face was twisted with despair. "Why should anyone listen to me?"

"Because Yahweh told them to," Deborah replied. "Barak, if you don't have confidence in yourself, have confidence in the God of your fathers. He has chosen you from the many for this work. As to why He chose you, that's a mystery. I have no idea why He chose me to prophesize, but I do my duty nonetheless."

"But—"

"Don't interrupt. I'm here because God told me to be here and because I know how miserable my life would be if I were to stop obeying His orders. I spent most of my life listening to myself. You couldn't have found a more self-centered person. But one day I heard a call. When I told people about it, they laughed at me. But I followed that call because anything else would have been more painful—more painful even than being mocked and scorned. So here I am, doing Yahweh's work, and I'm happy. It is very hard work, Barak, but I am happy."

Barak said nothing, but he appeared to be thinking about what she had told him.

Deborah took a deep breath. "Barak, you're wearing my voice out, forcing me to give these long speeches. Go back and do the work you've been assigned and make the best of it."

"But we're studying war with weapons of wood. We might all be slaughtered for our idealistic—"

"The weapons will come."

"I wish you would return with me and tell the troops that."

"I cannot. My place is here. You will return alone and follow Yahweh's commands, which I have transmitted to you."

Her voice had begun to rise in anger, causing Barak to hang his head, ashamed of his continuing weakness and doubt. When she saw his reaction, her voice softened, and she reached out and touched him on the forehead. "Barak, listen to me. You are right: Many young men will die before this war is over. But they will give their lives proudly under your command. In generations to come, your name will be blessed."

He turned and walked away, straightening his shoulders and wiping the tears from his eyes.

Huldah was in line not far behind Barak. To Huldah's surprise, Deborah recognized her immediately and greeted her by name. Then the seeress closed her eyes and seemed to sleep. When she stirred again, she stared at Huldah intently.

"I know why you're here," Deborah said, "even if you don't. You want me to make up your mind for you."

Huldah was not as haughty and aloof as she had been before. Her confusion and indecision showed. "I can't sleep," she said. "I'm tired and depressed all the time."

"Of course you are. You are carrying two heavy burdens, and your strength is not enough to support them."

"What can I do?"

"Lay them down."

"I can't," Huldah moaned.

"Nonsense. They're not attached to you like warts. You can walk away from them." Deborah smiled. "And when you do, you'll wonder how you managed, all these years, doubled over under their weight."

"You said 'burdens.' Two of them. I don't under—"

"One is your hatred and resentment of another and your refusal to forgive him."

Huldah stared at her.

"The other is your hatred and resentment of yourself and your refusal to forgive yourself."

Huldah looked at her in shock, unable to reply for a few moments. "How can I forgive? For years I was a whore in the worst brothel in Damascus. Recently I slept with the kinsman of my husband. I was abandoned by those who loved me . . . and now, out of vengeance, I am abandoning someone I once loved."

"Do you want me to pity you?" Deborah asked harshly.

"No, not pity—help."

"I can only point you in the right direction."

"You don't understand. My husband Pepi is alive. Pepi, the man I loved more than anyone on earth. But he's also the man I hated more than anyone on earth."

"Your time is up," Deborah said.

"Should I seek him out? Please help me. And if I find him, what should I say?" She grasped the seeress's arm. "Please, Deborah, I don't even know my own heart."

"Go. Do what you have to do," Deborah said before turning to the next person in line.

Even after several tries, Ishbak had failed to secure an invitation to join one of the rebel groups secretly training in the hills. But after he had been refused for a third time, he decided to take matters in his own hands and surreptitiously followed one of the recruits.

Thus he had punished his scrawny body for hours, hiking along a tortuous hillside path barely within sight of the man he was trailing. At last the man had disappeared over the crest of a hill and into a valley. Keeping as much out of sight as possible behind the rocks, Ishbak crept to the top of the hill and looked down.

What he saw astonished him. He had expected to find bumbling country louts milling about, banging away at each other clumsily with sticks, looking like large children mimicking real soldiers. Instead he witnessed as disciplined a weapons drill as he had ever seen in Sisera's camp, supervised by men who obviously knew what they were doing. The well-spaced ranks of paired figures were performing the kind of maneuvers one might expect from highly trained fighters. And their smooth lunges, parries, and reactions were accomplished with strength and lightning speed.

A shocking thought worked its way into his mind: *What if these bumpkins have a chance of winning?* What if they acquired weapons and defeated Sisera's lax, overconfident, badly managed legions? Looking at them, Ishbak could almost believe it might happen. If they ever got their hands on real spears, tipped with bronze or even iron, the sharp and disciplined drill they now practiced would hold them in good stead against any army in Canaan.

Have I wagered everything on the wrong side? If I betray the Israelites and Hazor loses, how long will I survive before someone finds me out?

Again he looked down at the strong, quick young recruits drilling in the valley and shuddered. Fear crept into his heart. He was risking his life . . . and for what?

Trembling, he sank back against the rocks and put one quivering hand on his rapidly beating heart. *What have I done?* he wondered. *How do I get myself out of this mess?*

He closed his eyes and prayed silently to every god he could think of, including the God of Israel and the entire Canaanite pantheon.

When he opened them again, he was looking into the hard eyes of an Israelite picket. The man was holding a pointed hardwood staff, which, with one stroke, he could drive right through Ishbak's head.

"What are you doing here?" the Israelite demanded, pushing the stick against Ishbak's neck. "Explain quickly, before I kill you."

"Jerah, you've done well," Deborah complimented. The two men Jerah had brought with him were as unlike each other as figs and olives: One was young, burly, clear-eyed, and strong. The other was thin and tired looking and walked with a pronounced limp. Deborah had never seen either man before, but she knew them immediately. "Ehud and Shemida. How glad I am to meet you both and to know that you have answered Yahweh's call."

Shemida inclined his head. "Just tell us what you want us to do."

Jerah, looking back at the queue of people that stretched down the hillside even as the shadows of late afternoon grew longer, brightened and said, "Will you excuse me, please? I think I see someone I know."

"We need men," Deborah said, studying the two newcomers. "And we need arms. Most of all we need the help of our brothers of the southern and central tribes to rid us of this monster Jabin and his lackey Sisera." She fixed her gaze on Shemida. "And we need an experienced organizer who knows how to make men work together."

"I will do whatever I can," Shemida agreed, "but what do we do about the arms we need?"

"I don't think we need to worry about that," Jerah's voice spoke up.

Shemida wheeled around to see a familiar figure accompanying Jerah; it was a man he had not laid eyes on in more than a decade.

"Pepi of Kerma," the tall man said to Deborah. "Hello, Shemida. By the end of the week you'll have enough arms for at least five thousand of your northern men."

Shemida and Pepi clasped forearms, while Ehud proclaimed his astonishment. Deborah, however, showed no surprise. She smiled placidly at Pepi.

"I didn't know how or when the news would come," she said. "But I knew that the moment we raised our fists for justice, Yahweh would place weapons in our hands."

"The weapons are a gift from the Children of the Lion," Pepi said. "They represent my family's appreciation for the friendship your patriarchs, prophets, and leaders have shown us over the years. Use the arms bravely. Death to the enemies of Israel!"

"Pepi has had a hand in the training of Barak as well," Jerah said.

"Yes, I know," Deborah replied. "God always sends us the friends we need, but not until we deserve them."

Shemida clapped Pepi on the arm in a soldier's rough gesture of friendship. "Thank you," he said warmly. "It's wonderful to have you back." Then he turned to Deborah. "When does Yahweh say we should attack?"

"As soon as possible," Deborah answered. "Before Sisera learns what our plans are and tries to stop us."

III

The man had drawn Heber the Kenite aside as if to share some secret with him, but now he seemed reluctant to speak. Instead he peered worriedly up and down the Megiddo streets, then escorted Heber into a dark alleyway.

"Sorry, but you can't be too careful these days," the stranger said. "Not only is it illegal to gather in support of our . . . organization, but spies are everywhere. Only yesterday we caught one of them spying on one of our drills. A craven little sneak named Ishbak."

"I don't know any Ishbak," Heber said, trying to pull away. "If I don't complete what I was sent here to do, I'll get in trouble. Now what do you want from me?"

"You're Heber the Kenite, aren't you?"

"Yes. But I've never laid eyes on you in my life. Who are you?"

"I'm Nahath. I . . . I have relatives who live near your wife in the Jezreel Valley. My people are of the tribe of Manasseh, and—"

"Israelites."

"Yes, the Hazorite yoke lies heavily upon us. As a man who's suffered at the hands of Jabin and Sisera—particularly Sisera—you'll understand how strong our feelings are against Hazor and its overlords. That's why we're planning an uprising against—"

"Uprising?" Heber stepped away from him. "Look, my friend, tell me no more. I'm an employee of the government you claim to oppose, and I can't do anything to jeopardize my position. I've been poor so long, and at last I have a chance to give my wife the life she deserves—"

The man stared at Heber as if he were insane. "But

it's Sisera I'm talking about! I thought you worked for Pepi of Kerma."

"Yes, but Pepi of Kerma has a contract with the government of Hazor."

"Then you don't know? Pepi is with us. He's working for our side."

"That can't be true!"

"It is. And as for your personal situation . . . is it possible that you don't know? I can't imagine that you'd know and not care."

Heber shook his head in puzzlement. "Know what?"

Nahath snorted in exasperation. "Your wife!"

With his strong tinker's hands, Heber grabbed the man by the front of his garment and pulled him close. "What has Yael got to do with this?"

Nahath twisted away and straightened his robe. "Your wife and Sisera," he said crisply, trying to regain his dignity. "Ask her. Ask her when you see her."

"Ask her what?"

"Never mind. Go with God, and good luck to you. But if you change your mind after you've talked to your wife . . . I run a little mill on the Kishon. You can always reach me there."

"Wait!" Heber cried.

But the man had vanished around a corner.

Heber continued to wonder about this strange encounter until he walked into the tent settlement that flanked the city gates. A crowd had gathered, and Heber, curious, tried to push his way to the front. Frustrated in his attempt, he asked someone what was happening.

"Gruesome sight. Ishbak seems to have gone and gotten his skinny throat cut. You don't want to look, my friend."

Heber nodded and backed off. "What did he do to get killed?"

Another man broke in, his face reddened by anger. "He sold out his people, that's what—his friends and neighbors. He sold them out to the Hazorite bastards. Ishbak got what he deserved. So perish all enemies of Israel!"

As Heber turned away he took one last look, and at that moment the crowd parted, permitting a view of a scrawny man dressed only in a loincloth, lying on the ground. He was covered with gore. His neck and chest were streaked with dried blood, and his sightless eyes stared at the sky.

Kish sat quietly on the ground. It was an hour before dusk, and the training session for the Israelite recruits had just begun. He was tired but contented. When he had started out for Damascus after meeting with the armorer Pepi and his kinsman Theon, he had been very skeptical about Theon's claims. But when Kish saw the weapons-packed warehouses in Damascus and certified that the arms were being loaded and shipped, he knew the time he had been waiting for all these past years had arrived: The Hazorite oppressors would pay in blood. Half dozing, he watched happily as the recruits went through their drills with the wooden weapons.

As the sun was falling below the western hills, one of the pickets suddenly cried out: "Hazorite patrol!"

Kish leapt to his feet and drew his short sword. A Hazorite spear flew out of the near darkness and pierced a sentry through his throat. All around him Hazorite soldiers rose from their hiding places and attacked the guards. The inexperienced Israelites, frightened and confused, took no action.

Kish ran among them. *Unblooded children!* He grabbed the closest trooper by the throat and pressed the sword against his neck. "Wouldn't you rather die honorably by a Hazorite sword than as a coward by an Israelite weapon?" he screamed at the frightened youth.

The bug-eyed boy nodded vigorously, desperately trying to twist away from the blade. Kish charged up the slope, dragging his reluctant companion with him. After only a moment's hesitation, the rest of the young Israelite troopers followed, grateful for the leadership and direction. The recruits were armed only with quarterstaffs and wooden spears; neither weapon had bronze or iron tips.

The Hazorite patrol, while numbering less than a quarter of the Israelites' strength, were fearfully armed.

The Israelites, led by Kish, did not attack as if they were underdogs. As they swarmed over the slope, their flashing staffs knocked Hazorites off their horses or killed them in their tracks, their brains crushed by ferocious and repeated blows of hardwood sticks. One by one the members of the Hazorite patrol were cut off, surrounded, and killed.

It was over as fast as it had begun. The Israelites, breathing heavily, rested and stared incredulously at the corpses, finding it difficult to believe that they, mere boys, had been the instruments of death.

Kish did not let the recruits rest long. He ordered them to strip the Hazorite bodies of every piece of usable equipment and then bury them naked in an obscure canyon.

The war had begun!

As an assistant armorer to the court of Hazor, Heber the Kenite had the privilege of quartering at the encampment Sisera had built on the slopes above the Jezreel Valley, and he decided to avail himself of it. After an early breakfast he headed eastward down the valley, following the track beside the Kishon River. He had bought some gifts for Yael and was eagerly looking forward to watching her face when she saw them.

The best presents of all, however, would be how well he was doing on his job, how much money he was making, and how soon the time would come when he could bring her north with him and buy a little piece of land of her own to grow vegetables. Perhaps they could even have a child. . . .

But as he rode, dark thoughts lingered in his mind— doubts about what the Israelite in Megiddo had tried to tell him. Was the man mad, or had he gotten Yael's name mixed up with someone else's? It was impossible that the stranger was talking about his Yael. She was faithful, the perfect wife.

Had she become disgusted by his shortcomings and turned to another man? He was, after all, the one who had failed to live up to her expectations. He had remained poor, while people to the right and left of them prospered. He had not been able to give her a home of her own, and they could not have afforded to raise a child if she had borne one to him. But all that was about to change. Yael would have pretty clothing and maybe even a servant.

Ahead, Heber could see the little community by the river, and he urged his horse down the path to the water. Pulling up twenty steps from his own tent, he dismounted, hobbled his horse, and strode to the door, carrying his sack of gifts.

A face appeared briefly in the doorway, but instead of coming out to meet him, Yael quickly retreated into the tent. "No, Heber!" she cried. "Don't come in!"

"Yael! I have wonderful news, and I've brought you presents." He walked in and found her cowering in a corner of the darkened tent.

"Please, Heber," she whimpered, "don't come any closer."

"What's the matter with you? I've missed you so. Come here and give me a real welcome." He reached up and pulled the curtain away from one of the smoke vents, allowing the morning sunlight to flood the tent. "Oh, no, no," he uttered.

Her eyes were swollen. Her face was a mass of bruises. Her mouth was bloody and misshapen. When he gently pulled her, weeping, into the light, he could see the welts that began on her neck and vanished under her robe. "Yael dearest, what happened to you?"

When the whole story had been told and he had swung from rage to weeping and back to rage, Heber went out to his horse and silently buckled on the sword he had made under Pepi's watchful eye.

Yael followed him and clutched at his robes.

"Please don't go after him, Heber! He'll kill you."

"Pepi's been teaching me how to use a sword," he said in a low, dangerous voice. "Don't worry about me, Yael."

"Heber! If you can still love me after what he did, please don't go."

"I'm doing this because I do love you, Yael. That monster has to die."

"But he's a professional soldier. He's killed many men. You're strong, I know, but in your heart you're a gentle man who doesn't want to hurt anyone. You're no match for a vicious and bloodthirsty savage. You have no idea how brutal he can be."

"Don't try to stop me."

"I have to," she said, sobbing. "Heber, if you get killed, I'll have nobody. I can't lose you. Promise me you won't challenge him. Please, Heber!"

Suddenly, the expression on his face changed. His eyes sharpened. He touched her gently on the side of her face. "Maybe there is another way, Yael. A man approached me yesterday. He asked me to help his cause. He even claimed that Pepi, my master, was on his side. Yes, this might just work. . . ."

IV

Rumors were beginning to spread through the northern kingdom: rumors of secret movements of large groups of men in the hills above Benjamin . . . rumors of militias training secretly in the wilderness . . . rumors of seditious behavior and uprisings in the vassal cities.

When a Hazorite spy was murdered and an entire patrol, sent out by Sisera to scour the foothills for illegal activities, disappeared, the Hazorite command could no longer ignore the possibility that the Israelites' threat should be taken seriously. Sisera, as was so often the case, was busy with the latest in a long succession of women—a young widow in Taanach, kept in submission by bullying and beating. So Lieutenant Telem took matters in his own hands: He hired new spies, only to lose contact with one immediately, while the others brought back vague confirmation of covert military activity. Telem suborned local officials; he captured and tortured young Israelites, hopeful of finding someone willing to betray his compatriots. He met with little success.

But when a caravan that had come down through the hills of Megiddo reported having seen an army of at least twenty-five hundred men moving stealthily along the mountain tracks toward the sea, Telem decided he could wait no longer.

He made one last desperate call on Sisera. The general was with the young widow, reveling in his complete control over her and making her serve him naked, like an Egyptian slave. Telem tried to ignore her shame and discomfort.

"Sir, something's happening among the Israelites. We have to take action now."

"Lieutenant," Sisera drawled, "you take things too seriously. You don't enjoy life as you should." The general snapped his fingers, and the naked woman began to massage his neck muscles. "You have to relax. The spineless locals don't have any revolt left in them. If they did, we'd have seen signs of it long ago. Look how easily we took their land to build the new encampment in Jezreel."

"That's another thing, sir," Telem responded. "The encampment is exposed to attack from three sides."

"Not to worry! It's in the perfect location for commanding the road between Ophrah and the sea. Just do your job and leave the planning to me."

"But, sir, we lost a whole patrol the other night. That's serious."

"Yes, yes, but the patrol was full of Jebusites and Hivites—the most disloyal bastards in the whole army. I warned you to get rid of them. They probably just deserted."

"Sir, if that were the case, they would have taken their horses and their gear. But one of the horses turned up at an auction a day later, and a trader reported having bought one of the saddles from a passing nomad."

"It would have been just like the thieving bastards to sell horse and gear both. I think you're overreacting. Ow! You bitch, that hurts!" He turned and grabbed the woman's arm and twisted it until she screamed—then he flung her aside.

Telem stood. His face was fixed and distant, and he could not look at either of them. "I'm sorry to have bothered you, sir," he said. "When can we expect you back in camp?"

"I don't know. Tomorrow, I suppose. I'm getting bored here. You look all out of sorts, Telem. Are you angry with my reaction to your news? Do you want me to shake like a palsied dog because your spies claim that the Israelites are training with wooden weapons? You're starting to sound like a woman who needs beating, Lieutenant. Don't you understand? I hate the Israelites. I despise them and their God. If they wish to mount one of their pathetic little revolts, fine. I'd love the opportunity to grind them into the mud once and for all!"

Pepi entered Hazor by the southern route, circling Lake Chinnereth. His business in the South had been profitable but not without danger. He enjoyed a great sense of accomplishment as he dismounted and led his horse to the stables, even though he knew it was possible that some spy had already betrayed him to Jabin.

In spite of the fact that Hazor might prove to be a death trap, he felt better than he had in a very long time. He felt alive again. He had committed himself. From this point on, he would have a double life.

At his forge he was surprised to find Melek in charge of the apprentices.

"Where's Heber?" Pepi asked.

Melek did not bother to hide his contempt for the Kenite who had supplanted him. "He was sent south to Megiddo. The tin shipment you ordered was held up. Since there wasn't anybody else available, a court administrator sent the Kenite to make new arrangements."

"And I'm sure he's doing a good job," Pepi rebuked sharply. "Have there been any messages for me?"

"Yes, sir. One from Nahbi, the king's personal messenger. You're to report to court the moment you return."

Pepi stiffened. *What if?* . . . But he forced himself to stay calm. "I'll go now. Is Sisera in the city?"

"No, sir. But Lieutenant Telem just returned from the southern encampment. That may have something to do with the summons, sir."

*   *   *

Telem had just presented himself before the king and was trying to explain why he had bypassed Sisera and was bringing the rumors of revolt in the South to the king directly. As Pepi entered the reception hall, Jabin was interrogating Telem.

"You say Sisera wouldn't pay attention?"

"No, Sire. He was . . . otherwise occupied."

"I see. And what makes you think your opinion should override that of your superior officer?"

Jabin noticed his armorer for the first time. "It appears we've got a case of insubordination on our hands, Pepi."

Pepi looked from one face to the other, and as he met Telem's eyes, he saw suspicion. *He knows,* he thought. *Or at least he suspects. Maybe he's heard something but doesn't dare speak up until he has proof. I'd better find out exactly what Telem knows.*

"Insubordination, sir? But Telem is renowned for his loyalty to Sisera."

"Judge for yourself. Telem says the South is full of rumors about troop movements and other strange doings."

"Troop movements, my lord?" Pepi asked. "If this were true, it would be serious indeed. But what kind of troop movements? Have the Philistines declared war? I can't think of any other military power that might be a threat to the periphery of our territory."

"Lieutenant," the king said, "explain if you can."

"Very well, Sire. Rebel groups are training in the hills. I heard from reliable sources that the Israelite irregulars who rose against Moab are on the march again and may be moving around the peninsula by the sea route."

"Whatever for?" Pepi asked. "You don't suppose they mean to attack the Tjekerites at Dor? That would be foolish. The Dorians have iron weapons. They'd make short work of the Israelites."

"No," Telem said, "the implication is that they mean to come into the Jezreel Valley from the sea."

"Ah!" Pepi raised a brow as he shot a doubting glance at the king. "Go on, please."

"One of my spies was murdered. Our patrol in the hills disappeared."

"Disappeared? But—"

"Leaving behind some of their gear, which turned up for sale a day or so later."

Someone's been careless, Pepi thought. "Surely you can't believe that the Israelites are transforming from sheep into lions!"

"That's exactly what I think, sir."

"And you brought this to Sisera's attention?"

"Yes. But he refused to take my warnings seriously. There was no recourse but to tell the king."

"So Sisera doesn't know you're here?" Pepi asked.

Anger blazed in Telem's eyes. "You as well as any man know Sisera and his ways. He can't sustain any lasting interest in anything but women."

"Telem!" Jabin said sharply. "That is a very serious charge!"

"Nevertheless, Sire, it needs to be made. The general spends little time in camp, and some weeks he hardly appears at all." He shot Pepi a hard glance. "You know about this, Pepi. Everyone else knows about Sisera and your assistant's wife."

Pepi's eyes narrowed. "And what version would you have the king hear?"

"He—he's got this mistress in Jezreel. She's the wife of Heber the Kenite."

Pepi's heart went cold. "Telem," he said. "I've looked into these rumors, and the woman is absolutely virtuous. There's not a jot of truth in this widespread story, and I'd appreciate your help in quashing it."

Pepi realized that he had spoken too rashly and without thinking in trying to protect Heber and his wife from dishonor. He reminded himself that he was now playing for larger stakes than his underling's reputation. It was counterproductive to dispute Telem when the man was telling the truth about Sisera . . . and when the truth would hurt the general.

On the other hand, it would be necessary to remove Telem, if possible. Although Pepi did not know if the lieutenant knew about his own betrayal of Hazor and newfound loyalty to the insurgents, Telem did have accurate information about the rebels' progress.

The hardness of Pepi's voice made Telem back off. "As you say, sir. I'm glad to hear there's nothing to it. But about the rest of this business . . ."

"I think we should reward Telem for his devotion to his work," Pepi suggested to Jabin. "And while he's been insubordinate and obviously can't work with Sisera anymore, he deserves recognition for his competence and vigilance."

"Well, yes, I suppose so. . . ." Jabin allowed.

"I suggest that he be promoted and sent as commander of the units in our northern territories. Moreover, Sire, I think that troops might well be transferred from other garrisons to bolster his new command. Other rumors are also prevalent. Traders I met in the Jordan Valley spoke of territorial ambitions nursed by the kings of Tyre and Arvad. They would dearly love to move on your domains, sir."

"Really?" Jabin asked. "An attack from the north?"

Pepi nodded. He looked at Telem's face and saw suspicion harden; but Telem would not dare contradict him—not if going along with this story meant a promotion and his own command. "It's too dangerous a possibility to ignore, sir. But with a fine man like Telem in charge of the northern territories and with, say, half the Hazorite forces sent north with him to guard our borders—"

"Pepi, you're invaluable! I'll do it!" Jabin said.

Pepi suppressed a huge sigh of relief. If Telem was out of the way and the local Hazorite forces were diminished, and if the arms arrived and could be distributed to the Israelites without attracting attention from Sisera, there might be a chance!

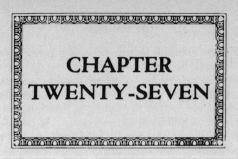

CHAPTER TWENTY-SEVEN

Gaza

The open-air inns of Gaza were all ramshackle establishments with bales for chairs and tent coverings for roofs. Most of them were attached to and shared kitchen facilities with private dwellings.

Because the inns never closed, they attracted everyone at all hours—some looking for excitement, some for food and wine, some for women, and some for a place to rest.

Nimshi and Micah sat in just such an inn after their second day of work. They were physically exhausted, and their backs and necks ached from the heavy labor. Their arms were knotted from using muscles they had not used in years. And they were dehydrated and headachy from working and sweating in the blazing sun.

"Welcome to a new life," Micah said bitterly as he buried his head in his hands.

"It's just temporary, Micah. Believe me, we won't be doing this kind of work much longer."

"You can bet your life on that," Micah agreed. "Gods, I could use a bath."

Nimshi ordered two bowls of wine and some bread—the flattish spongy cakes that were served with a thin film of honey spread over them. This particular inn was crowded but not raucous. It seemed to be a workingman's establishment, and most of the guests were tired and silent. Several had already fallen asleep in front of their food.

The wine, when it finally came, was bitter but cool. It seemed to have been cut with vinegar.

"Look at my palms—they're swollen and raw from lugging around those catapult carriages," Nimshi said, holding up his hands so that the fading light fell on them.

"At least we still have all ten fingers," Micah mumbled. Then he laid his head down on his hands and fell asleep.

Nimshi closed his eyes and relaxed.

They were both jolted awake by a hand slamming down hard on their table. Micah awoke and instinctively drew his knife. Nimshi was so startled he tried to leave the table quickly, tripped over himself, and fell heavily to the floor.

"I'm sorry, I'm sorry," boomed the voice of their boss, Arum, as he bent over and helped Nimshi up, dusted him off, and eased him back onto his seat. "As for you, put that knife away before someone gets hurt."

He sat down at the table, sniffed the wine in the bowls, scowled, and began to sing a song. The night was still young, but it was obvious that Arum had enjoyed too much wine already.

He yelled out for three bowls of strong, sweet Egyptian wine, then clapped Nimshi on the shoulder. "I like you boys. Not only do you work hard, but you have a sense of humor. After all, no one ever told me before that they were Children of the Lion—not when they look like they haven't eaten in five days." He laughed appreciatively. "I really must look stupid if you decided to try that story on me."

The wine arrived, and Arum pushed the bowls to the brothers. "Drink this," he said, "and you'll forget those aches and pains."

Micah sipped the wine. Nimshi tried it, and after a tentative tasting, he drank half the bowl in one gulp.

"There, didn't I tell you it was good? Now you listen to your old 'uncle' Arum. When you're in Gaza, always order Egyptian products—be they wine or food or clothes. Sure, the Philistines like to boast and show off their iron, gold, and silver—but when it comes to real quality, the Egyptians are the lords of heaven and earth."

Then Arum started to sing some erotic ditties, which embarrassed both brothers so intensely that they kept their faces in their wine bowls.

Nimshi found himself drifting off into wine-induced fantasies. He saw himself going to Egypt, to Thebes, and being acclaimed by thousands as he entered the city. Then he interrupted his dream and glanced up to see that Micah was growing more and more morose. Suddenly, in a burst of rancor, Micah flung his arm outward, sweeping the wine bowls off the table and onto the floor. The wine splattered off Arum, who jumped up, yelling, and then burst into laughter.

"I like you lads! You're always doing something stupid. Tell me another crazy story like the one about being Children of the Lion."

Micah reached across the table and grasped Arum's garment. He was going to strangle the large man.

"Leave him alone, Micah! What are you doing?" Nimshi shouted.

Micah released the garment. He glared at Arum for a long time and then, to Nimshi's horror, stood and disrobed, right in the center of the inn.

After the robe had fallen from his body, he turned slowly so that his back was to Arum, then pointed at the wine-colored lion's-paw birthmark, which marked all Children of the Lion.

Aram's face went pale. Nimshi quickly stood up and helped Micah back on with his garment. The two sat down immediately.

"Gods! It's true! You are who you say you are!" Arum shook his head in astonishment, then called for more wine. "I am ashamed of myself for doubting you. Forgive me, please, for offering you a job so beneath your station. Let me make amends. I can get you work that will pay you each five silver crowns a week."

"Doing what?" Nimshi asked.

"Working for an armorer named Dubai, who specializes in iron."

"In Gaza?" Micah asked.

The brothers were now hunched over the table, in-

terested, tantalized by the high remuneration Arum had
mentioned. They were down to their last few coins. Nimshi
had persuaded Micah to deposit all their assets with the
family bank in Jericho before embarking on their new life.
They were going to start out fresh, with little money, few
belongings, unencumbered by the past. But now reality
was upon them; they needed a solid income. . . .

"Not Gaza. Dubai is in the Wilderness of Judea, at
the Khareitun Caves, near the western shore of the Sea of
Salt. He is not difficult to find. Just proceed east from
Gaza until you reach the village of Tel Arad and then head
due north."

Nimshi's expression reflected his disbelief. "That is
the most desolate country on earth. Who in their right
mind would locate an iron forge there?"

"Someone who wishes to hide his work," Arum replied evenly.

"You're not making sense." Micah was angry. "Why
would an armorer hide his work? Everyone needs weapons. Everyone knows how weapons are made—even iron
weapons, now."

"All I know is that Dubai is a master. And if you ask
me more, I may say something that will get me into
trouble. Why question your good fortune? You boys want
to work at an excellent forge for extravagant wages? Then
go. If you don't, then shut up and drink your wine and
make sure you show up for work on time tomorrow morning at my forge."

Arum leaned over and continued in a conspiratorial
voice. "No one is supposed to know that something strange
is going on out there. Everybody is aware of Dubai's
operation, but no one knows any specifics. Maybe he
found gold out there. Maybe there's a royal brothel. Maybe
they're making siege machines or round swords or square
helmets. Who cares? The fact is, I heard they'll hire any
Child of the Lion or Chalybian who makes the trip."

The two brothers glanced at each other, then rose.
"We'll leave at dawn, Arum. Thank you."

Micah and Nimshi left quickly, their heads swimming
from the wine and their good fortune.

CHAPTER
TWENTY-EIGHT

Sea of Salt

It was a stifling night, and the moon was obscured by the clouds. Luti and Occa's campfire was only one hundred yards from the Sea of Salt. The smell of the sea hung heavy on the land. Warm breezes swirled over the baked ground. The sound of crickets and bats punctuated the night air.

Luti sat in front of the fire, watching Occa roast some roots he had dug from the rocky soil. She was very frightened and tried to hide her trembling.

The trip had started out well. From Damascus they had ridden swiftly south on their magnificent horses and soon entered the Jordan Valley. Mile after mile their horses had effortlessly taken them through the lush hills, fruit groves, and farms. She had not been plagued by the motion sickness that bothered her while riding a donkey in the early days of their journey.

As they approached the Sea of Salt, the terrain had changed. The temperature grew hotter, and the horses had slowed. But Occa had brought ample water, and the heat and the dryness could not diminish Luti's appreciation of the beauty of the landscape. It was a world of ancient rocks and baked soil and tiny dwarfed shrubs that seemed to cry out for water.

Then they had reached the southern limit of the sea and turned west for the last leg of their journey to Gaza.

Now, as Occa leaned toward her to offer her a root,
she shook her head at him; she did not want to eat. She
wondered if he thought he had her fooled. She knew that
instead of heading due west toward Gaza they had turned
north and were following the western shore of the Sea of
Salt. Could Occa really believe she had not noticed the
change of direction?

As she huddled in the flickering darkness, not five
feet away from the savage Bedouin with his jingling silver
ornaments, she tried to figure out what was happening.
Drak had told her she must get to Gaza, but the man
whom Drak had sent to protect her was evidently taking
her somewhere else.

Was he following Drak's instructions? Had Drak given
her false instructions, fearful that she could not be trusted,
and given the real instructions to Occa? That was what she
had thought when he had first altered the route and
purchased the horses to go south rather than go to the
coast.

What should she do? She studied the Bedouin. Who
was he? For the first time she had the feeling that she
would not survive, that forces of which she was not aware
were working against her . . . that it would have been
better had she died in Ur. That was a stupid thought, she
realized, a dangerous and counterproductive way of thinking.

Occa was now grinning at her from across the fire as
he chewed one of the roasted roots. His eyes flashed. She
looked away.

The trembling, which had stopped, began again. No,
she could not travel any farther with him. She did not
trust him. He was evil. He was taking her to her death.
He was going against the will of Drak. She glanced at him
surreptitiously. Having finished the roots, Occa was beginning to sway, signaling that he was close to sleep. His
eyes were closed.

Luti realized that she had to escape him this very
night, no matter what the risks. She would leave him one
of the horses and, taking no supplies but water, would try
to reach Gaza alone. She would do exactly what Drak had

told her. Had he not saved her life? Had he not shown her that enormous talents lay hidden in her hands?

The minutes passed; the fire died out. Occa drifted deeper into sleep. Luti waited. Her thoughts traveled back to Ur. How she longed to be close to the Tigris rather than this dreadful Sea of Salt. How she wished to be in Ur once again rather than in this harsh land.

When the last ember blinked out and Occa was fast asleep, she moved quickly and silently to where the horses were tethered by leather thongs on their legs. She started to untie one of the horses. It was hard work, and her fingers were not strong enough. She kept at it until the horse whinnied.

Luti blanched with fright and looked back at the sleeping Bedouin. His body shifted slightly. Why would she think he had heard? Occa was deaf. *Maybe he is not deaf,* she thought with a sinking feeling. *Maybe he can speak. Maybe he is not . . .*

She could no longer think coherently. The sweat was blinding her. Her fingers would no longer work. She left the camp without the horse and struggled through a series of steep, interlocking gulleys, which left her exhausted.

The night grew blacker. The floor and sides of the gulley cut her feet and legs, but she pushed on and entered a flat basin. There she rested and drank some water. She heard the sounds of nocturnal animals but could not identify them. Jackals? Wild asses?

As the night wore on she realized that she was totally and hopelessly lost. She had no knowledge of direction, where she was going or, worse, whence she had come. Each step she took filled her with trepidation that she was going away from Gaza rather than toward the city.

She rested again and drank more water. As she peered into the darkness she could see yellow lights. Were they the eyes of predatory animals? Were carnivores surrounding her? She heard a series of yelps. Wolves? Were they coming to get her? The yellow eyes now seemed closer.

Luti started to run, slipping and stumbling and rising again. She ran until she could not take another step. She sank to the ground. *I will die here,* she thought, and her eyes brimmed with hot tears.

Lying there in a heap, she fought her weakness and her fear. *I must keep going,* she thought. *I must not give up. Occa will be after me, with his long sword and the fiendish ornaments . . . silent, dreadful Occa.*

Slowly she stood and began to walk forward.

A hand snaked out from the darkness and grabbed her by the hair. She screamed. Another hand covered her mouth.

She stared wildly until her eyes focused. She looked into the eyes of a stranger with a hooded robe. Next to him was another figure dressed in the same manner.

He said something in a language she could not understand.

She shook her head.

He spoke again. "Who are you?" he asked in pidgin Greek, the trading language used all over the Great Sea and lands that bordered it.

This time she understood the question. Asa had taught her the language when they visited the markets to buy spice from the Greek traders.

The hand covering her mouth moved away so she could answer. She saw a long knife hanging from the belt of the stranger's robe.

She was too frightened to speak.

Slowly the man released his grip and stepped back. Now Luti realized that she had wandered into the men's campsite. A small fire was still burning.

"My name is Micah," he said, "and this is my brother, Nimshi."

"Luti," she quavered, praying that they meant her no harm.

"Are you alone?"

She nodded. The man called Micah then firmly took her by the arm, led her to the fire, and seated her on a rolled-up blanket.

"Why are you wandering alone in this wilderness?" Micah asked.

For the first time she could see his face; it was handsome, but he seemed very sad.

"I am going to Gaza," she replied.

Nimshi laughed and shook his head. "You are going in the wrong direction."

"I lost my way."

A breeze swirled around them. "It would be best," Nimshi suggested, lying down on the far side of the fire, "if we all sleep now and get acquainted when the sun comes up."

The three of them stretched out on the ground. Luti felt peaceful and safe with these strangers. She closed her eyes, but each time she almost drifted off to sleep, a frightening image invaded her dreams. She tossed and turned and thrashed. Finally, when she remembered the slaughter on the desert and the strange bird omens that had saved her, she sat up, folding her arms across her chest, and began to rock, as Occa did when he prayed.

"What is the matter?" Micah whispered. He was lying very close to her, and his face was etched with concern.

"Dreams. Memories," she replied.

"Would you like my robe?" he asked.

"No, thank you. I have no need of it."

"We have some fruit. Would you like some?"

"I am not hungry," she answered. There in the darkness an enormous sense of well-being enwrapped her, and it came, she knew, from being next to Micah.

"Where do you come from?" he asked. "Where is your home? You are very beautiful. I have never seen anyone in Canaan with skin or eyes like yours."

"I come from Ur, in the kingdom of Babylon. But my mother came from the steppes far to the north. My people were nomads, I think."

He started to speak but stopped and inclined his head. She realized that he wanted to ask her why she had traveled so far only to end up lost in the wilderness, and then he had perceived that she could not—or would not—answer. His consideration was overwhelming.

Luti could see that Nimshi was still asleep. The moon had appeared, but with Micah next to her, she felt no fear of the forbidding landscape. She pulled her long, black hair over her shoulder, and began to comb it with the only memento her mother had left her—a wooden comb.

"Would you let me do that?" Micah asked sheepishly.

"Do what?"

His face was very close to her. She studied his features—his dark eyes, the finely chiseled planes, the almost porcelainlike skin.

"Comb your hair."

Luti laughed. "Why?"

"I don't really know," Micah said. "I think it is because I have spent the last ten years of my life killing. And now I have started anew. And I need to do something . . . to feel something different, something gentle and life affirming."

She handed him the comb. He scooted around behind her and lifted her hair from her shoulder. Slowly, very slowly, he began to comb her hair. She felt a growing tenderness for him as he combed. Since she had grown to adulthood, she had never been this close to a man. What was she feeling? Why did she want him to continue combing her hair? Had he bewitched her? Or was she bewitching him?

"What if we never see each other again?" he whispered, and his breath was warm in her ear. "What if we have met for a moment in the wilderness, and when the sun comes up, you will disappear, and we will never be this close again?"

She could not answer the question. She started to tremble.

"Are you cold?" he asked.

"No," she replied, "I am frightened."

"Are you frightened of me?" Micah asked.

She turned and touched him gently on the cheek in answer. He took her hand and kissed her palm.

Luti pulled it back as if she had touched fire. *Why am I acting like this?* she wondered. *What is happening to me?*

"I am trembling, too, now," Micah whispered.

"I must go to Gaza in the morning," she said.

"Yes, I understand."

"We will never see each other again. And perhaps the name you have told me is a lie. And perhaps I am not named Luti."

"I'm not sure that is important." He moved closer and slowly opened her robe and lifted it from her shoulders. As it gathered around her waist, his hand lovingly circled her naked breast. She caught her breath and leaned forward, her hand touching his lips. Her caress prompted Micah to pull off his own robes, then unwrap his loincloth.

Suddenly she heard the tinkling of ornaments.

Occa leapt into their midst. His powerful foot smashed into Micah's face with a sickening thud, then he buried his sword into Nimshi's thigh. Blood and screams mingled in the dry air.

He picked up the dazed and horrified Luti. As he flung her over his shoulder she looked down to see Micah lying still on the ground. In the small of his back was the same mark she had—the lion's paw of the Children of the Lion.

PART
SIX

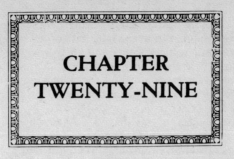

CHAPTER TWENTY-NINE

Troy

I

Two weeks had passed since the death of Achilles, but nothing changed in the war between the Greeks and Trojans. Achilles's brutish son, Neoptolemus, had arrived with his contingent, but too late to see his father alive. In a murderous rage, Neoptolemus immediately entered the battle, striking right and left at the Trojan ranks, but it was futile. The death of Achilles had, as predicted, taken the heart out of the Greeks, and the long war had once again settled into a bloody and increasingly bitter stalemate.

Both sides had lost the cream of their warriors, and on the Trojan side few great fighters were left; the army was comprised mainly of striplings and old men. And on the Greek side, Ajax had killed himself after an attack of madness, further dispiriting the troops who had already buried virtually all of their charismatic war leaders. The best Greek warrior remaining was the wily Odysseus. But to the growing annoyance of Menelaus, who had begun the war, Odysseus was making it clear that he was sick of the dispute and wanted a quick ending to it, even if it was not an unconditional Trojan surrender.

Almost every day Odysseus quit the battlefield to go down to the village and visit Epeius, the master carpenter. Phorbus alone was allowed to accompany him, and their comings and goings were conducted in the utmost secrecy. Although Menelaus's brother, Agamemnon, sent spies after them, the ever-vigilant Phorbus always found them out and returned them to their spy master, who reviled and beat them for their failure.

Then Agamemnon called for Philoctetes, the only man who knew the formula of the deadly poison Paris had used on his arrows.

"We need you, my friend," Agamemnon pleaded. "The war has gone on for too long. Come into the field with us. Paris always remains beyond our range. While he lives, the war will continue and our men will die from his poisoned arrows."

Philoctetes was unconvinced. "You want me to issue a challenge to Paris to meet me in the field, arrow for arrow? Why should I risk my life for you?"

"Because I will make it worth your while." Agamemnon clapped his hands, and seven beautiful girls were led in. "Look at the extraordinary Trojan slaves we have stolen for you."

Philoctetes smacked his toothless gums in delight.

"There is more," Agamemnon said. "Behold!" He waved at the horse pens, where twenty choice Trojan stallions pranced and snorted. "These are yours. And with them twelve tripods of the finest gold, stolen from the Trojan Palladium."

"I am impressed," Philoctetes said. "But—"

"And you will live in my palace with me and feast on the finest foods and wines and be waited on hand and foot. You will be treated with the deference accorded the kinsmen of the high king of Mycenae."

Philoctetes's ugly lips curled in a venal smile.

After the old man had agreed and gone off to admire his new possessions, Odysseus presented himself. "Do you think that having this murderous old fool kill Paris will end the war for us at last?" he asked. "My lord, your family does not have the reputation of being gullible."

Agamemnon frowned. "I can't think what else to do. Odysseus, advise me! I'm as sick of the war as you are."

"Go ahead with your plans," Odysseus suggested. "It'll be an advantage to have Paris dead. Once he's gone, we'll pack up and sail west."

"What? Leaving the war unwon?"

"So it will appear, and there will be great rejoicing in Troy."

"No! I won't hear of it!"

"And they will let down their guard, believing they are safe."

Agamemnon stared wide-eyed in excitement. "Go on."

What Cassandra needed most in her life now was a sane, predictable, safe succession of days. Instead the god Apollo returned to her, interrupting her life with falling fits. When she collapsed on the ground, her eyes rolled back into her head, and her mouth drooled, pronouncing gibberish.

She could not escape. The god's visits brought her blinding flashes of the depressing truth. She knew what was going to happen, but she could not talk about it. When she tried to warn her father, her tongue refused to work.

There were only two people in the world to whom she could talk, and the irony was that one of them was Paris, the person she most despised—and the other, Keturah, was now lost to her.

Cassandra had lived in isolation for most of her life, and as long as she had never admitted any other person into her heart, she had been able to live with her loneliness. But when she had opened up to Keturah, she had made herself vulnerable. How it hurt to be fully human! How it hurt to love. How it hurt not to be loved in return.

It was not that Keturah avoided her. The blind woman would obey dutifully if given an order. But if Cassandra tried to speak to her as a friend, Keturah would ignore her or cover her ears. She refused any longer to allow Cassandra to share her illusions with her—about Phorbus, about safety, about a time and a place where they would all live together as a family in happiness and intimacy.

As Apollo's visitations grew more horrible, obliterating any hope for escape or a life with Phorbus, Cassandra's need for Keturah's love grew keener. Days and nights passed in a restless frenzy. Cassandra became worn and haggard.

In desperation over the endless war, the Trojan women Andromache and Hecuba visited Helen. Andromache was the widow of Hector; Hecuba was Troy's queen. Hecuba got right to the point.

"Your desertion of your husband started this war, Helen, and it's your responsibility to end it. We think you and Paris should go to your husband and Agamemnon under a flag of truce and offer to return to Menelaus."

Helen looked insulted. "Do you realize what you're asking of me?"

"Do you realize what you've already required of us?" Andromache shot back. "I lost my husband because of you. Hector was a better man than Menelaus and Paris put together. Because of you, my child has no father and this horrid war shows no sign of ending. We're all growing old. Our children have come to adulthood never knowing peace—and all because of your selfish, irresponsible behavior."

Looking at Helen's peerless face, Andromache knew that the former queen of Sparta felt no guilt or responsibility. Worse, whatever the outcome of the war, Helen alone would survive and prosper. If Troy won, Helen would remain as Paris's wife and dominate life in the city. If Troy lost and Andromache and Hecuba and all the other Trojan women were dragged off into whoredom and slavery, Helen would return to Sparta as queen, as if nothing had happened. She would rule beside Menelaus and quite possibly would never give a thought to the ten years of horror her actions had brought on.

Paris stood atop the wall, looking down at Philoctetes.

"Paris!" the old man called. "You're young, and I'm old. Your arm is stronger than mine, and your eye is sharper. You can shoot straighter on your worst day than I can at my best. Why, then, do you avoid me and shoot your arrows from behind a wall? Come down and take your chances against my failing arm."

"If the odds are so strongly in my favor," Paris asked, "why challenge me? Do you wish to die, or do you have some trick?"

"No tricks—just you and me and a single quiver of arrows apiece. What have you to fear?"

Paris frowned, knowing he should be wary. Then he gave in to impulse, which he had not done since the day Helen had convinced him to steal not only her but the Spartan treasury.

That escapade had worked well enough, he decided, so why not accept the challenge? Anyway, he was tired of the fools who kept calling him cowardly.

He smiled. "Have the armies withdrawn. I accept."

II

Talus peeked around the corner into Cassandra's room and could not believe what he was seeing. When he returned to his mother's side he spoke in a low voice. "She's crying, Mother. The princess is sitting alone, wringing her hands and crying. Is something wrong, Mother? I've never seen her like this before."

"These are difficult times, dear."

Talus looked at Keturah. "There was a time when you'd have rushed to the princess's side if I told you she was unhappy. Now everything is different between you two."

She smiled at the sound of his voice. It was hard to believe he was only eleven years old. He was much more mature than other children his age, mainly because living in the palace had isolated him from other children. How sad it was that Iri had not lived to see Talus as a boy— as a very smart, sometimes exasperating eleven-year-old boy. In fact, she realized, it was time to tell him the truth.

"You can't be friends with the rich and powerful. They don't see things as we do. We can't have the same expectations of them."

"What happened, Mother, to make you think that way?"

"Talus, the princess has blasphemed against the memory of your father."

"But, Mother, you always told me that one should not be angry with the princess when she speaks wild words."

Keturah sighed. "There is more, Talus. I have never told you this, but Princess Cassandra wanted to adopt you, to take you away from me."

"I know that, Mother."

She was astonished. "How?"

"Many people told me. I would not have gone with her, though. I don't want to be a prince of Troy. I want only to be your son."

"You are a wonderful child," Keturah said affectionately, reaching out.

He moved into her embrace. "Mother, please go to her. She is so very lonely. I hate to see her cry!"

For a moment Keturah was tempted to tell him about her fears regarding Cassandra and Phorbus and the escape. But she had no proof, and her own thoughts were too confused. All she could do was repeat: "Rich people don't see things the way we do. We can't trust them."

"Please, Mother . . ." His voice was so pained that for a moment she wavered.

Then she said, "Talus, would you take me up to the wall and tell me what's happening in the field?"

Paris and Philoctetes circled each other on the battlefield. Their arrows were nocked, but their bows remained unbent.

"There are a dozen arrows in each quiver," Paris declared with a smirk. "Are we going to let the sun set before either of us uses a single bolt?"

Philoctetes's toothless smile mocked the handsome prince. "As you wish." He bent his bow.

Paris was poised, ready to leap out of harm's way. Then, cursing himself for inaction, he bent his bow and let fly an arrow at Philoctetes. To Paris's humiliation, as the arrow sped toward its target, the old man calmly bent his own bow and, without bothering to dodge, released a bolt.

Surprise rooted Paris to the ground. He felt like an unwilling participant in a nightmare. In the face of a lightninglike enemy, he could not get his body to move.

The arrow sped toward him, ever closer, until he could almost count the delicate feathers. In the distance he watched his own arrow go wide. But Philoctetes's bolt came directly at him. Why could he not move? Why could he not—

The arrow barely touched him. It grazed his wrist and did not even break the skin. He sighed with relief, then stopped. With blinding speed Philoctetes had nocked another arrow and let it fly. This one came at him more quickly than the first. One moment he saw it; the next it was gone.

Paris felt something strike him in the groin. He looked down in horror. The arrow had penetrated deeply and protruded from his crotch. The pain as it pierced his genitals was exquisite. He screamed shrilly and clutched himself. He fell to his knees, dropping the bow. He was going to die in agony.

The Trojans quickly surrounded Paris and fought off the Greeks who wanted to get their hands on the man who had caused the war. Troy's strongest warriors picked him up and carried him, shrieking in agony, from the field.

The irony of the location of the wound was immediately obvious. No one dared to mention it, however. The favor of the goddess Aphrodite had left him, which was serious, an event to inspire awe and fear, even when it befell a hated man like Paris.

The cynical Odysseus was the lone exception. He stood beside Agamemnon and Phorbus, watching. "So your brother has finally got his revenge," Odysseus said to Agamemnon. "What a terrible thing to be ruined that way and die knowing it. Don't think, however, that this ends the war for us. Losing Paris is not like losing Hector, Penthesilea, or the Nubian commander. Paris's death won't

affect Troy's morale. The Trojans did not think any more
highly of him than we do."

Agamemnon nodded. "All right, then. Go ahead with
your plan. I'll muster the captains to explain your strategy
the moment the army has quit the field." He narrowed his
eyes speculatively at Odysseus, and for a moment his
confidence wavered. "Are you sure this is going to work?"

Odysseus was tempted to confess that he really was
not sure. Instead he said, "Anything is better than squatting between Troy and the sea for another ten years of
slow death." He glanced at Phorbus and winked. "But it'll
work. Now I've got to get busy setting it up. Phorbus, get
down to the village and tell them we're ready. We move
at sundown."

Helen paused in the hallway and listened to Paris's
screams of agony. Prince Aeneas, standing outside the
door, saw the delicate look of distaste on her face and the
way she winced every time Paris cried out.

"Where did the arrow strike?" she asked.

Aeneas looked at her dispassionately. "In his manhood, my lady," Aeneas answered. "It went through his
genitals and into his thigh. The arrow had to be cut out of
his leg. He won't last long. In a few minutes the poison
will begin to work and kill the pain. Soon he won't be able
to feel anything below the waist."

She cringed as Paris screamed again. "I won't have to
look at it, will I? The wound, I mean?"

"No, my lady," Aeneas replied coolly. "They'll have
covered him up by now. You can go right in." His voice
turned as cold as his eyes. "On the other hand, you could
wait until the poison takes over and he stops screaming."

"Perhaps that would be better," she agreed quickly.
"Has he been calling for me?"

"As a matter of fact, no, he hasn't," Aeneas said.
"While he was incoherent he was calling for Oenone. I
don't think he's mentioned your name."

Helen's brows went up. "Oenone? The peasant wench
he deserted for me? Whatever could he want with a
common girl when he can have me?"

"I can't imagine—your compassion is nearly overwhelming," Aeneas said in disgust. "Look in on him or leave the poor man alone. I think the latter would be a blessing." He turned on his heel and stalked off.

Paris screamed again, and Helen shuddered dramatically before realizing that no one was watching her performance. She stood poised before the door for a moment, then shrugged and turned and walked rapidly down the hall, away from Paris's suite.

Phorbus returned at dusk from the village. A young Greek warrior accompanied him.

"They're moving it up now," the armorer informed Agamemnon and Odysseus. "By nightfall they'll be hauling it in from behind the trees. The wheels are rolling nicely. Epeius has done a good job."

"Take some credit yourself," Odysseus said, then turned to Agamemnon. "Phorbus suggested improvements in the design." He looked back at his friend. "Who's this with you? Is this Sinon?"

Phorbus nodded. "I've coached him, and he can recite the whole story backward and forward."

"Forward will do just fine," Odysseus said. "Now, lad, don't let the Trojans fluster you. They'll huff and puff at first, but if you tell the story the way Phorbus instructed, you'll seem like a man much put upon, and you'll have their sympathy. And when they understand what happened, they'll think you're their savior."

"I won't fail you, sir."

"Good lad." Odysseus looked at Agamemnon. "Our ships are loaded?"

"Yes. They're anchored off the coast now, ready to go."

"Good," Odysseus approved with the first big smile Phorbus had seen in months. "Let's have a drink on that—a drink to going home."

As dawn broke the next morning, the young guard atop Troy's city walls had slipped off to sleep. He was awakened not by the fresh pink light in the sky but by a harsh croak of seagulls flying out to sea to feed. He looked up and rubbed his eyes, expecting to see the same sight that met his eyes every morning. When he stood up and looked out over the plain, however, he gasped.

"Captain of the guard! Captain of the guard!" he cried in a high-pitched voice. "The Greeks are gone!"

There was no sign of the ships or of the great army that had camped on the beaches below Troy for the last ten years. In their place stood a towering wooden statue of a horse!

III

Within moments the city guard was roused, and a runner was sent to Priam. The old king struggled out of bed and up to the top of the wall. There he stood watching his men pouring out the city gates into what yesterday had been a field of battle.

Across the Scamander River there was no sign of the great flotilla—only abandoned, rotted hulks of ships, the charred remains of campfires, broken weapons, and heaps of garbage on which the gulls were feasting.

The captain of the guard spoke uneasily, watching the king's reaction. "This is the way the sentinel saw it at first light, Sire. Sometime during the night the Greeks must have packed up and gone away. And they dragged this statue up here. See, there are wheels to make the job easier. But just where it came from, or why they—"

"Captain!" came a call from below.

The captain excused himself and leaned far out over the wall to look down. "What is it?"

"We've found someone they left behind. Do you want me to bring him up for questioning?"

The captain looked at Priam. "Sire?"

Priam nodded enthusiastically. "Yes, by all means."

The prisoner said his name was Sinon, and he was very bitter toward the Greeks. He kept looking from the captain's face to Priam's, trying to figure out who might be more likely to sympathize with him.

"It was that cowardly bastard Odysseus, my lord." He gulped and started again. "Excuse me, I hadn't intended to use unseemly language before you like this, but whenever I think of what that man did to me—"

"It's quite all right," Priam said reassuringly. "Go on, young man."

"Thank you, Sire. I knew I was among gentlemen. Anyhow, I am a kinsman of Palamedes, who didn't get on with Odysseus, you know."

"I remember vividly," Priam said.

"Very well, sir. Anyhow, 'any kinsman of Palamedes's is an enemy of mine,' Odysseus says, and when it came time to choose a sacrifice to regain the favor of the goddess—"

"Wait!" the captain said. "Sacrifice? Goddess? Which goddess?"

"Sir, remember at the beginning of the war when Odysseus defiled that temple to Pallas Athene that you built outside the walls? Yes? Well, Calchas the seer decided we'd offended the goddess and had to atone for it."

"As he should," Priam said disapprovingly.

"Yes, sir. Well, the next thing you know they'd picked me for sacrifice, and—"

The captain interrupted. "What has this to do with their leaving? And with the statue out there?"

"I was coming to that, sir. They'd already decided in council that the war was a mistake and the only thing to do was go home."

"Hear, hear!" old Priam said. "Would that they had come to that decision a long time ago."

"Yes, sir," Sinon said. "And they had the horse made as a gift to the goddess, to give them good luck on their voyage homeward. Calchas said that human blood was required, too, and Odysseus chose me. I'd done him no harm! But they tied me up, put the sacred wreath on my head, and were ready to kill me. Thank the gods the soldiers hadn't tied the knots tightly enough, you see, and I managed to wriggle loose and hide. Rather than miss the morning tide, they took off without catching and killing me. I hope Calchas's prediction comes true; he said if they didn't kill me, they'd all return home to terrible fates."

"A wish with which we can all concur, eh, Captain?" Priam said, beaming.

"Yes, sir. But you, lad, what did you do next?"

"I couldn't think of anything to do, sir, but hide under the horse and, when the time came, throw myself on the mercy of gentlemen like you, sir."

The captain and Priam exchanged glances. "What do you think, sir?" the captain asked.

"I think that this young man has had a stroke of exceedingly good fortune," Priam said. "And I think he is going to be my personal guest at a banquet of thanksgiving tonight." He clapped Sinon on the shoulder. "You bring us luck, lad. You'll be richly rewarded for it." Priam raised both hands in supplication. His voice was clear and commanding. "Thanks be to the gods for peace! Tell everyone the good news! There's going to be a great feast tonight! Bring out the best food and wine! Kill the young lambs! Let there be feasting and thanksgiving and merrymaking! The war is over!"

The bells pealed, the horns blew, and the people hurried from the city, where they had been imprisoned for ten long and horrible years of siege. Men and women alike wept with joy and sang and danced on the blood-soaked field where so many of their loved ones had died.

Palace servants fanned out into the hills to butcher the animals that would be served at the great feast that night. Others went into the villages to secure the wine for Priam's festival of triumph. The word was spread: All vassals and friends of Troy were welcome at the evening's feast. Food and drink and dancing and lovemaking could be enjoyed without shame—all inhibitions were to be cast aside. The Greeks were gone! The city was safe! The gods had shown favor to the embattled city and its exhausted residents, and once more Troy would prosper and shed its light over the east.

*   *   *

Talus brought the news to Cassandra and his mother. "The war's over! The Greeks have sailed away!"

He was astonished by the bitterness of his mother's reply. "Now no one will come to take us away. Phorbus has dishonored his pledge to your father. He has betrayed the trust of a man who loved and adopted him. Now we will never go to the island your father called Home. We will live out our lives here. At least the Greeks have a home to go back to."

Cassandra said sadly, "I always thought Phorbus would return to Troy. Oh, I know he wouldn't have taken me—I'm too ugly. Men don't have anything to do with me and never will. But somehow I had the feeling he would rescue *you*." She started to say more, then she wilted and withdrew into herself.

As the musicians and dancers came through the city gates to serenade the crowd on the battlefield, a detachment of city guards dragged the great horse to the main gate. Four times the huge statue snagged on the raised threshold, but at last the soldiers, assisted by dozens of the enthusiastic citizens, managed to pull and push the horse into Troy.

They tugged the great hulking beast through the city streets toward the Acropolis, where it would be the centerpiece for the evening's festivities.

Cassandra was suffering from one of her spells. Talus restrained her as she thrashed on the floor, her eyes rolling back into her head, and tried to prevent her from swallowing her tongue.

Afterward, Keturah hovered dutifully by the princess's side, bathing her brow with cool water and speaking to the unconscious woman in soothing tones until she slipped into a gentle sleep.

Suddenly the dreams came back—horrible visions that made Cassandra sit up, screaming with mental anguish and physical pain. "No, please, Father, make it stop! Make them go away! Save me, please! Don't make me go with them!"

Keturah's face looked puzzled. What did her mistress mean? Had the Greeks not already gone? Was the war not over? Why did she have to be saved? Or was this merely lingering fear that would slowly fade, as security once more descended upon poor, embattled Troy?

IV

Helen wandered the halls of the palace in her most eye-catching clothes and to her surprise found that no one noticed her. For the first time since she had landed in Troy ten years before, she could walk among the people and fail to attract a single look. It was as if she was beneath even contempt, as if she were no longer human.

Shocked, she returned to her room and studied herself in the mirror. The reflection assured her that she had little to fear. Then what was wrong?

As she stood posing before the mirror, she became aware that she was not alone. She wheeled around to see Hector's widow, Andromache, standing in the open doorway, her arms crossed over her ample bosom, watching her with cold eyes.

"What's the matter?" Andromache asked. "Don't tell me; something has finally diverted the men's eyes from you."

"Get out of here," Helen grated, trying to retain her dignity after having been caught in an awkward moment.

"Find any wrinkles?" Andromache taunted. "Is your face beginning to fall? Are your teeth looking a bit long?" She paused. "By the way, they cremated Paris today. Not many people were there, and I think everyone would rather have postponed it, but the poor fellow was beginning to stink. Oh, yes, your absence was noticed by the few who bothered to attend."

Helen did not reply.

"I understand Paris never asked for you as he was dying. A good thing, too, because you never came to see him. He did ask to see his first wife—the *real* one. Unlike you, she came. And as he lay dying, she screamed at him for abandoning her for a shallow bitch like yourself. 'Shallow bitch'—those were her exact words. She screamed at him until she was hoarse and then rushed out into the night as if crazed."

"I don't know why you think I should be interested in—"

"Wait until you hear the rest: Today the woman was overcome with remorse. When they lit Paris's funeral pyre she jumped into the flames before anyone could stop her. She didn't even scream as the fire consumed her. I think she'd done all her crying."

"How disgusting."

"Oh, I don't think so; I thought it was noble. At least *she* truly loved him. At least *she* showed human feelings."

"I think you ought to go," Helen said through clenched teeth.

"You couldn't be bothered even to show up, could you? The man ruined himself and Troy for you, and you couldn't be—"

"Get out! I said get out!"

"My pleasure," Andromache said triumphantly.

Priam looked like a man from whom the weight of years had magically fallen. His step had a new bounce, and he walked around the palace beaming, speaking to the servants as if they were his equals.

Except for those preparing for the evening's feast, everyone had gone through the open gates and into the meadow, where they were singing and dancing. Down by the Scamander River, young men and women had undressed, dived into the stream, and were romping happily.

When Cassandra had finally calmed down and gone back to sleep, Talus had begged leave from his mother to watch the celebration. As he ran through the city streets toward the open gate, he passed the towering wooden horse. Curious, he stopped and kicked its wooden leg. The sound was solid. Then on impulse he climbed up to the platform that connected the legs with the wheels and stood on tiptoe to knock on the belly.

Here the sound was different. He heard a lingering echo and looked up. The belly was made of stout hard-wood planks.

Of course the figure would be hollow, he realized. What tree would be big enough to make a solid sculpture? How stupid of him.

Then Talus became aware of someone staring at him. It was the stranger Sinon, whom the Greeks had left behind. Why was Sinon looking at him with so peculiar an expression? Talus recognized the look: The Greek was afraid. Why should a soldier be afraid of a boy?

The celebration officially began at sundown. By Priam's express command everyone was welcome. All had shared the suffering of the Trojans and deserved to share in the celebration. Row after row of tables were set up in the city square, and endless lines of royal servants and slaves bearing heavily laden trays threaded their way down the halls from the palace kitchens.

As the cups of wine were passed around, rich man and poor man drank together and toasted each other's health as if they were brothers.

From the balconies above the square, music was played, and flower petals were tossed to the crowd. The sound of slaves singing resounded across the rooftops. Naked flute players, male and female, wound through the crowd, offering merry tunes. From time to time one of the revelers would pick up one of the musicians, toss him or her over one shoulder, and disappear into the darkened streets, the musicians laughing drunkenly all the way.

Priam tried to address the crowd, but he was full of wine, and his slurred words could not be heard over the din. The king did not mind. He waved his cup, spilling wine, until someone led him away.

Later, Princess Cassandra appeared on one of the balconies. Like Priam, she tried to speak. At first she was hooted down, but then she managed to get the attention of the assemblage.

"People of Troy!" she cried in a hysterical voice, only slightly slurred by the potions the palace magus had given her to calm her. "You stand in deadly danger! Apollo has spoken to me! He showed me a vision of the city filled with fire and blood! You have let death and destruction into the city! Wake up now before it is too—"

The spirit of egalitarianism that prevailed below and the general drunkenness had already formed a potent mixture. Someone tossed a half-gnawed animal bone at her; another added a wine cup, which overturned as it flew, splashing its contents all over. Cassandra drew back as the cup clanked against the wall beside her head.

"Don't ignore my warning!" she implored. "I saw death bursting out of the belly of that horse!"

Priam's attendants gently escorted her away. The last anyone heard was her shrill, crowlike voice warning: "You must listen to me!"

Talus watched and listened. Experience had taught him never to ignore Cassandra's prophecies, and now he pondered what she had meant. With the unclouded eyes of a child, he watched the drunken crowd and decided that something odd was happening and that the stranger, Sinon, had something to do with it. He decided to find the young Greek and stick to him like a barnacle to a boat.

He found Sinon in the great hall of the palace. Talus noticed that the Greek hardly drank. When the man on his left passed the wine cup to him, Sinon would take a sip, if that. Once Talus saw him pour out half a cup of wine when no one was looking.

When a fresh group of flute players came into the great room, one of the girls perched naked and amorous on Sinon's knee; surprisingly, he sent her away with a chilly smile. Even more alert, Talus noted that a boy musician, sidling up to Sinon and brushing up against the Greek's bare arm, got the same treatment.

Was the man a capon, or did he have other things on his mind? Talus, resolved to watch Sinon all the more closely, curled up behind a tall amphora and peeked out from the deep shadow.

As the night wore on, Talus dozed off. When he awoke, the floor was covered with unconscious Trojans who had drunk themselves to insensibility. The boy looked around. There was no sign of Sinon!

Panic-stricken, he rushed around the room, looking for the stranger, but none of the inert faces was his!

Talus cursed himself for having fallen asleep. He ran silently across the big room on bare feet and flew down the long staircase to the ground floor. He found not a single person who was awake and aware.

As he ran through the streets, he found the same situation. He scanned the city wall—the guards had either deserted their posts or fallen asleep, and the gates were wide open.

Talus's heart pounded with fear. He looked at the silhouette of the great wooden horse, which was outlined against the moon. In a panic he scrambled to the top of the city wall.

At first he saw nothing, but then a glimmer of light caught his eye. On the rampart where a guard should have been was Sinon, waving a torch. Talus knew it was a signal, which could easily be seen from well out to sea.

The boy dashed over to the far wall, nearer where the great horse stood. As Talus watched, Sinon affixed the torch to the rampart, ran to the statue, and climbed up the wheeled base and was knocking on the horse's belly— just as he himself had done before—but Sinon was knocking much more boldly.

The belly of the horse opened, and armed soldiers began to drop down silently from a door in its wooden stomach to the platform below.

V

Sinon's signal torch was visible to the Greek ships, which lay ready to lift anchor and return to Troy. The rowers who manned both sides of each black ship began to pull on their oars, and the Greek fleet moved to rejoin the warriors left behind in the belly of the great horse.

Far out to sea, toward Lemnos, a violent storm was brewing. In the distance, lightning rent the sky, revealing ships landing and the army marching rapidly up the slope toward Troy.

Although Talus managed to escape with his life in the confusion, the scenes of the butchery that he witnessed would, he knew, poison his dreams for as long as he lived: The Greeks, wielding sword and lance, descended upon the drunken, snoring Trojans and slaughtered them as they slept. Many invaders hacked and stabbed while others lit torches and fired the thatched roofs of the city's houses and businesses. The fires spread as Talus watched in horror. He knew he should be warning the city, but he stood paralyzed with terror atop the wall.

At last he forced his legs to move. He slipped down the other side of the wall, but a strong hand reached out and grabbed him by the hair.

Talus struggled in vain. "Let me go!" he screamed, flailing his small fists and kicking out at his attacker.

"Quiet, lad," a voice said. "Are you Talus? Gods, you favor your father! It is I, Phorbus!"

Talus nodded and hung limp as Phorbus set him down.

"I've come to get your mother and you and take you away. As an armorer I wasn't even supposed to be here tonight. I insisted on coming, because it was the only way I knew to reach you two before someone else did. Where is Keturah?"

"We'll never find her alive!" He began to cry. "Your people are murdering everyone in sight!"

"Quiet!" Phorbus urged. As he spoke, flames in the house across the way suddenly ignited something highly flammable, and the whole house exploded with a roar. Live sparks showered over them. "Come, we can't stay here, Talus. Keep your wits about you, now. I'm depending upon your help!"

They slipped down a deserted stairwell.

Talus looked at him warily. "I can lead you to Mother."

"No, right now I have to make it look as if I am participating in the seige. You find Keturah and lead her to a safe hiding place. The best place may be the roof of the palace. It'll take the Greeks a while to reach it. I'll come around from the far side. Don't panic. I'm here to rescue your mother and you, and I won't leave without you. Trust me, boy. Now go!"

The sounds of slaughter and the crackling of the fires finally roused the men of Troy. Those who could reach their weapons were now fighting desperately for their lives and their city. Phorbus fought his way toward the palace, where he saw a Trojan nobleman in his night-clothes and armed only with a poker, battling fiercely. Another man fought stark naked, armed only with a cere-monial spear pulled from the wall.

I've got to get out of here, Phorbus thought. *I've got to get up the stairs.* He parried an attack and sprinted for the stairwell. But as he did, he saw Ajax the Lesser, a mighty Greek warrior, go pounding up the steps ahead of him. Called the Lesser because he was so much shorter than Achilles's friend who was also named Ajax, he was a coarse, vulgar man. Phorbus knew that Ajax the Lesser would show no mercy.

Nearby, Achilles's hulking son Neoptolemus and Odysseus found old King Priam in a corridor. Odysseus would have spared the broken, elderly ruler, but Priam stepped forward to face Neoptolemus. His chin defiantly thrust out, he said in a regal voice, "Son of Achilles, before you go down this hall, you must kill me."

With a single stroke the young savage beheaded him. Odysseus winced but said nothing. Then Neoptolemus and Odysseus continued through the palace. They were preceded by Greek soldiers, who looked into the first open door. Inside, Odysseus recognized Andromache, who was holding her and Hector's son, Astynax, in her arms. As Odysseus watched, one of the warriors grabbed the child. The frightened boy barely had time to cry for his mother before the soldier hurled him out the window.

Odysseus made his way down the hall, trying to get away from Andromache's heartrending screams. This was war; this was the enemy who had kept him here, far from those he loved, for ten years. The only way to go home was to destroy the Trojans. He fought down the bile that rose in his throat, hardened his heart, and went about his work. He had resolved he would kill only men, but he could not stop the other Greeks from murdering women and children. Let them answer to the gods, he decided, for their own shameful deeds.

Phorbus reached the roof just in time to see Ajax the Lesser trying to trap Talus and Keturah. Standing between them and the Greek warrior was Cassandra, grasping a sword. She was still in her nightclothes. Her feet were bare, and her long hair was whipped wildly around her face by the growing storm winds. Her skinny arms were barely strong enough to hold the weapon, but she managed to point the blade at the man. When the Greek lunged toward her, she managed a clumsy parry. Then Phorbus interposed himself between the princess and the man reputed to be Greece's finest spearman.

"Leave them alone!" Phorbus demanded.

Ajax the Lesser glared at him, weapon at the ready. "A turncoat," he snarled. "Are you fighting for these Trojan dogs? Fight me, then!"

Phorbus glanced at Cassandra. "Princess! Get them over the wall and down the side. You know the way Iri and I used last time."

"Yes," she said, her eyes bright with hope.

She turned to Keturah and, with one hand on the blind woman's arm, led her to the wall. The princess picked up a coil of rope and tied an end around her friend's waist. As Phorbus watched, he believed for the first time that he would be able to save them.

Ajax the Lesser, however, took advantage of the distraction and attacked. He was quicker than anyone Phorbus, with his limited experience of fighting, had ever seen. The armorer was forced to give ground. He parried successfully but never had the opportunity to counterstroke. He watched Ajax's eyes as Iri had taught him to do so many years before.

Suddenly, without warning, the Greek's sword caught him a glancing blow on the head. Phorbus cried out and fell to his knees. He tried to defend himself, but another blow dazed him, and he pitched to the ground on his face.

Cassandra, meanwhile, was lowering Keturah down the wall with Talus's help when she heard Phorbus's cry. She ordered the boy to climb down when she felt Keturah touch the ground and let go of the rope. Once the child was safe, also, Cassandra turned around. The wind was now gusting across the parapets. Her hair swirled about her face, blinding her. Where was Phorbus? She couldn't see him. A strong gust of wind spun her around, twisting her nightgown around her legs. Her heart beat wildly— the ugly little Ajax with his powerful torso and malevolent expression was coming toward her.

So this is how it happens, she thought. She spoke quietly to her divine oracle: "You told me I would not escape, but at least Keturah and the boy are free. Thank you, Apollo, for that."

She sprinted barefoot through the formal rooftop gardens to the small temple of Pallas Athene on the far side of the roof. Few Greeks would dare to defile a temple by pursuing someone who sought sanctuary in it.

She grasped the statuette of the goddess in her arms, but Ajax's hand grabbed her hair.

"Dear goddess!" she cried. "Curse him for his blasphemy! Punish him!"

But Ajax the Lesser was not intimidated. He dragged Cassandra violently to her feet and smashed her across the face.

"Shut up," he ordered. "Or do you want to die now?"

By the time Phorbus, bleeding and groggy, staggered to his feet, he was alone. The dying city was in flames, and the fire was licking at the palace walls.

"Keturah!" he shouted, rushing to the far wall. He peered over the side. "Talus! Are you down there?"

"Yes, sir," a quavering voice piped. "Are you coming down?"

"Right away," Phorbus answered. Grabbing the rope, he wrapped it around his wrist. With one last look across the rooftop, he stepped over the side and rappelled down the face of the wall.

When he touched the ground, he saw a huge bulky figure move through the shadows and into the moonlight. It was Prince Aeneas, carrying his elderly father in his arms.

Aeneas stopped and stared at Phorbus. "If you want to try to stop me—" the prince challenged, about to set the old man down.

"No," Phorbus said, "get him to safety. I've no quarrel with you or with any Trojans."

The father and son moved on.

"Phorbus," Keturah said, pulling at his sleeve, "what happened to Cassandra?"

"I don't know," he replied. "Ajax attacked me and—"

"I'm so sorry," she whispered. "She may have given her life for us."

"If I can save you two, we'll be lucky," Phorbus said. "Let's pray that the Greeks left the boats unguarded down on the beach."

Far in the distance, as he led her and the boy down the slope, lightning bolts sent jagged white fingers into the water. The violent storm was getting closer, and thunder shook the chill night air. Behind him Phorbus felt the heat of the flames that were devouring the city, and the plain was almost as bright as day.

The storm was tossing the sea beyond Lemnos and moving slowly toward Troy. Huge waves nearly swamped Theon's boat. The mainmast, snapped in two by a bolt of lightning, crashed down into the rowers' pit and killed three of Theon's strongest oarsmen, leaving the galley unbalanced. Theon leapt into the pit and manned one of the oars, forever earning the respect of his crew. But not being able to stay safely out at sea, the vessel found partial shelter in a cove along the Lemnite coast, where it was anchored to windward to wait out the storm.

Theon watched the wind whip the waves as the rain whistled about him. He scanned the eastern horizon for signs of the dawn. How long would they be held up? he wondered. It would be unwise to sail for Troy now, even if the weather were calm. The mast must be mended. Besides, there was no sign of calm weather. The wind howled around him, and rain pounded on the deck. A thunderclap broke deafeningly close to the ship. The storm showed no sign of abating.

Fishermen sheltering in the same cove had news of ships moving along the Trojan coast. What could this mean? Theon wanted to know. Was the war over at last? Had the Greeks given up and gone home, leaving Keturah and the boy safe? Theon felt a sudden chill and pulled his robe more closely around him. No, somehow he thought the situation was more complicated than that.

PART
SEVEN

CHAPTER THIRTY

Canaan

General Sisera rode with only a pair of common soldiers to guard him, and in his red-hot anger and haste he had outdistanced them. Now he could not even see them atop the last ridge. Spurring his exhausted horse forward, he cursed them, the horse, and everything that stood between him and Hazor.

Then, as a final blow, the horse pulled up lame. Sisera dug his heels into the animal's flanks and flailed away at it with his whip, but the horse could go no farther.

Since Sisera was passing a once-prosperous Israelite farm in the foothills below Hazor, he dismounted. In the pen on the edge of the farmer's pasture, the general saw what looked like a serviceable mare. He took the saddle off his horse and, his eyes blazing with anger and disgust, thrust his sword into the horse's heaving belly and left it to bleed to death slowly. He stalked toward the farmhouse.

"You there!" he bellowed. "Come out and give me a hand!"

A young boy appeared in the doorway. "Who are you?" he asked.

"Your damned superior, you little bastard," Sisera yelled. "Bring me that mare and saddle her. Why are you just standing there? Get moving!"

The boy blinked. "I—I'd better call my father."

"There's no time for that," Sisera growled. "Get the

horse! Now!" His long arm reached out, and his powerful
hand closed on the boy's thin upper arm. "Saddle the
horse, or so help me I'll—"

"Yes, sir," the boy said, but still he did not move.

Sisera, taking his hesitance for insolence, slapped him
hard in the face. The boy's eyes filled with tears, and he
tried to run away; but Sisera held on to his arm.

"I—I'll get right to it, sir. It's just that the horse is my
father's favor—"

"Never mind!" Sisera said. "I'll get it myself. Out of
my way!"

The mare shied at first but ultimately allowed him to
force the bridle on her. He leapt up to her back, without a
saddle, and nudged the animal through the gate.

"What do I tell my father?" the boy called out.

For an answer Sisera galloped toward him. The boy
could not run fast enough and was trampled under the
horse's hooves. Sisera, a good horseman in fair mood or
foul, had the animal going at a dead run within half a
league and was soon within sight of Hazor.

"What do you mean he's not back yet?" Pepi demanded of one of his apprentices. "I gave Heber no extended leave of absence."

"I know, sir," the young man replied. "But he went
to Jezreel on an errand involving a tin shipment, and he
hasn't returned or sent word."

Pepi bit his lip. He did not like having Heber loose
out there. He had taken a great risk in coming back to
Hazor to get Heber to safety before the Israelites started
their revolt. Once that happened, it would be very difficult to prevent Heber from attempting to take revenge on
Sisera. The Kenite had no chance against that man. Pepi
tried not to show his concern. "Now that I'm here, I'm
declaring a holiday. Tell all the rest of the workers. They're
all to take a week off at my expense."

The man looked puzzled. "Why, thank you, sir!"

Pepi thought quickly. "Go now! Enjoy yourselves,
with my blessings." He was hopeful that they would all
obey him immediately and get to safety. But as he strode

away from the forges he himself had built but was now about to abandon, he felt a twinge of regret. *Will I be back?* he wondered. *Will I ever be able to return?*

King Jabin, agitated, continued to pace. "Tell me again," he said, glaring at his minister.

"Yes, Sire. Yesterday afternoon one of our informants arrived in the city and begged for sanctuary, saying his life was in danger because the Israelites had found him out. He said that they had already caught one spy—someone Telem had hired from Megiddo named Ishbak—and killed him, and the rebels had ambushed one of our patrols and wiped them out to the last man."

"Telem told me of that—an offense for which their wives and children will pay dearly," Jabin said. "But for some reason Pepi discounted Telem's credibility."

"Our informant," the official continued, "infiltrated one of the Israelite units, which had been training for an uprising. He claimed that a major attack was planned once their arms were delivered."

"Where can they have gotten enough arms to attack our main force in Jezreel?"

"Apparently the huge cache was a gift, Sire, from the family of Khalkeus of Gournia."

"Khalkeus? What grievance could he have against us?"

"That, Sire, is where Pepi comes in. He is a nephew of Demetrios the Magnificent, who built the trading company and chose Khalkeus as his successor." The minister let this sink in on a startled Jabin, then said, "And it seems to have been Theon, a kinsman of Pepi's and one of Khalkeus's associates, who authorized the weapons delivery." He paused again. "At the suggestion of Pepi, Sire."

There was a long silence. Finally Jabin spoke bitterly. "This is an act of treason . . . a betrayal of me and my people. Pepi shall pay for this. Is he still in the city? Bring him here!"

"Yes, Sire," the court official said.

"You've sent the message up north to Telem, ordering him to bring the army back here immediately?"

"According to the messenger, Telem left with his army for Hazor at dawn."

Jabin paced, fuming. "Bring that bastard Pepi here! Send someone innocuous, someone he won't be frightened of. Tell him . . . tell him I have a gift for him—that the king wants to see his favorite armorer. Whatever you do, don't let anyone scare off that traitorous bastard."

"As for Sisera," the official said, "I dictated the message myself. The army units in Jezreel are now on full alert, and in your name I told Sisera to get in touch with you immediately."

"You didn't tell him to attack?" Jabin asked.

"No, I wanted more specific information on how many men Sisera has and how soon Telem might arrive," the official replied. "Our sources told us that a major arms shipment is heading up from the Jordan Valley under heavy guard. We don't know if it's going to the Israelites or whether the delivery has been made by now."

At the sound of a commotion in the hallway, they looked up to see one of the city guards standing at attention in the doorway.

"What is it?" Jabin demanded.

"Sisera, Sire. He's been spotted coming through the gates."

"Sisera? Alone?" The minister was startled by the news.

Jabin gave a triumphant smile. "It's all coming together," he said. "Maybe we're in time, after all."

Pepi was disguised in the long robes of a Hivite and the customary head covering of a caravan owner. He had arranged for a fast horse to be ready for his use just outside the city; but now, as he approached the city gate, he worried about Heber. What if he had visited his wife and learned about Sisera? What if he had confronted the general?

As Pepi approached the guard at the gate, he pulled his head covering forward around his face. He did not want to be recognized—an army officer from the palace had been making inquiries concerning his whereabouts.

There was always the chance that someone had revealed his duplicity to the king, and the best course now was to take no chances.

Pepi knew it had been foolish of him to return to Hazor. Perhaps, he thought, he was too old to play the conspirator. He should have stayed with the Israelite army, even if, at this stage, there was no need for him. Since Shemida, along with many other veterans of Joshua's campaigns, had joined the irregular army, Pepi had been relieved of his need to train Barak. The young leader had made rapid progress in the use of arms; now all he needed was the blooding.

Just inside the city gates, Pepi could see someone dismounting from a lathered horse. When Pepi looked up to see who it was, his hood fluttered back, no longer covering his face.

"You!" Sisera grated, his jaw clenched. He reached for his sword.

CHAPTER THIRTY-ONE

Khareitun Caves, Wilderness of Judea

Luti had been tied to the pommel of her horse for twenty-four hours. Ahead rode Occa, looking back at her from time to time with his ugly grin. She was too numb and weary to feel any pain. Her mind was befuddled from flashing images: of Micah and the feelings he had aroused in her . . . of the birthmark she had seen on his back. Only when she remembered the horror of Occa's attack—the bloodshed and the sudden violence—did she open her eyes and stare around at the desolate landscape.

As the first light of dawn began to streak the Wilderness of Judea, the motion of the horse lulled her into a half sleep.

Suddenly the horse stopped, jolting her forward. She regained her balance and sat up. Occa stood grinning, holding her horse's bridle and pointing ahead. Then the Beduoin gently helped her down from the horse and cut her bonds, then whirled in some bizarre victory dance.

An astonishing sight assailed her eyes. The ground was broken into hundreds of small gullies and inclines. Mammoth rocks jutted out of the ground, and the faces of many of them revealed caves.

Beside the caves were sheds, and under each shed was a forge. The air was foul from their acrid smoke. She could see men stoking the newly lighted forges with charcoal and ore. Naked armorers and their assistants, waiting by each forge for the fires to grow white-hot, inspected their tools. Luti perceived the operation's overwhelming precision and order. Nothing seemed to be haphazard in the whole camp; everything was laid out for maximum productivity.

She remembered Drak's instructions: Get work in a forge and find the new kind of iron-and-wood chariot for the kingdom of Babylon. She was now certain that Occa had been given another set of instructions by Drak: Only the Beduoin had known their true destination, and he had succeeded in getting them there. She had speculated on this in Damascus and now knew that she had been right. It was tragic that she had doubted Occa's intent, for that insecurity had prompted her attempted escape, her meeting the two strangers, and Occa's subsequent violence against them. Occa was probably sworn to carry out Drak's mission, and without her, that mission was impossible.

She tried to push everything out of her mind and concentrate on what she needed to accomplish. Together, the pair mounted and rode into the ring of forges.

It had taken them a long time to find the man in charge, a fellow named Dubai. They located him studying a herd of goats, which was penned in front of a small cave filled with sacks of grain and other supplies. Dubai was a wiry, middle-aged man, unarmed and dressed in the short tunic of the Philistines. Around his neck was a leather amulet. His face and neck were burned dark from the sun. He was stern looking, but the hint of a smile played at the corners of his mouth.

He studied them for a long time, then addressed his questions to Occa. "Who are you? What are you doing here?"

"He neither hears nor speaks," Luti said.

"Fine. Then you tell me. What are a young woman and a Bedouin on expensive horses doing in the Wilderness of Judea?"

"I am looking for work."

Dubai laughed out loud and walked over to the horses, feeling their legs.

"This is an armorer's workplace. We don't have any

work for women unless you're whoring. You see our forges."
Then he smiled gently. "But you do have an eye for
horses. They are splendid animals. Where did you pur-
chase them?"

"In Damascus," Luti replied. "And I'm not a—a whore."

"You have come a long way."

"Yes, very long. That's another reason why you must
give me work."

"Another reason? What was the first one?" he asked,
laughing again.

Suddenly, before his astonished eyes, she unfastened
her robe and let it fall, turning as she did so. "I am a Child
of the Lion."

Dubai stared at the lion's-paw birthmark on the small
of her back. Then Luti put the robe back on and turned to
face him.

"I have always allowed Chalybians to work beside
me," Dubai said. "It would be a great honor to welcome
you. But do you take me for a fool? I have heard there was
only one woman who was a Child of the Lion, the great
Egyptian armorer, Teti. And that was generations ago."

"You are looking at another one," Luti said firmly.

"But it can't be." Dubai started to walk away. "This is
all nonsense!"

"Wait!" Luti cried out. Dubai stopped. "Let me prove
it to you."

The moment she said those words, fear struck deep
into her heart, for she had impulsively placed herself in a
terrible position. What if the gift in her fingers was gone?
What if it could not be called up without Drak's being
near her?

Dubai paced, obviously trying to make up his mind.
Finally he said: "Why not? Let's see what you have."

He walked away, with Luti following. The man led
her past the larger work areas and stopped in front of a
very battered, very old forge. He consulted with two men
who were toiling in the shed beside it.

Luti waited out of earshot. Then she glanced around
and realized that Occa was nowhere to be seen.

Dubai motioned for her to come closer. "See those

tongs and the mallet? Good! Now the men are going to pour molten iron into that mold, which turns out long rods. If you're a Child of the Lion, you'll have no trouble beating it into a perfect circle, like a . . . chariot wheel. Of course, I expect it to be flawless."

The heat from the open pit was beginning to singe her eyebrows. She picked up the tongs and the mallet and stared at the mold. The realization came over her that this time there would be no magic. The tools were alien to her; everything in the shed and on the forge was meaningless. She felt an enormous wave of fatigue. She had traveled so far to fulfill Drak's plan, but it was for nothing. She looked at Dubai. The man was grinning from ear to ear.

A rustling could be heard from outside the shed. Luti and Dubai turned to see Occa standing before them. Instead of his Bedouin robe, he wore a strange-looking, full-length coat made of bird feathers.

"The feathers of the nighthawk," Luti whispered.

Her body drew upon some unseen power source. She smiled and turned back to the molten iron, which was now being poured into the mold. Her fingers felt as if they were becoming the talons of a hawk.

It was dusk in the wilderness. The setting sun shot red rays through the rock and shrubs. Nimshi lay against the side of a small hill. His wounded leg had started to bleed again in spite of the dressing of mud and herbs that Micah had placed on it. At least the fever had broken, and the delirium had abated for the moment. He vaguely remembered babbling and weeping and enduring a pain so severe, he could not see straight. He was ashamed to be such a burden to Micah, but he could no longer depend on himself. His idealistic plans had turned to dross.

From where Nimshi lay, he observed his younger brother at the top of the hill, pressed against the earth so that he would not be seen. Nimshi had wanted to return to Gaza after the Bedouin's attack, but there was no stopping Micah, who sought vengeance. He was determined to track down and kill the Bedouin and rescue the girl. He had carried Nimshi mile after mile while tracking the horses.

Micah moved silently down the hill and squatted near Nimshi. "Has the pain returned?"

"Yes," Nimshi replied, wondering how much distress Micah himself felt; the side of his face was grotesquely swollen from the Bedouin's kick, and it looked as if Micah's cheekbone was broken.

In the dim light, Micah peered into Nimshi's thigh wound and then mixed and shaped another patty of dirt, roots, and saliva to place on the wound.

"What were you looking at?" Nimshi asked.

"The forge."

"Dubai's forge?"

"The very same."

"Then we can get food and water and medicine there," Nimshi said, overwhelmed by relief. He finally admitted to himself that he had thought he would die for lack of care.

"No, we can't."

"Why not?"

"Because the girl and the Bedouin are there, and I am going to sneak in to kill him."

"Can't you forget it, Micah? We don't know why the Bedouin went crazy. Maybe that girl is his wife. And I need to be looked at by a physician."

He winced as Micah began to dress his wound. Nimshi could see by the set of his brother's face that he would not forget or forgive. He would get his vengeance or die in the attempt. The pain now started to come in waves, and he lost consciousness. . . .

When Nimshi awoke, it was pitch dark. He could make out Micah's crouching form. He had removed his long knife and was whetting it against a stone. It sounded like an animal in pain.

"Sleep, Micah, sleep," Nimshi whispered.

"I am thinking."

"About the girl? Have you fallen in love, Micah?"

Micah did not answer.

"What a mistake this has all been," Nimshi said in

anguish. "I took you away from the Israelites because your life was filled with terror and death and brutality. And look what I led you to: a barren wilderness of—"

"Stop talking, Nimshi," Micah said sourly. "You need rest and quiet."

"When will you go to the forge?"

"Soon. We will stay here for a day or so. I will go in alone. You will wait here for me."

"Are you going to bring the girl back?"

"I don't know. Go to sleep. You always ask too many questions."

"When will *you* sleep?"

"When the demons leave my brain," he said, then laughed. But it was not a sound of happiness, and it chilled Nimshi to the core of his being. Was this the hidden legacy of the Children of the Lion?

"Only a Child of the Lion could have hammered out a perfect iron wheel so quickly." Dubai bowed low and presented both Luti and Occa with a bowl of special wine. "It is an honor to be your employer."

It was dark, but Luti was no longer tired. She had slept all afternoon, after the magical powers had once again expressed themselves through her fingers. Before she fell asleep, she had tried repeatedly to thank Occa because the coat of nighthawk feathers, set in the configuration of her zodiacal sign, had conferred the powers on her. She knew that; Drak had taught her so.

But Occa was oblivious to her praise. He had just grinned, and the silver ornaments pinned to his cheek had tinkled.

"Was your dinner to your liking?" Dubai asked now.

"Yes. The cook told me we will be fed twice a day, in the morning and the evening."

"But there is always goats' milk for the armorers," Dubai told her.

"You have been most kind." Luti felt light-headed and powerful.

Dubai bowed again, his eyes twinkling. "No, it is you who have been so kind as to allow me to work with a Child

of the Lion. Now I must express my appreciation. I want
to show you something beautiful, which you will soon be
working on."

He motioned for them to follow. Luti and Occa fell in
step behind Dubai. As they strolled through the night,
past the banked fires of the forges, past the small bonfires
where the armorers and their helpers rested, the thought
came to her that there existed occult powers in her that
she had not even tapped.

Who am I, really? she mused. *Am I a reincarnation
of the goddess Astarte?* The thought was so absurd that
she laughed out loud, and Dubai turned around to stare at
her, perplexed.

They entered an enormous cave in which no fire was
burning. The threesome moved deep inside and stopped
at the edge of a large antechamber lighted by oil lamps.

"What you see here must never be discussed," Dubai
warned.

Something was very strange about the floor of the
room; it was not uniform in its appearance. One strip was
muddy, the next strip sandy, the next strip rocky, the next
strip made of crushed gravel. It was as if someone had
turned the cave's antechamber into a cloth of many colors,
an area of many surfaces.

"Now watch," Dubai whispered, the excitement rising in his voice.

From the far side of the huge area a horse-drawn
chariot emerged. It was a fighting chariot of iron, manned
by a driver in the front and two soldiers in the rear. The
vehicle's back was open.

Luti knew little about weapons of war in general and
chariots in particular. But even she could see that there
was something unusual about this chariot. It was much
higher along the sides and much deeper. But it was the
wheels that startled her. They were twice the diameter of
ordinary chariot wheels and were very thin—so thin that
they seemed to be made out of iron pounded to the
fineness of a spider web.

"You see," Dubai whispered in her ear, "the wheels
are double rimmed with wooden guards. It is like having

four wheels, two on each side, with the wooden center acting as ballast. Now watch how it works."

The chariot driver urged the horse forward, and the vehicle picked up speed. Faster and faster it went. Luti had never seen an object move so rapidly. And it was not slowed by the mud, sand, rock, or gravel.

Such intense joy suffused her body that she had to will herself not to cry out. This was the chariot Drak had spoken about! This was the reason for their mission!

She turned toward Occa. His eyes were sparkling. He reached out one hand, and she grasped it in solidarity.

Micah stood pressed against the stone fifty yards from the three watchers in the cave. The shadows hid him. He had covered his face and body with dirt the moment Nimshi had fallen asleep, so no light would reflect off his skin.

He had been about to leap from the shadows and onto the Bedouin to drive his long knife into the man's throat. Then he had planned to take the girl and flee. But that was before he had seen the chariot. He realized immediately that it was revolutionary in its design and possibilities for warfare.

He remained where he was, clutching the long knife so tightly that the muscles of his hand began to cramp. Sweat drenched his body as he gazed at Luti. The woman was so lovely. And the Bedouin was there for the taking. The very thought of his steel blade penetrating the soft flesh of that barbarian was delicious, like eating a very ripe, sweet fruit. But he could not act. He seemed paralyzed. It was like that moment before he had slit the belly of the Moabite tyrant.

He closed his eyes. The gleaming wheels of the racing chariot still flashed in his mind. A powerful thought occurred to him. The Israelites! What would it mean to them if he could bring this wondrous war chariot to Hazor? They would be able to duplicate it and smash Jabin—smash anyone who oppressed them.

He opened his eyes and slid the long knife back inside his robe. Where were his true loyalties? Did they

rest with Israel? With Nimshi? With the Children of the
Lion? Or did his allegiance belong to Luti? To his vengeance? To the future? The past? Where? To whom?
Why, at the moment of triumph, when he was close to
love, to taking revenge, why did he think of the Israelites?

The chariot was slowing. He could see Dubai and
Luti leaning close, talking. The woman was radiant. When
he had been with her, she acted frightened and shy and
confused. But now her beauty shone through the cave,
reflecting along the gloomy walls, in each shadow, and
resting on his body like a cloak.

He had to get back to Nimshi before his brother
awoke. He had to think about how to steal the chariot.
There was some time, but not much. There were virtually
no defenses at the forges except their isolation in the
wilderness. It would be easy to sneak into the camp tomorrow night and take the vehicle. For just a moment, he
had a fantasy of returning to the Israelites' base camp,
behind the reins of a war chariot that would bring them
awesome power. The Israelites would greet him with even
more joy than when he had returned after the assassination of Eglon.

Micah bowed his head. Was that what he craved? To
be worshiped? To be loved as a hero? The thought shamed
him. He pressed his body closer against the walls of the
cave and breathed deeply. Everything would have to be
resolved quickly.

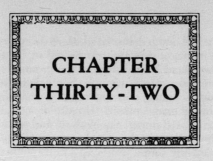

CHAPTER THIRTY-TWO

Canaan

I

Pepi's eyes met Sisera's and locked. When the Hazorite general came at him with the first pass of the sword, Pepi, weaponless, slipped to the side and brought his big armorer's fist down on Sisera's forearm, numbing it enough to make him drop the sword.

Realizing the guards would come running as soon as they heard a commotion at the gate, Pepi snatched up Sisera's sword and with one swift motion stabbed it at the general's midsection. But the general's armor—the armor that Pepi had made for him—stopped the blade.

Sisera cursed and grabbed at the sword. As Hazorite soldiers pounded toward the combatants, Pepi battered Sisera's hand away and swung with the sword again, catching the general in the head with the flat side. Pepi turned just in time to duck a blow from one of the soldiers. Sliding under the guard's weapon, he buried Sisera's blade in the guard's unprotected belly.

The man's falling body pulled the sword from Pepi's hand, leaving him unarmed once again. He ducked a roundhouse swing by the second guard and punched him hard in the groin. The man doubled over in pain. Out of the corner of his eye Pepi could see Sisera on hands and knees, groggy but trying to rise. Without hesitation the Child of the Lion made for Sisera's horse and leapt onto its bare back. He nudged the tired mare around and got it moving in the right direction. As he did so, an arrow sped past his cheek and buried itself in the ground.

Pepi risked a glance over his shoulder: Bowmen stood atop the wall, aiming down at him. As the horse hit its stride, another arrow passed so close that it tore Pepi's head covering. He ripped the cloth off and tossed it to the wind as the animal settled into a steady gallop along the high road leading south.

Heber had joined the revolt along the Kishon River. Standing beneath towering Mount Gilboa and watching the armies of the Israelites as they marched full strength for the first time, he was impressed with their numbers, even if their skill remained to be proved. Now, if only the weather would hold. . . .

Heber looked up at the dark clouds in the west. The chilly air foretold a storm. If the army were to make a move, now was the time. Why were they waiting?

A figure detached itself from the first column and rode up the path toward him. It was the man they had called Shemida.

"You're the armorer, aren't you?" he asked. "Pepi's assistant?"

Heber nodded. "Have you seen my master?"

"No. I heard that he'd gone to Hazor, looking for you. That's a dangerous place for him now. I just got word that someone has informed Jabin about the revolt. The Hazorites won't be the sitting target we expected."

"Is the attack going to be called off?" Heber asked.

"No," Shemida said, "we've committed ourselves. If we lose heart now, Jabin's forces will wipe us out."

"I looked at the weapons Theon gave you. They're good. Not the sort Pepi made for Hazor, but they'll meet the test."

"Thanks be to God."

"But after Sisera put up a fuss, Pepi was ordered to make iron chariots for Hazor. They're going to be your most serious problem."

"The chariots and the army's superior numbers," Shemida said.

"Superior numbers? But I thought Telem's new command had withdrawn half the Hazorite force to the northern marches."

"That's correct. But our spies tell us that Telem's been recalled. If he gets his troops down here to Jezreel in time to head us off, we'll have a difficult fight."

"But you don't seem to be worried."

Shemida smiled. "The odds were unfavorable in almost every battle Joshua fought against the Canaanites. We have an unbeatable advantage: Yahweh is on our side."

"Then what are we waiting for?" Heber asked. "If time is so important, why aren't we attacking?"

Shemida sighed. "Barak hasn't arrived yet. We can't move without him."

The day after Heber had found Yael beaten and ravaged by Sisera, the Kenite had thought clearly enough to move his wife and her belongings well out of the valley and harm's way. She now lived in a small hill community with Kenite tinkers. This group gathered every year on the slopes where runoff from Lake Chinnereth spilled over and formed the Jordan. Her loyal friend, Basemath, had relocated with her.

The encampment was on no major trade route, so Yael was surprised when she looked into the valley and saw a caravan making its way down a narrow canyon from the east.

"I recognize that caravan," Basemath said. "I've seen its banners before. It's from Damascus."

Yael put down the jug she was carrying and sat with her friend on a flat rock. "Damascus? Basemath, where would you have seen a Damascus caravan? They never passed through our valley."

"I saw it in the Benjamite hills when we went to see Deborah. As a matter of fact, I wouldn't be surprised if it was the same one. Yes! Look, Yael! There's the same elaborate carrying chair. Remember that rich woman who came to see Deborah? That's hers."

"I wonder what she's doing here. We probably should warn her against going into the Jezreel Valley, with the war about to break out there."

Basemath looked at the western sky. "She'll have other problems if she continues today; that storm is about to break. She'd be safer on the high ground than in a river valley."

Yael frowned worriedly. "That's also true for the Israelite soldiers. Oh, I hope Heber doesn't go to war with them! Helping them with arms repair is one thing, but I can't bear the thought of his fighting, getting hurt or even—"

"Pray to God," Basemath urged fervently. "I do, Yael. Ever since I talked to Deborah."

"Wait," Jabin said to his general. "Once Telem arrives with the northern forces, then you can move together in full strength and smash the Israelites to pieces."

"No." Sisera was pacing, full of nervous energy and rage. He kept touching the egg-sized lump on his head, although he forced himself not to wince. "No, Jabin, I'm going south now with whatever guard you can send with me. Telem can catch up to me later. I'm going to crush those Israelite bastards. And when I find that bastard Pepi—" He felt the lump again.

"Maybe I'll come along," Jabin said. "I'll destroy every Israelite village myself! I'll impale every man, woman, and child. I'll teach them to resist my supremacy. We'll use the Israelites as an example that won't soon be forgotten."

"Meanwhile," Sisera said, "I have to make sure they don't mount a sneak attack on my garrison in the Jezreel Valley. The spy said that the Israelites have over ten thousand men. Curse it! I wish your informants had gotten the news to you sooner and that your message had reached me sooner."

"I had no idea they were putting together that large a force."

"Well, it's too late now," Sisera grumbled. "I've got to get back to my men in Jezreel and make sure they're ready to fight. I have enough soldiers to stand against an army of ten thousand, even if it were comprised of regulars and not the ragtag crew they are."

"Don't get too confident," Jabin advised. "The Israelites have been training intensively."

Sisera grinned. "But they've never faced real swords in the hands of men who mean to kill them."

"That's just it," Jabin replied. "There is a solid cadre of men who *have*. They brought up Ehud and the men who smashed the Moabites; they're blooded. Don't forget, our army has been inactive for the last five years, except for minor occasional raids."

Sisera glared at him. "My men will fight. They're trained. They're blooded. They have been taught to fight to the death. And I'm leading them."

"As you say," Jabin said, taken aback by Sisera's belligerent tone but not wanting to exert his kingly authority by pointing out his general's disrespect. "Go now. I'll follow with the northern troops."

"I'll send the cavalry on first. They'll make good time. The rest of our northern army can back us up and help mop up once the southern contingent has broken the Israelite advance."

Deborah had never been on a horse before, and the speed at which Barak was riding the animal down the road frightened her more than the idea of the upcoming battle. "Please," she begged, hanging on to Barak for dear life. "Not so fast!"

"Don't worry!" Barak called over his shoulder. "Hold tight, and you'll be safe. I may be new at soldiering, but I was born in the saddle. We'll be there in an hour."

She shut her eyes tightly so as not to look at the ground flying past beneath them. Behind them was the detachment of recruits Barak was leading south, strung out in a line and galloping at full speed.

Barak's request that she accompany him into battle was a disappointment to her. There was no reason for it—it was not her place. But he seemed to need confirmation of his mission. . . . Her presence was vital to making him feel confident. She could not make him understand that Yahweh was on his side, with or without her. He never understood that she was merely the voice through which Yahweh spoke; she was of no significance whatsoever. Yahweh was Lord of Heaven and Earth, and His will would be done.

She clenched her teeth and hung on tighter. She had told all this to Barak before she finally agreed to come along. Yet, he insisted on her appearance as a tangible sign of Yahweh's blessing. In vain she had warned him that her presence would overshadow his; future generations would remember only that a woman had led the revolt against Sisera. She would be remembered, and Barak would be forgotten.

Deborah did not care whether or not anyone remembered her, as long as Yahweh's favor did not leave her. When the battle was over and the enemy had been vanquished, she would not ride in triumph through Hazor like a queen or a conqueror. She would head southward— this time on foot!—and return to her husband, children, and grandchildren and would, the next morning, take her usual place under the palm trees.

How she longed to be there now! Eyes closed, heart pounding, she gripped Barak's waist and wished the day and the battle were over.

II

The track narrowed in the hills above Lake Chinnereth, and the ground became treacherous. Pepi had pushed the stolen mare to the limit and then, with the last of his purse, bought a crossbred nag not much larger than a pony from a Canaanite farmer in the high country.

His seat had been a steady one in the foothill country; but now, in the rocky heights, on a mount that did not know the road, Pepi should have slowed to a walk or even dismounted and led the animal. Unfortunately the necessity to convey the information that Jabin knew of the revolt was so great that he dared not slow down. He threaded his way down the winding track, his eyes fixed on the path ahead.

The sun would set soon. Pepi hoped against hope that the blow he had given Sisera had delayed the general's plans—either to return to the Hazorite encampment or to meet with the king. But in his heart he knew that Sisera would put the Hazorite army machine in motion before he, Pepi, could reach the Israelites. If Sisera made contact with his army before nightfall, Hazorite troops might already be moving into position to attack.

In the back of Pepi's mind was the nagging worry that his army of recruits was not sufficiently prepared to fight against anybody, much less against Sisera's tough professionals. He had done his best, but there had not been time to transform them into skilled soldiers.

With these worries in mind, he stepped up the pace, abandoning caution . . . forgetting that he did not know the terrain . . . ignoring the lengthening shadows that were making the ground more difficult to judge.

When the horse moved into a trot, Pepi hunkered low over the animal's neck, urging it to greater speed. The horse shied. Pepi was off balance, and as the horse broke step, he pitched forward over the nag's neck and fell heavily into the animal's path.

Pepi threw up his arms to protect his head, but one of the animal's flailing hooves caught him a glancing blow to the temple. He felt a blinding pain, and then everything went dark as he slipped into nothingness.

The trader Ammuk of Carchemish had lingered overlong in Damascus, enjoying the fleshpots of the city, only to find that he had missed his caravan to the coast. As a result he had shopped around the city for another, but when none of his usual sources had turned up a new caravan, he had asked around in the stews.

There he had learned that Huldah, widow of Ephai, had mounted a caravan headed for the port of Acco. He

quickly made contact with Huldah's assistants and paid
them handsomely to allow him to ride with her column.

The fare was still a bargain—at least that was what he
had believed then. Now he was not so sure. When the
caravan had halted at the mouth of the Jezreel Valley,
Ammuk had waited patiently at first. Then he angrily
pulled his horse to the side and made his way up the line.
When he reached the scout at the head of the caravan, he
saw that armed men were blocking the path.

"What's the matter?" he demanded of the scout. "Why
aren't we moving?"

"Hostilities are about to erupt between the Israelites
and the Hazorite army."

"Nonsense!" Ammuk scoffed. "Let me talk to them."
He urged his horse up the path only to be stopped by a
strapping young man in civilian dress, bearing a spear.

"I'm sorry, sir," the young man said. "I've orders not
to let anyone through. If the fight breaks out, we can't be
responsible for your safety. I recommend you tell your
people to make camp for the night and forget about getting to the coast on this road."

"What is happening?" Ammuk asked. "A rebellion
against Hazor?"

"Yes, sir. It's no time for a caravan to be passing
through the valley."

Ammuk nodded. "I'll inform the caravan leaders."

He turned quickly and made his way back down the
line to Huldah's litter. Ephai's widow was infuriated by
the delay.

"What are you doing out of line?" she demanded
when she saw him. "Get back to your place."

Ammuk neither dismounted nor moved. He spoke
very quietly. "There is no chance of going on tonight or
tomorrow, either, perhaps."

To his surprise she nodded. "I know. I've sent a
messenger ahead. But when they find out who I am,
they'll let me through."

He shook his head. "I doubt that. The road is closed.
We'll have to head south and follow another route to the
sea."

"We're not taking a detour," she declared. "We'll make camp now and wait for my messenger's return."

He looked at her in disbelief. What was she thinking of? In the distance, dark clouds blocked the sun. In the air was the thick smell of rain.

When Barak's horse slowed to a walk, Deborah could breathe normally. She loosened her death grip on the young man and spoke in a voice that held little of her usual authority. "Are we here?"

"Yes," Barak replied. "We'll camp for the night and then see how things look in the morning."

She knew immediately that something was wrong. "Can I get down?" she asked. "I'll feel better with my feet on the ground. If I never get on a horse's back again, it'll be too soon."

He dismounted and helped her down, then started toward the huge encampment spread out before them.

She put her hand on his arm. "Wait!"

He turned. "But I've got to confer with—"

"No. Something very disturbing and frightening has just been revealed to me. Yahweh has put the thought in my mind. Barak, the army can't camp here tonight!"

"What?" he asked, aghast. "It's almost sundown. And there's a storm coming!"

"You've got to move now!" Deborah's words sparked with urgency. "Otherwise the Hazorites will hit you while you're advancing tomorrow. It is imperative that our troops get into position tonight! Take the best ground and be waiting for Hazor in the morning! If they are waiting for us, we'll be doomed."

"But—"

"If you weren't going to listen to me, why did you make me come with you? If you forced me to endure that terrible ride only to ignore what I tell you, I'm going to be very angry."

Barak looked down at her. Her usually calm brown eyes were blazing. Her middle-aged body seemed to have lost its softness and roundness. "Deborah, you know I'd never ignore anything you had to say, especially not at a time like this. But moving at dusk, with a storm ready to hit—"

"The weather won't change until we're situated. And the moon will provide enough light for us to move safely. Trust me, Barak: We have to be in place before Sisera moves up."

Her last-minute change in strategy made Barak agitated at first; then he became resigned. "It makes some sense. If we were in position at dawn—"

"Listen to me. It's becoming increasingly clear now." Deborah's voice was oddly abstract, as if she was speaking to a large gathering of men, rather than to Barak alone. "Sisera's infantry will hit us from the west as soon as it's light. Jabin plans to bring the reserves down from Hazor, to come up behind us and to catch us in a pincer movement."

"From behind?"

"Yes, his cavalry, including those iron chariots. But if we're on the high ground between here and Sisera's army, everything will be all right."

"Are you sure? We'll be caught between them. It sounds like a disaster."

"Trust me, Barak. Jabin won't arrive by the time Sisera attacks. If you can handle Sisera . . ."

The enormity of the task became clear to Barak, and he felt a sinking sensation in the pit of his stomach. If he could handle Sisera!

The horse, moving about curiously, the bridle dragging from its friendly nose, woke Pepi. He tried to sit up, but the stabbing pain in his head forced him down again. He closed his eyes and felt the world spin beneath him.

After some minutes Pepi's head cleared. He remembered what had happened and realized he had been foolish. Slowly, cautiously, he tried to sit up. This time the pain was less severe. He achieved a sitting position, but he had to fight a dizziness that threatened to overwhelm him.

He looked to the west. The sun had disappeared beyond the far hills. Soon it would be dark—no time to be up here alone. He had to join his Israelite allies before one of Sisera's scouts found him.

Pepi pulled his feet under him and slowly, unsteadily, stood up. With one hand on the horse's flank to stabilize himself, he looked at the path he had used to thread his way down the slope. He inadvertently jerked his head to one side, causing the terrible throbbing headache to come again. It almost drove him to his knees.

He held on to the horse's flank until the agony ebbed, then he looked back along the track. A great body of troops, their banners waving, was moving along the path.

He thought hard, but pain and confusion clouded his mind. How far behind him were they? When would they catch up with him?

He took hold of the horse's bridle and put a calming hand on the animal's neck. Could he mount in his present condition? He had no choice; he had to get down into the valley and warn the Israelites: Jabin was coming! Not tomorrow, but tonight!

III

Think this through! Pepi chastised himself silently. *You must do something. Warning them is not enough.*

He tried to think, but the throbbing in his head was unrelenting. If he managed to warn the Israelites, they could protect their flanks but little else. Jabin would still fall on them in the morning. In the meantime Sisera would have mobilized his hordes and would hit the Israelites from the west. Trapped between the two arms of the Hazorite attack, the Israelites would be cut to ribbons.

If he could delay Jabin's force, however, Barak might be able to dispense with Sisera.

His head pain blinded him. He held his temples between his palms and cursed his infirmity. It had been so long since his last attack, he had dared to hope that he was cured. Poor Tirzah! She had never forgiven herself for throwing that rock at him. His blackout reminded him of

her, his one true love. If he had not been recuperating
from one of his blackouts in Ashod . . . if his messenger to
Tirzah had not been murdered on the road between Ashod
and Jerusalem . . . if he had been able to warn her, she
would never have been abducted in Jerusalem! How he
missed her! Pepi shook his head grimly. Why was he
lingering here, thinking of the past? The danger was now.

He squinted up at the rocky heights, but just tilting
his head sent pain slicing into his skull. Through the haze
of agony he studied the rock face. He looked down to
where the path was narrow; only one man at a time could
pass. If he could engineer a landslide and block the way, it
might be hours before the Hazorite army could clear the
trail or find some other route into the valley.

He put a calming hand on the horse's neck and stroked.
"My friend," he said, "somehow I've got to mount you and
get up there. Stand still, friend. Let's see if I can do that
without blacking out again."

When Sisera rejoined his army, he found it unpre-
pared to move out. His absence and Telem's transfer to
the northern command had left the troops to languish
under inexperienced and incompetent leadership. He let
his wrath fall on everyone. Two pickets were whipped and
staked out on ground infested with ants and scorpions.
Sisera personally beat into senselessness one of his
underofficers and cursed out six others.

Finally he faced his three senior officers by the light
of a campfire. His dark eyes reflected highlights from the
leaping flames and seemed to glow.

"You lazy bastards have cost me the element of surprise," he snarled. "Now I'll have to attack in the morning, when the enemy will be ready. If we lose this battle
because of you, so help me, I'll have your hides stretched
out on wagon wheels."

"Sir," said Ikkesh, commander of the first troop, "this
will never happen again. I understand your anger, but
wouldn't it be more productive if we spent the night
discussing the strategy for tomorrow?"

The two other senior officers waited for Sisera to

explode again in anger, but the general was too tired from his long ride and the beatings he had administered to his underlings. He let it pass. "What do you suggest?" he asked.

"Well, sir," Ikkesh began, "obviously the earlier we're out on the field the better. I suggest we shake the troops out an hour before dawn—but make certain they've prepared their kits and weapons tonight and will be ready to move."

"Good," Sisera approved. "Go on."

"Thank you, sir. I suggest we split the advance into three columns: One can hit the Israelites head-on; the other two can come at them from the flanks, and—"

"No," Sisera interrupted. "We're going to move the whole unit against them. It will terrify those bumpkins to see an army the size of ours advancing on them. We'll batter them until they break, and when Jabin comes up behind them with the chariots—"

"But, sir, what if Jabin's force doesn't arrive in time? Moving iron chariots along that mountain track—"

"Don't worry, Ikkesh. The king will be with us in plenty of time."

"Yes, sir. But what if he isn't? We ought to allow for every contingency."

At any other time this disagreement would have provoked Sisera's fury, but now he kept his anger in check. He looked from one face to the next: Ikkesh, Huram, Lud. "Remember, you're going up against farm boys who, until now, have never held a real sword. What's there to worry about? We'll smash them on the first assault. We probably won't need Jabin at all."

As he spoke, the first raindrop fell on his arm. Cursing, he brushed it off.

The rain was enough to halt the progress of the Israelite army down the Jezreel Valley toward the sea. Barak looked disgusted, but Deborah, walking beside him, put her small hand on his forearm.

"Have faith, young man. It will be all right."

"But I'll have to halt the advance."

"Of course," she agreed, unperturbed. "Make camp here. It's raining on the Hazorites, too, you know. If we can't move in the rain, neither can Sisera."

"I suppose you're right," Barak conceded. "Captain! Make camp here." Still, when he turned back to Deborah, she could see his frustrated expression in the moonlight. "We didn't make the high ground."

"Then Yahweh wants us to camp on the low ground," she replied, "and it will turn out to be the better camp-site. We are not in charge. Don't you understand?"

"How can the low ground be better? One of the first things Pepi taught me was—"

"I don't doubt Pepi's knowledge, but who is expert in matters of war? Pepi of Kerma or the God of Moses and Joshua? Who has sent us so obvious a message about where He wishes us to camp? Pepi or Yahweh?"

Barak wanted to scream at her and grab her by the shoulders and shake her until her teeth rattled. He caught himself, and in the end he realized that there was nothing to do but return her calm smile.

Flashes of lightning split the sky in the distance, followed by dull booms of thunder. The rain pummeled Pepi as he balanced precariously on top of the hill and pushed his shoulder against an overhanging rock. He could not budge it.

He glanced at the horse standing patiently nearby and shook his aching head. "If only I could figure out some way to harness your strength, my friend," he said, "but there seems to be no way."

He looked back down the track. Jabin, having found no place to stop and make camp, appeared doomed to push ahead to the foothills, rain or no rain. If the king succeeded, the Israelites would lose the battle before it began.

Pepi peered up at the great rock. What would Moses have done? Many years before, during the great trek through the wilderness, Pepi had watched the Israelite leader face one seemingly insurmountable problem after another; and every time the impossible suddenly became possible. What had Moses done? Of course, he had prayed to his God, but . . .

Pepi frowned and wiped the rain out of his eyes. If he prayed, as Moses had prayed, what harm could possibly come of it? After all, in this case Yahweh's aims and Pepi's were the same. He closed his eyes and prayed as Moses had prayed—with all his heart, with all his soul, and with all his might. He prayed for Yahweh's help.

The rain continued to pour down, rushing in rivulets around the base of the rock. Pepi was soaked to the skin, and his feet had sunk up to the ankles in soft mud. Suddenly the ground under him shuddered. Alarmed, Pepi reached out for the horse, grabbing its bridle and resting one hand on its broad flank, as much to steady himself as to calm the animal.

As he watched, the great rock before him slowly sank into the earth. The cliff beneath it seemed to have dissolved, and the rock slid down the cliff. At first its descent created a low rumble, and then the rumble gathered volume.

The horse shied, but Pepi held on tightly to the frightened animal. The sound grew to a roar. Pepi inched closer to the edge of the cliff to see what was happening. As he peered over, a bolt of lightning brightened the sky. Then came a deafening crack of thunder, a blast so ear-splitting it obliterated the roar of the landslide.

For a moment, in the glow of the lightning, he could see what had happened: The rock had dislodged half the mountainside's rubble. The sandstone, undermined by the heavy rain, had tumbled after the great rock on its disastrous course down the hillside. The track he had ridden on was now buried under a mountain of debris.

Pepi gaped in awe. Something miraculous had happened. Could it have been because—? No, that was ridiculous. The landslide did not occur just because it solved his problem. It was merely a fortuitous coincidence. Surely. . . .

But as Pepi thought about it, he knew for a certainty that what had happened for him had happened for Moses so many times. But why him? How could the prayer of an unbeliever change the course of a war?

But it *had* happened. Now Jabin would be forced to make camp, and in the morning the king would be faced with finding a new route into the Jezreel Valley, which would likely entail doubling back.

Suddenly Pepi was bone weary. His head hurt, and nothing in the world seemed as important as wending his way down into the valley, finding shelter, and sleeping. Perhaps the Israelite army would be there and would take care of him. He pulled the horse closer and clumsily mounted, then nudged the animal forward cautiously. Before committing his total attention to the dark path in front of him, he closed his eyes and thought, *Thank you. Whoever you are.*

IV

Storms swept across the broad expanse of the Great Sea. Enormous banks of black clouds driven by gale-force winds moved eastward, dumping their rain on the first landmass they reached. Storm after storm ravaged the area. The winds and rain drove ships aground and drowned men by the hundreds.

Along the Canaanite coast waves battered the docks and inundated cities, cutting off islands like Tyre and Arvad from the mainland. Just as the first storm was beginning to abate, the next came ashore.

Inland, after a night of driving rain, the silence awoke Sisera. He sat up and looked around. "Telem!" he called out peevishly. Only then did he remember that Telem had been promoted and taken from him.

As he swung his bare feet over the side of his cot and set them down, he landed in a puddle that had leaked under the corner of his tent. He cursed. "Ikkesh!" he cried. "Lud! Huram! Get in here."

A guard stuck his head into the tent. "Sir?"

"Bring the officers to me!" he yelled. "What are you gaping at, you idiot? Get them for me! Now!"

The guard blinked and disappeared. Sisera found his boots and reached for his clothing. Looking through the flap, he saw a slight tinge of pink in the sky. The storm had passed; there was no time to waste. He had to fall on the Israelites and wipe them out!

Still naked, he stood in the dim light and looked down at his body. His nightmares had reminded him of what he had tried to forget—he had become impotent ever since his last meeting with the Kenite woman Yael. He remembered his stallionlike prowess during that last time with her. He savored the memory. Whipped into submissiveness, she had been the perfect mate for acting out his fantasies.

Other women had failed to kindle his flame, even when he resorted to extraordinary means of arousal. Merely beating the women had not been enough. Sisera frowned. He clenched and unclenched his fists, feeling the strength and suppleness in his arm muscles.

Was he becoming dependent on the Kenite woman? Never before had he been attracted to only one woman. When the battle was over, he would summon her to his bed. Her husband could be easily disposed of, and then he could have her whenever he wanted.

Something was so delicious, so inviting about the fear in her eyes when she saw him. Just thinking of her, he could sense his flesh stirring. Yes, he would set her up in a house with guards to make certain she did not escape. And he would keep her chained to the bed and forbid her any clothes, so that he would always be able to think of her naked and ready for him.

Naked and ready, afraid and shamed. He knew how prudish her people had become, how deeply humiliating it would be for her to wait naked. As a Kenite, she had absorbed many of the Israelites' peculiarities.

Israelites! He snarled at the thought of them. What gall to rise against him like this! He would crush them! He would break them! He would make an example of them, so none of the other upstarts in the region would get any

ideas. He would choose one village—maybe even a city—
and burn it to the ground, killing everyone in it. He
would do to them what Joshua's legions had done to his
own people!

But even as he contemplated his slaughter, the girl
was in his mind again. Having her all to himself would
provide a comfort that had escaped him through most of
his violent life. She would serve his needs and sleep with
him, and when he went into the field again, he could
think of her at home waiting for him. He would always be
in complete control. The blunders of his subordinates, the
malice of his rivals, or the stupidity of Jabin would never
intrude. She would exist for no reason other than to serve
him, to fulfill his every wish, to cater to his pleasure. And
to fear him.

He shuddered with delight at his fantasy, then began
to dress for the day's battle.

Before dawn the servant Yabamat came to wake
Huldah. She shook her mistress gently and then stepped
back. It would not be the first time she had awakened her
lady too early and been beaten. But this time Huldah sat
up, rubbed her eyes, and asked, "What is it?"

"Mistress, you told me last night to make certain you
were up and about by dawn."

"Yes, I want the whole caravan awake. And when
you've passed that message along, come back and dress
me. Why are you standing there? Do as I told you."

But Yabamat stood her ground, though timidly. "Mistress, a stranger, ill and shivering, wandered into camp
during the night. We took him in."

"You know I left orders that no strangers be taken
in."

"Mistress, he claims to have vital news for the army.
He asked us to get it to Barak and Deborah."

"What kind of news?"

"I don't know, but Ammuk the trader said I should
tell you about it."

Huldah frowned. "Ammuk is a nuisance, but he's not
stupid. If he says it's important . . ."

*   *   *

When Huldah emerged from her tent, the sky was already light. Ammuk was waiting for her.

"Greetings," he said with a bow. "This stranger has quite a story to tell. He claims that the Hazorites were coming down behind the Israelites, along the lakeshores. But during the night he managed to cause a rockfall that will delay Hazor at least until late afternoon."

"I'll send a runner to Barak," she said.

"I've already taken the liberty of doing so in your name," Ammuk replied smoothly. "Now don't get angry. It was either that or awaken you in the middle of the night."

She snorted at him but nodded. "I suppose you're right. Who is this stranger?"

"I didn't ask, and he didn't offer. He's very ill, incoherent with fever. He's in one of the tents now. He was out all night in the rain and has a bad cut on his head."

"I suppose I should have a look at him," Huldah conceded. "If he's telling the truth, he's done us all a favor: If the Hazorites had come down the lakeside trail, they very likely would have mistaken us for a weapons caravan and attacked us."

Ammuk led her down the long line of neatly arranged tents. All around they could hear the sounds of men breaking camp.

The trader paused before one of the shelters. He held aside the entrance flap, and Huldah swept past him and went inside. At the far wall of the tent a young woman bent over a cot on which a man lay covered with blankets.

"Let's have a look at this fellow who saved our caravan," Huldah said, and nudged the girl aside and stood looking down at the stranger.

It took a moment before she recognized his face. Then she felt as if she had been punched in the stomach. Her knees went weak, and she breathed in great gulps of air. Memories flashed before her eyes: of the first time she had seen him, so young and strong, the first man who could look her in the eyes . . . of when she had thrown the rock at him, thinking he was an Israelite trooper bent on rape and pillage . . . of that first horrible night in the brothel in Damascus, when she had prayed that he would rescue her.

Tears filled her eyes as the memory assaulted her: Her left foot had been chained to the bed. She was naked, frightened, and confused. A filthy trader as hairy as a bear had lumbered into the room. They had no language in common. When she tried to push him away, he had kicked her hard in the chest. She was half-conscious, lying on the floor, and he had had his way with her again and again, beating her afterward each time.

When the morning had come she had watched the trader through swollen eyes as he dressed. Smiling, he had tossed an extra coin on the floor beside her and then left. For hours she had lain there, staring at the small round coin. Never before or since had she wanted so much to die. Never before or since had she so hated the world and men. And she had blamed it all on the man who lay now before her.

She recovered her equilibrium and bent down over him. His face was drawn, his breathing difficult. She touched his forehead. He was burning with fever. She closed her eyes, remembering their first year together. How handsome and loving Pepi had been! Their days had been filled with joy; their nights had been filled with passion. They had existed together in a bubble of contentment and optimism, oblivious to the horrors around them—the horrors that would soon destroy their love.

She knelt and placed her lips by his ear. "Pepi," she whispered, drawing the name out in a long and heartfelt sigh.

He opened his eyes and looked at her. "Where am I?" he asked in the broken, desperate voice of a dying man. "How did I get here?"

"Pepi, darling, don't you know me?"

He squinted at her. "No. Where am I?" He tried to raise his head but fell back.

Tears coursed down her cheeks. "Oh, Pepi," she said softly, and put a hand on his forehead and stroked it soothingly. "Don't die, darling. Please, not when I've found you at last."

His eyes fixed on the ceiling of the tent, and then fluttered shut. His breathing deteriorated into hoarse gasps.

Huldah's messenger reached Barak, Shemida, and Deborah just as the army was preparing to march. "My mistress says that Jabin's army has been held up," he reported. "There was a landslide, and the king had to find another route."

Deborah smiled. "Barak! Didn't I tell you he would be delayed? Now you can concentrate on fighting Sisera. Why won't you learn to trust me?"

"Wait," Shemida cautioned. "Before we start rejoicing, there is a second road through the hills. It's three leagues west, and while it's rough and rocky and will require care if his chariots are to cross it, it is passable—or at least it was before the storm."

"Where does it rejoin this road?" Barak asked.

"Only about a league west of here. But it will still take some time to double back to it. We ought to be past it well before he arrives—if we move now."

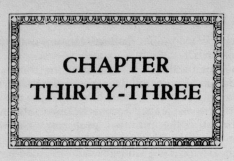

CHAPTER
THIRTY-THREE

Khareitun Caves, Wilderness of Judea

The sun was at its zenith now, and Nimshi's wound was beginning to fester again. Unable to help, Nimshi watched as Micah skinned and gutted the small rodent he had caught in a snare. Then his brother built a little fire in a sand pit and quickly roasted the meat along with the intestines. Micah ate ravenously, while Nimshi picked at his small portion.

"I know you left the camp last night, Micah," Nimshi finally said after they had sought shade beneath a rock ledge.

Micah just grunted and refused to speak.

"Tell me," Nimshi continued, "did you get your vengeance? Did you kill the Bedouin?" Nimshi looked around. "And where is the young woman? Did she refuse to accompany you after you murdered her kidnapper . . . or was he her companion or her husband?"

"I killed no one," Micah muttered.

Nimshi stared at the waterskin lying between them. There was only enough for one more day in the wilderness. Micah would have to get some water from the forge area, perhaps from the man named Dubai, whom they were supposed to contact for work.

"I found out why they are paying such high wages for armorers," Micah said, cleaning the blade of his long knife.

"That's why you sneaked into their camp with your face blackened last night?" Nimshi asked. "To find out about their pay scale?"

"Nimshi, listen carefully." Micah sheathed his knife and spoke with urgency. "They have built the prototype of a chariot."

"So what?" Nimshi shifted his position, trying to ease the burning pain in his thigh.

"It is a vehicle of such power that—"

"Come on now, Micah. All chariots are the same. They're like swords—only as good as the men who wield them. Or the horse that pulls them."

"No! Believe me! I saw it! It is twice as fast as the swiftest iron chariot I have ever seen. It has thin double wheels supported by wooden joints, and it rides over any surface. Even in deep mud the chariot moves quickly because the double wheels keep it from sinking like the normal chariot."

"I'm happy for them. What does that have to do with our situation?"

"Whoever possesses that chariot holds the power. A hundred of those chariots, drawn by good horses and manned by experienced three-man teams, can control this entire region. No existing army could stand against them— even those armies that have the conventional iron chariots."

The pain in Nimshi's thigh was throbbing. Again he turned slightly. "So what, Micah? Since when have you become a military strategist?"

"If the Israelites owned such a chariot, they could smash Hazor and anyone else who oppressed them. They would be able to control all of Canaan again, in spite of the disunity among the tribes."

"A dream," Nimshi replied sourly. "The Israelites don't have the skill or capabilities to duplicate chariots of iron from a prototype. And surely not one that, according to you, has so many new features. You're dreaming, Micah."

His brother looked bitterly at him, then grew silent. He took out his knife again and began to play with it.

"Is that what you are going to do, Micah? Steal that chariot and take it to the Israelites?" When Micah did not answer, the fury rose in Nimshi. "When will this all-consuming loyalty to those crazed people end? What have the Israelites done for the Children of the Lion? For Pepi? What have they done for you except to turn you into an assassin?"

Micah looked up. "Yes, you're right; that is all I know—how to kill. You're always right, Nimshi, even regarding things about which you know nothing."

"Tell me, Micah," Nimshi requested gently. "Help me to understand. Why is your loyalty to them rather than to me, your blood brother? You and I have started on a new life together. All right, things have not gone well. But that will change. Think of the future, Micah. The Israelites represent your past . . . and a bloody past it was."

The pain was so great, Nimshi could not speak anymore. He closed his eyes and began to weep. Micah moved to him quickly and dressed the wound again.

"Forgive me, Nimshi," he said softly, "but I must do this. I will go in there again tonight, steal the chariot, and return here. Together we will bring it to the Israelites. That, I promise, will be my last service for them. Then we can embark once again on our new life." He embraced his brother, and they clung to each other in the heat of the wilderness.

Finally, Nimshi pushed his brother away. "I will not say anything more about how the Israelites have corrupted you into violence. If you wish to take the chariot to them, I cannot stop you. And I have no choice but to follow. But I have great forebodings about your decision." Nimshi turned to ease a stab of pain in his wound. "If we return north, you may never escape their power over you. Our plans will become dust."

Micah did not reply.

Luti and Occa waited until the moon was high, packed up their belongings, then carefully shaped their bedrolls as if sleeping figures were in them. It was time for them to carry out the mission with which they were entrusted: to bring the chariot back to the kingdom of Babylon.

They walked very slowly at first, crouching low, waiting for their eyes to grow accustomed to the night. They located the cave into which Dubai had brought them the night before. Inside was the gigantic antechamber that contained the many ground surfaces used to test the chariot.

Luti scanned the far wall, trying to remember just where the chariot had entered. They crossed the room and searched the rocky wall for a passageway. It was Occa who discovered it, his strong hands gliding along the rock until the lever was found, and then—behold!—a passageway opened in the very rock itself.

The tunnel was narrow and low, but there was enough room for a single chariot. They followed the path for a long distance, moving slowly in the pitch dark.

At last they approached a lighter, wider section of the passageway. Occa stopped Luti by touching her arm. They moved carefully, step by cautious step, until the path widened into a high, vaulted area of the cave. In the center was the chariot, and beside the vehicle was an armed guard. A spear rested on his shoulder, and a sword hung in his side scabbard.

Where are the horses? Luti wondered, then she realized that there had to be another opening from the cave to the outside. Each cave probably had dozens of secret entrances and exits operated by hidden levers in the stone, just like the one that had opened up the tunnel they had followed.

Pressed against the wall to avoid being spotted by the guard, she stared at the chariot. She marveled at the remarkable wheels and remembered how well they had drawn the vehicle. It would be wonderful when Occa and she finally delivered the prototype to Drak.

She turned to find that Occa had put down their bag of belongings and vanished. Startled, she realized he had climbed up the side of the wall, like a fly. He gestured to her with one hand, and she understood immediately what he wanted.

She stepped into full view and called out to the guard. "I'm hurt. Help me, please!"

The guard was taken aback, but he stepped away

from the chariot. "Who are you? What are you doing there?"

"I'm hurt. Please hurry." The guard came toward her, holding the spear by his side. The moment he entered the area where the path began to narrow, Occa pushed away from the wall and landed on him. The guard never saw his murderer. Occa silently drove his sword through the guard's chest, and the man died before the scream on his lips could burst forth.

There was no time for sorrow or horror. They picked up their bag of belongings, then stepped over the corpse, hurried into the vault, passed the chariot, and searched for a lever or opening. It would be too risky to go back the way they had come, into the antechamber and then out the front entrance of the cave.

They found nothing. Their fingertips were raw, and sweat blinded them. Luti staggered back and dropped to the ground; she had to rest. Occa squatted beside her. His customary grin was gone.

Looking up, Luti realized that slivers of moonlight were filtering into the vault. This was a good sign: Once they found the opening, they would be free in the wilderness; they were at the end of this particular cave system. But first they had to find the exit.

Occa nudged her. She turned to him. In his hand he held some dried fruit. As she reached out to take one, a scream of rage echoed through the vault from behind her. She turned toward it just as a figure burst past her.

With a gasp Luti pressed herself against the cave wall, seeking safety. She could not see the assailant's face; it was covered by a hood. His first two lunges with a long knife had cut into Occa's face and shoulder. But the Bedouin quickly recovered, dropping his bag of belongings to hold his curved sword high with both hands.

Her heart beat fiercely as she watched the two men circle each other warily. Could she help Occa? No, she could do nothing—fear paralyzed her.

Occa feinted low, then swung the sword high, missing the stranger's neck by inches as he danced away. As they circled, Luti could hear their labored breathing and smell their acrid sweat. The Bedouin lunged again, and this time the stranger sidestepped and kicked Occa in the leg, sending him sprawling. The Bedouin scrambled desperately, trying to rise, but he slipped and sprawled again. His grip on the sword loosened.

Luti heard the sickening crunch of breaking bones as the robed attacker landed hard on the Bedouin's wrist. Then he drove the blade of the long knife through Occa's neck. Blood spurted out. Luti watched in horror as the Bedouin's eyes rolled back. His mouth opened, he convulsed, and then he was still.

His murderer pushed back his hood. Luti gasped again when she saw it was Micah. He reached down, pulled his knife free, and wiped the blade on Occa's robe. Then he turned.

Luti found her voice. "You!"

"Quiet," Micah said. "We are in danger."

"Are you mad? What have you done?"

"I have killed the man who hurt my brother and who took you from me."

Luti was trembling uncontrollably. When she buried her face in her hands, Micah moved beside her, and she felt his hands stroking her back.

"I have thought about nothing but you," he whispered, "every waking moment of every day since the Bedouin took you from me. Even when I was asleep, I dreamed of you."

"I don't want to see any more blood." She started to cry. His hands on her face evoked a flood of emotions. She loathed him at the same time as she loved him. She wanted him to go away, and she wanted him to come closer.

"Listen, Luti. We must stay here for several hours. The chariot horses are left unguarded for about an hour before dawn. We'll leave then, hitch some horses to the chariot, pick up my brother, who lies over the ridge, then go to the Israelites."

"Who are the Israelites? I am on a mission to obtain this chariot for Babylon. I am sworn to carry it out! And you have murdered the man who led me here! My companion!"

"The Israelites are my friends, Luti. They desperately need this vehicle!" Micah stood to pull Occa's body away from Luti and half covered the corpse so the throat wound was no longer visible. Then he said: "We have other things to talk about."

She stared up at him. Did he not understand what she had said?

He came back to her and placed his hands on the sides of her face. "That first moment I saw you, I loved you. Do you understand me?"

She angrily brushed his hands away. He stroked her hair. She started to push him away again, but instead she held on to him. He pulled her to her feet, and they stood together, embracing. She could feel his love through his flesh. It seemed to flow across to her, to spread throughout her.

He was right, she knew—from that first moment there had been something so special, so charged and beautiful between them, as if some supernatural force had sent them to meet . . . as if their destinies had been linked by the gods themselves. Yes, she loved him.

"Lie down beside me, Luti," he whispered into her hair. "The worst is over. In a few hours we will be away from here."

She stretched out next to him. His arms were strong and comforting. It was all over, she realized. Her mission had failed. She had done her best and could do nothing more. Let these people called the Israelites have the stupid chariot. Let poor Occa rest in peace, and may Drak forgive her for her disloyalty.

"Do you remember what happened when you wandered into my camp?"

"Yes," Luti whispered.

"Do you remember how I touched you?"

"Yes."

She felt his hands opening her robe. Then he drew her closer. She felt his mouth on her breast. A thousand little darts of shame and pleasure coursed through her body. What was she doing with this stranger? Why did she want him to touch her?

Her hands went into his garments, seeking his flesh. Maybe, she thought, this was the reason for all her pain. Maybe this was what the gods had planned for her—to love a man and be loved by him.

Something broke free within her—her love for this stranger seemed to burst through all her defenses and fears. She kissed his face again and again. And then he entered her. She could not breathe for a moment—his weight was crushing her. Then she moved wildly and felt a tide of joy and love sweep over them.

When she awoke, Micah lay next to her. The moonlight was still filtering down through the vault. She did not know how long she had been sleeping. How many hours were left, she wondered, before they could obtain the horses? She leaned over and let her lips gently touch Micah's. He stirred but did not awake.

Her eyes fell on the body of Occa. *Poor, strange man*, she thought. She wondered if he had any family. What funeral rites would have been offered him had he been among his own people? The thought pained her, and she realized that the least she could do was cover his face.

Carefully, so as not to wake Micah, she crept to the body. Blood had spurted during the death throes, and it was caked all over his face. She picked up the hem of his robe and began to wipe the dried blood from his cheeks.

Something strange was happening: The blackened skin was peeling from his face!

Astonished, she began to probe gently with her fingers, then pulled at the silver ornaments dangling from his lifeless cheek.

A large flap of skin lifted to reveal a tattoo of the morning star. The dark skin was a mask, which had begun to dry and curl when Micah had slashed the Bedouin's face.

She pulled harder. Finally, the entire mask fell away.

Luti could not believe her eyes. She was staring at the corpse of her archenemy, Banniselk, priest of Astarte.

At first, she was dumbfounded. *Think*, she told herself. *Think simply and clearly. Why would Banniselk wear a disguise?*

There was only one reason: He wanted to fool both Drak and her. Why? One possibility emerged: Banniselk fooled Drak in order to get directions to the secret forge. And he had to fool her so she would gain employment, as planned. Banniselk was no worker of metal; only she, with the help of Drak's cloak of feathers, could gain entry to the forge.

Then a chill shook her body. Banniselk wanted the chariot for himself, for his own power-hungry factions in Ur. He would have murdered her the moment she was of no use . . . and that meant the moment they were out of sight of the forges.

Another thought occurred to her: If Banniselk intended the chariot for his own faction, then Drak, too, was in danger. Drak, her savior, needed the chariot to stay alive.

She turned to stare at the sleeping form of her lover. Micah had brought her joy, but old Drak had become her mother and father. He needed her; Ur and all of Babylon needed the chariot.

Micah told her that the horses outside the cave were unguarded just before dawn. She could harness them to the chariot by herself. But how could she find the exit? And how could she slip away without disturbing Micah?

He would be wakened if she moved the chariot. What then? She could not overpower him.

She stared at Occa. Where was the cloak of feathers? Probably in Occa's bag, which he had dropped when Micah attacked him. She found the bag, and her fingers fumbled with the string. Inside was the cloak of nighthawk feathers and a length of hemp rope.

Luti closed her eyes, knelt, and pressed her face against the feathers, and prayed fervently for strength, wisdom, and skill.

A mantle of power seemed to slip over her body. She felt calm and light-headed. She knew exactly what she must do. She walked back to Micah and hunkered down beside him. Her hands were skilled and silent as she bound his wrists and feet. He felt nothing. Her touch was so light, so magical, that he remained fast asleep.

She hurried to the walls, and in seconds her roving hands found a secret lever. A large section of cave wall creaked open.

In the moon glow she could see the horses stabled outside. Past the horses she could see the outline of the dark hills. The guards had indeed vanished. She grabbed hold of the chariot and began to pull it toward the light of dawn.

As Luti pulled the chariot out, Micah woke. He raged at her to untie him. He begged her to loosen his bonds. He cried out that he loved her. But Luti would not listen. She led the chariot out and harnessed the war-horse to it, then, knowing she would need them, tied several more horses behind the chariot. Only once she stared back into the cave at her lover writhing in his bonds. But Drak and Ur were waiting for her. They were her first responsibility. The tears streamed down her face as she urged the horses away, north to Damascus. Micah's pleas quickly faded.

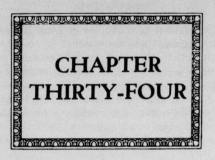

CHAPTER THIRTY-FOUR

Canaan

I

As Barak's raw, untested soldiers moved forward from their positions in the eastern end of the valley, Sisera's hardened professionals were advancing along a broad front down the Plain of Esdralon. Sisera had given them a rousing speech, and this, as much as the harsh warnings of their commanders, had whipped them into a killing frenzy.

Thus, when Barak's force reached the center of the valley, they found Sisera's men already occupying the high ground they themselves had hoped to hold. Barak stopped to confer with Shemida and his cadre of veterans.

"What can we do?" Barak asked. "If we charge up that slope, the Hazorite bowmen will cut us down before we've reached the crest of the hill."

Shemida frowned, thinking. Then he waved for Deborah to join them. "What do you think?" he asked her.

Deborah shrugged. "God has yet to speak to me of this."

"Then it's up to us mortals to think of something," Shemida said. "Does anyone have any ideas?"

He studied the circle of blank faces. No one spoke.

"The clouds are gathering in the west again," Deborah remarked. "I think it will rain."

Shemida looked around. "You're right," he said

dismissively. An idea of which even Joshua would have been proud was forming in his mind.

Struggling, sweating, and cursing, Jabin's cavalry, joined by Telem's troops, finally reached the crest of the hill. They had hauled the heavy iron chariots up the twisting road to the spine of the ridge, and now they stood poised for the descent.

"Can you see the Israelites down in the plain?" Jabin asked Telem.

"No," the commander said, shaking his head. "I sent a runner ahead to find them. I suspect that Sisera's and the Israelites' armies are to the west of us."

Jabin permitted himself a fierce smile of triumph. "I told you it was a great idea to march all night! Now we stand a good chance of closing in behind them and catching them between us and Sisera, just as we planned."

"Yes, sir," Telem agreed. "But will our men be able to fight? Look at them. They've been wrestling heavy chariots all night. They're exhausted."

"Exhausted?" Jabin asked testily. "Nonsense! They're as fresh and fit as when they left."

"*Your* cavalry may be fairly fresh," Telem said, "but my command has marched twice as far as yours. Our only hope is to crush the enemy in the first charge, sir. If the fight goes on longer, my men will begin to fold."

Jabin's eyes narrowed. "Don't worry, we'll strike at the Israelites quick and hard. They won't know what hit them."

Telem raised his eyebrows slightly but said nothing. He looked to the west, where black clouds were boiling up over the low hills. Thunder rumbled in the distance. "Whatever you say, sir. We'll give it our best."

"What are the Israelites doing? Why don't they attack?" Sisera shaded his eyes with his hand.

Lud, his left-flank commander, hesitated. "Why, they seem to be falling back, sir. That doesn't make any sense. Why would they come all this distance and then turn tail and run?"

"Why not?" Sisera asked gleefully. "Cowards! I knew they'd be. Damned foreign swine."

"I beg your pardon, sir," said Ikkesh, the second-in-command. "Cowards or no, they're getting away."

"Then what are you standing here for?" Sisera asked. "Attack!"

Behind him the deep growl of thunder was louder, and the orders to pursue the retreating enemy could hardly be heard over the howling wind.

"Don't turn and face them too quickly," Shemida advised Barak.

"But how will I know when to fight?" Barak asked.

"I'll tell you when to turn and make your stand. Now they're coming down the hill. They've divided up into three fronts. The left wing of their attack—that'll be on your right as you face them—have pulled ahead. I don't know why Sisera would allow such a stupid maneuver. I suppose he's convinced we're running away, so it doesn't matter."

Barak looked worried. "I can hear them."

"Look straight ahead," Shemida said. His horse shied; he yanked hard at its bridle and put a calming hand on its broad neck. "Act as though you want to get out of here as fast as you can."

The Israelites continued their quick march across the field without looking back. Behind them the Hazorite army spread out, advancing in a hopelessly disorderly fashion, officers and men alike making no effort to maintain battle formation because their enemy was already running like whipped dogs.

"Just a little farther," Shemida said. "When we go over the crest of the hill ahead, our army will be out of Hazor's sight. Then, when they come over the top, let them find you facing them and ready to kill. Remember, sell every piece of land as dearly as you can."

"Right," Barak said.

Shemida saluted and set off to the sidelines at a brisk trot, not looking back, as if he were bolting for home.

As the wind continued to rise and the thunder echoed hollowly in the distance, the first drops of rain fell.

The rain soaked the cursing Hazorites, who were maneuvering the heavy iron chariots down the precipitous path. Jabin dismounted and led his horse ahead of the column until he reached an outcropping of rock overlooking the valley floor. He inched toward the edge of the rock and looked down through the rain.

"Telem, come here."

The commander arrived at the run.

"Look, Telem! Sisera is down there, and the Israelites are retreating. It's a rout."

Telem studied the situation. When he finally spoke, his voice was cautious. "Sir, they may be falling back to prepared positions. Look: They'll be invisible behind the rise, and when Sisera comes upon them, they'll hold their ground!"

Jabin's eyes widened. "Are you saying that Sisera is running into a trap?"

As Telem and Shemida predicted, when Sisera's screaming hordes came over the top of the ridge, they faced a wall of arrows. The first men fell immediately. The next rank raised their bucklers to fend off the shower of arrows but were overrun by the men behind them.

From the ranks of the Israelites came a low cry of long-suppressed rage. It began quietly among the young soldiers, spread quickly, and grew louder. At first there were no words; then someone shouted: *"Death to Hazor!"*

As the Hazorites continued to come over the top of the hill and collide with their own halted advance, the Israelites attacked in force.

Deborah watched from the sidelines, flanked by two bodyguards drawn from the ranks of the older fighters whom Shemida had drafted. Shemida stood on a projecting rock and watched the fight. "Come, Deborah. See your handiwork."

"It's no handiwork of mine," she said frankly. "I was

only following Yahweh's orders." She shivered as the rain intensified. "As were we all, I suppose. It was my job to mobilize you and Barak. It is Barak's job to fight the war. But we are no more than the weapons of God."

Shemida chuckled. "You sound like my old master Joshua. He would never take credit for anything. He always said that he was no more than an arm animated by Yahweh."

"I never met Joshua, but I understand how he thought. There are only two ways to deal with the voice of God telling you what to do: One is to say no and lose Him forever; the other is to say yes and ask no questions."

Shemida smiled. "That, too, sounds like Joshua. I didn't envy my master, and I don't envy you. God has given you a difficult task."

A white flash of lightning lighted the skies. Deborah shuddered and shut her eyes against the rain that pelted her.

Shemida turned to look up the hillside beyond. His face grew ashen. Men were lowering chariots down the hill on ropes. Jabin's army had arrived sooner than expected!

II

Sisera's army, marching across the ridge to find themselves facing fierce resistance, lost its momentum. Screaming officers hurled rank upon rank of men against the immovable Israelite line in a futile attempt to dislodge it from its position.

Sisera, cursing, beat fleeing soldiers back into line with the flat of his sword. He charged the crest after gathering around him a loose squad of proven regulars. The general's sword flashed right and left as his feet slipped and skidded on the muddy slopes. As men fell before his assault, he drove ever forward, hacking and slashing.

He looked through a gap in the line and saw Jabin's army slowly descending into the valley with their chariots. Sisera let out a fierce cry of triumph, and he attacked with renewed fury, crying out to his men: "Jabin's come! Jabin's here!" But his words were carried away by the high winds.

Strangely, the general could clearly hear the young Israelites' commander's huge voice carrying through the pounding rain, ordering reserve units to handle the attacks from the right and left flanks. He was headed for Sisera, hacking his way through the Hazorite ranks before him.

Beneath his excitement Barak felt surprised. He had thought himself a man ill suited to warfare. But now, with a real enemy before him—an enemy at whose hands his people had suffered great oppression—he found himself relishing his newfound prowess. No matter how many times he grew weary from swinging the heavy sword, fresh strength would suddenly flow into his arm, and all fatigue would vanish. Never in his life had he felt so powerful and so focused. War was seductive. Never had he felt so close to his companions, to every Israelite who had picked up a weapon.

The Israelite soldiers, who until a few days before had never held a real sword in their hands, had taken surprisingly well to fighting. They continued to drive the Hazorite forces back, all along the line.

Suddenly the driving wind took a chill turn, and the rain became hail, which hammered mercilessly on his helmet. He redoubled his efforts, fighting his way toward the Hazorite general.

"Sisera!" he bellowed. "It is I, Barak! Come to me, Sisera, oppressor of women! Come to me, you coward!"

The rear ranks of the Israelite force suddenly became aware of the Hazorite cavalry units forming up on the rainy plain. They passed the word forward, and a unit of Barak's infantry turned to face the ranks of horse-drawn chariots. When the Israelites saw the iron vehicles and the barrel-chested horses, they trembled with fear. If Jabin hit them from the rear and Sisera rallied, they could be crushed between the two claws of the Hazorite army. These iron chariots were demon beasts. They could smash all before them. No weapon could stop them. They were relentless scythes whose only harvest was mutilated corpses.

The Kishon River was swollen with the runoff from the many wadis that fed it. The river had risen to twice its normal height and four times its normal width. Floodwaters swept bushes and trees before it; even the tents of nomads had been smashed by the current and swept downriver toward the sea.

The rising waters began to inundate the approaches to the ridge on which the Israelites had made their stand against Sisera and awaited the crushing blow from the Hazorite cavalry. The rivulets poured down, turning the lowland soil into slick, slippery mud.

The Hazorites faltered and floundered as they tried to cut their way up the slope and destroy the insurgent army. Unable to maintain their footing in this quagmire, they were quickly cut down.

As Jabin's chariots prepared to attack the Israelites from the rear, they discovered a new problem: Telem pulled his chariot ahead of the line, and the wheels sank into the mud. Even the powerful charger was mired. Telem cursed and yanked at the reins. The horse only churned up the mud and sank deeper. When the commander used his whip, the animal stumbled and almost fell.

"What's going on?" Jabin demanded. He pulled his chariot forward only to have it sink up to the axle.

Seeing their leaders helplessly stuck in the mud in a driving rain sent panic through the other chariot drivers. They backed their animals onto firmer ground.

"Where are you going?" Jabin howled against the wind and the drumming rain. "Get me out of here!"

The ground unexpectedly gave way beneath the front rank of chariots, and they sank. The panicked horses reared, and one chariot tipped over, throwing its occupants into the mud.

The Israelites, seeing their enemy's weakness and sudden vulnerability, attacked. Yahweh's storm was emasculating the wheeled demons, and the mud was slowing their force and finally stopping them. The Israelites raised their spears and shields over their heads and screamed their triumph. Then they moved in on their enemy.

Barak lunged and impaled the last man who stood between Sisera and him. But one of his own soldiers stepped into the breech and attacked Sisera. Barak recognized the attacker as Heber, the young armorer who had recently joined them.

"Do you know me? Do you know who I am, you cowardly pig?" the Kenite screamed at the Hazorite general. He grasped his sword with both hands and started his swing, shouting Yael's name.

Sisera laughed insolently and, with a quick-footed, strong-wristed parry, disarmed the young man with insulting ease. He was about to finish him off when his sword caught Barak's blade. The Israelite stepped between Heber and his nemesis.

"Let me have him!" Barak yelled to Heber over the roaring wind.

Sisera blinked the rain out of his eyes. He knew whom he was facing. "Your size won't help you here, country boy. Nor will your Deborah!"

He punctuated his words with a furious attack that drove Barak back. The young leader parried wildly and was unable to counterattack. Finally he used his own superior strength to pin Sisera's sword for a moment.

"You're a dead man," Sisera growled, bringing his knee up savagely and smashing it into Barak's groin.

Sisera stepped back as Barak clutched himself and bent double with pain. He lunged to kill Barak. But the act was never completed. Sisera was stabbed in the forearm by Heber, who had picked up his weapon and thrust blindly.

Sisera howled in agony. His right hand was useless. He grabbed his sword with his left hand.

"To me!" he called. Instantly he was surrounded by his elite guard, who fought while he fell back, cursing the pain.

*   *   *

The wind howled down from the hills and brought with it sheets of blinding rain. The gusts waxed and waned. Shields were flattened against bodies by the wind's force.

The Hazorite cavalry, sunk in the sea of mud, tried valiantly to fight off the infantry attack. The iron sides of Hazor's chariots protected the soldiers' legs from Israelite swords and spears. But when the Israelites began over-turning chariots and slaughtering the occupants, the chari-oteers leapt off their perches, only to sink into the mud under the weight of their body armor.

The Israelites, wearing only leather vests, hunted them down. No mercy was shown. Their spears impaled the Hazorites through neck and limbs and face—wherever the body armor was absent. The enemy was crushed into the mud, blood mixing with the thick brown sludge. Wind whipped the hair of the fallen Hazorites once their helmets were dashed aside. Rain washed their frothing wounds, but the blood bubbled up again.

Some of the Hazorites managed to escape their pur-suers, only to see the swollen waters of the raging Kishon bearing down on them. The wave swept along, carrying uprooted trees, houses, and drowned and bloated animals.

Many men threw down their weapons and raced for the safety of high ground, but Shemida and his old guard were waiting and showed no mercy.

Watching the battle from a safe place, Deborah ex-plored her feelings. As a seeress, she accepted the blood-shed as Yahweh's plan. Tyrannical Hazor was the enemy and deserved to die. As long as there were evil regimes in the world, soldiers would die overthrowing them. She fought back tears as she saw the carnage. She had to be as strong as Barak—even stronger!—for this was the will of Yahweh.

Sisera was in too much pain to fight. He grasped the hilt of his sword weakly in his left hand and watched his army disintegrate.

The officers of the doomed cavalry unit had found their way into his ranks. He could see Telem and Jabin fighting desperately. As he watched, Barak, tall and straight, engaged Jabin, attacking fiercely. The big man's superior strength was too much for the king, who fell back. When Jabin missed a parry, Barak's blade pierced his neck.

At first it looked as if the king was through. But Jabin recovered and picked up an abandoned battle-ax. Now the king, bleeding profusely, and Barak faced one another, isolated from the ranks. Sisera watched as Telem slipped away to safety.

Barak was holding his sword with two hands and swinging it repeatedly at the king, only to have it blocked each time by the hilt of the battle-ax.

Sisera knew that Jabin could not withstand the pressure much longer. He had to break out of the circle and destroy the timing of Barak's strokes.

Again and again Barak's sword crashed down. Jabin crumbled a bit more with each blow. His body armor was soaked with blood. Barak was relentless.

He will not last much longer, Sisera thought as the king found it harder and harder to block the slashing sword with his ax. Then it ended. Jabin's arms simply could not be lifted. The ax could not block the sword. Barak's weapon sliced through the muscles and tendons of the king's neck, half severing his head. His body fell into the mud.

Sisera realized with horror that the rabble was winning. His army was doomed. And if the army was doomed, he was doomed along with them. Unless . . .

He looked around, frightened. Through the rain he saw the horses Shemida and Deborah had tethered on the slope. A narrow path led up to them. If only the track had not turned to treacherous mud like everything else! . . .

With no hesitation he bolted, keeping his eyes on the horses. Twice he slipped and fell. His mind was full of terror and pain as he pressed forward. Finally he reached the horses and flung himself on the back of the smaller one. Cursing the animal's unsteady footing, he urged it up the rocky slope and away. Sisera did not look back.

III

At last the driving sheets of rain lessened and became drizzle, and the leaden skies were no longer split by lightning. Afterward, no one was able to say when the wet, muddy, ugly battle in the Jezreel Valley turned into a victory for the Israelites or when the victory became a rout. No one ever knew how many men and horses had been ground into the mud.

To the east the renowned cavalry of the Hazorites had been destroyed by the very weight of the iron chariots Pepi had made for them, and the charioteers were slaughtered or drowned. To the west, the once proud army of Sisera now fled, terrified, and the Israelites dispatched each deserter with deadly efficiency. No mercy was expected or shown. A vulture began slowly circling the field. He was soon joined by others.

Barak and his men had commandeered Sisera's remaining horses the moment he saw the general escape. The Israelites trailed him up the treacherous slope, but at the top they saw no sign of him. One of the scouts dismounted and studied the landscape, and after a few moments he pointed to the path that led due east along the lone line of the ridge.

Barak urged his horse forward. "I'm going after him!"

From the slopes Deborah and Shemida watched the bloody mopping-up of the enemy force.

"You know," Shemida said, shaking his head, "I had my doubts. This was a miraculous victory. If Barak had known my fears, he'd never have been able to succeed."

Deborah smiled. "I'm not so sure about that. Men have many ways of expressing bravery. As for me, I didn't have to be brave at all. I just passed the word along: Yahweh told me that He would deliver the Hazorites into our hands. What had I to fear? Besides, I didn't have to do any fighting." She looked with respect at Shemida. "You doubted and feared, yet you went ahead. That requires great bravery! And what Barak feared most was his own inability to act, his own weakness. But he fought. He, too, is a very brave man."

Shemida permitted himself a small, knowing smile. "God gave you weapons no man has any defense against: You've a golden tongue. When the songs are written about our victory, your name will be sung louder than Barak's."

"And a pity, too," Deborah said. "Not that it will matter to Barak—he'll end up the same uncomplicated man he was when we first met. He doesn't want fame or glory; all he wants to do is return home and resume his life."

"That's not going to happen," Shemida predicted. "Barak will wind up ruling over northern Canaan, whether he likes it or not." He seemed to realize something and shot a sharp glance at Deborah. "Unless by some chance you—"

She laughed. "I refuse to rule anyone. I have enough difficulty just deciphering Yahweh's messages."

Shemida chuckled. "That's what Barak said when we started training him, and he's just won an important battle. We think we know our own capacities, but the only one who truly knows our limits is the God Who made us."

The rain had stopped. The sun had come out, drying the rocky road that threaded along the ridge top. Sisera pushed his horse into a trot.

The shock of what had happened to the Hazorite army was just beginning to sink in. Gone were the days of easy living, of having men jump to obey his every order. Gone were his power and command and all the attendant benefits. Until he managed somehow to reestablish himself, he would be no better than the next man. Having lost his authority, the great Sisera would have to show deference to the rich and influential. He would have to mind his manners and watch his mouth. He would have to subdue his passions.

It was unfair that these bumpkins could defeat an army as superbly trained and conditioned as his own. How had it happened? It could not have been his own fault. He had led them with his usual skill, and they had fought bravely enough . . . at first, anyhow.

The more he thought of what had transpired, the more he realized that the blame fell on the extraordinary weather. That, and the fact that his men had been weighted down by their bronze armor, and Jabin's cavalry had been bogged down by the enormous weight of the now-useless iron chariots that Pepi had made for him. If it had not rained . . . if he had ordered his men to turn out in their normal gear rather than in their ceremonial armor . . . if Jabin had arrived an hour earlier . . . If . . . If . . .

The accursed weather! Had it been a spell cast on him by that witch Deborah everyone kept talking about? Deborah! If only he could get his hands on the bitch's throat!

If . . .

He cursed, spat into the dust, and urged the horse to go faster. If he could reach the Jordan Valley by sundown, perhaps he could make it all the way to Damascus tomorrow. He could find work as a mercenary there. In a city of that size, along the trade routes, someone always needed a soldier or, at worst, a bodyguard. Yes, Damascus tomorrow.

Suddenly he felt more tired than ever before. If only there was some place he could find sanctuary for the night and rest. But he could not stop now. The Israelites would have set some murderer on his trail. He could not stop until dark.

If only he had a friend in the Jordan Valley—a comrade or a relative he could stay with. Just one night, and then he would move on to find a new life, in which he would trust neither kings nor comrades. He would play them all off against one another. That was the only way to handle people. As for that Kenite Heber, a time would come for revenge. He would pay Heber back for stabbing him. If he ever ran into the Kenite's wife again, he would take his revenge on her. He savored the thought of mutilating her.

But then his growing fever, brought on by the still-bleeding wound, forced him back to the reality of his mistakes. Like a fool he had trusted Telem and Jabin. The only one he had suspected had been Pepi. He would give a fortune to have Pepi in his hands right now! He would kill the man slowly, savoring the armorer's pain, taking pleasure in the traitor's every scream.

Pepi sold them all out. Pepi and that assistant of his, the tinker who had wounded him. *Will I ever be able to use my arm again?* The thought was so frightening he suppressed it. Pepi had gone over to the other side. The man had to die, even if it meant sending an assassin back to Canaan once he had gotten himself set up in a new life. He would see that the bastard paid!

Huldah had sent to one of the Jordan Valley settlements for a physician, and by midafternoon one had found his way to her camp.

He examined Pepi and then turned to her. "May we discuss this outside?"

Huldah led him into the sunshine. "He's dying, isn't he?"

The physician nodded grimly. "He could go at any time. I found an old scar. . . ."

"Yes, that wound almost killed him years ago. He's been living on borrowed time."

"I was afraid of that. You say he's not clear in his mind now?"

She shook her head sadly. "No. He should know me but doesn't; I was his wife."

"A pity, but don't pressure him. He can't stand a shock now."

She caught her breath. The thought of his dying now was like a pain in her breast. She brought herself under control. "Thank you. If you'll see my assistant, he'll take care of your fee."

"Send for me if he gets worse."

But they both knew if Pepi were to get worse, there would be no need for a physician.

What an irony: For years she despised his very name. Now fate had brought him back to her. For what? To die? She walked slowly back inside the tent.

To her surprise, he was alert and looking around. "Who's there? Come here and let me see you."

She moved into the lamplight and looked in his eyes. "Are you feeling better?"

"Tirzah?" he asked, incredulous. "Oh, gods, Tirzah, is that you?"

IV

Barak reined in his horse and stared along the ridge line. He had lost Sisera's trail. With Jabin dead and Sisera fleeing, only one major task remained: to destroy Telem and Jabin's other surviving staff officers. If Hazor would rise again, it would be behind the strong sword arms of Telem and his able comrades.

He wheeled his horse around and quickly picked up Telem's trail, along the track above the flooded plain of Jezreel. Barak smiled. Telem would be a great prize because he was the most competent of Hazor's commanders. The young Israelite began to see signs of the officer's fatigue: The man had shed his armor one piece at a time—greaves had gone by the wayside, then his breastplate; and finally his bronze helmet, fouled with mud.

Barak was no longer unsure of himself. He redoubled his efforts on the trail. How strange were the ways of God, he marveled. For example, he had suddenly found new strength whenever he needed it. Deborah was right; this battle had been preordained, and he had been chosen to lead the army to victory. Everything was preordained by Yahweh. Barak feared no longer.

He came around a ledge of rock to find himself within a spear's cast of Telem. The officer was alone. His uniform was bedraggled, and he had lost one boot in the mud; his hair was disheveled, and his shoulders slumped with fatigue.

"Are you ready to die?" Barak asked, sliding off the horse and drawing his sword.

In an instant, the fatigue seemed to vanish from Telem.

He drew his sword and stared around to see if Barak was accompanied by others.

"I am alone," Barak told him.

A grim smile played at the edges of Telem's lips. Barak realized that the man facing him, no matter how tired now, had earned his excellent reputation. He had been Sisera's second-in-command and had then been promoted to the northern command. It was Telem whom the king had chosen to lead the cavalry in that desperate attack on the muddy plain.

Barak knew he was facing a trained swordsman, a combat veteran, a young man who had fought the best and lived to tell about it. The only other swordsman of Telem's capabilities he had faced was Sisera—and if it had not been for Heber's timely intervention, Sisera would have killed him.

Barak, however, felt no fear or confusion. If Yahweh had ordained that he would live, it would be so. If Yahweh ordained that Telem would kill him, so be it.

Telem began to circle. Barak was calm. He could see Telem's fierce eyes as they studied him. Barak recalled the strategy one of Joshua's veterans had told him to implement when fighting a quicker man: "The only way strength can overcome speed is through exhaustion."

Telem attacked. His thrusts and footwork were lightning quick. He moved like a snake, attacking and withdrawing, each time hopeful of striking beneath Barak's guard.

Barak stood relaxed, parrying each thrust with the strength of his arm alone.

But the long day of battle began to slow Telem. All the reserve energy he had summoned for this new combat was quickly expended, and he took on the look of a broken soldier. Still he circled the larger, stronger man, and still he lunged with a fast sword, only to be shaken to his bones as the Israelite blocked the thrust.

As the deadly game progressed, Barak realized that Telem would die at his hands. It was such a clear epiphany that he felt no urgency. It was as if whatever he did, even if he kept his guard down, Telem would die.

Finally, all the strength left the Hazorite officer. He
stood gasping, his sword arm trembling, his legs barely
able to support his weight.

He nodded to Barak as if accepting his defeat. Then
he threw back his head and tried to give one last Hazorite
war cry. It came out a raspy croak. Quickly, he removed
the small dagger from his belt and in one smooth motion
slit his own throat.

Barak stood unmoving. He stared with remorse at the
fallen body; in a different time and different place, he and
Telem might have been friends. Then he approached the
body and gently laid Telem's sword on his breast.

Now, he said to himself, *there is only Sisera!*

Huldah was struck dumb by Pepi's recognition of her.
She sank to her knees beside his cot and buried her face in
her hands. For the first time in years, she surrendered to
the emotions she had denied herself ever since her abduction. Her shoulders heaved, and she shook with violent,
rending sobs.

Pepi sat up weakly and reached for her. "Tirzah,
won't you speak to me? What's the matter?" But the effort
brought pain, and he sank back on the pillow exhausted.

Huldah wiped her eyes and looked at him. She had
imagined how she would feel if she ever found him, and
she always thought it would be pure, unadulterated anger.
He had let all those unspeakable things happen to her! He
had not rescued her from oppression and degradation! But
now she felt no anger. Instead she felt shame and self-
loathing for what she had been and what she was now.

"What's the matter?" he repeated. "Why won't you
speak to me? I've wanted to find you for so long. . . ."

She swallowed. "And I've wanted to find you. But,
Pepi . . . some terrible things happened to me. I don't
know if I can face you if you ever find out what I did."
Then she realized she could not burden him in what might
be his last hours. She took his hand between hers. "Forgive me, Pepi. Nothing matters except that we have found
each other."

She removed her robe and draped it over him. Her

arm touched his forehead, and she was shocked at how hot his skin was. She stroked his fevered brow.

He tried to smile. "You look so . . . elegant. You look like a queen."

She returned his smile. "I've become rich. Perhaps even as rich as you." She patted his hand. The armorer's once-powerful hand was weak. He was dying right before her eyes, and she could do nothing about it—except, perhaps, be brave and say nothing that would sadden him.

"How did the battle come out?" he asked.

"The Israelites won," she replied. "Your own action saved them—that and the rain. If Jabin's army had caught them from the rear, Sisera might have beaten them."

Pepi shook his head sadly. "I did the Israelites great injustice. I tried to make up for it before dying." He saw the pain in her eyes. "You don't have to pretend. I know how I feel. But I'm happy. I made peace with the Israelites, and I got to see you again."

"Oh, Pepi, why did we have to be apart all these years?"

He squeezed her hand weakly. "At least we had some time together, didn't we? Some people never—" His voice was growing weaker. "Come closer," he whispered. "My words don't seem to have any wind behind them."

"Just tell me you love me," she asked. "As you once did. Please." She struggled to suppress her sobs. "And . . . forgive me."

His hand rose to touch her hair. His eyes closed. His chest rose and fell with effort. "We will see each other again. I love you. Nothing to forgive." His hand fell to his side.

She rubbed his hand, but there was no life in it. "Pepi, don't leave me! Don't go! No, please don't die! Pepi!"

On his wan face was a peace she had never seen before. Now she was truly alone, as she had never been even in her worst days.

The sun was setting. Sisera's horse had given out hours before, and he had abandoned it. As he wandered

through the well-kept farmlands south of the lake, it was
impossible to tell he was a soldier. He had cast off his
armor and uniform. All he kept was his sword, which was
rolled into the cloak he carried under one arm. If no one
recognized him, he might find shelter for the night.

He was so weary he could hardly put one foot in front
of the other. He approached a tent with a woman standing
by the entrance. Everything was beginning to become
indistinct in the dusk, and it was as if he were moving
through a dream.

He felt as if he was going to a home he had often
dreamed of, a place where he would always be welcomed,
where he would be met with love and forgiveness and
compassion, a place where he could find rest and sleep
and wake refreshed and whole.

He squinted at the woman in the doorway. It was his
little plaything from the Jezreel Valley, the one who was
married to the armorer. Somehow it was entirely fitting
that she should be the one he turned to in his hour of
need. Looking at her gentle face, his heart warmed to her.

"Yael," he pleaded, "I'm so tired. My throat is dry. I
need a drink of water and a place to lie down."

She gestured for him to enter. As he staggered through
the tent entrance, his eyes fastened for a moment on the
curve of her neck. He stopped and closed his eyes, letting
his mind wander over her body, remembering her round,
firm breasts and smooth, naked thighs.

Sisera stiffened as he recalled how her husband had
wounded him. His desire to mutilate her returned. The
memory of the taste of her blood came to his mouth. He
recalled how he had once latched on to her nipples with
his teeth until she had screamed and begged for mercy.
He would take her now, as he used to! He would rip off
her robe and ravage that sweet young body until her will
to fight was broken.

But he could not move toward her. He could not
speak. The pain and exhaustion had taken his manhood
from him. He stared at her.

She gave him an odd smile, and her voice was strangely
soft. "Yes, Sisera. Come inside. I'll get you some fresh

buttermilk. Lie down over here. Poor man, you look exhausted. Rest, don't think of anything."

He lay down on a simple mat and placed his head on the crude lambskin pillow. All his bones and joints ached. For a moment he felt a stab of fear.

"I can't rest now," he said, trying to sit up. "Men are after me. If I go to sleep—"

She put a gentle hand on his shoulder. "If anyone comes, I'll tell them I've seen no one."

He sank back down. "Thank you." His body was relaxing. He felt sleep, healing sleep, coming on. His breathing deepened. . . .

Yael faltered only once. Then she remembered what Deborah had told her: When the time came, he would be delivered into her hands, and she would know what to do.

She forced herself to concentrate on the fact that earlier today he might have been fighting her husband and trying to kill him. She thanked God that a runner had come through the area to spread the news that the battle had been won and the power of Hazor broken forever. The runner, however, knew nothing of Heber's fate.

She looked around the tent for a weapon when Sisera's breathing deepened further. She saw the mallet she had used to drive the tent stakes and, lying beside it, one of the stakes. She went over and picked them up. Trepidation momentarily paralyzed her. Then she straightened, realizing that she would not sleep well again if she did not act, that she would condemn other women to suffer the same horrors she had endured if she did not carry out her task and murder her tormentor.

Yael shuddered, then she firmed her resolve. For a moment she watched the rapist's face. How curious—there was no peace in him even when he was asleep.

She inched closer and touched the point of the metal stake to his temple. He was facing her. She took a deep breath, picked up the heavy mallet in her other hand, and raised it high. With all her might she struck downward.

It was done. Revolted, she flung the mallet away and fled from the tent, screaming. "Basemath!" she cried.

Her friend hurried from the adjoining tent, and Yael ran into her arms.

"It's over," Yael said, weeping. She cringed and fought down the bile rising in her throat.

"Then we must finish it properly," Basemath replied in a matter-of-fact voice. "I'm proud of you, Yael!"

She walked back inside her tent and came out again carrying a large ax with a stone blade.

Yael did not move. "I can't go back in there," she said, casting a nervous glance at her tent.

"Come, Yael, he's dead. He can't hurt you now. We must bring Deborah proof that Yahweh's will was done."

Yael reluctantly followed her friend.

V

Shortly after dawn of the next day, the conquering Israelite heroes marched into the little valley. Within a twenty-four-hour period they had broken the ten-year domination of Hazor. And now from the cities and towns and rolling foothills, their countrymen came to praise them for what they had done in the name of Yahweh.

Drums beat and trumpets blew as men, women, and children gathered to greet the army. Barak marched at its head and Deborah, small and unpretentious, walked by his side.

As they entered the Jordan Valley, a small, lone figure stood timidly in the middle of the path of the victory column. Barak frowned and called the column to a halt.

"Get her out of the way," he demanded, "and then find out why she's here."

But Deborah put a hand on his arm. "That's Heber's wife. I think I know why she's here. Come with me."

As they approached the young woman, Deborah smiled reassuringly, but Yael did not smile back.

"Yael," Deborah said, "your husband's in the rear ranks. He's all right, and he helped to secure the victory."

"Thank God," Yael whispered, then looked from Deborah to Barak. "If you're still looking for Sisera . . ." she began in a curiously detached voice.

"Sisera?" Barak asked, his hand automatically reaching for his sword. "Where is he?"

"He came to me, as he had come to me before. And Deborah, it was as you said: God told me what to do." Yael nodded toward the wrapped bundle that lay at her feet. Then she unrolled it with her foot.

Barak's jaw dropped when he saw the severed head of Sisera. The tent stake still protruded from his skull.

"*You* did this?" Barak asked.

Yael nodded.

He shook his head in amazement and gestured to a soldier to remove the bundle. "Come," he said to Yael, "you will march beside us." Then he turned to Deborah. "When the songs are sung, everyone will remember the women—you and Yael. That is as it should be. Women suffered the worst at Sisera's hands. It's fitting that he died at theirs."

Deborah put a comforting arm around Yael's shoulders. "I know it couldn't have been easy for you, even though your action had Yahweh's blessings. Put it behind you now, my dear. Yahweh will help you to forget."

Barak turned and faced the column of soldiers. "All glory to Yael, the victor!" he cried in a powerful voice that carried all the way back to Heber. "All hail the slayer of Sisera the tyrant! And all praise to Yahweh, Who guided her hand!"

It was a day for feasting and thanksgiving. Now the carefully hoarded secret foodstuffs the farmers and herdsmen had been hiding from Jabin's tribute collectors quickly appeared, and the cooks prepared a victory feast. The musicians brought their instruments, and there was joyous singing and dancing. Someone broke into one of Jabin's storehouses and brought out amphorae of wine the Hazorites had extorted from the local vintners.

As Barak went from unit to unit congratulating his men, Heber sat holding Yael's hand and beaming at her.

"I am very proud of you." Then his smile faded. "But I have some bad news. A rich woman who owns a caravan now camped in the valley says my master, Pepi, is dead." He smiled sadly. "Somehow I knew we weren't going to get rich. But Pepi gave me a profession. I'm not a tinker anymore. I can do my own work, and pretty well, too." He thought for a moment. "We may become rich, after all!"

Deborah stepped close to them. "Excuse me. I heard you say the rich woman told you Pepi was dead."

He nodded.

"Are you certain? Did she mention Pepi by name?"

"Yes," he replied.

She thanked him and walked briskly away.

Huldah was supervising the loading of the pack animals when she saw Deborah bearing down on her.

"I see you've heard. We found each other, but—"

"You talked to him before he died, didn't you?"

"Yes," Huldah answered, "but there was not enough time. I wanted to say so much, but I couldn't. He was too weak." She shook her head. "I remembered him as being so strong. But he was terribly frail at the end."

"Men are frail," Deborah responded. "They like to act as though they are strong, but the slightest fever can carry them away. They go out and fight the world for us, but all they accomplish is getting themselves killed or maimed. Men can't save us from anything; we have to do that ourselves. But they're a gallant lot, though, and because we love them, we allow them their self-delusions."

Huldah nodded. "Their dreams of power, of controlling their destinies, of protecting their loved ones . . . it's all foolishness. But I suppose there are worse dreams to have. Oh, Deborah, I had such awful thoughts about him! I blamed Pepi for my ordeal, but he did search for me. He did his best. He had his own problems. He felt terribly guilty about letting me down and about his vindictiveness toward the Israelites."

"But he redeemed himself, Huldah. He saved us." Then Deborah looked at the other woman sharply. "Pepi dealt with his guilt. How are you going to deal with yours?"

Huldah's face fell. "I . . . I don't know. I thought I'd risen above . . . what happened to me. But it seems the more of a shell I try to build, the more vulnerable I become. I feel as worthless now as I did when I was a whore without a scrap of cloth to cover me. No, I feel worse. At least then I could blame others for my predicament. Now I loathe myself."

Deborah put a hand on Huldah's cheek. "You have to go on with life. Pepi's dead. You wouldn't have had him for much longer anyway. The damage was done long ago."

"Yes, by that rock I threw at him!" Huldah said bitterly.

"Don't think about that now. And don't think about what might have been, either. Think only about what can be."

"My life is over."

Deborah shook her head. "Far from it, my dear. You're a very rich woman. In addition to your own fortune, you have inherited Pepi's." The seeress smiled. "I have the feeling that Heber has been left something by Pepi as well. Heber knows nothing about it, of course, but maybe you could seek out the family representatives in one of the big cities and facilitate a transfer of funds."

"Certainly I'll ask. But what shall I do—"

"The country here is poor, and many people suffer terrible hardships. Yael, for instance, has a friend, a good-hearted but plain young woman. As a favor to me you could give Basemath a monetary gift that will attract a husband."

"I will."

"You might relocate here. There are many services you could perform. The traders cheat the people. With your business sense, you could intervene and represent them honestly in their dealings."

Huldah's face was thoughtful.

Deborah continued, "There's a colony of Kenite tinkers down by the river. Their homes were destroyed by the flood."

"Yes, I can help them."

"And there are thousands of victims from ten years of Hazorite oppression."

"I—I used to hate your people. They had done such terrible things to me."

"And you harbored a burning hatred also for Pepi's clan. That's too much anger to carry in your heart, Huldah. Give it up. We are human and fallible. No one is any better than anyone else. God certainly did not choose the Israelites because we are better than the rest of mankind. But your problem was never with them; it was with yourself. Forgiving yourself is very difficult." She pressed Huldah's hand warmly. "Practice forgiving others, particularly your enemies, and everything that follows will be good."

She stood on her tiptoes and embraced Huldah. Then she turned to go.

But Huldah held her back. "May I see you again?"

"Of course. Just look for me under the palm trees between Ramah and Bethel." She laughed. "But bring something to eat and drink. The lines are long these days."

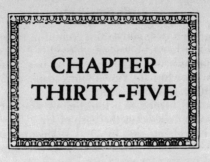

CHAPTER THIRTY-FIVE

Damascus

It was one hundred and thirty miles as the crow flies from Dubai's forge in the Wilderness of Judea to the bustling city of Damascus. Luti made the journey in two days, driving the chariot only at night and hiding and resting the horses during the day. She had crossed to the east bank of the Jordan River just north of the Sea of Salt and drove into the desert before she turned north. In that way she had avoided the numerous settlements of the more fertile areas.

One of the horses died of convulsions just south of Jerash, but Luti could not slow her pace. All during the journey she had the feeling that she was being pursued, that horses and men were only moments behind. She pushed herself relentlessly. From dawn to dusk she felt the pain in her heart at betraying Micah, and her thoughts were consumed with reliving their brief moments of passion. Yes, she loved him. But she loved Drak and Babylon more.

During daylight, while she was in hiding, she tried to plan her journey from Damascus to Ur. Would she be able to retrace her steps? Would she be able to navigate the great desert from Damascus to Ur without a Bedouin guide? Would she and the horses survive the blistering heat?

When she saw the spires of Damascus in the distance,

she stopped and dropped to the ground in prayer. At least the first leg of her trek was completed.

As she rose, two riders closed on her. She leapt into the chariot to whip the horse and escape, but the riders had already grasped the bridle.

Luti's fear turned to astonishment when she saw that the men were dressed in the garb of Ur.

"We have been sent by Drak to ensure your safety," one said. "We have been patrolling the approaches to Damascus, waiting for you."

Luti had no choice, so she submitted to their escort toward the city.

Luti found Drak waiting for her on the outskirts of Damascus in a makeshift camp with a large, well-armed contingent. After delivering the chariot to him, she wrapped herself in a blanket and slept for twenty-four hours without interruption.

When she finally awoke, Drak was beside her on a large cushion. Within reach was a wooden tray filled with fruit and bowls of milk. He looked very old and terribly sick, and one of his eyes was half-closed from infection. But he had obviously covered her with several blankets while she slept.

"What a brave woman you are," Drak approved, smiling kindly at her.

His compliment warmed Luti. She drank milk from one of the bowls. It was tart, unlike the milk of Ur. But she would soon be home.

"I never expected to find you here, waiting for me, Drak. I thought I would have to travel the desert by myself."

Drak painfully bent over and placed the wooden tray on the ground. "I've been in Damascus for a while. I left Ur the moment I realized that Banniselk had deceived me. You cannot imagine how frightened I was for your safety when I discovered that the Bedouin I had sent along with you for your protection was a man sworn to destroy you. But he had been sent to me by a man I trusted. That man has since met with a most unfortunate accident. Banniselk and he were conspirators. My so-called friend convinced me that Occa was the man for the job."

"Why had you given him a different set of directions from the one you gave me?"

"Merely a precaution. Forgive me. I knew all the time where the forge was, and it seemed to me that the less you knew, the better. I entrusted 'the Bedouin' with the real route."

"And the coat of nighthawk feathers?"

"I showed the Bedouin what to do with it once you entered the forge area and had to prove your worth. I trusted him. His disguise fooled me so completely that I would have trusted him with everything I hold dear."

"How did you find out that Occa was actually Banniselk?"

"From an informer, thank the goddess. There is much strife in our nation now. The fools don't realize that the more they fight with one another, the more vulnerable we all become."

His words confused her. "Why did Banniselk want the chariot?"

"It is a very long story, and I am not sure I know all its complexities. It is clear now that the priests of Astarte were engaged in a conspiracy to turn the southern cities into an independent state, taking orders no longer from the northern capital but from the cult. Above all, they were determined to destroy all traces of the god Marduk in the south. Possession of the chariot would have afforded them tremendous leverage. You have done a great service to Babylon, Luti."

"It wasn't I who killed Banniselk."

"Then who?"

"A Child of the Lion."

Drak's eyes widened in astonishment. "You met another Child of the Lion? With the same birthmark?"

"Yes. His name was Micah."

"Did he know who you are?"

"No, and I never told him any more than my name." She turned away from Drak for a moment as painful memories overwhelmed her. Then she turned back toward him. "I don't know why I never told him. I'm sorry now. I left him tied up in the chariot's cave. He was probably killed when the chariot was discovered missing."

As Luti nibbled some fruit and drank more milk, she briefly explained all that had transpired in the Wilderness of Judea. It was only the murder of Banniselk that she described in any detail. When she was finished, Drak was silent for a long time.

Finally he asked: "To whom did you say this Micah wished to deliver the chariot?"

"To the Israelites."

"Then Micah himself was not an Israelite?"

"No. He was their friend."

"The Israelites," Drak noted, "had no need of secret weapons in their recent battle against King Jabin. Word has come in that the Israelites destroyed the Hazorite army."

"If Micah still lives, that news will make him very happy."

"Tell me more, Luti, about your powers with the birds."

She described what had happened in the desert at the beginning of her trip and how she had interpreted the omen of the ravens on the family's corpses to mean danger and how that interpretation had saved her life. Then she told Drak about her meeting with the armorer Dubai and how Occa had worn the same coat of feathers Drak had used to help her master the metal.

"And what about the chariot you have so bravely brought us?"

"I saw it being tested."

"Was it fast?"

"Like the wind, over a variety of surfaces. It moves over mud as if it were glass."

"Good, Luti. There is a lot of mud along the Tigris."

"When will we leave for Ur?"

"Perhaps this afternoon."

"I feel as though I have been away for years. I feel that when I go back I will recognize no one, and no one will recognize me."

"Tell me more about this Micah."

She sighed. "There is nothing to tell. But it is strange that we met in the wilderness, as if it had been our destiny . . . as if some force had driven me from my land and he from his, only to meet without warning or motive or intent. I just stumbled into their camp."

"Did you dream before you met him?"

"I can't remember. Why do you ask?"

"Because you are a woman with great powers. We now know that."

"You flatter me, dear Drak."

"Are you sure he didn't speak about being a Child of the Lion?"

"Not a word. He said nothing, and I said nothing. I saw his birthmark only by chance."

"Why didn't you ask him about it?"

Luti did not answer. She stared at the pack animals of the caravan—short, powerful horses with shaggy manes. They seemed to accept their fate stoically as the heavy burdens were strapped on them. Only one beast was being difficult, and that was the one to which the waterskins were being fastened. *How odd,* she thought, *that the one carrying the most pleasing burden would be the only one protesting.* She looked back at Drak.

The old man was smiling at her kindly. "Now, young woman, you must rest again. You'll need all your strength for the trip home. You will not be returning to a hovel in Ur or to a job in the flax fields. In your absence I have made all the transfers. You are now one of the wealthiest women in Ur, and you have earned it. Babylon will be eternally grateful to you. Our armorers will reproduce the chariot, and when the kingdom is again invaded, the might of Babylon will shine forth."

They sat together in silence for a long time. Then, inexplicably, Luti began to weep.

"What is the matter, child? Why are you weeping? Have I offended you in some way?"

"No, it's not that," she said between sobs.

"Then tell me."

"I just feel terribly sad." She closed her eyes. She did not care about the wealth that awaited her. She did not

care about the eternal gratitude of Babylon. All she could
think of was Micah and those precious moments in the
cave. But she could not tell Drak. She took the old man's
hand and held it tightly.

   One day, she thought, *if Micah is alive, I will be with
him again.*

CHAPTER THIRTY-SIX

Wilderness of Judea

It had taken Micah hours to loosen the knots on his wrists and escape from the caves, luckily before anyone from the forges discovered him. When he had returned to his brother, he had refused to speak.

Nimshi had questioned him again and again. Where was the chariot? Why were there welts on his wrists and ankles showing that he had been bound? Why was blood splattered over his robe? But Micah had not answered. He had pulled the robe over his head and slept.

Now it was midmorning. Micah was awake but maddeningly silent. Nimshi offered him the last of the water.

"Why won't you tell me what happened, Micah?"

"Nothing happened," he snapped. "As you see, no chariot accompanied me."

"But the blood and the marks on your wrists and ankles—?"

"I paid back the Bedouin who wounded you."

"How?"

He withdrew the long knife. "With this, through his throat."

"Why, Micah? Why was that necessary?"

Micah exploded. "Look at your festering leg! You can't even walk. That's why."

"And the girl?"

"What about her?"

"Where is she?"

Micah did not answer. He turned away from Nimshi and laid his stomach on the baked earth.

Nimshi shook the near-empty waterskin. They had no food at all. Nimshi realized that if Micah had murdered the Bedouin in the forge area, they would never be welcomed there; on the contrary, they would probably be arrested. And while his leg wound was showing signs of healing, he could not walk back to Tel Arad, much less to Gaza. They were trapped in the wilderness.

Suddenly Micah started to laugh crazily.

Nimshi shook him. "Are you mad? There is nothing funny about our situation."

"I was thinking about when we were children in Jerusalem."

Nimshi shook his head. There was no talking to his brother now; he was no longer making sense. He had been acting crazy ever since that girl had walked into their camp, and whatever had happened in the caves during the night had made him more bizarre. Nimshi crawled up the hillock to stare down at the forge area. Smoke hung over it like a blanket.

Micah continued to babble about their childhood, but after a while Nimshi closed his ears. He turned and stared to the north, toward Jerusalem. From where he lay he could see far in the distance, where the rocky, parched wilderness began to give way to green hills.

Something was moving out there. He blinked and tried to shield his eyes from the ferocious sun. "Look, Micah," he cried. "Visitors!"

Micah curtailed his reminiscences and joined his brother on the hillock. "Where?" he asked.

Nimshi pointed. There were two men, one armed with a spear, and five horses.

"My guess is that they are making a delivery to the forge," Micah said.

"Ore? Charcoal?"

"No, the sacks look like grain. Maybe dates."

Micah filled his leather purse with stones, then started to stand, but Nimshi pulled him down. "What are you doing? If you murdered the Bedouin in the forge last night, maybe they know about it."

"How could they possibly know? They are just arriving from the north. I'm going down there and ask for some bread and water. Don't worry."

"What about the blood on your robes?" Nimshi asked.

But Micah was already striding off.

Micah approached the small pack train slowly and stopped about twenty feet away. The first guard, the one with the spear, dismounted swiftly, in the manner of a trained soldier. The second guard gathered the reins of the packhorses as a precaution.

"Who are you?" the guard demanded gruffly.

"Root digger," Micah explained, "from the coast." It was common for men to travel into the Wilderness of Judea to dig up medicinal roots, which brought a good price in all the cities of the Philistine League.

The guard warily pointed his spear at Micah's blood-flecked robe.

Micah laughed. "Oh, this. My companion drank too much wine. He thought his foot was a root, and I had to sew him up. We need some bread and water until we get back."

"Why don't you get it from the caves?"

"Those people are touchy and don't like strangers nosing around. They're building some new chariot that rides in the sky without horses. You just spit on the wheels, and off it flies."

Both guards laughed appreciatively. Then the nearer one apologized. "We'd like to help you, but all this is contracted food. Every ounce is measured. If we're short, we pay."

Micah studied them. They were not Israelites. He guessed they were displaced Moabites who had intermarried with the tribes that remained on the west bank of the Jordan. They were wearing long gowns made of skins, and their feet were bare.

"I will give you five gold crowns for a bag of grain and two skins of water."

The two guards were astonished by Micah's generous offer. One of them laughed nervously. "Say that again?"

"You heard me. Five crowns for one bag of good grain and two skins of water."

"You must be very hungry."

"And thirsty," Micah confirmed. "But I want to see that the grain has no maggots and that the water is fresh."

The guard with the spear squatted on the ground, and Micah hunkered down beside him. The other guard went to the animals and removed a bag of grain and two waterskins, which he carried to Micah and placed on the ground.

Micah drew out his long knife and made a small slit at the top of the grain bag. He poured some grain into his hand, sifting it carefully and studying its color, and then tasted it.

"Well?" asked the guard with the spear.

"Looks good. Now for the water." One of the waterskins was handed to him. He drank deeply. It was clean, fresh water. He took the other skin and tasted the water in that, also. He nodded.

"It's time to see your coins," the guard said.

Micah smiled and stood up. He removed his heavy leather purse from his robe and opened it slowly. The guards watched eagerly for the gold coins.

Suddenly Micah stepped back and swung the purse savagely, smashing the leather object into the head of the closest guard. The guard fell over with a muffled cry, and blood gushed from his nose. The man died almost instantly. Micah was on the other guard in an instant, his long knife driving up between the man's ribs and into his heart.

Then he picked up the guard's spear and waved it triumphantly.

Nimshi, pressed against the hillock, turned away in horror. Why had Micah murdered those travelers? They did not need all the water and grain. They didn't need all the horses. Now they were both fugitives. They would not be safe in Gaza or anywhere else. He cried bitterly in frustration. The new life had turned into a nightmare. Micah was a monster, created by the Israelites.

Then Nimshi understood the weird logic in Micah's behavior. The only people who would welcome Micah among them were the Israelites. Micah had made certain that when he went north, Nimshi would have to go with him.

What was this strange and powerful bond between the Israelites and the Children of the Lion? When would that bond be severed? The questions were too deep for him to ponder now. He gathered the remaining objects from the campsite and limped slowly toward his brother, who was dancing gaily over the corpses.

PART
EIGHT

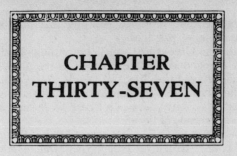

CHAPTER THIRTY-SEVEN

In the Aegean

I

The repairs on Theon's boat had been extensive and time-consuming. He had watched as the ships leaving Troy braved the rough seas and sailed past him one by one. And he worried as they disappeared into the brooding storm clouds of the east. Finally the violent weather had hit, sweeping in from the sea and bringing towering waves and terrifying winds.

When a second day had passed without a sign of renewed storms, Theon ordered his men to right his careened vessel and drag it to the water. At Troy he beached his boat on the same shore where the Greeks had encamped for ten years during the siege of the city. At last he stood before the burned-out hulk that had been Troy the Magnificent, the most beautiful city in the Greek-speaking world.

It was a heartbreaking sight. The massive wooden gates had been torn down and burned. The towering walls were blackened with smoke. As he looked past the city at the dull skies and dark clouds, the enormity of Troy's destruction almost overwhelmed him. How could a place that had been so vital end up as smoldering ashes?

He took a squad of men into the abandoned city, where they walked through the desolate, litter-filled streets, experiencing the emptiness, sensing that ghosts walked the same somber passages.

After the Greeks had stolen everything of value, looters had descended, to strip Troy of every piece of wood that had survived the fires and take it to their villages for fuel. The dead had not been buried, but scavenging animals had been busy, and now there were only scattered bones with shreds of flesh.

Theon turned to his first mate, Strabo. "Look at this pile of bones. Greek or Trojan? It's strange how we all look alike under the skin."

"Right, sir," Strabo responded. "All we know is that they're men. The women were carted off; by now they'll be slaves or whores. Only a lucky few will be wives."

Theon frowned, thinking of Keturah and her son. "And what of the children?" he asked. "I don't see many small skeletons here."

"The children would have been dragged off with ropes around their necks—the healthy ones, anyhow. They'd make good slaves. You could get a long lifetime of work out of them."

Theon's frown turned to a scowl as he continued up the grand staircase of the palace. He shivered at the dreary, ominous emptiness. A great nation had died here, and with it, great traditions and beauty. Troy had been a city-state devoted to justice and fairness; its people held great love and respect for its rulers and its laws. For generations there had been neither revolt nor rebellion. Troy had been a haven of art and music and graceful architecture, an environ of peace and harmony.

Now there was nothing left. Its warriors were dead, and its women and children were chattel. Its riches were dispersed, like the inhabitants, to the far corners of the world. How vulnerable and ephemeral was civilization! This could happen anywhere. Many Greek soldiers would no doubt return to cities fallen or ready to fall—a spirit of violent change was loose in the world—and in time little would remain of their own city-states but broken rubble and a few words in a half-forgotten song.

"Captain!" A shout interrupted Theon's brooding

thoughts on the inexplicable rise and fall of civilizations. "We've found someone!"

Theon and Strabo hurried in the direction of the voice. They found themselves staring down a long hallway; at the far end a door stood ajar. One of Theon's men stood next to it.

As Theon approached, his men led out a frightened-looking old man, white-haired, bearded, frail. His ribs protruded as if he had not eaten in a long time. In his wild eyes was a look akin to madness.

"Whom have we here?" Theon asked gently. "Can he talk?"

"He says his name is Cleomedes," the soldier answered. "He claims to have been Priam's armorer. It's possible, sir. Look at his hands. They've got the right calluses, although he doesn't look strong enough for such work."

"I'm sure he's starving," Theon noted. "Look, my friend—Cleomedes, is it?—we'll happily feed you. In return, I'd like you to answer our questions. You may even wind up with a bit of money as well, to buy a warm place to sleep."

Cleomedes looked furtively from face to face. "Water," he croaked.

Theon called to one of his men for a waterskin.

The old man gulped the liquid eagerly, losing much of it down his chin and chest. Then he wiped his mouth and breathed heavily.

"Now," Theon said, "where has everybody gone? And why are you alone still alive?"

"I got hit on the head," Cleomedes explained. "The Greeks must have thought me dead, and they left me alone. When I awoke I saw the invaders killing the men and hauling away the women. I was afraid they'd see me, so I stayed quiet. But I did see Ajax—the lesser one—carrying away Princess Cassandra." He said her name with hatred.

"What happened to the blind woman?" Theon asked. "The one in Cassandra's service?"

"Keturah?" the haggard old man asked, hungrily eyeing

the waterskin. Theon passed it back to him, and he took a deep drink. "I think I saw Keturah and her son outside the palace, with that Greek fellow who tried to slip in and spirit them away once before."

"Phorbus?"

"Maybe. I never knew his name. They were with Aeneas when I saw them."

"Prince Aeneas? He escaped? I thought all the Trojan nobles were killed."

"Aeneas escaped with his father. It began to rain very hard, and they vanished into the groves. I couldn't see them anymore. I hid and didn't come out until everyone had gone."

Theon looked at Strabo with relief. "So Keturah and the child got away. But where might they have gone?"

As Cleomedes took yet another drink, he studied Theon carefully, obviously trying to determine whether or not he was to be trusted. "They left while all the Greeks were in Troy," the old man finally said. "They probably found an unguarded boat on the beach."

Theon nodded thoughtfully.

Cleomedes drank again before speaking. "If they sailed, they were in for trouble. The storm was the most violent I can remember. The rain saved a bit of Troy by putting out the fires."

Theon frowned. "If they were trying to sail those heavy seas in a small boat when that first real blow hit, with no one but the boy to help Phorbus—"

Strabo interrupted. "I thought Cleomedes said they were with Aeneas."

"No," the old man corrected. "I saw them split up. Aeneas was carrying his father on his back, and he looked as if he knew exactly where he was going. Anyway, young Talus would have been more help than you might think. He was a smart lad, strong and quick minded. If Phorbus knew how to sail and could instruct the lad, they might have been able to manage."

Theon tossed the man his purse. "Thank you. You've been a great help. Come on," he said to the others. "We'd better get to sea ourselves while we've still got the tide."

*   *   *

But a new storm caught them just as they were getting under sail. It was as if the sea's wrath were lamenting Troy's death. The wind yanked the lines from the sailors' hands, making it impossible to control the boat. Between the towering waves that crashed down over the sides, the men saw flashes of lightning. The thunder became deafening. The craft sailed up the side of one gigantic wave and down the next. Once on the crest of the wave, the boat seemed suspended in midair for a terrifying moment before the sickly plunge into the trough.

When the rain came down in earnest, half the crew had to bail for dear life. There was no time to think about fear or nausea. Everyone was occupied with the urgent task of keeping the boat above water. One sailor was washed overboard, but the others could do nothing to save him. Theon held tightly to the mast and squinted through the driving rain.

At the top of one wave, the boat nearly capsized. It heeled sharply, slamming Theon into the mast. He heaved up his guts and nearly blacked out—but he still hung on.

The storm raged. There was no hope of holding a course. All anyone could think of was surviving and praying that the boat would not run aground on one of the rocky inlets that dotted the coast.

Theon thought of Keturah and the boy, tossed and battered by seas even worse than these. Had they survived? Would *he* survive? He thought then about his wife, his twins, and finally Huldah. Would he see any of them again?

A wave lifted the ship high. For an instant it seemed to float, and then the sea rushed up to meet it with a terrifying crash. There was the sound of splintering wood as the boat was torn apart. Beams, timbers, and sails went flying.

The mast, weakened by the last disaster, broke in the vulnerable place and killed three sailors as it swept along the leeward rail. An enormous hole gaped in the side of the vessel, and water poured in as the wind howled and the rain beat down.

Theon tried to hang on to the broken shaft of the mast, but the sea easily whisked him away. The boat was sinking fast. It spun round and round, faster and faster in a furious eddy. Theon struggled for breath, but the whirlpool sucked him down . . . down . . . down.

His lungs and ears were bursting. He could not hold his breath any longer. Powerful forces, like a giant hand, tore at his body. How long had he been underwater? He was about to give up, open his mouth, and drown when he suddenly shot to the surface. He was propelled above the waves, where he gasped for air, and then fell face first back into the water. The breath was knocked out of him, and he sank. But his tired limbs churned away once more, and he rose to the surface.

Around him the storm was still roiling. The waves raised him up only to cast him down. The rain pelted the churning water. Lightning crackled in the sky. A wave overwhelmed him, but this time when he resurfaced he saw a sturdy spar and managed to grab it. It supported his weight, and he held on with all his strength. He scanned the waves but could see no other survivors.

The storm continued to pummel him mercilessly. Theon drifted. Where he was, he had no idea, but he managed to hold on to the spar with one hand and unhook his sword belt with the other. He let the heavy sword sink, then used the thick leather belt to lash himself to the spar so it could not be pulled from his grasp by a wave.

His resolve was weakening as well as his flesh. Was this the way it was going to end for him? Drowned like a pathetic rat who had fallen from a ship? His weakness shamed him. He stared up into the blackened sky and cursed. "Do your worst, damn you!" he cried. "Kill me if you—"

His words were drowned by a wave that plunged him in a deep trough, then dumped debris on top of him. Timber from his own boat knocked him unconscious, but the buoyancy of the spar propelled him back to the surface.

When he awoke, he struggled to hold his head above water and coughed up salt water. But his mind was addled from the trauma to his head. He remained unaware and uncaring of the passing of time or of anything except the desperate struggle to remain afloat.

At last the storm abated. No longer tossed by waves, his spar drifted into a sheltered cove on one of the many islands along the coast. Finally, his dangling toes touched bottom. The spar washed onto a beach. He lay on the sand and fell asleep, exhausted.

When he regained consciousness, he was still lashed to the spar. With difficulty he unhooked his belt and rolled free. Where was he? He looked around to see that the beach he was lying on fronted a lovely, shallow lagoon.

He sat up, groggy, bruised, and battered. Every bone and muscle ached. He was naked, his clothes torn off by the raging sea. He struggled to his knees and tried to stand, but his legs were too wobbly. He fell to his hands and knees and shook his head, trying to clear it.

He vaguely remembered being on a sailing craft and having the boat come apart on him. Where were the others? There must have been others aboard. Then came the greatest shock of all. He could not remember his name, or where he had come from, or where he was going.

He forced himself to stand. He scanned the empty horizon, then turned to the land. The inlet was covered with scrub, making him feel optimistic about finding fresh water and something to eat. There must be people. There must be!

He held his head in his hands. Suddenly he felt dizzy, and he sat down to keep from falling.

Who am I? he thought desperately. *In the name of all the gods, who am I?*

II

"Princess! Princess!" the voice urgently whispered. Cassandra turned toward the sound, her chains rattling in the dank hold of Ajax the Lesser's ship. The vessel rolled mightily on the huge swells, but a sliver of moonlight

filtered through the timbers. The storm had abated for the
time being, and the thunder and lightning had ceased.

Cassandra had been assaulted by the vulgar Ajax,
then thrown to his underlings to be raped. Twelve other
Trojan women lay there, also chained. Bales of plunder
stolen from Troy were scattered throughout the hold,
interspersed with the ravaged women—gold and silver
ornaments, vases, grain and dried fruits, and jars of oil.

Cassandra heard the voice again, but her eyes could
not pierce the darkness. "Who is there? Who's calling
me?" she asked.

"I saw the blind woman escape, Princess, with her
child and a handsome stranger in Greek garb. They took a
boat out to sea just beneath the palace. Be happy, Princess; your blind friend is free, as is her boy. They do not
share our fate." And then the voice was silent.

Cassandra bowed her head. Tears slid down her blood-
caked, swollen face as sobs wracked her broken body. She
was weeping with joy. It was a miracle they had eluded
the forces that had swept onto the beaches.

Brave, wonderful Phorbus, she thought. Now he would
guide her friends Keturah and Talus home. Odd, she
thought, that only now, debased and bloodied, did she
understand the enormity of her love for them. They represented the life she never could have. They enjoyed simple
pleasures and endured common hatreds. They had passion
and friendship.

A sound came from one of the bulkheads. The women
shrank back into their chains, fearful that the Greek beasts
were coming for them again. But it was only the wind or
perhaps a rat.

Cassandra started to speak to the woman who had
given her the good news. But the words were never
uttered. A sudden, painful convulsion shook her body,
causing the chains to rattle against her bones. She closed
her eyes tightly. She knew what was going to happen—
Apollo was coming to her. In the midst of her pain and her
fear, a divine seizure was taking control. Her body trembled so violently that the women close to her struggled to

get away, moving to the farthest length their chains would allow.

White froth bubbled to her lips, and she opened her eyes to see a magnificent figure standing in the black hold. Light blazed from the beauty of his body. His long hair shone, and the bow he carried and his hooded quiver of arrows were made of beaten gold. He was naked. In one hand he held a gorgeous black vase.

"Blessed Apollo," she whispered to the god.

He did not answer.

She reached out with her chained arms for his aid.

He did not move to help her. Nor did he speak. He raised the graceful vase over his head, then let the object fall. It shattered to a thousand pieces. Then he was gone!

Cassandra sat up, crying out for him to reappear. But the god had irrevocably departed. She looked around, bewildered, then reached out along the floor. Her hand found the shattered shards. She picked a piece up and held it to her cheek.

She suddenly realized why the god had not spoken: There was nothing to say. She knew what the shattered vase meant. Her life was ended. This ship was doomed. It would never reach Greece. It would fly apart in another storm, as had the black vase. Her eyes pierced the darkness to search out the faces of her companions who would die with her.

"Oh, my sisters! Oh, Trojan women!" she cried out. For the first time in her life she felt compassion.

Helen had lost track of the time. Had it been two days since she had sailed from Troy on Menelaus's ship? She was locked in a small but clean room. The drunken revelry aboard the ship had ended. No longer were loutish sailors screaming through the locked door at her that she was a bitch and a whore and that Menelaus would pay her back for her cheating ways. One sailor had sung her a particularly disgusting ballad about an adulterous wife who ran off with a beautiful young man only to discover that her lover was really a horned goat.

She longed for a bath and a mirror and some scented

oil for her hands. She was still wearing her Trojan garb—
the long white dress with the slit in the bodice from neck
to navel and a single golden necklace against her flawless
skin. She had lost her slippers on the beach when she had
been carried to the boat.

The night came, and moonlight filtered through the
room. She lay down on the small, well-made bed and slept
peacefully.

She was awakened past midnight by a cold, strong
gust of wind that swept across the room. She sat up.
Someone had opened the door and entered. Then the
door shut.

"Who are you? What do you want?" she demanded in
a firm, regal voice.

Then her eyes focused. Her hand flew nervously to
her neck and grasped the necklace. It was Menelaus! He
was standing just inside the door, a sword in one hand. He
had aged greatly these ten years. His beard and hair were
streaked with white, and he had lost weight. But his eyes
were still the same—leering, cruel, and contemptuous.

They stared at each other in silence across a ten-year
gulf of war and betrayal.

"Do you remember who I am, my dear?" he asked,
his voice dripping with barely controlled violence. His
fingers tightened on the hilt of his sword.

She did not answer.

He swung the sword in a fury, bringing the blade
down on the small table and shattering it.

She drew back in fear.

"Tell me who I am!" he shouted.

"You are Menelaus, king of Sparta."

"Who else am I?" he roared, pointing the sword at
her neck.

"You are Menelaus, admiral of the Greek fleet, general of the Greek army. You are Menelaus, conqueror of
Troy."

He swung the sword again with a fury, so close now
to Helen that she could feel the current of air the blade
displaced.

"Who else?" he shouted.

"My husband," she whispered.

The sword came down hard, taking a chunk out of the floor. He stood in front of her, breathing heavily. He stank from wine and sweat.

"Why, Helen, why? How could you leave my bed for that scatterbrained young fop? How could you betray your throne?" His voice was pitiful now.

She stood for the first time, having realized that the danger was past, and slipped off her gown. She had him in the palm of her hand. In a few minutes, she knew, it would be as if the Trojan War had never been fought. It would be as if none of his companions had died. It would be as if he had never been shamed. She took his free hand and guided it to her naked breast.

"Gods, you are so beautiful," he whispered, dropping the sword to the floor.

She smiled and lay back down on the bed.

Frantically, he began to undo his tunic.

Helen turned her eyes toward the wall. She could stomach his loathsome body, she decided, until they got back to Sparta and she was reestablished as queen. Then she would discreetly look for a new lover. She would look for a literate, beautiful young man in the court of Sparta who would do anything to share the bed of the most beautiful woman in the world.

Far out to sea, Phorbus and Talus raised the sail on their stolen, storm-beaten boat. Talus had proved to be an apt little sailor in the midst of the threatening winds and rain. Now that the storm had passed, Talus clearly enjoyed the feel of the strong pull of the wind as the sail spread and billowed. They set their course for the open sea.

Phorbus glanced at Keturah, who sat quietly in the stern, and called out to Talus, who was proudly manning the tiller for the first time: "Hold her steady, lad! We're bound for Home!"

"Home?" Keturah asked. "I've dreamed of it so many times, but the dream has never come true. Now I can't even call up my fantasies about the legendary island."

Phorbus nodded. "I know what you mean. Iri told me fabulous stories of the magical island and of the wonderful life you and Talus will have there."

But Iri was dead and that dream with him. Phorbus was fairly certain that even though Iri had left him in charge of making the dream come true for Keturah, she probably did not believe in it anymore.

She had told Phorbus that she was done with dreaming. Dreaming was for bewildered, otherworldly people like poor Cassandra. Keturah had shuddered as she and Phorbus wondered about Cassandra's fate.

Now, while Phorbus watched, she clung more tightly to the side of the boat. The sails filled above them. Overhead the gulls cried. The sun had come out, bringing a new day and what, Phorbus prayed, would be a new beginning.

Epilogue

The winds calmed, and a seductive softness gentled the evening air. The clouds drifted away, and the night was ornamented with a million stars. The desert birds withdrew to sleep, while small nocturnal animals came to the oasis to feed. It was a time of peace.

The Teller of Tales spoke. "Thus came calm after the storm. The winds of war no longer blew either in Troy or in Canaan. Men laid down their swords or beat them into plowshares. The weary Greek soldiers headed home after their long siege, and the children of Israel put away the weapons with which they had destroyed Hazor. And a young woman, carrying the lion's-paw birthmark, entered Babylon in triumph to gain her just reward.

"Yet all was not peaceful," he said, his tone altering subtly, gaining an edge. "Even as they put down the implements of war, the world was changing. From far across the Great Sea, new waves of the Sea Peoples swept into Canaan, taking over the cities of the northern coast. From far to the south, a new Egyptian king set sail for the lands of the Crescent, bent once more on extorting tribute from Canaan and its neighbors. And new enemies from the Great Sea threatened the shipping empire of the Children of the Lion, which had long reigned supreme in seafaring trade."

He held up a cautionary hand. "And as everyone

dreamed of peace, new oppressors arose. The nomadic tribes of Midian swept across Canaan, seeking revenge for the day in the distant past when Joshua's army had defeated them and drove them deep into the desert. Disarmed and off-guard, the Israelites were no match for the nomads' lightning attacks. There came a day when Israel was a slave nation once more, and the mighty Children of the Lion were homeless, penniless, and adrift in a hostile world. The old heroes were gone. It was time for new ones to arise!

"Disruption and change swept through the land. Those once high were now low. Those once at peace were now at war. The rich were now poor.

"And those who had been lost were now to find themselves.

"Tomorrow," he said, bowing and backing away into the darkness. "All these things you shall hear tomorrow."

The best-selling saga of the Children of the Lion continues with a new generation . . .

Here is an exciting preview of **THE TRUMPET AND THE SWORD,** Volume Fourteen of the *Children of the Lion* Series, by Peter Danielson.

On sale in 1992, at bookstores everywhere.

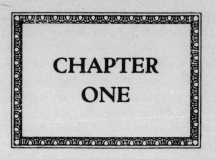

CHAPTER ONE

Canaan

The donkeys moved slowly on the path, stepping gingerly on the sunbaked earth. What little vegetation remained from the effects of the drought was burned brown by the relentless heat. The trees by the side of the path were too stunted to provide any shade for the beasts or their riders.

The lead rider, called Gideon, dismounted and drank sparingly from a small bladder of water. "We'll rest here," he told his servant, Purah.

Gideon looked too poverty-stricken to have the luxury of a servant, and his appearance did not deceive. His robe was tattered and filthy. A short sword hung in a worn scabbard on the belt that secured his robe. On his back were a bow and a quiver with only two arrows remaining. His once-magnificent leather sandals with high straps were now missing many thongs and as a result flapped loosely on his feet. Around his neck was a plaited rope, which was attached to a trumpet. His tall frame was haggard and thin; the brown, gold-flecked eyes were deep in the skull. His soft brown hair was matted with dust and sweat.

"Bring me some dates," he ordered Purah, who had just climbed off his own donkey and was standing on the path.

"There are none left," Purah said, removing his master's shield from his back and hanging it on the donkey. The servant's feet, shod only with palm fronds, were scorched by the hot earth.

Purah had been with Gideon's family for many years. He had been treated well during their long-past days of affluence and now remained to share what little they had. He wore a tattered skin around his middle, and two water bladders hung around his neck. He was a small, wiry man with eyes that squinted. His face was lined from the sun and the wind, and his long oily black hair was fastened with a leather thong at the nape of his neck.

"It is meat, not dates, I want anyway," Gideon responded. He thought for a moment, then added, "Maybe I'll eat the donkey." He laughed uproariously at his own joke.

Purah smiled grimly. "Sir, wouldn't it be better if we moved on? There is no food to be found here, and we are too close to the river. The Bedouins have been raiding this area often."

Gideon pulled his sword from his scabbard with a flourish. "Shame on you, Purah, to be frightened by the Midianites. I am here to protect you. If we see an enemy, I will make soup out of him." He waved his sword dramatically and menacingly in a circle, then slipped it back into its sheath.

Purah watched his master's antics in patient silence.

"The trouble with you, Purah," Gideon continued, "is that your fear of the Midianites prevents you from thinking straight. You believe they are the cause of the Israelites' problems; but it is the drought that has once again destroyed us as a proud people. The land has dried up; the rains have vanished; the flocks have died. Look at me! Ten years ago I was feasting with my family on the booty from Hazor. Now we are all starving. We have been forsaken by Yahweh and by the land. As for the Midianites, they are just mosquitoes who have crossed from the east bank of the Jordan because there is no more blood to suck there."

Purah replied with his usual deference, "Yes, my lord, you are right. My mind is clouded by fear."

"And you sound sad as well," Gideon remarked. "You need to be cheered up. And music is the only thing that can make a person forget an empty stomach."

Purah shuddered. He did not think he could survive another assault from his master's trumpet. Not now.

"Perhaps, sir, you should preserve your strength for the journey back," Purah suggested fervently.

"Nonsense. Music gives strength to musician and audience alike."

Purah closed his eyes and leaned wearily against his donkey when he saw Gideon put the horn to his lips. If only he could find some acceptable way to stuff up his ears . . .

The first sounds from the horn caused Purah to feel even more despair. Gideon was playing an Israelite march that had been composed during Joshua's time. It had always given Purah a headache. If he had to listen to Gideon's trumpet, he preferred the southern love songs. But Gideon did not know too many of those. Purah shut his eyes tightly, gritted his teeth, and tried to think about a refreshing bowl of cool goat's milk, something he craved but had not tasted in months.

When the piece was finished, Gideon smiled broadly, very pleased with himself. He let the trumpet hang loose on the cord around his neck and started to mount his donkey. "Now that the music has refreshed us we can journey again, Purah. Mount up! Mount up!"

But Purah did not move. His entire body had become rigid as he stared directly down the path.

"What's the matter with you, Purah? Mount up!" Gideon ordered. He slid off his donkey again as if planning to shake his servant out of his sudden torpor.

"Your sword, sir!" Purah whispered desperately from between clenched jaws.

Then Gideon turned and saw what had transfixed his companion. It was a fearsome sight. Two immense white camels were kneeling shoulder to shoulder on the narrow path not more than fifty feet away. They were adorned with magnificent woven bridles and halters. Their limbs were muscular and lean, their eyes were clear, and their beautifully shaped heads were held erect. And on the back of each beast sat a Midianite warrior.

The Bedouins wore long black robes, and white sashes covered the lower half of their faces. From the left ear of each man dangled brilliant gold earrings, hammered fine into intricate patterns and burnished carefully until they captured the sun's light and reflected it in shimmering waves.

"Your sword, sir!" Purah hissed again urgently. The servant's hand rested on the edge of his master's shield as he waited for the sword to be drawn. Then he could bring the shield up.

"Maybe it would be better to talk to them," Gideon whispered back.

The Midianites easily swung their long legs over the backs of their kneeling camels and started to walk toward the two Israelites. Curved swords were sheathed in jeweled scabbards on their backs, and each man carried a dagger at his waist. They wore nothing on their feet, so they moved silently, like predators.

Purah's hand began to tremble, and his heart was beating so fiercely he thought it would leap out from his chest.

"Run, Purah! Run!" Gideon shouted, and they wheeled around to flee—only to discover that a dozen other Midianites had emerged from the sides of the path to form a circle around them. The Israelites stopped short, trapped.

A Bedouin left the circle, strode up to them, spat forcefully in their faces, then screamed, "Kiss the ground, pigs! You are standing before Oreb and Zeeb, warlords to King Zalmunnah." The Bedouin's curved sword cut through the heavy air an inch from their faces.

Purah could feel the hot wind from its path, and he and Gideon fell to their knees and kissed the ground, holding their mouths against the hot baked earth until they choked and their eyes were filled with dust. They were well aware of the men to whom they were bowing: Oreb the Raven, a one-eyed butcher, and Zeeb the Jackal, whose right hand was twisted into an ugly claw from a childhood mishap. Gideon and Purah knew of these two most feared Bedouins whose names had come to symbolize torture and death among the Israelites.

"Have mercy on us! For the love of God have mercy upon us!" Gideon begged. "We have nothing of value. We are just two humble travelers searching for food for our starving children." He held out trembling hands in supplication.

The two warlords strode arrogantly around the prostrate Israelites, ignoring Gideon's plea and inspecting them as if they were livestock.

"They are worthless," Zeeb said in disgust. "Zalmunnah wants gold from this raid."

"I say we bury them alive up to their necks and let the ravens pluck out their eyes," Oreb suggested.

"We don't have time," Zeeb responded. "I'll slit their throats and be done with it." He drew out one of his daggers and dug the point into Gideon's bowed neck.

"Wait," Oreb said. "There's a horn around his neck. It might be amusing to have this Israelite play for us." Oreb turned to his Midianite troops and called out: "Do you want to hear a song?"

They shouted their approval of Oreb's idea. One of the troopers shouted, "And let's see a dance."

Oreb dragged the two Israelites to their feet. "This pig will play," he ordered, pointing at Gideon, "and this pig will dance."

Purah had never danced a step in his life; but in spite of his fear-weakened knees, the moment he heard the first cacophonous notes from Gideon's trumpet, he began to leap up and down and sideways, trying to imagine the steps of a dancing girl. He ground his hips and swung his pelvis. He shimmied his shoulders with his head thrown back. He wiggled his rump and kicked his legs and twirled.

The Midianites jeered and hooted and threw dirt and stones at the pathetic pair.

When the performance was finally over and the trumpeter and dancer fell exhausted to the ground, Oreb and Zeeb kicked them into near unconsciousness, accompanied by the cheers and laughter of their soldiers. "Come back again," Zeeb yelled at them, "when you have learned some new tunes."

The Midianite troops mounted their white racing camels and followed Oreb and Zeeb northward, where there were still crops to be stolen, livestock to be slaughtered, Israelite women to be raped, and gold to be unearthed from hidden caches after their owners were tortured into disclosure.

As the camels raced effortlessly over the parched land, the Bedouins' beautiful earrings tinkled in the dry, hot wind.

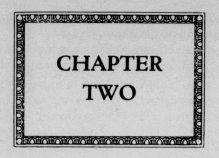

CHAPTER TWO

Island of Home/Aegean Sea

The young man Talus stood with bowed head before the freshly dug grave. There were now two graves on that mountain trail: One was Keturah's, his mother, who had died two years before. The newly dug grave was for Phorbus, Talus's adopted brother. There had not been much left of poor Phorbus to bury. The sharks had taken chunks out of the body before it had washed up on shore.

Talus wept softly as he remembered his brother's last days. Phorbus had become delusional and then totally insane, believing that his long-dead lover, Myrrha, was swimming across the Great Sea to him from her battlefield grave in Troy. And then one morning Phorbus had climbed to the highest point of their uninhabited part of the island called Home, leaped into the sea, and swum out, supposedly to join his beloved.

Talus stepped back from the grave and looked toward the brush that lined the trail. He spied some yellow wildflowers and plucked a handful to scatter on both graves. Then he jogged down the trail, his short, broad body eating up ground in easy strides. He had the same sloping, powerful shoulders his father had had, the great armorer Iri of Thebes, who had died trying to rescue his family from captivity in Troy.

When Talus reached the small shack where he, his mother, and Phorbus had lived in total isolation from the other residents of Home, he rummaged frantically through the root cellar until he located an old bronze sword, an anvil, and a pair of prongs. He dragged these to a small outdoor bellows and began to fire it, working furiously to get the blaze hot enough so he could work and keep his mind occupied. He did not want to dwell on the frightening fact that now he was totally alone. Memories were all he had left—memories and two graves.

How different it had all been ten years before, when the three of them had miraculously escaped from burning Troy and reached the island home of their kinsmen—Children of the Lion. They were expecting the wealth and privileges and respect due them as the family of Iri of Thebes. They were anticipating the acceptance, love, and protection of Khalkeus of Gournia and all his retainers.

But upon their arrival, they had gotten nothing but ten years of hardship, near starvation, and isolation . . . ten years of living with the bitter knowledge that they could never leave their island prison because they had no ship, no money, and no contact with Khalkeus and his court. They built themselves a crude hovel, using materials found on the shoreline. Their shack was on the desolate end of the island, and they had been forced to live like wolves, eating gulls and rodents and roots and berries. No wonder Phorbus had lost his mind and his mother had wasted away from sadness.

Talus worked the bronze sword for hours, beating it into various shapes. And then, when he was totally exhausted, he picked up the now-useless weapon and flung it as far as he could into the woods. Then he sank down on the ground beside the small forge and slept.

When he awoke he found himself staring at bowls of olives and cheeses and small pieces of salted meat set onto the ground not more than five feet from him. He stretched and looked up to see the two young visitors who had brought the food. The twins stood silently a few feet behind the bowls. It was almost impossible to tell the brother and sister apart.

During these missions of mercy they just stood at a distance and watched him eat voraciously. They always seemed to enjoy seeing him devour the food. No matter how many times they brought him the food and no matter how pure their intentions, the twins Hela and Gravis inadvertently made him feel like a swarthy savage, like a leopard in a cage. He was barefoot and grimy and long-haired, and his only garment was the skin of a mountain wolf. The twins, however, were dressed elegantly and identically in expensive lemon-yellow linen tunics, which almost matched the color of their carefully trimmed golden hair. They wore calfskin boots beautifully embossed with beadwork.

It was difficult for Talus to accept the fact that the three were blood relatives, but he knew it was so; the beautiful twins before him were the children of Theon and Nuhara, and they bore the same lion's-paw birthmark on their lower back as he did.

Talus chewed a small piece of tasty meat. It was more delicious than anything he could scrounge up on his own. Phorbus, while he was sane and alive, had accepted food from Hela and Gravis with bitter reluctance.

"Guilt offerings," he had told Talus. "It was their mother, Nuhara, who told her father, Khalkeus, that we are imposters. It was the greedy Nuhara who prevented us from seeing Khalkeus and pleading our case that Iri's fortune—his share of the Children of the Lion's commercial enterprises—is rightfully ours. She would never have gotten away with this if poor Theon were alive! But now Nuhara's children secretly bring us food to assuage their guilt."

Phorbus is dead, Talus thought philosophically, *and I am hungry, and I don't really care why Hela and Gravis bring the food.* The only thing he was sad about was that they seemed unable or unwilling to converse with him.

Talus finished the food, licked the bowls clean, and brought them to his benefactors.

"Next time, please bring me some big fat juicy grapes, red ones," he requested. His eyes twinkled with offered friendship as he handed the bowls back.

Talus suddenly realized that he had never been so near to the twins. Up close, their eerie beauty was almost overwhelming. And they smelled beautiful, as if they had bathed in wildflowers. Talus found himself unable to look away from their gaze. He glanced from one to the other and then back again. A growing excitement filled his heart, as if he were embarking on a journey that promised both great beauty and terrifying danger. Their eyes were magnificent wells of—

A sharp pain abruptly stabbed through his right leg, and he collapsed to his knees. Convulsed, he held out a hand for help, but neither twin moved. The pain vanished as suddenly as it had come, and he stood up. But the pain came again—this time putting his left leg into spasm. He fell flat on his face.

What was happening? He looked up. The twins were staring straight ahead, their lean, majestically clad bodies ramrod straight. He was awed by their presence and wondered if he had ventured too close to them physically and they had rightly responded with some demonic power to thwart his arrogance.

"What are you?" he cried out. But the twins had turned and were moving off to begin their long trek back to the populated, civilized part of Home. Talus could see that they were holding hands. He shuddered.

"What are the people in the square saying?" Nuhara asked the young, dark-skinned woman kneeling beside her chaise.

"They are frightened," replied the young woman, whose name was Allomander. She was painstakingly painting her mistress's toenails with a mellow red dye imported from Egypt.

Nuhara smiled contemptuously and folded her arms across her breasts. She was still wearing her sleeping robe. Although her lustrous black hair had specks of gray and her small, perfectly formed face was lined at the mouth and brow, she was still a very beautiful woman. "Of what are the fools frightened? Plague?"

"No, my lady. It's just that many of them haven't received their wages in weeks. They are starving. Many are in danger of being put out of their homes."

"Is that all?"

"No, my lady. They are frightened because they see so few ships in our harbor. The walls of their dwellings are crumbling, the warehouses and shops are falling into disrepair, and even this palace, which was once so magnificent, has become ugly to the sight."

Allomander's explanation was cut short by ferocious sounds in an adjoining room. A man was shouting, and then objects crashed against the walls and floors. Servants screamed and wept. Nuhara and Allomander listened but did not move to investigate. They knew that Khalkeus of Gournia—head administrator of the commercial empire of the Children of the Lion . . . chosen successor to the great Demetrios . . . a legend in his own time for his daring and cunning as a feared high-seas pirate—was drunk again.

"My father is obviously enjoying himself," Nuhara noted without concern, and then returned to her questioning of the servant. "What are they saying about me?"

Nuhara rarely left the palace. The small villages and squares that radiated from the palace to form the inhabited section of Home were alien territory to her. She had never even entered the warehouses or the workshops or the accounting offices—the lifeblood of the vast shipping concern.

"Nothing, my lady, except that you are still beautiful."

"Liar!" screamed Nuhara. Enraged, she lashed out with one well-formed foot and sent the bowl of precious dye spinning across the room.

Allomander, splattered with the dye, stood trembling by the chaise. She was afraid to speak and afraid not to speak.

By concerted effort, Nuhara calmed down. She remained quiet for a long time, then she carefully removed from her neck a single strand of beaten gold, so fine it seemed to be made of tiny golden raindrops. She dangled it in front of the young woman. "If you tell me the truth, it shall grace your neck," Nuhara whispered.

Allomander, wide-eyed, her face stained red, gulped and straightened. Possession of such an expensive and beautiful ornament was beyond her wildest dreams. "The people say, my lady, that you never really mourned Theon when he was lost at sea. They say that the only man you ever loved was your father, Khalkeus of

Gournia. And they say that you are destroying Home."

Nuhara dropped the necklace onto the floor. After the young woman grabbed it up and ran from the room, Nuhara clapped her hands. Within seconds a eunuch named Strabo appeared, bowing.

"Clear this mess up," Nuhara ordered, pointing to the spilled dye, "and then bring in someone who can finish my toes properly."

Strabo, a huge man wearing a sailor's vest and a scarf around his thick neck, bowed and trotted off to do his mistress's bidding.

Nuhara sank back into the chaise. *What fools they all are,* she thought. *They think I am the worm destroying the golden apple. What would they think if they knew that the worm is a god, and my drunken father is the priest of that god?* She closed her eyes and, frightened for a moment, wrapped the robe tighter. It was, she knew, a very treacherous game she was playing.

★ WAGONS WEST ★

This continuing, magnificent saga recounts the adventures of a brave band of settlers, all of different backgrounds, all sharing one dream— to find a new and better life.

☐	26822-8	INDEPENDENCE! #1	$4.95
☐	26162-2	NEBRASKA! #2	$4.50
☐	26242-4	WYOMING! #3	$4.50
☐	26072-3	OREGON! #4	$4.50
☐	26070-7	TEXAS! #5	$4.99
☐	26377-3	CALIFORNIA! #6	$4.99
☐	26546-6	COLORADO! #7	$4.95
☐	26069-3	NEVADA! #8	$4.99
☐	26163-0	WASHINGTON! #9	$4.50
☐	26073-1	MONTANA! #10	$4.50
☐	26184-3	DAKOTA! #11	$4.50
☐	26521-0	UTAH! #12	$4.50
☐	26071-5	IDAHO! #13	$4.50
☐	26367-6	MISSOURI! #14	$4.50
☐	27141-5	MISSISSIPPI! #15	$4.95
☐	25247-X	LOUISIANA! #16	$4.50
☐	25622-X	TENNESSEE! #17	$4.50
☐	26022-7	ILLINOIS! #18	$4.95
☐	26533-4	WISCONSIN! #19	$4.95
☐	26849-X	KENTUCKY! #20	$4.95
☐	27065-6	ARIZONA! #21	$4.50
☐	27458-9	NEW MEXICO! #22	$4.95
☐	27703-0	OKLAHOMA! #23	$4.95
☐	28180-1	CELEBRATION! #24	$4.50